The TRAITOR QUEEN

BY TRUDI CANAVAN

The Magician's Apprentice

The Black Magician Trilogy
The Magicians' Guild
The Novice
The High Lord

Age of the Five
Priestess of the White
Last of the Wilds
Voice of the Gods

The Traitor Spy Trilogy
The Ambassador's Mission
The Rogue
The Traitor Queen

TRUDI CANAVAN

The TRAITOR QUEEN

Book Three of the TRAITOR SPY TRILOGY

orbit

www.orbitbooks.net

ORBIT

First published in Great Britain in 2012 by Orbit

A CIP catalogue record for this book
is available from the British Library.

Hardback 978-1-84149-595-8
C format 978-0-356-50109-3

Typeset in Garamond by Palimpsest Book Production Limited,
Falkirk, Stirlingshire
Printed and bound in Great Britain by Clays Ltd, St Ives plc

Papers used by Orbit are from well-managed forests
and other responsible sources.

MIX
Paper from
responsible sources
FSC® C104740

Orbit
An imprint of
Little, Brown Book Group
100 Victoria Embankment
London EC4Y 0DY

An Hachette UK Company
www.hachette.co.uk

www.orbitbooks.net

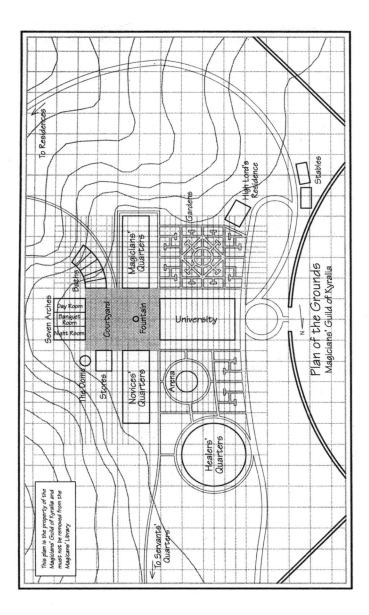

Plan of the Grounds

Magicians' Guild of Kyralia

To Residences

Stables

High Lord's
Residence

Gardens

Magicians'
Quarters

Baths

Seven Arches

Day Room

Banquet
Room

Night Room

Courtyard

Fountain

University

The Dome

Stores

Novices'
Quarters

Arena

Healers'
Quarters

To Servants'
Quarters

This plan is the property of the
Magicians' Guild of Kyralia and
must not be removed from the
Magicians' Library

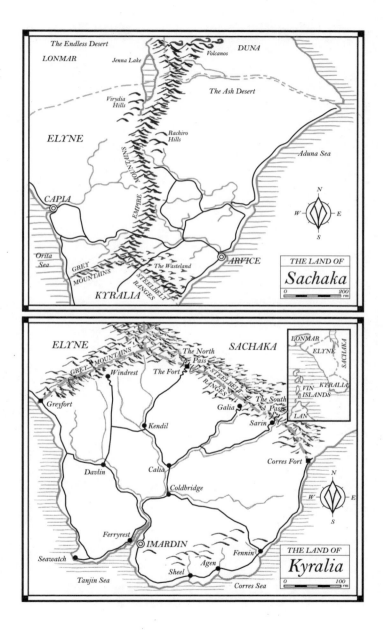

PART ONE

CHAPTER 1

ASSASSINS AND ALLIES

There is a mistaken belief, in Imardin, that printing presses had been invented by magicians. Anyone unaware of the workings of presses and magic could easily gain the impression, from the spectacular noise and the convulsing actions of the machine, that some sort of Alchemy was taking place, but no magic was required so long as someone was willing to turn the wheels and operate the levers.

Cery had learned the truth of the matter from Sonea years ago. Prototypes of the machine had been presented to the Guild by the inventor and the Guild had embraced it as a fast and cheap way of making duplicates of books. A printing service was then offered to the Houses for free, and to anyone from other classes for a charge. The impression that printing was magical was encouraged to deter others from starting their own trade. It was not until people of lower-class origins entered the Guild that the myth was dispelled and printing presses began to appear in the city in significant numbers.

The downside to this, Cery reflected, was the boom in popularity of the romantic adventure novel. A recently published one featured a rich heiress rescued from her luxurious but boring life by a young, handsome Thief. The fights were laughably implausible, nearly always involved swords rather than knives, and the underworld was populated by far too many good-looking men with impractical ideas about honour and loyalty. The novel had given a portion of the female population of Imardin an impression of the underworld that was a long way from the truth.

Of course, he had said none of this to the woman lying in bed beside him, who had been reading to him her favourite parts of these books every night since she had agreed to let him stay in her cellar. Cadia was no rich heiress. *And I am no dashingly handsome Thief.* She had been lonely and sad since her husband's death, and the idea of hiding a Thief in her basement was a pleasant distraction.

And he . . . he had all but run out of places to hide.

He turned to look at her. She was asleep, breathing softly. He wondered if she really believed he was a Thief, or if he simply fitted well enough into her fantasy that she didn't care if it was true or not. He was not the dashing young Thief of the novel – he certainly didn't have the stamina for the adventures described, either in bed or out of it.

I'm getting soft. I can't even walk up stairs without my heart thumping, and getting out of breath. We've spent too much time locked away in cramped hiding places and not enough time in fighting practice.

A muffled thump came from the next room. Cery lifted his head to regard the door. Were Anyi and Gol awake? Now that he was, he doubted he'd sleep again for some time. Being cooped up always led to him sleeping badly.

He slipped off the bed, automatically pulling on his trousers and reaching for his coat. Slipping one arm into a sleeve, he reached for the door handle and turned it quietly. As he pushed it open Anyi came into view. She was leaning over Gol, a blade catching the light of the night lamps, poised ready to strike. He felt his heart lurch in alarm and disbelief.

"What . . . ?" he began. At the sound, Anyi turned to look at him with the enviable speed of youth.

It was not Anyi.

Just as quickly, not-Anyi's attention moved back to Gol and the knife stabbed downwards, but hands rose to grab the assassin's wrist and stop it. Gol surged up off the bed. Cery was through the door by then, but checked his stride as a new thought overrode his intention to stop the woman.

Where's Anyi?

He turned to see that another struggle was underway over at the second makeshift bed, only this time it was the intruder who was pressed to the mattress, holding back the hands that held a knife hovering just above his chest. Cery felt a surge of pride for his daughter. She must have woken in time to catch the assassin, and turned his attack against him.

But her face was stretched in a grimace of effort as she tried to force the knife down. Despite the assassin's small size, the muscles of his wrists and neck were well developed. Anyi would not win this trial of brute force. Her advantage was her speed. He took a step toward her.

"Get out of here, Cery," Gol barked.

Anyi's arms were forced back as her concentration was broken. She sprang out of reach of the assassin. He leapt off the bed and dropped into a fighting stance, whipping out a long, thin knife from within a sleeve. But he did not advance on her. His gaze moved to Cery.

Cery had no intention of leaving the fight to Anyi and Gol. He might one day have to abandon Gol, but this was not that day. He would never abandon his daughter.

He had slipped his other arm into the coat sleeve automatically. Now he stepped backwards and feigned fear, while reaching into the pockets, and wriggled his hands into the wrist straps of his favourite weapons: two knives, the sheaths fastened inside the pockets so that the blades would be bare and ready when Cery drew them out.

The assassin leapt toward Cery. Anyi sprang at him. Cery did too. It was not what the man expected. Nor did he expect the twin knives that trapped his own. Or the blade that, well aimed, slid through the soft flesh of his neck. He froze in surprise and horror.

Cery ducked away from the spray of blood as Anyi withdrew her knife, knocked the assassin's knife from his hand, then finished him with a stab to the heart.

Very efficient. I've trained her well.

With Gol's help, of course. Cery turned to see how his friend was faring and was relieved to see the female assassin lying in a growing pool of blood on the floor.

Gol looked at Cery and grinned. He was breathing hard. *So am I*, Cery realised. Anyi bent and ran her hands over the male attacker's clothing and hair, then rubbed her fingers together.

"Soot. He came down the chimney into the house above." She looked at the old stone stairs leading up to the basement door speculatively.

Cery's mood soured. However the pair had got in, or found them in the first place, this was no longer a safe hiding place. He scowled down at the dead assassins, considering the last few people he might call on for help, and how they might reach them.

A small gasp came from the doorway. He turned to see Cadia, wrapped only in a sheet, staring wide-eyed at the dead assassins. She shuddered, but as she looked at him her dismay turned to disappointment.

"I guess you won't be staying another night, then?"

Cery shook his head. "Sorry about the mess."

She regarded the blood and bodies with a grimace, then frowned and peered up at the ceiling. Cery hadn't heard anything, but Anyi had lifted her head at the same time. They all exchanged worried looks, not wanting to speak unless their suspicions were true.

He heard a faint creak, muffled by the floorboards above them.

As soundlessly as possible, Anyi and Gol grabbed their shoes, packs and the lamps and followed Cery into the other room, shutting the door behind them and lifting an old chest into place before it. Cadia stopped in the middle of the room, sighed and dropped the sheet so that she could get dressed. Both Anyi and Gol turned their backs quickly.

"What should I do?" Cadia whispered to Cery.

He picked up the rest of his clothes and Cadia's bedroom lamp, and considered. "Follow us."

She looked more ill than excited as they slipped through the trapdoor that led to the old Thieves' Road. The passages here were filled with rubble and not entirely safe. This section of the underground network had been cut off from the rest when the king had rebuilt a nearby road and put new houses where the old slum homes had been. Though it was not quite within the borders of his territory, Cery had paid an old tunneller to dig a new access passage, but had left the old ways looking abandoned so that nobody would be tempted to use them if they did find them. It had been a handy place to hide things, like stolen goods and the occasional corpse.

He'd never planned to hide himself here, however. Cadia

regarded the rubble-strewn passage with a mix of dismay and curiosity. Cery handed her the lamp and pointed in one direction.

"In a hundred paces or so you'll see a grate high on the left wall. Beyond it is an alley between two houses. There'll be grooves in the wall to help you climb up, and the grate should hinge inward. Go to one of your neighbours and tell them there are robbers in your house. If they find the bodies, say they're the robbers and suggest one turned on the other."

"What if they don't find them?"

"Drag them into the passages and don't let anyone into the cellar until the smell goes away."

She looked even more ill, but nodded and straightened her back. He felt a pang of affection at her bravery, and hoped she wouldn't run into more assassins, or be punished some other way for helping him. He stepped close and kissed her firmly.

"Thank you," he said quietly. "It's been a pleasure."

She smiled, her eyes sparkling for a moment.

"You be careful," she told him.

"Always am. Now go."

She hurried away. He couldn't risk staying to watch her leave. Gol moved forward to lead the way and Anyi remained at the rear as they made their way through the crumbling passages. After several steps something slammed behind them. Cery stopped and looked back.

"Cadia?" Gol muttered. "The grille closing as she climbed up to the street?"

"It's a long way for the sound to travel," Cery said.

"That wasn't the sound of a grate on bricks or stone," Anyi whispered. "It was . . . something wooden."

A rattle followed. The sound of disturbed bricks and stones. Cery felt a chill run down his back. "Go. Hurry. But quietly."

Gol held his lamp high, but they could only manage breaking into a jog now and then with so much rubble on the passage floor. Cery bit back a curse more than once, regretting not tidying things up a little bit more. Then, after they'd continued along a straight section of tunnel, Gol cursed and skidded to a halt. Looking over the big man's shoulder, Cery saw that the roof ahead had collapsed recently, leaving them in a dead end. He spun about and they hurried back toward the last junction they had passed.

Anyi sighed as they reached the turn. "We're making tracks."

Looking down, Cery saw footprints in the dust. The hope that the pursuit might follow the tracks down to the dead end was dashed as he realised that Gol's now led down the side passage, leaving plenty of evidence they'd backtracked.

But if there's another opportunity to set down false tracks . . .

None came, however. Relief surged through him as they finally reached the connecting passage to the main part of the Thieves' Road. Once again he regretted not anticipating the situation he was in: while he'd disguised the entry to the isolated tunnels, he'd made no effort to conceal the exit from anyone exploring within.

Once the door was closed behind them, they looked around at the cleaner, better-maintained passage they were standing in. There was nothing they could use to block the door and prevent their pursuers from leaving the old passages.

"Where to?" Gol asked.

"South-east."

They moved faster now, shuttering the lamps so that only the thinnest beam of light illuminated the way. Once Cery would have travelled in the dark, but he'd heard stories of traps being set up to defend other Thieves' territories, by enterprising robbers or by the mysterious Sligs. Even so, the pace Gol set was precariously fast and Cery worried that his friend would not be able to dodge any dangers he hurried into.

Soon Cery was breathing hard, his chest aching and his legs growing unsteady. Gol drew ahead a little, but slowed after a while and looked back. He paused and waited for Cery, but his frown didn't fade and he didn't move on as Cery caught up.

"Where's Anyi?"

The lurch Cery's heart made was like a stab of pain. He whirled around to see only darkness behind them.

"I'm here," a voice said quietly, then soft footsteps preceded her out of the gloom. "I stopped to see if I could hear them following." Her expression was grim. "They are. There's more than one." She waved a hand as she hurried closer. "Get going. They're not far behind us."

Cery followed as Gol raced onward. The big man set an even faster pace. He chose a twisting route, but they did not lose their pursuers – which suggested they knew the passages as well as he and Cery. Gol drew closer to the Guild passages, but whoever followed was clearly not sufficiently intimidated by magicians to let their prey go.

They were nearing Cery's secret entrance into the tunnels under the Guild. *They won't dare follow me there.* Unless they didn't know where the passages led. *If they follow, they'll discover that the Guild leave their underground ways unguarded.* Which meant that Skellin would find out as well. *Not only will I never be able to escape that way again, but I will have to warn the Guild. They will fill the passages in and then our safest way to Sonea and Lilia will be gone.*

He regarded the Guild passages as an escape route of last resort. If there was any alternative . . .

Twenty strides or so from the entrance to the Guild passages a sound came from behind, confirming that the assassins were close. Too close — there would not be time to open the secret door before they caught up. When Gol slowed to look back at Cery — his eyebrows raised in a silent question — Cery slipped past him and headed in a new direction.

He had one other alternative. It was a riskier one. It might even lead them into greater danger than that which they fled. But at least their pursuers would be in as much danger, if they dared to follow.

Gol, realising what Cery intended, cursed under his breath. But he didn't argue. He grabbed Cery's arm to slow him, and took the lead again.

"Madness," he muttered, then raced toward Slig City.

It had been over a decade — nearly two — since dozens of street urchins had made a new home in the tunnels after the destruction of their neighbourhood. They soon became the subject of scary stories told in bolhouses and to terrify children into obedience. It was said that the Sligs never ventured into the sunlight and only emerged at night via sewers and cellars to steal food and play tricks on people. Some believed that they had bred into spindly, pale things with huge eyes that allowed them to see in the dark. Others said they looked like any other street urchin, until they opened their mouths to reveal long fangs. What all agreed on was that to venture into Slig territory was to invite death. From time to time someone would test that belief. Most never returned, but a few had crawled out again, bleeding from stab wounds delivered by silent, unseen attackers in the dark.

Locals left out offerings, hoping to avoid subterranean invasions of their homes. Cery, whose territory overlapped the Sligs' in one corner, had arranged for someone to put food in one of the tunnels every few days, the sack marked with a picture of his namesake, the little rodent ceryni.

It had been a while since he'd checked to make sure they were still doing so. *If they haven't, then I'm probably not going to get a chance to punish them for it.*

Soon he spotted the markers that warned they were crossing into Slig territory. Then he stopped seeing them. He could hear Anyi's quick breathing behind him. Had the assassins dared to follow?

"Don't," Anyi gasped as he slowed to look over his shoulder. "They're . . . right . . . behind . . . us."

He had no breath to utter a curse. Air rasped in and out of his lungs. His whole body ached, and his legs wobbled as he forced them to keep jogging onward. He made himself think of the danger Anyi was in. She would be the first one the assassins killed if they caught up. He couldn't let that happen.

Something grabbed at his ankles and he toppled forward.

The ground wasn't as flat or hard as he expected, but heaved and rolled, and muffled curses were coming from it. Gol – now invisible in utter darkness. The lamps had gone out. Cery rolled aside.

"Shut up," a voice whispered.

"Do it, Gol," Cery ordered. Gol fell silent.

Back down the passage, footsteps grew louder. Moving lights appeared, filtering through a curtain of roughly woven fabric that Cery did not recall encountering. *It must have been dropped down after we passed it.* The footsteps slowed and stopped. A sound came from another direction – more hurried footsteps. The lights moved away as their bearers continued in pursuit.

After a long pause, several sighs broke the silence. A shiver ran down Cery's spine as he realised he was surrounded by several people. A thin beam of light appeared. One of the lamps. It was being held by a stranger.

Cery looked up at a young man, who was staring back at him.

"Who?" the man asked.

"Ceryni of Northside."

"These?"

"My bodyguards."

The man's eyebrows rose, then he nodded. He turned to the others. Cery looked around to see six other young men, two sitting on top of Gol. Anyi was in a fighting crouch, a knife in both hands. The two young men standing on either side of her were keeping a safe distance, though they looked willing to risk a cut if their leader ordered them to take her down.

"Put them away, Anyi," Cery said.

Without taking her eyes from them, she obeyed. At a nod from the leader, the two men climbed off Gol, who groaned with relief. Cery rose to his feet, turned back to the leader and straightened his shoulders.

"We seek safe passage."

The young man's mouth quirked into a half-smile. "No such thing nowaday." He jabbed a thumb toward his chest. "Wen." He turned to speak to the others. "This name I know. One who leaves food. What we do?"

They exchanged glances, then muttered words to which he shook his head: "Kill?" "Free?" "Worm?" one said, and Wen looked thoughtful. He nodded. "Worm," he said decisively.

Somehow this resulted in nods, though whether of acceptance or agreement Cery couldn't tell.

Wen turned to Cery. "You all come with us. We take you to Worm." He gave Gol back his lamp, then looked at one of those who had been sitting on the big man. "Go tell Worm."

The young man scampered off into the darkness behind Wen. As Wen turned to follow, Anyi reached out and took her lamp back from the youth holding it. Two of the youngsters hurried forward to join their leader Wen and the rest took positions at the rear.

No one spoke as they walked. At first Cery only felt an overwhelming relief at simply not running any more, though his legs were still shaky and his heart was beating too fast. Gol looked as winded as he did, he noted. As he recovered he began to worry again. He'd never heard of anyone meeting with a Slig called Worm. Unless . . . *unless Worm isn't really a man, but something they feed trespassers to.*

Stop it, he told himself. *If they wanted us dead, they wouldn't have hidden us from our pursuers. They'd have stabbed us in the dark or led us into a dead end.*

After walking for some time, a voice spoke in the darkness ahead, and Wen grunted a reply. Soon a man stepped into the light and the group stopped. He stared at Cery intently, then nodded.

"You are Ceryni," he said. He extended a hand. "I am Worm."

Cery held out his hand, unsure what the gesture meant. Worm grasped it for a moment, then let it go and beckoned. "Come with me."

Another journey followed. Cery noticed that the air was growing humid, and from time to time the sound of running water came from a side passage or behind the walls. Then they stepped out into a cavernous room filled with the rush of water, and it all made sense.

A forest of columns surrounded them, each splaying out to form a brick archway that joined with its neighbour. The whole network formed a low ceiling that suggested draped fabric or a faren's web. Below this was no floor, but the reflective surface of water. Their guide was now walking along what appeared to be the top of a thick wall. The water flowed past on either side. It was too dark to tell how deep it was.

Fortunately the path was dry and not at all slippery. Glancing back, Cery saw that the water flowed into tunnels which, by the slant of their roof, descended even further under the city. On either side he saw other wall tops, too far away to reach by leaping. The only illumination came from the lamps they carried.

The water itself was surprisingly free of floating matter. Only the occasional oily slick passed them, mostly smelling of soap and fragrance. The walls bore patches of mould, however, and there was an unhealthy dampness to the air.

A cluster of lights appeared ahead and Cery soon began to make out some sort of large platform bridging two of the walls. Several people were sitting on it, and a low murmur of voices echoed in the vast room. Beyond the platform Cery made out dark circles within a lighter area, and eventually picked out enough detail to see that they were more tunnels, this time set higher up and with water spilling out into the vast underground pool.

Their footsteps set the platform creaking as they followed Worm onto it. Looking at the people, Cery saw that none were older than their mid-twenties. Two of the young women nursed babies, and a toddler was tethered by a rope to the closest column, probably so that he did not scamper off the platform into the water. All stared at Cery, Gol and Anyi with wide, curious eyes, but none spoke.

Worm glanced at Cery, then gestured at the water outlets.

"This lot come from the Guild Baths," he said. "Further south there are sewer pipes and those up north are both sewers and drains from the kitchens. But here the water is cleaner."

Cery nodded. It wasn't a bad place to settle, if you didn't mind being underground and constantly surrounded by dampness. Looking to either side he made out other platforms, populated by more Sligs, and narrow bridges linking them.

"I never knew this was here," he admitted.

"Right under your nose." Worm smiled, and Cery realised how right the man was. This part of Slig territory ran under Cery's own area. Cery turned to face him.

"Your people hid us from people who wanted to kill us," he said. "Thanks. I would never have trespassed if I'd had another choice."

Worm tilted his head to one side. "Not the Guild tunnels?"

So he knows I have access to them. Cery shook his head. "It would have shown them to my enemy. I'd have had to warn the Guild about that, and I don't expect to like what they'd do about it. I'm guessing you would not like them snooping around down here either."

The man's eyebrows rose. "No." He shrugged, then sighed. "If we'd let the one who sent the hunters after you find you, he would find us too. Once he takes your things there is nothing stopping him from taking ours."

Cery regarded Worm thoughtfully. The Sligs were far more aware of the goings-on in the world above than he'd have expected. They were right about Skellin. Once he held Cery's territory he'd want control of the Sligs too.

16

"Skellin or me. Not much of a choice," Cery said.

Worm shook his head and scowled. "He won't let us 'lone, like you do." He nodded toward the tunnels. "He will want those because he wants what they lead to."

The Guild. Cery shivered. Was this a smart guess by the Slig leader, or did he know of Skellin's specific plans? He opened his mouth to ask, but Worm turned to stare at Cery.

"I show you this so you know. But you can't stay," he said. "We will take you out in a safe place, but that is all."

Cery nodded. "It's more than I'd hoped for," he replied, putting all his gratitude into his tone.

"If you must come back, speak my name and you will live, but we will take you out again."

"I understand."

Worm held Cery's gaze for a little longer, then nodded. "Where do you want to go?"

Cery looked at Anyi and Gol. His daughter looked anxious, and Gol looked pale and exhausted. Where could they go? They had few favours left to them, and no safe place within easy reach. No allies they could trust or risk endangering. *Except one.* Cery turned back to Worm.

"Take us back the way we came."

The man spoke a word to the youths who had rescued Cery and his companions. Worm gestured to indicate Cery should follow them; then, without voicing a farewell, he walked away. Taking that as a Slig custom, Cery turned also.

The journey out of Slig territory was slower, which Cery was grateful for. Now that fear and relief had both passed, he was tired. A gloom settled over him. Gol was dragging his feet, too. At least Anyi had youthful stamina on her side. Cery began to recognise the walls around them, then the Slig guides melted away into the darkness. The lamp Cery was carrying spluttered and died as it ran out of oil. Gol did not protest as Cery took his lamp and led them to the entrance to the Guild passages.

When they had slipped through and the door was closed again, Cery felt much of the tension and fear leave him. They were safe at last. He turned to Anyi.

"So where is this room you and Lilia meet in?"

She took the lamp, leading him and Gol down the long, straight passage. After a side turn, they reached a complex of rooms connected by twisting corridors. An unwelcome memory rose of being locked in the dark, imprisoned by Lord Fergun, and Cery shivered. But these rooms were different: older and with a feel of deliberate confusion to the arrangement. Anyi took them into a room cleaned of dust, with a few small wooden boxes for furniture and a pile of worn pillows for seating. At one end was a bricked-up chimney. She set the lamp down, then lit a few candles in alcoves carved into the walls.

"This is it," she said. "I'd have brought in more furniture but I couldn't carry anything big and I didn't want to draw attention."

"No beds." Gol settled down onto one of the boxes with a groan. Cery smiled at his old friend.

"Don't worry. We'll sort something out."

But Gol's grimace didn't soften. Cery frowned as he noticed that Gol's hands were pressed to his side under his shirt. Then he saw the dark stain, glistening in the candle light.

"Gol . . . ?"

The big man closed his eyes and swayed.

"Gol!" Anyi exclaimed, reaching his side at the same time as Cery. They caught Gol before he could fall off the box. Anyi dragged pillows over.

"Lie down," she ordered. "Let me look at that."

Cery could not speak. Fear had frozen his mind and throat. The assassin must have stabbed Gol during the fight. Or perhaps before he woke up, and Cery had only seen Gol stop the second stab.

Anyi bullied Gol off the box and onto the pillows, pulling his hand away and peeling back the shirt to reveal a small wound in his belly, slowly seeping blood.

"All this time." Cery shook his head. "Why didn't you say anything?"

"It wasn't that bad." Gol shrugged, then winced. "Didn't start hurting until we were talking to Worm."

"I bet it does now," Anyi said. "How deep do you think it went?"

"Not far. I don't know." Gol coughed in pain.

"This could be worse than it looks." Anyi sat back on her heels and looked up at Cery. "I'll get Lilia."

"No . . ." Gol protested.

"It was only a few hours until dawn when we left Cadia's house," Cery told her. "Lilia might be at the University already."

Anyi nodded. "She might. Only one way to find out." She raised an eyebrow at him questioningly.

"Go," he told her.

She took his hand and pressed it over the wound. Gol groaned.

"Keep pressure on it and—"

"I know what to do," Cery told her. "If she's not there at least get something clean to use as a dressing."

"I will," she said, picking up the lamp.

Then she was gone, her footsteps fading as she hurried into the darkness.

CHAPTER 2

SUMMONED

"Should I take Mother's blood ring?" Lorkin asked as Dannyl walked through the open doorway of his rooms in the Guild House.

Dannyl looked down at the ring of gold Lorkin held, a globe of red glass set into the band. *If something should go wrong during this meeting with the Sachakan king it would be good if we both have a way to communicate with the Guild,* he thought. *But if things go that badly both of our blood rings could be found and taken, and could be used as a tool of torture and distraction against Osen and Sonea.*

That was the limitation of blood gems. They conveyed the thoughts of the wearer to the magician whose blood went into their making. The disadvantage was that the creator couldn't stop sensing the thoughts of the wearer, which was particularly unpleasant if the wearer was being tortured.

This had been done to his old friend and mentor, Rothen, by one of the Sachakan outcasts – known as Ichani – who had invaded Kyralia twenty years before. The man had caught Rothen but, instead of killing him, he'd made a gem from Rothen's blood. He had put it on every one of his victims so that Rothen received a flood of impressions from terrified, dying Kyralians.

Of Black Magician Sonea and Administrator Osen, who would be most affected if their ring was taken? Dannyl shivered at the obvious answer.

"Leave it," he advised. "I'll have Osen's ring. Give Sonea's to me and I'll hide it, in case they read your mind and learn of it."

Lorkin looked at Dannyl, an odd, half-amused expression on his face. "Don't worry, they won't read anything from me," he said.

Dannyl stared at the young magician in surprise. "You can . . .?"

"In a limited way. I didn't have the time to gain the skills the Traitors have at tricking a mind-reader. If someone tries it on me they won't succeed, but they'll know they aren't succeeding."

"Let's hope it doesn't come to that," Dannyl said. He took a step back toward the door. "I'll go hide this and meet you in the Master's Room."

Lorkin nodded.

Dannyl hurried back to his rooms, ordered the slave to leave and stop anyone entering, then looked for a place to hide the gem. *Lorkin can block a mind-read!* Ashaki Achati, the Sachakan king's adviser who had been Dannyl's friend since he had arrived in Arvice, had said the Traitors had a way of doing it. How else did their spies, posing as slaves, avoid detection? *I wonder what else Lorkin hasn't told me.* He felt a stab of frustration. Since returning to Arvice, Lorkin had been reluctant to say anything about the rebel society he'd lived with for the last few months. Dannyl understood that his former assistant had been entrusted with secrets he couldn't reveal without risking many lives. *But it gives the impression that his loyalties now lie with them more than with the Guild and Kyralia.*

21

The young magician had begun wearing robes again, so he clearly still considered himself a Guild magician – despite telling Dannyl, back when they had met in the mountains, that the Guild should act as if he'd left it.

The legs of Dannyl's travel chest were carved to look like tree stumps, with rough, twisted bark. Dannyl had cut out one of the twists with magic, making a small hollow behind it, in case he ever needed to hide Osen's ring. Easing out the twist, he set Sonea's ring inside, then plugged the hollow closed again. Then he set off for the Master's Room, the part of a traditional Sachakan house where the head of a family greeted and entertained guests.

The Guild had never officially declared that Lorkin was no long a member, despite the awkward situation this had created between Sachaka and Kyralia. Aside from avoiding the pain this would have caused Sonea, the Higher Magicians did not want to appear to give up on finding wayward magicians too quickly. However, there had been a danger that doing nothing would make it seem as if they condoned Lorkin's association with the rebels, which would strain relations between the Allied Lands and the Sachakan king.

Coming back to Arvice might have eased that strain, except for the fact that the Sachakan king badly wanted to know what Lorkin had learned about his enemy. He was about to be disappointed.

As soon as he knew the young magician had returned, King Amakira had sent orders forbidding Lorkin to leave the city. Dannyl had expected a summons to the palace to come soon after, but several days had passed with no further messages. No doubt the king had been consulting with his advisers.

Including Ashaki Achati, if his absence is any indication.

The adviser had not visited or sent any messages since the day he, Dannyl and Tayend had arrived home from their research trip to Duna. At the thought of the journey, Dannyl felt anger simmering. Tayend had manipulated Achati into taking him with them, then deliberately and successfully prevented Dannyl and Achati from becoming lovers.

Funny how that has made me want us to be together more, when before we left I was hesitant, and doubtful about the political consequences of such a relationship.

The fact that Tayend's reasons for interfering were the same as those that had caused Dannyl to hesitate in the first place, and that the current situation was exactly the sort that would make such an affair awkward, did not make it any easier for Dannyl to forgive him for interfering.

Dannyl could not help hoping it was only the situation with Lorkin that kept Achati away, rather than that the man had given up on him.

He also could not help feeling a pang of guilt. Whether he and Achati were lovers or not, there would always be secrets they must keep from each other. Secrets like the Duna people's proposal for an alliance or trade agreement with the Guild. That matter had been all but forgotten since Lorkin had returned. Once, the Guild would have been excited by any chance to acquire a new kind of magic, but the prospect of the same trade with the Traitors, who would be a more formidable ally, had eclipsed that.

Dannyl did not know exactly what the Traitors had told Lorkin to communicate to the Guild. Osen had decided that it was best that Dannyl did not know, in the unlikely event that his mind was read. Dannyl frowned. *Osen must know that*

Lorkin can block a mind-read. Lorkin isn't going to tell me anything he hasn't already told Osen.

Arriving at the Master's Room, he saw that Lorkin was already there. He, Tayend and Lady Merria, Dannyl's assistant, were sitting on stools, talking quietly. They got to their feet as Dannyl entered.

"Ready?" Dannyl asked Lorkin.

Lorkin nodded.

Tayend gave the young magician a serious look. "Good luck."

"Thanks, Ambassador," Lorkin replied.

"We've both been asking our Sachakan friends what they think the king will do," Tayend added, glancing at Merria. "Nobody wants to predict anything, but they all hope the king won't do anything to upset the Allied Lands."

"And do they think I should break my promise and tell all about the Traitors?" Lorkin asked.

Tayend grimaced in reply. "Yes." Merria nodded in agreement.

Lorkin's lips twitched into a brief smile. "Hardly surprising." But despite his apparent humour, his eyes were hard. Dannyl was suddenly reminded of Black Magician Sonea. Thinking of how stubborn Lorkin's mother had been at his age, Dannyl felt a little better about Lorkin facing the questions and bullying of the Sachakan king. *Let's hope bullying is all he tries.*

"You be careful, too," Merria said.

Dannyl realised she was looking at him, and blinked in surprise. She had been giving him dark looks since he'd returned, letting him know that she hadn't forgiven him for not taking her to Duna. He wasn't sure how to respond to her concern, especially since he didn't want to think about what would happen to himself should matters take a turn for the worse.

"I'll be fine," he told her. "We'll be fine," he added. Tayend was looking at Dannyl in a concerned way that Dannyl did not want to think about either, so he turned towards the corridor leading out of the Guild House. "Well, let's not keep the king waiting."

"No," Lorkin said softly.

Dannyl looked over to Kai, the man who was now his personal slave. Merria had learned from her friends that it was a typical ploy of slaves to switch tasks a lot, since it was harder for a master to find the right slave to punish for a particular error if many different slaves could be responsible. The more slaves you saw the harder it was to remember their names, and if you couldn't remember a slave's name it was harder to order them punished.

Merria had demanded that each occupant of the Guild House have one or two slaves dedicated to meeting their needs. But though the arrangement was closer to having a servant there were still disadvantages. A servant asked questions. A servant would tell you if something was impossible or difficult to do. A servant didn't throw himself onto the floor every time he came into your presence. Despite having had some irritatingly argumentative servants over the years, Dannyl would rather that than the inconvenience of unquestioning obedience.

"Let the carriage slaves know we're ready, Kai," Dannyl instructed.

Kai hurried ahead. Dannyl led Lorkin down the corridor to the front door. As they stepped out, bright sunlight dazzled Dannyl's eyes and he lifted a hand to shade them. The sky was blue and cloudless, and there was a warmth and dryness to the air that, in Kyralia, he'd have associated with the onset of summer. Here it was only early spring. As always, the slaves threw themselves onto the ground. Dannyl ordered them to rise, then he and Lorkin climbed on board the waiting carriage.

They rode in silence. Dannyl considered all that Osen had told him to say, and to avoid saying. He wished he knew more of what Lorkin and the Guild planned. Not knowing the full truth made him uneasy. All too soon the carriage turned into the wide tree-lined avenue leading to the palace, then pulled up outside the building. The slaves clambered to the ground and opened the door.

Dannyl climbed out and waited for Lorkin to join him.

"Pretty," Lorkin said, gazing up at the building in admiration. *Of course, he hasn't seen the palace before*, Dannyl thought. Looking up at the curved white walls, and the top of the glittering gold dome just visible above, he remembered how impressed he'd been the first time he'd visited. He was too worried about the coming interview to feel admiration now.

Turning his attention to the entrance, he led Lorkin inside. They strode down the wide corridor, past the guards, out into the huge, column-filled hall that served as the king's grand Master's Room. Dannyl's heart began to beat faster as he saw many more people were present than at any time when he'd met the king before. Instead of a cluster of two or three people here and there, there was a small crowd. Judging by their highly decorated short jackets and confident poses, most of them were Ashaki. He counted quickly. *About fifty.*

Knowing that there were so many black magicians surrounding him sent an unpleasant chill down his spine. He concentrated on keeping his face impassive and his walk dignified, hoping he was hiding his fear successfully.

King Amakira was sitting on his throne. Though old, he looked as tense and alert as the youngest of the Sachakans in

26

the room. His eyes never left Lorkin until Dannyl stopped and dropped to one knee. Lorkin, as instructed, followed suit.

"Rise, Ambassador Dannyl," the king said.

Dannyl stood up and resisted looking at Lorkin, who was obliged to remain kneeling until told otherwise. The king's gaze had shifted back to the young magician. His gaze was intense.

"Rise, Lord Lorkin."

Lorkin got to his feet, looked at the king, then lowered his gaze politely.

"Welcome back," the king said.

"Thank you, your majesty."

"Have you recovered from your journey back to Arvice?"

"I have, your majesty."

"That is good to hear." The king looked at Dannyl and a kind of cold amusement crept into his eyes. "Ambassador, I wish to hear Lorkin tell how he came to leave Arvice, live with the Traitors and then return."

Dannyl nodded. "I expected you would, your majesty," he replied, managing a smile. He turned to Lorkin. "Tell him what you told me, Lord Lorkin."

The young magician gave Dannyl an amused, almost reproachful look before he turned back to the king. Dannyl suppressed a smile. *If he tells them what he told me, he'll hardly be telling them much at all.*

"On the night that I left the Guild House," Lorkin began, "a slave crept into my bed and tried to kill me. I was saved by another slave, who convinced me that assassins would return to finish me off if I didn't leave with her. My rescuer, as I'm sure you've guessed, was not really a slave at all, but one of the Traitors.

"She explained that the society she belonged to was formed before the Sachakan War, when a group of women were driven to unite by their ill treatment in Sachakan society. The war forced them into the mountains, where they became a new people, rejecting slavery and inequality between men and women."

"They are ruled by women," the king interrupted. "How is that equal?"

Lorkin shrugged. "It's not a perfect arrangement, but still fairer than any I've encountered or heard of."

"So you went to their base?"

"Yes. It was the safest place to go, what with the assassins still hunting for me."

"Could you find it again?"

Lorkin shook his head. "No. I was blindfolded."

The king's eyes narrowed. "How big is their base? How many Traitors are there?"

"I . . . I can't really say."

"You can't or you won't?"

"It wasn't the sort of place where you can easily guess how many people are around."

"Take a guess anyway."

Lorkin spread his hands. "More than a hundred."

"Did you gain any impressions of their fighting strength?"

Once again, Lorkin shook his head. "I never saw them fight. Some are magicians. You know that already. I can't tell you numbers, their strength or how well trained they are."

A movement among the Ashaki near the throne attracted Dannyl's attention, and his heart skipped at he recognised Achati. The man met Dannyl's eyes briefly, but his only expression was one of thoughtfulness. He leaned closer to the king and murmured something. The king's stare didn't waver from Lorkin, but his eyebrows lowered slightly.

"What did you do while with the Traitors?" he asked.

"I helped treat the sick."

"They trusted you, a foreigner, to heal them?"

"Yes."

"Did you teach them anything?"

"A few things. I learned a few things, too."

"What did you teach them?"

"Some new cures – and I learned several from them, though some require plants we don't have in Kyralia."

"Why did you leave them?"

Lorkin paused, obviously not expecting the question so soon. "Because I wanted to return home."

"Why didn't you leave sooner?"

"They do not usually let foreigners leave. But they changed their minds in my case."

"Why?"

"There was no reason not to. I hadn't learned anything important, so I couldn't reveal anything important. When I left, they made sure I'd never be able to find my way back."

The king regarded him thoughtfully. "Even so, you've seen more of the Traitors' base than any non-Traitor has before. There may be details you do not understand the significance of. These rebels are a danger to this country, and may one day be a danger to other lands in this region, including yours. Will you consent to a mind-read?"

Lorkin went very still. The hall was quiet as he opened his mouth to answer.

"No, your majesty."

"I will enlist only my most skilled mind-reader. He will

not search your thoughts, but will allow you to present your memories to him."

"I appreciate that, but I am obliged to protect the knowledge taught to me by the Guild. I must refuse."

The king's gaze moved to Dannyl. His expression was unreadable. "Ambassador, will you order Lord Lorkin to cooperate with a mind-reader?"

Dannyl took a deep breath.

"With respect, your majesty, I cannot. I do not have the authority to do so."

The king's eyebrows lowered. "But you have a blood ring that allows you to communicate with the Guild. Contact them. Get the order from whoever has the authority to give it."

Dannyl opened his mouth to protest, but thought better of it. He must look as if he was trying to be cooperative. Reaching into his robes he took Osen's ring from his pocket and slipped it on a finger.

—*Osen?*

—*Dannyl*, came the immediate reply. The Administrator had said he would arrange to be unoccupied while the meeting with the Sachakan king took place, and Dannyl detected no surprise at his communication.

—*They want the Guild to order Lorkin to submit to a mind-read.*

—*Ah. Of course. They won't believe a word he says.*

—*What should I tell them?*

—*That only Merin has the authority to order it, and he will only consider it once he has had a chance to interview Lorkin personally and privately.*

Dannyl felt a chill. The only way the Kyralian king could make his wishes clearer would be to abandon formality and demand Amakira send Lorkin home. —*Nothing else?*

30

—Not for now. See what Amakira says to that.

Dannyl slipped off the ring and, keeping it in one hand, looked up at the king of Sachaka and conveyed Osen's message.

Amakira stared at Dannyl for what felt like a long, long time. When he finally moved, it was preceded by a shifting of his jaw muscles that hinted at the anger the message had roused.

"That is inconvenient," he said quietly. "And forces me to question whether I must cast aside efforts at cooperation between our nations for the sake of protecting my own – or at least reduce my efforts to match that of Kyralia's." He pursed his lips, and turned to look at two of the Ashaki. "Please escort Lord Lorkin to the prison."

Lorkin took a half-step backwards, then stopped. As the two Ashaki approached, Dannyl moved forward.

"I must protest, your majesty!" Dannyl exclaimed. "I ask on behalf of the Allied Lands that you honour the agreement—"

"Either Lord Lorkin goes to prison, or Lord Lorkin goes to prison and Ambassador Dannyl leaves Sachaka," the king said, loud enough to drown Dannyl's words.

—Let them take him.

Dannyl almost gasped aloud in surprise at the voice in his head. He realised he was gripping the ring tightly, allowing the gem to touch his skin and therefore conveying his thoughts to Osen.

—Are you sure?

—Yes, the Administrator replied. *We hoped this wouldn't happen, of course, but we'd rather not lose Lorkin and have you expelled from Sachaka. Go back to the Guild House and start nagging Amakira to let Lorkin go. We'll be doing everything we can from this end.*

Dannyl felt his heart sink as the two Ashaki stepped past him and stopped on either side of Lorkin. The young magician looked resigned and worried, but when he met Dannyl's eyes he managed a wan smile.

"I'll be fine," he said. Then he let the two men lead him away.

Dannyl turned back to the king.

"Take him if you must, your majesty, but do not harm him," he warned, "or any chance of a peaceful alliance between the Allied Lands and Sachaka will be much harder to achieve in the future. That would be a great shame."

Amakira's stare did not waver, but his voice was quieter as he spoke.

"Go back to the Guild House, Ambassador. This meeting is over."

Even before Sonea opened her eyes, she knew it was too soon for her to be waking up. Turning toward the screen over her bedroom window, she frowned as she saw early morning light reflected on the wall behind it. The light at this time of day always had a quality that distinguished it from the late evening glow, and told her that she had only been asleep for an hour or two.

A knocking from the main room told her why she was awake.

Groaning, she threw her arms over her eyes and waited. Every morning, except on Freedays, Black Magician Kallen stopped by to escort Lilia to lessons. Most of the time the novice prepared for her day at the University quietly enough not to wake Sonea. But it had taken Kallen some time to work out, after Sonea pointedly mentioned several times that she usually took the night shift at the hospice, that he should knock *softly*.

He appeared to have forgotten this morning.

The knocking came again, even louder. Sonea groaned again. Why wasn't Lilia answering the door? Sighing, she threw off the bedclothes and forced herself into a standing position. She ran her hands through her hair to straighten it, grabbed an overrobe and threw it on over her bedclothes. Entering the main room, she headed for the door, tossing a little magic out to turn the handle.

As the door swung inward, a frowning Kallen looked up and saw her, and his eyebrows lowered further. His gaze flickered to her overrobe and back up to meet her gaze, his expression not changing.

"Good morning, Black Magician Sonea," he said. "Sorry to disturb you. Is Lilia here?"

Sonea looked toward Lilia's closed bedroom door on the other side of the room, then walked over to it. She knocked quietly, then louder, then opened the door. The room was empty. The bed was made, however, so clearly Sonea's aunt and servant, Jonna, had been and gone.

"No," she said, returning to the main door. "And no, I don't know where she is. When I do, I'll let you know."

"Thank you." Kallen looked decidedly unhappy, but he nodded and stepped away from the door.

Closing the door, Sonea headed back towards the bedroom, then stopped. It was unusual for Lilia to be absent of a morning. It was not in her nature to misbehave or cause trouble, but she still needed watching over because she had proven to be easily led astray by others.

Perhaps not as easily as in the past, though. After all, being tricked into learning black magic by your closest friend so she could frame you for the murder she committed has got to make you consider carefully who you trust. Not to mention discovering that Lorandra, the rogue magician who had helped Lilia escape from prison, intended to return that favour by turning Lilia over to her son, the infamous Thief, Skellin, so that Lilia could teach him black magic.

While Sonea trusted Lilia not to *willingly* get into serious trouble again, she might unwillingly do so. Sonea was also obliged to look as though she was keeping an eye on all other black magicians. Though she wasn't officially Lilia's guardian – that was Kallen's role – letting the girl stay in her rooms had given everyone the impression she had taken responsibility for her.

Looking around the room, Sonea saw the corner of a slip of paper under the water jug on the side table. She walked across the room and picked it up.

Left early to meet a friend. Tell BMK I will go straight from there to class. Lilia.

Sonea sighed and rolled her eyes, but her annoyance soon passed. The message was probably not for her, but Jonna. The servant hadn't seen it – or wasn't able to wait around to meet Kallen – or else had tried and failed to find him.

The friend was probably Anyi, who had saved Lilia from being handed over to Skellin. Since Anyi was Cery's daughter, Sonea wasn't entirely convinced the girl wouldn't lead Lilia astray in some way.

Cery wouldn't let the girls get into trouble. Even so . . . I wonder why Lilia is meeting Anyi at this time of day – and where. Sonea put the note down. She knew that Anyi was entering her rooms the same way that Cery occasionally did: through a hidden doorway in the guest room. But for Lilia to leave to meet Anyi meant they were getting together elsewhere, and that *was* something to worry about. As a new black magician, Lilia was forbidden to leave the Guild grounds.

Perhaps she went back through the hatch with Anyi. The passages beneath the Guild were forbidden to all but the Higher Magicians, officially because they were unstable and dangerous but mainly because there was never any *good* reason for anybody to be down there. That wasn't what worried Sonea the most about Lilia leaving to meet Anyi, however.

Skellin wanted Cery dead. That meant that anybody who helped him was a target. So far Cery had been able to conceal the fact that Anyi was his daughter. Officially she was still a bodyguard, but that still meant she was a target. Lilia might be able to protect herself with magic, but if the attacker was Skellin or his mother, Lorandra, she would be in trouble since both were magicians.

Has she left because Cery needs her help? But surely he'd contact me first. She frowned. Lately Cery had been hard to find, and when they did manage to meet he looked gaunt and anxious. She suspected he was polishing the truth about his efforts to find Skellin, and was only succeeding in keeping himself out of the rogue Thief's reach.

Sighing for a third time, Sonea went back into the bedroom, but not to sleep. It was unlikely she would do more than lie awake, now that she had both Cery and Lilia to worry over. She washed and dressed, drew a little magic to soothe away weariness, and was making a cup of raka when someone knocked on the main door again.

Catching herself about to sigh again – she had sighed far too much already today – she looked over her shoulder and opened the door with magic.

Administrator Osen stepped into the doorway. She blinked in surprise.

"Administrator."

"Black Magician Sonea," he said, inclining his head politely. "May I come in?"

"Of course," she replied, turning to face him. He closed the door. "Would you like some raka or sumi?"

He shook his head. "I have some bad but not entirely unexpected news."

She felt a sensation uncomfortably like all her inner organs turning to water. *Lorkin.*

"How bad?"

Osen's lips thinned in sympathy. "Not the worst news. I'd be more direct, if that was the case. Lorkin refused a mind-read. King Amakira demanded he be ordered to submit to one. King Merin refused. Amakira sent Lorkin to prison."

A chill ran down her spine and her stomach flipped over. An image of Lorkin chained up in a dank, dark cell sprang into her mind and she felt nauseous. In her mind's eye he was a frightened boy. *But he isn't. He's a grown man. He knew this might happen, and still refused to betray the Traitors. I have to trust his judgement that they are worth saving.* She forced her attention back to Osen.

"What now?" she asked, though the Higher Magicians had discussed this eventuality many times before.

"We work towards freeing him. We being the Guild, the king, and the Elyne king. If Lorkin is right, and he can prevent them reading his mind, then we must convince

Amakira that letting him go is the easiest path towards learning more about the Traitors. That's where your role begins."

Sonea nodded and felt a belated relief. Her task to meet the Traitors on behalf of the Guild had become more complicated when it became clear King Amakira wouldn't let Lorkin leave Sachaka until he had learned all he could from him. The Guild had decided to send her to Arvice as well to negotiate her son's release. This worsening of Lorkin's circumstances could have made them change their minds.

Because the Higher Magicians had decided that only a black magician would receive the respect needed to negotiate with the Sachakan king, that meant choosing between her and Kallen – Lilia being too young and still a novice. They had good reasons not to choose either of them. While the Sachakans regarded women as having less status than men, and being Lorkin's mother might leave her open to blackmail, Kallen's addiction to roet made him potentially unreliable and just as vulnerable to coercion.

And perhaps knowing that I have killed Sachakans before, and would be prepared to do so to save my son, may also nudge Amakira towards releasing him.

Of course, the Sachakan king might threaten to harm Lorkin in order to gain something from her, but there wasn't much he could gain from that. She did not know what they wanted to find out, and could not order him to speak. All she could do was promise to try to persuade him to, if they let him go.

Unless, of course, he gives in to torture first. But she didn't want to think about that. She turned to Osen.

"So when do I leave?"

*   *   *

Faint light spilling out of a doorway ahead told Lilia that she and Anyi were nearly at their destination. Dodging rubble in the corridor, she followed her friend to the opening and into the room beyond.

Cery was sitting on one of the old wooden boxes Anyi had found to use as seats. Under his hands, lying on some of the threadbare pillows from the pile Lilia and Anyi had so often lounged upon, was Gol. Even in the dim candlelight she could see he was pale. She brought her globe light closer and brightened it. His brow was slick with sweat and his stare was feverish with pain.

Lilia stared down at him, paralysed with doubt. *Do I know enough of Healing yet to save him?*

"Just . . . try," Anyi urged.

Glancing at her friend, Lilia nodded. She made herself kneel down beside Gol. Cery's hands were pressed against Gol's abdomen, stained with blood.

"Should I take the pressure off?" Cery asked.

"I . . . I'm not sure yet," Lilia admitted. "I'll just . . . look."

She pulled away more of Gol's shirt, placed a palm on his bare skin, then closed her eyes and sent her senses outward and into his body.

At first all was chaos, but she drew upon what she had been told or read, and on exercises designed to make sense of all the signals. The first thing that was obvious was the pain. She nearly gasped aloud as she picked that up, and was proud that she did not lose focus. Pain was easy to stop. It was one of the early lessons taught to Healers. Once she'd tackled that, she looked for other information. Her mind was drawn toward the damaged part, where essential liquids were being lost, and others that were dangerously poisonous were trickling into healthy systems.

His guts have been nicked by the blade that stabbed him. He'd have died already if the leak had been much larger. Clearly that's what I have to fix first . . .

Drawing magic, she fed it into the rupture so that the edges of the wound knit together, healing faster than they could ever have done without intervention.

Now I have to stop the blood leaking out. But before I do, there's this poison from the guts and the blood pooling inside him to deal with. Use one to help wash out the other. She hoped Cery and Anyi weren't panicking as she used magic to force the liquids out of the wound. There was a little more resistance to this than she'd expected. Then she remembered that Cery was still pressing on the wound. She concentrated on her own body enough to gain control of her vocal chords.

"You can stop now," she made herself say.

She saw the blood begin to flow again, and was forced to concentrate hard to align and Heal the separated flesh and skin. Remembering warnings from her teachers, she checked within to make sure there were no internal rents causing bleeding to continue within. A few tubes needed fixing. Easily done.

After a final check, she drew her senses back to herself, took a deep breath and opened her eyes. Gol's face was no longer rigid with pain. He looked up at her and smiled.

"Better?" she asked.

He nodded. "Yes. But . . . tired. Very tired." He frowned. "Thirsty."

"You will be. You've lost blood and there might be some inflammation from the poison."

"The blade was poisoned?" Cery asked, alarmed.

"No, but his gut was sliced into. What's inside acts like a poison if it gets into the rest of the body."

Cery regarded the big man thoughtfully. "You're not going to be any good for fighting practice for a while." He looked at Lilia. "How long until he fully recovers?"

She shrugged. "I'm not sure, but faster if he can get good food and clean water." She looked at Anyi. "If you come with me I'll see if Jonna left anything back in the room. There'll be water, at least."

"You're already late for classes," Anyi pointed out. "You should go straight to the University."

"In these?" Lilia looked down at her novice robes. They were scuffed and dirty from climbing down the narrow gap within the Magicians' Quarters walls that allowed her to slip out of Sonea's rooms and into the underground passages. Normally Anyi brought some old clothes for her to change into, but this time she'd arrived empty-handed. They couldn't keep them in Sonea's rooms in case Jonna, Sonea's servant, found them. Lilia hadn't wanted to risk that Gol might die while she tried to find something else to change into.

Anyi looked at Lilia's robes. "Can't you use magic to fix them?"

Lilia sighed. "I can try. Depends how bad they are. It might take longer than going back."

Anyi inspected her. "Doesn't look too bad. Nothing you can't explain away as having tripped and fallen into a hedge."

"What about getting food and water?"

Anyi shrugged. "I'll do it."

"Sonea will be in her rooms all day."

"She works the night shift at the hospice, right? So she'll be asleep."

"And if she isn't? Or she wakes up?"

"Then I'll tell her I dropped in to visit you and I was hungry."

"If it's just water we need, I know of a few leaky pipes,"

Cery said. He looked at Lilia sternly. "But we'll be in a worse situation if you miss classes or someone realises you've been roaming around under the Guild. We're going to be stuck here for a while, and need you free to visit us, Lilia."

She looked from him to Anyi. He was right, of course. While classes seemed unimportant compared to keeping her friends safe and well, skipping them would only rouse suspicion. Once more she cursed herself for giving in to curiosity, and trying the instructions on using black magic in Naki's book. Nobody had paid her any attention when she had been an ordinary novice. She sighed and nodded. "All right. But I'm coming back tonight with dinner for you all."

"How are you going to manage that?" Cery asked, one eyebrow rising.

"Oh, Jonna is always telling me to eat more, and leaving me little snacks to have while studying. Tonight I'm going to be unusually peckish."

CHAPTER 3

QUESTIONS

L orkin suspected the relief he felt was premature, as the Ashaki interrogator ushered him out of the room. Their path looked as if it would be a reversal of the one they'd taken that morning, from the cell Lorkin had been sent to upon leaving the palace hall, to the room he'd been questioned in. Perhaps they were finished for the day. Perhaps it was night outside. Lorkin's stomach had been his only indicator of the passing of time, and it wasn't a particularly good one. During moments when not knotted with anxiety it growled quietly with hunger.

The interrogator, who hadn't introduced himself, led the way, his assistant following behind Lorkin. Lorkin only knew that he was an Ashaki because a guard had addressed him as such.

They reached a corridor that Lorkin remembered well, because it sloped downward into the prison area. Once again he wondered why there were no stairs, but now the answer became clear: a prison guard was pushing a trolley towards them. On the trolley lay a very thin, very old man wearing nothing but a white cloth from his waist to his knees. As the interrogator moved past, Lorkin stole a look at the old man's face, then looked closer.

Is he dead? The chest didn't rise or fall. The old man's lips were bluish. *Looks like it.* He scanned hurriedly for wounds but spotted none. Not even marks where manacles might have encircled wrists. *Perhaps he died of old age. Or illness. Or starvation. Or black magic . . .* He resisted he urge to reach out and touch the corpse, and to use his Healing senses to search for the cause of death.

At the end of the sloped corridor they entered a wide room. Manacles hung from walls, red with rust. A pile of similarly tarnished metal objects lay in one corner — shapes that might suggest torture devices to frightened imaginations. In contrast, the bars that criss-crossed the alcoves along two sides of the room were a dull black, without a hint of age or weakness.

Three larger cells took up the longer wall of the room, and five small ones along the shorter. Only two were occupied: one containing two middle-aged men and the other a young couple. Two guards sat near the main room's entrance with another man dressed in a more sombre version of the usual Ashaki male garb. The latter nodded at the interrogator, who returned the gesture.

Prisoners rarely stayed more than a few weeks, Lorkin had been told. Even if judged guilty. Magicians were too much trouble to keep locked away, and non-magicians were simply sold into slavery. The interrogator hadn't said whether the magicians were freed or executed.

That's part of the game, Lorkin thought. *Constant hints at dire consequences if I don't cooperate, but no direct threats. Yet.*

The man had gone on to wonder aloud whether Lorkin qualified as a magician, in the Sachakan sense, since his magical knowledge was incomplete. Did not knowing higher magic make Lorkin a half-magician? Keeping a half-magician prisoner might still be more troublesome than it was worth. Still, it had been done before, though not here. With Lorkin's very own father.

If he was trying to insult me it was a weak attempt. Surely he knows that Guild magicians don't see our lack of higher magic as any kind of deficiency – rather it is a more honourable state. I suppose pointing out that my father was once a slave was his true aim.

Even so, that fact wasn't the source of humiliation to Lorkin that it would have been to a Sachakan noble. Akkarin had been enslaved by an Ichani, outcasts who were an embarrassment and annoyance to the rest of Sachaka – and an indication of weakness in their society. Lorkin did not point this out, though.

Aside from a few other attempted jibes, the interrogator had spent the day asking questions and pointing out how bad it would be for Lorkin, the Guild and peace between Sachaka and the Allied Lands if Lorkin didn't tell him everything about the Traitors. There were only so many questions that could be asked, and versions of the same warning, so the man had repeated himself a lot.

Lorkin had also repeated, apologetically but firmly, his refusal to answer. He did not want to get chatty, and risk inadvertently giving them any information they could use against the Traitors. Eventually he decided his refusals were only going to be ignored, so he stuck to saying nothing. It wasn't as easy as he'd thought it would be, but he only had to think about how much harder it would be to resist torture and his resolve hardened. Still, they hadn't tried to read his mind yet, so they didn't know it wouldn't work – so long, that is, as the Traitors' mind-read-blocking gem lying under the skin of his palm did its job. Perhaps King Amakira remained reluctant to harm relations with the Allied Lands by doing so. Perhaps he hoped Lorkin would give in to questioning and threats.

Reaching the gate to the cell Lorkin had been locked in previously, the interrogator waved him inside. The gate closed. Lorkin turned back to see that the Ashaki in the sombre garb had approached them.

"Done?" he asked.

"For now," the interrogator replied.

"He wants you to report."

The interrogator nodded, then led his companion away.

The newcomer looked through the gate at Lorkin, his eyes narrowing, then moved away. Lorkin watched him glance around the room, his gaze resting on a simple wooden chair. The chair rose in the air and floated to a position in front of Lorkin's cell, then settled upon its legs.

The well-dressed man sat down and proceeded to watch Lorkin.

Being stared at was not something Lorkin particularly relished, but he figured he would have to get used to it. He looked around the cell. It was empty but for a bucket for excrement in one corner. He hadn't eaten or drunk anything all day, so he felt no need to relieve himself strong enough to draw him into using the bucket while being watched.

Eventually I'll have to. Better get used to that idea, as well.

With no other choice, Lorkin sat down on the dusty floor and rested his back against the rough wall. He'd probably have to sleep on the floor, too. The stone was hard and cold. At least it was sufficiently cool here for his robes no longer to feel uncomfortably hot. It was easy to warm the air with magic, but cooling it involved stirring the air, preferably past water.

He thought back to the moment he had donned robes again after months living as a Traitor. It had been a relief at first. He'd appreciated the generous style of garment and the soft, richly dyed fabric. As the Sachakan spring brought hotter days, he'd begun to find the robes heavy and impractical. When he was alone, in his room at the Guild House, he'd taken off the outer robe and worn only the trousers. He'd begun to long for simple, economical Traitor clothes.

That longing was probably as much to do with wishing he was back in Sanctuary. Immediately memories of Tyvara rose and he felt his heart lighten. The most recent recollection, of the last night they were together, with her naked and smiling as she taught him how lovers used black magic, set his pulse racing. Then older memories rose. Like the way she moved when in Sanctuary, secure and confident – taking for granted the power her society granted her. Like the direct stare that was both playful and intelligent.

He also remembered her before then, as she'd led him across the Sachakan plains toward the mountains, protecting him from Traitor assassins and them both from capture by the Ashaki. She'd been tired and difficult to talk to, yet had impressed him with her determination and resourcefulness.

He sent his mind further back to a memory of her in her guise as a slave of the Guild House. Shoulders hunched and eyes downcast, confused by his attempts to befriend her. He'd been attracted to her even then, though he'd told himself he was only fascinated by her exotic looks. But no other Sachakan woman had drawn his eyes in the same way, and he'd seen plenty of beautiful ones in both Arvice and Sanctuary.

Sanctuary. I actually miss the place, he realised. *Now that I've left, I can see that I liked it there, despite Kalia.* Memories of being abducted, locked away, bound and gagged while Kalia searched his mind for the secret of magical Healing darkened his thoughts, but he pushed them aside. *Kalia is no longer a Speaker. No longer in charge of the Care Room*, he reminded himself. *The Traitors have their flaws, some more than others, but all in all they're good people.* Being stuck working with Kalia in the Care Room, worrying about her manipulations and how he was going to convince the Traitors to trade with the Guild, had distracted him too much to truly appreciate their way of life.

His abduction had been the action of a small number of less scrupulous Traitors. He suspected not all of Kalia's faction would have condoned her actions. Most of them wouldn't have been willing to break Traitor laws as Kalia had, even if they agreed with her. They only thought the way they did out of a desire to protect their people. Their fear of the outside world was well ingrained after centuries of hiding in the mountains.

While he wasn't quite ready to forgive Kalia for stealing Healing knowledge from him, he could hardly begrudge her the desire to be able to use it to save the lives of Traitors. *Still, she was planning to kill me and claim I'd attempted to flee Sanctuary and froze in the winter snows. That's not something I intend to forgive.*

As compensation for what was taken from him, Queen Zarala had decreed that he be taught how to make magical gemstones. He'd learned a kind of magic the Guild had never heard of. It was the dream of finding new, powerful magic that had led him to volunteer as Ambassador Dannyl's assistant in the first place. Looking back, he smiled at his own naivety. The chances

47

of finding something had been ridiculously remote. And yet he had.

His hopes of finding magic that might render black magic obsolete, or at least provide protection against it, hadn't been fulfilled, however. The potential in magical gemstones to negate the need for black magicians was in turn negated by the fact that a stone-maker needed to learn black magic in order to create them.

He felt his smile fade and a knot of worry form inside his stomach. *What will the Guild do when they find out that I know black magic? Will they forgive it, once they understand I could not have learned stone-making otherwise?*

He had considered all possible consequences, and had hardened himself to the worst of them: the possibility they would exile him from the Allied Lands, as they had done his father. It would hurt, but would also free him to return to Sanctuary and Tyvara, which wasn't too bad an outcome. Apart from one thing.

Mother is going to be disappointed in me. No – more than that. She'll be devastated.

Which was why he hadn't said anything about it to Ambassador Dannyl or Administrator Osen yet. It was one piece of news he would be putting off for as long as possible. Osen *had* decided that nobody should be told anything more than necessary, in case the Sachakans did start reading minds. Even so, Lorkin knew he couldn't avoid Sonea finding out forever.

But when she does, I'd rather she didn't hear it from anyone else. It's not going to be easy to tell her, but maybe if I do it myself it'll be easier for her to hear.

* * *

Cery had lost count of the times he'd woken up, but this time he knew there was something different about the waking even before he gathered enough awareness to name what it was.

Light. After Anyi had returned with a little food and water taken from Sonea's rooms, which they had given to Gol, they'd decided to sleep. To avoid using up all the candles, they'd blown them out – but not before Cery had tricked Anyi into giving him her matches. He hoped that robbing her of a source of portable light would keep her from exploring the passages while he was asleep. Though she assured him she knew most of them now, she had to agree that the lack of maintenance and repair had left many unsafe.

The pile of old pillows had been divided between the three of them. Though he had enough to protect him from the cold, hard floor, keeping them together was a challenge. If he changed position, one would inevitably skitter off into the darkness, and he'd have to grope around to find it and stuff it back underneath him.

I wonder if anyone is living in my old hiding places, enjoying the fancy furniture and drinking my wine, he thought as he sat up. Though broken sleep had left him aching with weariness, he was relieved to be giving up on trying. The light outlined the doorway and was brightening. He heard a familiar voice call out, "It's just me!"

They could have the wine and the luxuries. All he wanted now was a warm fire and a comfortable bed. And for those he loved to be safe.

The loved ones of a Thief are never safe.

A stab of pain went through him, savage despite its familiarity. For a moment all he could see was a memory of his wife's and sons' bodies, but he closed his eyes and willed the vision away.

Will I ever stop remembering? Or will it stop hurting to remember?
Guilt rose at the thought. *I shouldn't want to, but I can't do anything
to change their deaths and I won't be able to protect Anyi if I let grief
and anger distract and control me.* He sighed. *And I'd rather remember
them whole and happy than . . . than that.*

The source of the light entered the room. Dazzled, Cery
looked away from the globe of magical light to the young
woman standing below it. Lilia smiled at him and held out a
basket.

"I told Jonna that Anyi might be visiting. She brought some
extra food. I took a bottle of Sonea's wine – not from the
expensive ones. Well, not the *really* expensive ones."

Anyi leapt to her feet, kissed Lilia on the cheek and grabbed
the basket.

"You're a treasure, Lilia," she said, sitting down on one of
the wooden boxes and rifling through. "Buns! Meat-filled and
sweet ones." Then her nose wrinkled. "Urgh. Fruit."

"It's good for you and easy to carry," Lilia told her, but she
was looking at Gol. "You look better."

Cery turned to see his friend sitting up, nodding and
stretching. A thoughtful look crossed Gol's face. "Still tired,
though."

She nodded. "My books says your body will take a couple
of days to replenish the blood you lost. Depends how much
you bled. If you do start feeling sick again let me know. It
might be some poison was left. I should be able to Heal you
if there is."

"A few days." Anyi looked at Cery. "Is that going to be a
problem?"

Cery held out a hand for a meat-filled bun, took a bite and
chewed as he considered. He still had loyal people out there.

They would start to worry if he didn't contact them. They might even assume he, Gol and Anyi were dead. What would happen if they did? Cery had no illusions that they'd stand up to Skellin. Most likely the rogue Thief would take control of Cery's territory. Not personally. He'd arrange for an ally to take over.

"Let them think we're dead," Gol said.

Cery looked at his friend in surprise. He hadn't expected this. *What* had *I expected? That Gol would try to get up and pretend to be healthier than he is, rather than be the reason I lost my territory? Or that he'd tell me to abandon him here? All very noble. Am I so vain that I expect my friends to sacrifice themselves for me?* Cery frowned. *No, it isn't that. It's that I didn't expect Gol to give up before I did.*

"Next time you won't get away," Gol said. "We were lucky this time. I've been lying here trying to decide who told Skellin's people you were at Cadia's house. Who betrayed us? Did they have any choice? You can't stop Skellin blackmailing and bribing your own people. He's got too many allies, too much money. You've already . . . ."

". . . already lost your own territory," Cery finished. He felt bitterness rising. But it was an emotion too familiar and worn out to do more than make him feel tired. It had crept in after Selia and the boys had been murdered, and he had grown used to it.

"Let them think you're dead. Maybe Skellin will get smug, let his guard down. Maybe with nobody else fighting him, other people will try. Maybe they'll set him up. Betray him to the Guild."

It was tempting. Very tempting.

"You want to stay *here*?" Cery asked, pretending disbelief.

"Yes." Gol looked at Anyi and Lilia. "What do you think?"

Anyi shrugged. "We can block off the entrance to the Guild passages – collapse them if you think it's safer. There are passages that come out in the forest, so we have escape routes. Well, ones that don't lead into the Guild buildings, that is." Anyi glanced at Lilia. "We'll work out ways to get food and water down here."

Lilia nodded. "I'm sure Sonea would help."

"No, we can't tell her." Cery paused, surprised at the conviction in his own voice. *Why don't I want Sonea's help?* "She won't like it. She'll want to smuggle us out of the city. She'll tell Kallen." He didn't entirely trust Kallen, and it wasn't only because the man was a roet addict.

"She wouldn't," Lilia said, though her voice lacked conviction.

"Cery's right," Gol said. "Sonea's leaving for Sachaka. She'll either want someone else high up in the Guild to know we're here, or she'll move us out."

"So . . . if you don't want Kallen to know either," Anyi said, "then you won't be able to work with him any more."

"No." Cery turned to Lilia. "But he doesn't need us to tell him that. We can say it's safer if we communicate through messages, which Lilia will send."

"We won't have anything useful to tell him if we stay here and have no contact with your people," Anyi pointed out.

"No, but he'll keep us informed as to what's going on out there," Cery replied, "before he gives up on us as a source of information. And hopefully we will find a way to be useful again – which we won't if Sonea sends us away."

The four of them exchanged looks, then nodded.

"Well, first Lilia and I need to find solutions for the most basic needs, like food and water," Anyi said decisively, straightening. "And then to make things safer and more comfortable down here."

Cery smiled at the determined look on her face. If he let her, she would take charge of them all. "No," he disagreed. "That's not what we'll do first."

She looked at him, frowning in puzzlement. "No?"

He nodded at the basket. "First we eat."

If there was a code of etiquette that allowed Sachakans to refuse entry to an unwanted guest, Dannyl wished he knew what it was. It wasn't that he didn't want to see the Ashaki who was coming down the entrance passage of the Guild House. He yearned to see the man. But he suspected that the visitor was here in his official capacity, and that was something Dannyl was not looking forward to.

Being friends with the enemy certainly complicates matters.

As Achati entered the room, Dannyl searched the man's face for some hint of good news, despite knowing the chances were slim. He was surprised when he saw regret and apology there. He'd expected a carefully maintained neutral expression.

"Welcome back to the Guild House, Ashaki Achati," Dannyl said, falling back on Kyralian manners.

"I wish it were under more amicable circumstances," Achati replied. "This is an official visit, but I also wish it to be an informal one between friends, if that is still possible."

Dannyl invited Achati to sit, taking the main chair for himself. "That depends on how the official part goes," he replied wryly.

"Then let's get the official part over with first." Achati paused to regard Dannyl. "King Amakira wants you to persuade Lorkin to answer all questions regarding the Traitors."

"I doubt I would succeed."

"Would he refuse if you ordered him to?"

"Yes."

"And this is acceptable?"

"It isn't his choice, or mine."

"But he is your subordinate. He should follow your orders."

"That depends on the orders." Dannyl shrugged. "We do not have a . . . a custom of unquestioning obedience in the Guild, or even outside it. Except in the case of royalty, but even then advisers have the right to advise – to give their opinion and recommendation without reprisal – though they still must obey orders even if they disagree with them."

"You are also an Ambassador – and not just a Guild Ambassador. Until Ambassador Tayend arrived, you spoke for all the Allied Lands, too. Though you no longer speak for Elyne, you still represent the rest."

"Yes, I speak for them." Dannyl spread his hands. "But I cannot make decisions for them."

"So you are saying that only one of the monarchs of the Allied Lands could order Lorkin to answer questions?"

"Only the Kyralian king. Monarchs of other lands and non-ruling royals cannot give orders to Kyralian magicians."

Achati's eyebrows were high. "How do you maintain order?"

Dannyl smiled. "Most of us are smart enough to know that disorder would lead to a loss of freedom and prosperity. Those who don't . . . well, the rest of us keep them in line. Like the general rule against magicians involving themselves in politics. Though it's not strictly enforced, maintaining the appearance that it is being followed restricts the more ambitious of us."

As Achati paused to ponder this, Dannyl took the opportunity to ask a question.

"Has King Amakira considered that Lorkin may not have any information to give? After all, why would the Traitors have let him return to Arvice if he knew anything that might harm them?"

Achati looked up. "Why doesn't he answer our questions, then?"

"Perhaps it is a test."

"Of what? Lorkin's loyalty to the Traitors?"

Dannyl frowned at the suggestion that Lorkin had changed his loyalties. "Or to Kyralia. Or perhaps it is not a test of Lorkin at all."

Achati's eyes narrowed. "It is a test of King Amakira?"

Dannyl spread his hands. "And the Guild, King Merin and the Allied Lands."

"Put us in a position of conflict and see what happens?" Achati nodded. "We have considered that."

"Though perhaps Lorkin believed that he could return to Kyralia via Arvice, because he didn't think King Amakira would break his agreement that all Guild magicians would remain free and unharmed in Sachaka."

Achati's expression hardened. "So long as they did not seek to harm Sachaka." He looked at Dannyl directly. "Do you honestly believe Lorkin's withholding of knowledge about the Traitors will not harm my country?"

Dannyl held his friend's gaze but, not prepared for such a direct question, he felt the mix of guilt and suspicion that the question roused shift something in his own expression. Achati would have seen it. He would know if Dannyl lied. So best to answer with a different truth.

"I don't know," he replied honestly. "Lorkin has only discussed what he knows with Administrator Osen."

Achati frowned. "Did he tell you why he returned?"

Dannyl nodded and felt himself relax a little. "To go home. He particularly wants to see his mother. Of course, we did not know if he would ever return, so after months of worry she is anxious to be reunited with him as well."

"I imagine she is," Achati replied, standing up. He sounded sympathetic, but his expression was a mix of amusement and defiance. "The sooner Lorkin answers our questions, the sooner that will be."

Dannyl rose. "What will King Amakira do if he doesn't?"

Achati paused to consider his answer. "I don't know," he replied, his apparent honesty and helplessness a mirror of Dannyl's.

"The Allied Lands will view the reading of Lorkin's mind as an act of aggression," Dannyl warned.

"But hardly something to go to war over," Achati replied. "Sachaka has prospered for centuries without trade with the lands to the west, thanks to our links with lands over the eastern sea. Without training for all in higher magic, your magicians are hardly a threat. We don't need you. We don't fear you. You were only ever an opportunity we wanted to explore."

Dannyl nodded. "Thank you for your honesty, Ashaki Achati."

Achati waved a hand dismissively. "I said nothing that wasn't already obvious." He sighed. "Personally, I hope we can resolve this in a way that does not ruin our friendship. Now I must go."

"I, too," Dannyl replied. *The friendship between us, or our countries? Or both?* "Goodbye for now."

The Ashaki nodded, then disappeared down the corridor leading to the Guild House entrance. Dannyl sat down again and considered the conversation. *'We don't need you. We don't fear you.'* Why had anybody ever thought Sachaka would want to join the Allied Lands?

"How'd it go?"

Looking up, Dannyl saw that Tayend was hovering in the doorway. He sighed and beckoned. His former lover hurried across the room and sat down, leaning forward with almost childlike eagerness. But Tayend's gaze was sharp and his curiosity was as much from his need as an ambassador to stay up to date on political matters as from a love of gossip.

He is genuinely concerned about Lorkin, too, Dannyl reminded himself. A memory rose unexpectedly of Tayend playing with Sonea's son as a small child, back when he and Dannyl used to make social visits to the Guild more often. Tayend had had a knack of keeping children occupied and entertained. He found himself wondering if Tayend had ever wished he had children of his own. Dannyl had never wanted them, though he . . .

"So?" Tayend urged.

Dannyl brought his attention back to the present and, taking care not to give away anything the Guild wanted concealed, began to tell his fellow Ambassador what Achati had asked, and revealed.

CHAPTER 4

PREPARATIONS

A full day had passed since the news of Lorkin's imprisonment. That alone had made sleeping difficult, but the sudden shift to a daytime routine also did not help. After a restless night, Sonea felt muzzy-headed and had to draw a little magic to soothe away a nagging weariness. But one benefit of her new routine, Sonea discovered, was that when she emerged from her bedroom Lilia was still in the main room, eating a morning meal.

"Black Magician Sonea," the girl said, clearly surprised to see Sonea.

"Good morning, Lilia," Sonea replied. "How are you? Did Black Magician Kallen track you down yesterday?"

The girl nodded. "Well. And yes."

Sonea moved to the side table and began making herself a cup of raka. "How are your lessons going?"

Lilia winced, but then put on a cheerful expression. "Good. I think Black Magician Kallen wishes I was doing better, though. I told him I wasn't good at Warrior skills, but I don't think he guessed how 'not good' a novice can be."

Sonea chuckled sympathetically. "I wasn't very good at them, either."

The girl's eyes widened. "You . . . but you . . ."

"Won a formal challenge and defeated invading Sachakans. It's amazing what you can learn when you have to. Still, I did have a wonderful teacher."

"You won . . .?" Lilia blinked and straightened. "Which teacher was that?"

Taking her raka to the main table, Sonea sat down and helped herself to a sweet bun from a platter. "Lord Yikmo. He died in the invasion."

"Oh." Lilia's shoulders dropped. Then she looked up again. "A formal challenge?"

Sonea smiled. "A fellow novice who was making life difficult for me."

"He accepted a challenge from a black magician?"

"It happened before then. I don't recommend it as a way of dealing with annoying novices. Only as a last resort, and if you're confident of winning." She paused as a thought occurred to her. "Are any novices giving you a hard time?"

Lilia shook her head. "No, they ignore me most of the time. That's fine. I understand why they avoid me. And I have Anyi."

Sonea felt a pang of sympathy, and gratitude toward Cery for allowing Anyi to visit. "Well, if any of the novices are friendly toward you – properly friendly, not a trick – then don't turn them away too quickly. You'll be working with them soon enough."

"I know."

Lilia looked resigned, but not unhappy. Finishing the bun and raka, Sonea rose and sighed. "Will you be all right staying here on your own while I'm gone, Lilia?"

The girl looked up. "Of course. With Jonna and Black Magician Kallen looking after me, how could I not be?" She frowned. "You're the one who is going to be in danger, Black Magician Sonea. You . . . you will be careful?"

Sonea smiled. "Of course. I have every intention of coming back. After all, I want to see your graduation." She moved to the door, then paused and looked back. "I won't be working at the hospices now, so I'll probably be coming and going a lot. I'll make sure I knock before entering, in case Anyi has snuck in to see you."

Lilia nodded. "Thanks."

Leaving her rooms, Sonea found the Magicians' Quarters corridor busy with magicians. She returned respectful nods and greetings on her way out. The courtyard outside was crowded with novices and magicians, some making their way to and from the Baths, others heading toward the University, and more than a few simply enjoying the early spring sunshine.

Heads turned toward her as always. There was something about black robes that drew the eye. Not even the white robes of the High Lord or the blue of the Administrator attracted as much attention. Novices might notice and watch them pass, bowing respectfully as they were meant to do to all graduated magicians, but they did not stare and take a step back as they did for Sonea and Kallen.

And every time they do, I remember Akkarin, and how everyone did the same to him, though they didn't know, as I did, that he practised black magic. He wore black only because it was the colour of the High Lord then, but since it also marked him as the most powerful magician in the Guild I guess that made him as intimidating as a Black Magician is now.

She suppressed a sigh, ignored the stares, and headed toward the University.

Once inside she chose the passage through the centre of the

building rather than the main corridors on either side. Stepping out of this into the Great Hall, she looked up at the glass-panelled ceiling three levels up, then at the rough stone of the original Guildhall building standing proudly within the vast room. *There won't be another Meet before I leave*, she realised, slowing her steps. *This might be the last time I see this place.*

She stared at the building, then shook her head and quickened her stride again. *Only if everything goes terribly wrong*, she amended.

Reaching the end of the Great Hall, she passed through the other end of the central passage then turned into the right-hand side corridor and stopped at the first door. At a tap from her knuckles the door swung inward, and she stepped into Osen's office.

The Administrator was sitting at his desk, facing two magicians who had turned to regard her. High Lord Balkan inclined his head respectfully and murmured her name, as did Osen. The third magician was becoming more familiar to her.

"King's Adviser Glarrin," she said, nodding to him first before turning to the others. "High Lord. Administrator."

"Black Magician Sonea," Glarrin replied.

He was in his sixties, she knew, but looked younger. Though he was officially the king's military adviser in matters relating to magic and the Guild, he also handled peacetime international relations. A second King's Adviser handled domestic matters – mostly political wrangling between the Houses. *A task I don't envy him.*

"Please sit," Osen said. He gestured to three chairs, which slid closer and into a half-circle before his desk. They all sat down. Osen leaned forward onto his elbows. "We're here to discuss how Black Magician Sonea should go about negotiating the release of her son. First I have some news from Ambassador Dannyl."

Sonea felt her heart skip a beat.

"Ashaki Achati, the king's representative that Ambassador Dannyl has established a friendly relationship with, visited the Guild House last night," Osen continued. "He relayed the king's desire for Dannyl to persuade Lorkin to answer questions about the Traitors. Dannyl, of course, repeated that he was in no position to order Lorkin to. Ashaki Achati would not say what would happen if Lorkin did not talk, but he did make it clear that Sachaka feels no great reluctance to sever friendly ties with the Allied Lands. It was not a threat, Dannyl assures me, but a statement of fact. They do not need to trade with us or feel we would be a threat as an enemy."

"Is it a bluff?" Balkan asked.

"Perhaps," Glarrin replied. "It is too close to the truth, however. I would not want to test it. Sachaka doesn't need us just as we do not need it, but we would both lose some lucrative opportunities if stricter restrictions on trade were imposed."

"So reminding them of the wealth they may miss out on is all I can do?" Sonea asked.

Glarrin pursed his lips in thought. "It would not hurt to point out that the Allied Lands seek trade with Sachaka rather than rebels. That might at least reassure them that we don't plan to side with their enemy."

"Of course, the fact that we *are* seeking trade with the Traitors should not be mentioned," Balkan added, with a chuckle.

"Of course not." Sonea smiled. "Though should I hint that we might consider such a possibility, should Sachaka prove uncooperative . . . and perhaps unreliable when it comes to upholding agreements relating to the safety of Guild magicians?"

"No," Glarrin said. "They will not take kindly to that sort of threat. I . . ." He paused, his eyes focusing on a distant point. "The king asks if the Traitors can be contacted – if they can do anything to help us. After all, they can't have planned for Lorkin to be imprisoned."

The Kyralian king and Glarrin must be communicating via a blood ring, Sonea realised. *That one little magical trick of Akkarin's has become very popular since the Guild decided using one wasn't technically using black magic.*

"We can try," Balkan replied. "Dannyl's assistant, Lady Merria, has established a way to send messages to the Traitors."

"We won't get an answer before Sonea leaves," Osen pointed out. He looked at Balkan. "Sonea should leave a blood ring of hers here. Should she carry a blood ring from one of us as well?"

"Whoever gives her a ring risks seeing the secret of black magic in her mind."

"Not if she's wearing Naki's ring." Osen pointed out.

Sonea nodded. The ring Lilia's former friend had used to stop her mind being read also protected the wearer from access via a blood ring.

Balkan nodded. "It will be useful if Sonea can contact us when she chooses – but Dannyl already has a ring of yours. Would it be better to give her one from me?"

"If the Sachakans seize them, then they can annoy the both of us." Osen shook his head. "She should take one from me."

Sonea hid her amusement at his choice of words. If someone got hold of Osen's blood ring, the malicious things they could do with it wouldn't be designed to annoy him. Then she sobered. *As they could to me, if they got hold of the blood ring I gave Lorkin.* Thankfully Osen had told Lorkin not to take it to the meeting with the Sachakan king. *If they had it, all they'd have to do is torture Lorkin while . . .*

"When will I be leaving?" she asked, to turn her thoughts somewhere less frightening.

"Tomorrow night," Osen said. "We'll call a Meet tomorrow and ask for volunteers to give you magical strength. We've decided to let it be known that Lorkin has been imprisoned by the Sachakan king and we are sending you to negotiate for his release."

"Amakira has given us the perfect excuse to send you to Sachaka," Glarrin said. "You are to try meeting with the Traitors as well, though it would be best if you did it after Lorkin was free – even better if he was home – in case the meeting is discovered." He frowned and looked away, then smiled. "The king asks how Lilia's Warrior training is going."

Balkan grimaced. "Lilia is no natural Warrior. Her reflexes and comprehension are good, and her defence strong, but she shows no initiative in battle."

"Ah," Sonea said, smiling. "A familiar problem."

Glarrin looked at her and raised an eyebrow.

"I was much the same," she explained. "If only Lord Yikmo hadn't been killed in the Ichani Invasion. He was good at teaching reluctant novices."

"Lady Rol Ley had studied Yikmo's methods," Balkan said, his expression thoughtful. "She teaches many of the standard classes all novices attend, so she will know Lilia's strengths and weaknesses."

"She sounds like she could help," Sonea said. "I'd offer to if I wasn't about to leave."

"Maybe you can when you get back," Osen said. "Is there anything else we need to discuss."

"Nothing that can't be relayed through blood rings," Glarrin said. "We should not delay Sonea's leaving more than necessary."

Osen looked at her. "Is there anything you must do before you go?"

She shook her head. "Nothing."

"Then you had better let your assistant know he'll be leaving tomorrow night."

She stood up. "If we're done here, I'll do that next."

Final-year Warrior classes had never been a part of Lilia's plans for the future. According to the University standards, she had achieved the minimum level of understanding and skill required for a novice to graduate. She ought to be off in the Healer's Quarters learning advanced techniques, but instead she was being roundly trounced by novices destined to be the next generation of red-robed magicians.

They were finding her presence in the class fascinating. It wasn't every day that a novice or magician got to practise fighting with and against a black magician. They didn't even seem to mind that she wasn't good at it, because the lessons were mostly demonstrations with little actual magic used. She wasn't allowed to take and store power – not even if that power was given willingly. But she had to admit that, when the lessons didn't involve her making decisions or taking the initiative, she found them as interesting as the other novices did.

Black magic certainly changed the dynamics of fighting. She'd have thought being able to steal magic from a person would be the most useful black magic ability in battle, but it wasn't. It still required her to get close enough to that person to cut their skin and break their natural barrier against magical outside interference. By the time she had worn an enemy down enough to do this, there was little magic left to take.

Being able to store magic was a much bigger advantage. It was disturbing how it made non-black magicians redundant, once they'd given their power to a black magician. It was also frightening to realise how important it made her, over the others. And more of a target.

When it came to actually engaging in a fight, she nearly always made the wrong decisions, acted too soon or hesitated too long. As her latest attack on the "enemy" scattered ineffectually off his shield, Black Magician Kallen called a halt.

"Better," he told her. He looked around the Arena. The tall spires supporting the invisible barrier of magic that protected everything outside from the practice bouts within were now casting shorter shadows on the ground. "That's enough," he said, looking at the trainee Warriors. "You may go."

They all looked surprised, but did not argue. Kallen waited as they left through the short tunnel entrance, then walked beside Lilia as she followed them.

"Wait, Lilia," he said as they emerged.

He said nothing as the other novices strode away, but then sighed. Looking up at him, Lilia saw that he was scowling, but his expression smoothed as he noticed her looking at him. She looked down and waited for his assessment.

"You're improving," he said. "It may not feel like it, but you are learning how to respond to different challenges."

"I am?" She blinked at him in surprise. "You looked so . . . disappointed."

His mouth thinned into a grim line and he looked over at the University. "I am merely annoyed at my own deficiencies."

Looking closer, she saw a tension in his face. Something about his eyes brought a sudden jolt of pain as a memory of Naki rose. Naki with that same distressed look about her, which usually led straight to the lighting of her roet brazier.

A shiver of realisation ran down Lilia's spine. She had smelled roet smoke on Kallen, wafting from his robes, once or twice before. Never before a Warrior lesson, thankfully. She did not like the idea of fighting against or relying on the shield of someone taking a drug that reduced their ability to care about their actions.

If he hadn't smoked any roet before this lesson, was he now craving it as a result? Was that why he'd ended the class early?

Taking a step away, he opened his mouth to speak. "Well that's all—"

"I have a message from Cery," she said.

He stopped, his gaze sharpening. "Yes?"

"He was attacked. Someone betrayed him. He has had to go into hiding and let people think he's dead. You won't be able to meet him for a while. It's too risky."

Kallen's brows lowered. "Was he injured?"

She shook her head and felt a small pang of gratitude at his concern. *Not what I would have expected. Maybe he isn't as cold and rigid as I thought.* "One of his bodyguards was, but he's fine now. He asks that you not tell anybody that he is alive, and that you send messages through me and Anyi."

"You see Anyi often?"

She nodded.

His eyes narrowed. "You aren't leaving the Guild grounds to see her, are you?"

"No."

He regarded her thoughtfully, as if pondering whether she was lying or not.

"Cery would like to know if you have made any progress in finding Skellin," she told him.

"None. We're following a few leads, but nothing promising has come from them so far."

"Anything I can ask Cery about?"

The look he gave her did not conceal his scepticism. "No. If I find out anything that he needs to know, I will pass it on." He looked toward the University again. "You may go now."

Lilia suppressed a sigh at his dismissal, bowed, and walked away. After several paces she looked back, and caught a glimpse of Kallen before he disappeared behind the University building. From the angle of his path, she guessed he was heading for the Magicians' Quarters.

Off to have a dose of roet? she wondered. *Did he avoid telling me anything about his hunt for Skellin because he doesn't think Cery or I need to know, or was it going to take too long, keeping him from the drug?*

And why don't I have this craving for it? She hadn't smoked roet for months. The smell of it sometimes made her want it, but not in a way that overcame her determination never to use it again. Donia, the bolhouse owner who had helped Lilia hide from Lorandra and the Guild, had said it affected people differently.

I'm just lucky, I guess. She felt a pang of unexpected sympathy for Kallen. *And he obviously isn't.*

"Tell us what you know and you can go free."

Lorkin could not hold back a chuckle. The interrogator straightened a little at his reaction, his eyes brightening.

"Why do you laugh?"

"I could tell you anything. How would you know it was the truth?"

The man smiled, but there was no humour in his eyes. *He knows I am right.* Meeting the man's eyes, Lorkin felt a chill run down his spine. There was a sharpness to them. A patience that suggested he would enjoy the hours of interrogation to come. That he was just beginning. This was only the second day of many to come.

They hadn't tried to read his mind yet. Something was holding them back. *A reluctance to damage relations with the Allied Lands?* But then why lock him up in the first place?

They can't have dismissed the idea entirely. Eventually they would try it. Once they attempted and failed to read his mind, they would realise they had sacrificed good relations with the Allied Lands for no benefit. With restraint for the sake of diplomacy abandoned, nothing would stop them torturing him – but they would face the same problem: not knowing if what he said was true.

Perhaps they would verify his words in other ways. Perhaps they hoped imprisonment, discomfort and fear would drive him to give them permission to read his mind.

He almost wished they'd get it over and done with. He was tempted to offer a willing mind-read, to speed things up. Instead he thought of a range of ridiculous lies he could tell the interrogator. It would be fun, at least temporarily, to lead the man on for a while. *But not yet*, he told himself. *It's only the second day. You can hold out for much longer than this.*

The interrogator's companion appeared in the doorway carrying a bowl. Glancing at him, the Ashaki questioner smiled, then looked back at Lorkin.

"Tell us something about the Traitors – just one small thing – and we'll give you something to eat."

A delicious smell reached Lorkin's nose. His stomach clenched then growled with hunger. He'd been given water that morning, which he'd sipped cautiously, but still no food since being brought down here. He had resisted using Healing magic to dull the growing hunger, not wanting to use the magic that Tyvara had given him. It couldn't be replaced, and he might need it.

The smell of the food was strong and set his head spinning. He thought of the lies he'd considered telling them, and felt a strong impulse to speak rising within him. Osen had said he should avoid revealing that his mind could not be read for as long as possible. Leading the interrogator along a false path might delay that.

Don't be ridiculous, he thought. *It might distract him for a short while, but the more I test that man's patience the sooner he'll give up on persuading me to speak. Tyvara would expect me to have more willpower than this.*

She also intended him to use the magic she'd given him to protect himself. It would never get him out of the prison, or stop an Ashaki torturing or killing him, but it could help him resist these less direct attacks on his determination to keep silent.

Closing his eyes, he drew a little magic and sent it out into his body to dull the gnawing in his stomach and stop his head from spinning.

When he opened his eyes, the interrogator was watching him closely. The man stared at Lorkin thoughtfully, then beckoned to his assistant. The pair of them, with a great display of relish, began to eat.

CHAPTER 5

SPECULATION AND SECRETS

The servant who had answered Sonea's knock had told her Lord Regin was at a meeting with Black Magician Kallen. She had asked him to inform her when Regin returned, then retreated to her rooms for a much-needed cup of raka.

The wait was excruciating.

This is ridiculous. I chose him to be my assistant. I've worked with him before. But since he had agreed to travel with her to Sachaka she had begun to worry that she had chosen too quickly. He had all the right qualifications for the role: he was intelligent, a strong magician, a well-trained Warrior, adept at political manoeuvring, and fiercely loyal to the Guild and Kyralia.

But will we get along?

Everything had been fine between them when he had helped her in the hunt for Lorandra. He'd been remarkably easy to work with. But this time they would be together day and night, week after week, with no respite from each other.

Well, that's not entirely true. Once we get to the Guild House in Arvice we'll have two other magicians to talk to as well as the Elyne Ambassador.

In the meantime, they would be stuck with each other's company. Though she did not distrust Regin as she had at the beginning of the hunt for Lorandra, it was impossible for her to forget the pain and humiliation he had subjected her to as a novice.

That is in the past. He has been nothing but respectful and supportive these last twenty years. He even apologised, during the Ichani Invasion. Am I unable to accept apologies? It is silly of me to carry around this resentment.

A knock at the main door made her jump, even though she was expecting it. She put down her cup and rose, walking to the door as she willed it open with magic. Regin's servant bowed.

"Lord Regin is home, and awaits your visit."

"Thank you," she said.

Stepping past him, she closed the door and headed down the corridor to Regin's rooms. As she reached his door she paused to take a deep breath before knocking. The door opened. Regin inclined his head.

"Black Magician Sonea," he said. "Please, come in."

"Thank you, Lord Regin," she replied.

She moved inside. The room was sparsely furnished, and most of the contents looked new. She saw nothing that appeared long-treasured or personal. Regin gestured to a chair.

"Would you like to sit down?"

Sonea regarded the chair and shook her head. "I better not take up too much of your time, considering what I have to tell you." She met his gaze. He was watching her with an intense stillness. An expectation. Suddenly the lack of personal belongings made sense: he'd known he might be leaving soon so why bring them here? "We'll be leaving tomorrow night," she told him.

He let out a small breath, looked away and nodded. She

caught a fleeting expression and felt a pang of guilt. *I haven't seen him show apprehension since the Invasion.*

"If that is too soon, or you feel that your obligations are here, it is not too late to change your mind," she told him, keeping her tone formal to avoid sounding like she was questioning his determination or any suggestion she might consider changing his mind cowardly.

He shook his head. "It is not too soon. In fact, the timing is perfect. I have no other obligations than to do my job, which is to be useful to the Guild and Kyralia. It's rather nice to actually *be* useful for once. This is the sort of task we Warriors are trained for, and yet most of the time we strive not to be needed."

Sonea looked away and felt a pang of sympathy at the slight hint of bitterness in his voice. *No other obligations. He really has cast off all familial ties.* The ruthlessness of his revenge on his wife for her numerous adulterous affairs had entertained the Guild gossips for weeks. He'd given his two properties to his daughters, both married to respectable and wealthy men, and requested rooms in the Guild. This had left his wife homeless and with no money, forcing her to live with her family.

Rumour was that she had attempted to kill herself after Regin had sent her last lover away. Her lover, on the other hand, had simply found another wealthy woman to seduce. Despite this and the shame of being returned to her family like faulty goods, Wynina had made no further suicide attempts. Sonea didn't know whether to feel sorry for her or not. Sometimes she wondered if being married to Regin had driven the woman to such extremes.

Perhaps he is well-behaved in public, but goes back to being the nasty brat he was as a novice in private.

73

Perhaps she would find out, on this journey. Not that their time together would qualify as "private". The purpose was too important, and would still be so even if Lorkin wasn't a prisoner.

"I can now tell you the reason for the journey," she said. Regin's head lifted and his gaze snapped to hers. "Tomorrow everyone will be told. Lorkin returned to Arvice. Before he could leave for Kyralia, King Amakira summoned him and, when Lorkin would not answer questions about the Traitors, he imprisoned him."

Regin's eyes widened. "Oh, I am sorry to hear that, Sonea." He grimaced in sympathy. "They're sending you to negotiate his release, then? You must be impatient to leave." He took a small step toward her. "I will do everything I can to help."

His expression was so earnest that the familiar anxiety that came every time she thought of Lorkin began to return. She looked down and pushed the feeling away.

"Thank you. I know you will."

"If we are leaving tomorrow . . . we have barely begun the process of adding to your strength. Do you want me to give you power now?"

Something within her clenched, and she felt her face warming. She glanced at him and away.

"No," she replied quickly. "Tomorrow there'll be a Meet, and Osen is going to ask for volunteers. Wait until then."

"What is Osen going to tell everyone?"

"Only what I've told you."

"Only?" Regin let out a soft sigh. "Be careful, Sonea."

She looked up at him, then realised her mistake. She had given away to him that there was more to the journey than Lorkin's imprisonment. That tiny piece of information might endanger both of their lives, should a Sachakan magician read it from his mind.

Too late now. I must be more careful in future.

But the frightening truth was, if Regin wound up in the hands of a Sachakan magician who wasn't prevented by politics and diplomacy from reading his mind, there was a good chance Sonea would be too. Though Naki's ring would prevent her own mind from being read, she did not know how long she would hold out against someone determined to torture information out of her.

Especially if they used Lorkin to persuade her.

Though nothing had happened he hadn't expected, Dannyl still felt anger and humiliation simmering inside. He hoped that it hadn't shown. He'd endeavoured to remain calm and polite throughout his short visit to the palace, but he could never tell if he was successful or if his true feelings were somehow obvious – or that his feigned calm was taken as an indicator he'd been successfully ticked off.

Ironically, the decision he'd made to call off the search for Lorkin, which had cost him respect among the Sachakan elite, was making it harder to protect the young magician now. There had been more than a few smirks on the faces of those who'd witnessed the denial of his request to see Lorkin.

If I'd let the search continue, the chances are I and the Ashaki who'd helped me would have been killed by the Traitors. Lorkin would have had no help at all when he returned to the Guild House.

But that wasn't entirely true. The Guild would have sent a replacement Ambassador. One whose reputation hadn't been besmirched by cowardice. Which might have been better for Lorkin's predicament.

No. If the Traitors had been forced to kill a Guild magician, Lorkin may not have returned to the Guild House at all. He may not have even been allowed into Sanctuary for fear that he'd seek revenge for my death.

Though . . . the idea of anybody seeking revenge for his death felt unlikely and ridiculous to Dannyl.

A faint rhythm of bare heels on the floor came from the direction of the Guild House entrance. Dannyl stopped pacing the Master's Room and turned to face the sound. The door slave, Tav, emerged from the passage and threw himself on the floor with his usual overly dramatic flair – a habit that Tayend had noted about the man a few weeks before.

"The Elyne Ambassador has returned," Tav gasped.

Dannyl nodded and waved to indicate the slave could get up and go and do whatever door slaves did when not announcing arrivals.

The sound of a door closing reached him, then footsteps. Tayend smiled briefly as he emerged from the passage, then shook his head.

"No luck," he said.

Dannyl let out the breath he'd been holding. "Well, thanks for trying."

Tayend sighed. "It's early days," he said. "If we are persistent, perhaps he'll relent. I pointed out that you can hardly persuade Lorkin to speak if you never get to talk to him."

Dannyl frowned. "Is that wise? Hinting that we might consider it could be dangerous."

"Not if I say it. And I was only pointing out the fault in his logic."

"I'm sure he'll be *so* pleased you pointed out his weak logic in front of everyone."

"Oh, there was nobody else there to hear — and he seemed to enjoy it."

Dannyl felt his heart sink even further. "You gained a *private* audience with him?"

"Now, now. Don't be jealous." The Elyne smirked, then waved a hand. "Let's have some wine and something to eat, eh?" He turned, beckoned to a slave, and began to give the man specific instructions.

Moving over to the stools, Dannyl sat down. Tayend might not have been able to see Lorkin, but the king had made the effort to see him personally. *Maybe it's because Tayend is an Ambassador who speaks for his king and country, while I am mainly a mouthpiece for the Guild.*

He doubted that made a lot of difference. When it came down to it, King Amakira was annoyed with Kyralia and the Guild, not Elyne. It made sense he'd treat Tayend with the same respect as he always had.

"Ah. Wine," Tayend said as a slave hurried in with a bottle and goblets. He sat down next to Dannyl and waited until the slave had served them and left before leaning closer to him.

"Merria told me this morning, after you left, that she has discussed the situation with her female friends. They are going to stir up objections to this dangerous treatment of a foreign magician," he murmured.

Dannyl felt his mood lighten a little. "And . . . the other contacts?"

"Will pass on our message. They aren't unaware of Lorkin's predicament, apparently, but they didn't say whether they could do anything about it."

"I hate to think what they would do, if they could." Dannyl

shuddered and sipped at the wine. "They might kill Lorkin to ensure he won't talk."

"They won't," Tayend assured him. "They must have known there was a chance this would happen. They would not have sent him here if it would be disastrous for them."

"Perhaps because they had people in place to kill him if it did happen. He might be dead already."

Tayend shook his head. "The king assured me Lorkin is being well cared for."

"He could be lying."

"Yes, he could." Tayend sighed. "We can only hope he isn't." The Elyne's brows creased. "I keep thinking about one possibility, though I can't see any advantage in it for the Traitors, so I suspect I'm seeing conspiracies where there are none."

"What is that?"

"That the Traitors knew Lorkin would be imprisoned by the king. That they meant for it to happen."

"Why would they do that?"

Tayend looked at Dannyl and shook his head. "That's what I can't work out. Except . . . maybe they want the peace between Kyralia and Sachaka strained. Maybe they want to ensure our countries don't make any promises to help Sachaka defend itself against them."

Dannyl felt a shiver run down his spine. "You think they might be planning something bigger and more direct than spying and assassination?"

"It must always be considered." Tayend smiled grimly. "What doesn't make sense is: if they are, it could have the opposite effect. They're gambling that we don't agree to something like that in order to free Lorkin." He took a sip of the wine, his expression serious. "If it came to civil war, who do you think would win?"

"I have no idea." Dannyl shook his head. "We don't know enough about the Traitors."

"Then I hope Lorkin does know more than he claims, because if the Allied Lands do get dragged into a war we could easily end up picking the losing side – or find we can only win by doing the majority of the fighting, and suffering the greater casualties."

A knot of cold had formed in Dannyl's stomach. *Lorkin will have told Osen all he knows about the Traitors, so if Lorkin knows they're planning a civil war then Osen does too.* As Dannyl considered all Osen's instructions so far the knot tightened. When slaves began to file into the room carrying platters of food he felt too sick to eat, but he made himself select from the plates, put food in his mouth and chew. *Why? Because slaves made it. People who have no choice about their life put effort into this, and it seems thoughtless and wasteful to let that go to waste.* Then he felt the knot loosen a little. *The Traitors don't approve of slavery. Civil war might bring freedom.*

But it would come at a cost. It always did.

As Gol walked back into the room, Cery breathed a silent sigh of relief. His friend's movements were careful and he grimaced with pain as he sat down, but otherwise he was looking much better than he had two days ago.

"It's going to get nasty in there soon," Gol muttered.

"I know," Cery agreed. "But it'll have to do for now."

They'd chosen another room to relieve themselves in. The roof and walls looked stable enough, and Cery had brought in a pile of dirt with which to cover their leavings, but it was only going to be a temporary solution.

Asking Anyi to stay and watch over Gol for a while, Cery had explored the small network of rooms and passages nearby. It had been a long time since they'd been occupied. He knew that the late High Lord Akkarin had used them to store things, but the only items there now that were old enough to be from that time weren't valuable: mostly empty boxes like the ones they were using as furniture. He'd found lamps of a style that would have suited the oldest houses in Imardin, if they hadn't been distorted with rust, and broken shards of pottery from vessels that would have been worth a fortune for their age and rarity if they'd been whole.

The walls of these rooms were a combination of brick and stone. There were patches of brick filling in gaps between the stone, and brick walls dividing up larger stone-walled rooms, suggesting that perhaps the rooms had been originally all stone, and the brickwork had been added to repair and adapt the spaces.

In one room someone had scratched words on the wall. "*Tagin must die*", he'd made out easily, as the letters were large and deep. "*Indria must be won*", was smaller. A broken patch began with: "*Higher magic is the ca . . . and must b . . .*" In another, larger room with a collapsed ceiling at one end, a list of names had been carefully carved into a stone slab leaning out from a wall. He didn't recognise any of the names, but they were preceded by the titles "Lord" and "Magician". Odd that they used both. He thought he could make out a date at the base, but he could not get the candlelight to reach that far and there was no way he was going to stretch under a large and heavy slab that looked as if it might fall at any moment.

Returning to their refuge, Cery had let a restless, pacing Anyi continue her explorations of the passages. He remained with Gol, and they talked about what Cery had found and of the past until Gol grew sleepy. Sitting in silence didn't bother Cery as much as he'd thought it would, so long as he didn't let his mind fix on unpleasant memories. It was restful and quiet, and for once he wasn't worried about assassins creeping up on them.

Well, not completely unworried, he amended.

As if challenging his shaky belief in their safety, soft footsteps came from the passage outside. He rose to his feet, and felt a rush of relief when Anyi appeared in the doorway.

She was grinning widely, and stooped to pick up their nearly-empty water bucket.

"I've found a leaky freshwater pipe under the University," she told him. "It's closer than the one you knew about, but just as slow. It'll take a while to fill this. Be better if we had two buckets — one to leave there while it fills. Or I could try to make the leak worse."

Cery shook his head. "They might notice and investigate. Let's see if Lilia can get us another bucket. Or something less leaky."

She nodded, then tucked the bucket under her arm and walked away.

He sat down again and felt his mood lighten a little. At times he doubted that they could live here at all, let alone comfortably. There was so much they had no access to. They relied entirely on Lilia for food — but thankfully not for water. They had nothing but a pile of old pillows, a few boxes and the cold floor to sleep and sit on. It wasn't too cold, and the air didn't appear to be getting stale.

The tap of footsteps reached him again, but whoever was

approaching made no effort to be quiet. They were wearing boots or some other kind of sturdy shoe, but walked lightly.

Lilia. He smiled to himself. Helping her had proven to be very beneficial. He would never have left her floundering out in the city's underworld on her own anyway, but not handing her over to the Guild straightaway had gained him a very useful ally. *And Anyi likes her a lot.*

A bright floating globe of light preceded Lilia into the room. She was carrying a bundle and a large glass flask, and smiled as she saw Cery. But as she looked around the room her cheerful expression faltered.

"Anyi?"

"Collecting some water," he told her. "She found a leaky pipe."

"Not a drainpipe, I hope." She carefully set the bundle on an upended box and began to unwrap it.

"She says it's clean," he replied. He blinked in surprise at the amount of food she'd brought. Bread, a lacquered box of two layers, the lower portion filled with slow-cooked meat and the top one with seasoned vegetables. Since servants had to transport food to the magicians in their Quarters, they always used practical, tightly lidded heat-retaining containers. Though this would feed no more than three people, it was more than one person ought to have needed. "That's . . . that's your dinner?"

"And Sonea's," she told him. "Lord Rothen asked her over for a last meal together, and it was too late to tell Jonna."

"What smells delicious?" another voice asked.

Lilia grinned as Anyi entered the room. "Dinner. I brought some lamp oil and candles, too."

"Ooh!" Anyi drew a box closer and grabbed a chunk of bread. Somehow Gol had woken up and got to his feet without groaning, and was leaning over the food.

"Won't the servants notice if you eat enough for two people?" Cery asked, helping himself.

Lilia shrugged. "Jonna is always trying to get me to eat more, and she's used to Anyi dropping by and eating everything in sight."

"Hai!" Anyi protested.

Lilia chuckled. "She doesn't mind."

"What about you?" Gol asked, looking up at Lilia and gesturing at the food.

"I ate extra at the midday meal," the girl replied. "And snuck some bread and fruit into my bag to eat later."

"This last meal Sonea and Rothen are having. Just how 'last' is it?"

Lilia's expression became serious. "She's leaving tomorrow night. It's official, too. She's going because Lord Lorkin returned to Arvice, and the Sachakan king put him in prison when he refused to betray the Traitors."

Cery felt his stomach sink. To learn your child was in prison . . . *Still, at least he's alive and no longer trapped in a secret city of rebels. That's one step closer to home. After all these years of maintaining peace and benefiting from new avenues of trade, surely the Sachakans won't endanger it all by killing a Guild magician.*

He had to admit, he didn't know enough about Sachaka to be sure.

"I'm glad we didn't tell her we were here," he said. "She doesn't need to be worrying about us as well."

Anyi nodded. "It'll be easier for Lilia to help us now she doesn't have to worry about Sonea finding out."

"But Sonea's the only one who would defend us if the Guild found out we were down here," Gol said, shaking his head.

"What about Kallen?" Anyi asked, looking at Lilia.

Lilia shrugged. "I wouldn't want to rely on him."

"Then we'd better make sure we aren't discovered," Cery said. "Have you spoken to Kallen? Did he have any news for us?"

"I have, and no," Lilia replied. She sighed. "He doesn't seem inclined to confide in me."

"You'll just have to win him over," Anyi told her.

As Gol slurped up the last of the sauce in the meat section of the pot, Cery wiped his hands on the edge of the cloth the food had been bundled in.

"In the meantime," he said to Lilia, "you need to check Gol. If he's healing up well then you need to come with me to the entrance to the Guild tunnels. None of us is going to be truly safe until we find a way to block it so that no Thief's man could get through. If that means collapsing the roof, then that's what we'll have to do." He turned to Anyi. "Then I want you to show me these escape routes. Maybe they'll take us close to where servants toss out things magicians don't use any more."

The girls both grinned. "A bit of exploring sounds like fun," Lilia said.

"Don't you have some studying to do?" Cery asked.

Her face fell. "Do I ever *not* have studying to do?" She sighed, then looked at Anyi reproachfully. "You get to have all the fun."

Anyi shook her head. "You don't get to say that until I have a nice soft bed down here and regular steamy hot baths."

Lilia's eyes widened in mock apology. "Actually, now that you mention baths and body odour—"

Though she was clearly expecting it, she still only just managed to dodge Anyi's punch to her arm. Chuckling, she slipped out of reach and headed toward Gol.

CHAPTER 6

PERMISSION GRANTED

The two middle-aged men were still in their cell when Lorkin returned from his second day with the interrogator, but the couple who had been imprisoned there had gone. Once again water had been left for him, but no food. Hunger had made it difficult to sleep until he gave in again and soothed it away with magic.

It was impossible to tell what time it was. No windows allowed in light to indicate day or night. Lorkin had to rely on the routine of the interrogator and watcher to measure the passing of the days. When he woke he noted that the watcher was still in place, gazing at him with alert eyes but no expression. Sitting with his back to the wall, Lorkin entertained himself with mental games and memories.

A sound eventually drew his attention. Footsteps warned of someone approaching. The watcher turned away, then stood up. Lorkin sighed quietly and got to his feet, bracing himself for another day of questions and hunger.

Instead of the interrogator, a male slave appeared holding a tray on which lay a bowl, a lump of bread and a goblet. Lorkin could not help feeling his heart skip with hope as the watcher examined the items then stepped forward to open the gate to his cell.

The slave's eyes remained downcast as he stepped inside, lowered the tray to the floor and backed out again.

The watcher paused to regard Lorkin thoughtfully after he'd relocked the gate. Lorkin waited until the man returned to his seat before approaching the tray. He picked it up and carried it to the far side of the cell.

The bowl was full of a cold, opaque soup. The goblet contained wine. There were no utensils.

If any of this is poisoned, I won't know until I try eating it. I've never had to Heal away poison before. It'll use up more of Tyvara's power than simply quashing hunger. Should I risk it? Do I need to eat badly enough?

The particles in the soup were settling to the bottom, leaving most of the liquid clear. But the growing sediment was not forming a flat layer. It clung to something lying at the bottom. Something square and thin. He felt a tingle run down his spine.

Aware that the watcher was observing his every move, he drew a tiny amount of magic and used it to gently nudge the particles away from the object. At first the soup clouded at the slightest stirring, but soon it settled allowing him to confirm what he'd suspected.

The object was a piece of paper.

'Boil soup to make safe. Bread good. Wine bad.'

Beneath was a squiggle. It would have been taken as a flourish or hastily drawn initials by someone else, but Lorkin recognised it as one of the code signs the Traitors had told him to look for.

They know I'm here, he thought, his heart lifting in relief and

86

hope. *They're going to get me out of here.* But even as the thought crossed his mind he knew he could not expect that much. The prison was under the very palace itself and guarded by Ashaki and the independent, fiercely loyal guard class that was unique to this place.

It was nice to know the Traitors were trying to help him, though. Drawing more magic, he set the soup boiling. That at least explained to the watcher why he'd been staring at it so intently. He still drank it slowly and paid attention to his body in case the note was a clever lie. The bread was stale, so he dipped it in the soup to soften it.

He didn't touch the wine. Would the interrogator, or whoever had poisoned it, wonder how Lorkin had known to avoid it, or would he assume Lorkin simply didn't want his senses fogged by wine during the next session?

Not long after he'd finished eating, the slave returned for the tray. Lorkin held it up for the man to take. The slave's gaze rose to meet his.

"Lord Dannyl says King Merin wants you to tell them everything," the man said, his words barely a whisper.

Lorkin nodded to show he understood, and turned away so that the watcher would not see his smile.

As if I'd believe that! They must think I'm stupid, if they think I'd accept such an order from anyone but Dannyl himself. Even then . . . I'd have to consider that Dannyl was being blackmailed or threatened.

Administrator Osen had given Lorkin a code word as well, in case the Sachakans tried something like this. Forcing the smile from his face, Lorkin leaned back against the wall and waited for the interrogator to arrive and the day's questioning to begin.

* * *

The Foodhall was almost vibrating with noise, despite the midday meal finishing some time ago. Lilia resisted the temptation to roll her eyes at the other novices. The sudden announcement that lessons had been cancelled for the afternoon while the entire Guild attended a Meet had sent them into a mix of giddy exhilaration at their unexpected freedom and excited speculation as to the cause of the meeting.

Lilia already knew the reason for it, but nobody was asking her and she had much more important things to worry about. Like keeping Cery, Gol and Anyi fed and supplied with lamp oil and candles. Lilia had decided Jonna, Sonea's servant, was the key to both. She had to find a way to persuade the woman to bring more supplies these things to Sonea's rooms, without it sounding suspicious.

It was easy enough to smuggle small items into the tunnels. The lacquered boxes that servants used to carry food could be lowered down the gap in the wall of Sonea's room using magic. Larger items like whole pieces of furniture weren't going to fit in the narrow space, however. Perhaps they could use other entrances to the tunnels. She had heard that there were some in the University.

Even if she did find another way in, most of the furniture in the Guild was old and valuable so likely to be missed. The servants' furniture might be less precious, but they lived and worked away from the areas magicians and novices frequented. If Lilia wandered over to the servants' quarters, or even slipped into the kitchens beside the Foodhall, she'd stand out like, as her mother would say, "a prince at a beggar's ball".

I need to find cast-offs that nobody is using. They'll probably be broken, but I suppose we can try to fix them. We might have to pull

*them apart and reassemble them anyway, to get them into the tunnels.
I'd have to get hold of some wood and nails — and tools. Hmm, if
I'm going to do that, maybe we could smuggle wood in and make
furniture from scratch.*

"Look, it's the black novice."

The words were spoken loudly and from close by. Lilia looked
up and met the eyes of the speaker. He was Bokkin, a tall
novice — a lowie who liked to bully those weaker than him.
None of the lowies protested too loudly because he was bold
enough to pick on the snooties as much as the lowies.

He'd stopped to lean on a nearby table, the usual group of
followers hovering around him. She doubted they actually liked
him. More likely they allied themselves with him to avoid
being his target.

"Got anybody killed lately?" he asked, his lips twisted in a
sneer.

She tilted her head to the side and pretended to consider.
"Well, no actually."

"What are you going to do with yourself now that Black
Magician Sonea is leaving?" He pushed away from the table.
"You'll be all alone in her rooms. Got a new girlfriend? Or do
you want to see what a man's like for once?" He strutted up
to her table and thrust his groin close to her face. "How about
I show you what you've been missing?"

So they know Sonea's leaving. Lilia leaned back and looked up
at him. She'd considered that someone might try to take
advantage of the situation, but hadn't expected anyone to test
her so soon.

"You never showed any interest before." She stood up slowly,
staying close so that her face ended up near to his, and stared
straight into his eyes. "Must be the black magic that changed

your mind. You're attracted to it, aren't you? The thrill of danger. I've been told to watch for people like you."

He opened his mouth to speak, but she grabbed his face, fingers digging into the flesh of his jaw. At the same time she pushed at him with a sharp jab of magic, forcing him to stagger backwards before he could summon up the magic to resist it. She followed and pressed him back against the edge of the next table.

"You know what's going on in that Meet? Black Magician Sonea is taking power from every magician in the Guild. Using black magic. One day – maybe one day soon – I might do that to you. You'll have no choice. King's orders. Do you really want to give me reason to make it as unpleasant as possible?"

He stared back at her, his face pale. She let go and wiped her hand on the front of his robe. The novices around her were silent, and the silence was spreading. She did not take her eyes from Bokkin, but she could see in the edges of her vision that faces were turning toward her.

"You had better hope she returns," she told him. She turned her back, picked up her bag and the pieces of fruit and spiced bread rolls she'd collected for her evening meal, and left the hall.

As she stepped into the corridor she felt a rush of triumph.

That'll get them talking. And worrying about the reason for Sonea's trip to Sachaka, but they'll wonder about that anyway. I'm not going to let anyone think that her leaving makes me vulnerable.

If the only future she had was to be restricted to the Guild grounds, groomed to be a protector of the Allied Lands and the main target of any enemy who might attack, then she wanted to be treated with respect in return.

Failing that, with people like Bokkin who are too stupid to remember who'll be risking their life for him, I'll settle for being feared.

From her seat at the front of the Guildhall, Sonea watched the gathering magicians and struggled to keep her breathing slow and even.

What will they do? Is twenty years of getting used to the idea of black magic long enough for them to agree to take part in it? Will they consider my mission to free my son justification enough?

It would have been easier to dismiss these questions if the other Higher Magicians hadn't also expressed the same concerns earlier. None could predict the outcome of the Meet. All had thought some magicians would refuse to give their magic and some would not, but their opinions differed greatly on the likely numbers of either.

On both sides of the long hall, magicians were taking their seats. As always, patches of green, red and purple formed where friends of the same discipline gathered together. The dominant colour was the Alchemist's purple, but the numbers of Healers had grown in the last few decades and there was plenty of green around the hall. Though more Warriors existed than ever before, red robes were still in the minority. This didn't worry her, though. While most magicians dedicated their energies to something more useful, she knew that the majority of them still maintained their fighting skills in their spare time.

At the front of the hall the Higher Magicians waited. Only Administrator Osen was missing from the tiered seats. As always he would address the room from the Front, the area before the Higher Magicians. Sonea looked at the row of seats above hers. The king's chair was empty, but both King's

Advisers had joined the Meet – which was unusual. Adviser Glarrin met her eyes and nodded; Adviser Rolden, who had been present twenty years before when she and Akkarin had been judged and exiled, glanced at her and frowned.

Looking down, Sonea noted how the Higher Magicians in the lower tiers of seats kept casting glances upward. From his place among the Heads of Studies in the bottom row, Rothen met Sonea's eyes. He looked grim, but managed a reassuring smile.

Their dinner the night before had been shadowed by frightening possibilities. She knew he was wondering if this was the last time he'd see her. It was another fear to add to the worry that he'd never see Lorkin again. He'd offered to go with her. She'd reminded him that he knew too much about her other reason for the journey. He'd nodded, then said that he would take comfort from the fact she had chosen a reliable assistant.

Looking around the hall, she searched for Lord Regin and found him sitting, as she'd expected, near the front. He looked serious and aloof. This might have been a deliberate mask of his true feelings, but it was hard to tell. He always looked serious and aloof.

I hope Rothen is right about him. Well, of course he is. Regin takes his responsibility to the Guild, Kyralia and the Allied Lands much too seriously to jeopardise our task.

Which meant, no matter how unpleasant things got between them, he would obey her orders.

Most of the magicians had settled in their seats now. Administrator Osen strode out in front of the Higher Magicians and a gong rang to mark the beginning of the Meet.

The room immediately quietened.

"At this Meet here today we have an exceptional situation to discuss and deal with," Osen began, "and, as such, the course of action given to us will be unique in the history of the Guild." He paused and looked around the room. "As you may already know, Ambassador Dannyl travelled to Sachaka some months ago to serve in the Guild House of Arvice. He took with him the young magician Lord Lorkin, who had volunteered to be his assistant.

"Not long after settling in Arvice, Lord Lorkin was saved from assassination by a slave. The slave was a spy for the people known as the Traitors, Sachakans who have lived separately to the rest of the country for hundreds of years. To evade future attacks on his life, this slave helped Lorkin flee to the Traitors' secret home.

"There Lorkin learned more about these people. They reject slavery and though they use black magic they appear to live peacefully. They have a network of spies throughout Sachaka – though from all I have heard the main aim of their spying is their own protection.

"Recently Lorkin sought to return home. On arriving in Arvice he was summoned by King Amakira and ordered to reveal all he had learned of the Traitors. Knowing that he must give any such information to King Merin first, Lorkin refused. Though this was made clear to King Amakira, and he agreed when we sent the first ambassadors to Sachaka that they will answer to their own king, he sent Lorkin to the palace prison."

Sonea felt her stomach sink. No matter how many times she heard it spoken, the thought of Lorkin in a dank cell made her heart shrivel.

The hall had grown quiet. *Funny, I expected there to be protests and anger. I think they're mostly too shocked to speak, though I'm not sure whether they're more appalled at the audacity of Amakira daring to imprison a Guild magician, or at the possibility this might lead to another conflict with Sachaka.*

"The king has approved our request to send a negotiator to seek Lorkin's release," Osen continued. "We chose our negotiator carefully, considering who might have the greatest influence on the Sachakan king. The Sachakan prejudice against magicians who do not know black magic narrowed our choices." Osen turned to look up at the Higher Magicians and held out his arm toward Sonea as if offering her a hand out of a carriage. "We chose Black Magician Sonea."

She felt her skin prickle and her face heat as hundreds of gazes shifted to her. A murmur of voices filled the hall. Resisting an urge to look down and away, she stared back at the assembled magicians, heart beating a little too fast. *What will they do?*

Osen's outstretched hand beckoned. Swallowing a sigh, she rose and started to descend the steep stairs to the Front.

"But the advantage in sending a black magician will not count unless that black magician is as powerful as we can make her," Osen continued. As Sonea reached his side, he glanced at her once then turned to face the assembly. "The permission of the king has been granted for Black Magician Sonea to gather strength for this mission. We call for volunteers to give their power to this cause."

The hum of voices that had been gathering now grew louder, swelled, then diminished again. Osen, judging their mood, raised his arms and the room fell into a restless quiet.

"This is the first time such permission has been granted, and thankfully not for the reason we have long feared. We have learned, in the last twenty years, that black magic need

94

not involve barbaric rituals and unpleasant bloodletting. Though this fact is taught to our novices and such reassurances given to all else, there may be some for whom this is not clear. I call upon Black Magician Sonea to explain."

Sonea drew in a deep breath and worked magic into the air before her to amplify her voice.

"Sachakan magicians cut the skins of their slaves because their slaves are not magicians and can't offer up their power. They do the same to their victims in war because their victims are hardly going to offer up their power willingly. The ritual of higher magic in our past was a symbolic gesture of an apprentice's submission to his master, and no longer relevant."

She managed a smile, though she suspected it would look more grim than reassuring. "I only require a magician to draw and send power to me so I can take it and store it. That is all. The giver need do nothing more than a trick taught to every novice in their first year of University." She looked around the hall. *That's really all the explanation it needs*, she thought, but as Osen began to turn away from her she thought of something else.

"It seems only a small thing to ask of each of you," she said. "A day's strength. But if it leads to the freeing of my son you . . . at the least you'll have my own and my son's heartfelt gratitude."

Osen nodded. "And you'll have ensured the safety of a member of the Guild, a citizen of Kyralia and the Allied Lands, while securing ongoing peace with Sachaka. Which is no small thing at all." He turned to face the tiered seats. "We will begin with the Higher Magicians."

Sonea felt her heart skip as High Lord Balkan rose and descended from the tiered seats, followed by several other

Higher Magicians. As Balkan approached, a voice called his name from the side of the hall. All turned to see that King's Advisers had come down from the highest row.

"Would you permit me to be the first," the adviser asked Balkan. The High Lord smiled and stepped aside, gesturing to Sonea.

"The king sends his best wishes," Glarrin told her. He held out his hands to her.

Taking them, she nodded. "Please convey my thanks in return, Adviser." She felt her skin tingle as he sent power to her. Drawing it inward, she felt a slight sensation that told her she now held more magic than her natural limit, but when he was done she could not judge how much power he had given her.

Glarrin stepped away, bowing slightly toward Balkan. Sonea looked up at the tall Guild leader. He regarded her with a familiar slightly surprised expression. *As if he has as much trouble thinking of me as a Higher Magician as I do of him being High Lord. Though Balkan is a competent leader, only Akkarin will ever fit the title in my mind.*

She took his hands and power, and slowly the rest of the Higher Magicians took their turn. All but Kallen. Osen had decided that a few magicians should still retain their full strength at the end of the meeting. When the last of the Higher Magicians stepped away, Sonea turned to face the hall.

And felt her heart stop.

All of the seats were empty. Every magician was standing in the centre of the hall, waiting. *Well, it's possible that those who don't intend to volunteer have slipped out already*, she told herself. But the crowd that waited was too large for many to have decided not to participate.

She realised she had stopped breathing, and heard a gasp escape her mouth as the first magician stepped forward.

Regin. His eyes brightened with unexpected humour as he reached out to take her hands.

"You really don't know how much people respect you, do you?" he murmured as he sent her magic.

"Respect me?" She shook her head. "They're not doing this for me. They're doing it for a fellow magician and Kyralia."

"That as well," he admitted. "But it's not the only reason."

He gave her a lot of power. At least it seemed that way. She watched him walk away, looking for indications of physical weariness and worried that he would be tired at the start of their journey that night, but the next magician stepped forward and she had to turn away.

And then the next, and the next. Healers, Warriors, Alchemists. Men and women. Old and young. Magicians from the Houses and all other classes. They all spoke a few words, wishing her luck, expressing their hopes that Lorkin had been treated well and would be released, even warning her to watch out for Ichani when crossing the wasteland, and urging her to come home safely. Overwhelmed and surprised, she struggled at times to appear calm and dignified. At one point she felt a wave of sadness as she suddenly remembered another time, standing in this hall while magicians filed past. Then, they had been tearing her robes and those of Akkarin as they spoke ritual words of banishment.

Because we learned black magic in order to defend Kyralia. How much things have changed.

When finally a magician moved away and she found there were no more waiting, she felt a great relief and weariness. She nearly laughed aloud at that. This taking of power was supposed to make her stronger, not tired. She focused on the power within her, detecting that a glow of magic was escaping from her control. Remembering Akkarin's instruction, she strengthened the barrier of influence lying at her skin, and felt the leakage stop. Then she considered the power within.

Aside from knowing her strength had been boosted, the only way she could guess at how strong she'd become was to add up the number of magicians who had given her magic. She wasn't even sure how powerful the average Guild magician was. *I haven't held this much power since the Ichani Invasion, when the poor people offered their strength in preparation for the battle ahead.*

Osen was still standing beside her. The hall was empty but for him, Regin and Rothen. A gong rang out, indicating the end of the Meet despite most of the magicians not being present to hear it.

"What time is it?" she found herself asking.

Osen considered. "I believe the University gong rang a short while ago."

She looked at him in surprise. "That late?" She looked at Regin. "It's nearly time to load up the carriage."

"You have a few hours still." Osen smiled. "You should both eat a good meal before you go."

Sonea felt her stomach knot. "I'm not sure I can."

"That'll disappoint everyone."

She frowned at him. "Why?"

His smile widened. "The Higher Magicians have a farewell dinner waiting for you in the banquet room. You didn't think we'd let you go without saying goodbye, did you?"

She looked at him in amazement. Osen chuckled. "Come on, they're all in the Night Room having a drink while they wait for you to join them."

CHAPTER 7

A DIFFERENT APPROACH

"The roof is unstable here," Anyi said.

Looking up, Cery noted the cracks in the walls and the slight sag in the roof. Fine roots matted the passage ceiling – perhaps from a tree above.

"If we have to use this escape route, and Lilia is with us," Anyi continued, "we could get her to collapse it when we're all far enough past, to stop anyone following us. Or we could rig it up to collapse. Lilia could help us by supporting it with magic while we install weights and ropes that we can operate from further down the tunnel."

Cery nodded. *I like the way she thinks.* "We'll ask her."

"Now, where does this go?" Anyi grinned and hurried past the unstable area, leading Cery down an increasingly deterior-ated passage. It ended not at a tunnel entrance, but where a tree had fallen through the roof and blocked the way. A weak, grey light filtered through a hole between two of the great roots. Bricks and rubble, smoothed by accumulated dirt and moss, provided a rough ramp up which Anyi scrambled.

She peered out, then looked back at him and beckoned. Picking his way up to her, he took her place and peered up through the hole.

A forest surrounded him, lit by pre-dawn light. He sighed as he remembered taking Sonea through the Guild forest many years ago – before she had been captured by the magicians – so she could watch magic being performed and perhaps learn to control her powers. It hadn't worked, of course. Only another magician can teach a novice how to handle magic safely. But they hadn't known that then.

So much has changed, Cery thought, *but thankfully the forest is still here.* He extinguished his lamp and set it down, then climbed out of the hole. Anyi followed.

"Where in the Guild do you think we are?" she whispered.

He shrugged. "Probably north of the buildings, since the southern part of the grounds are hillier than this."

"The servant quarters are to the north."

"Yes."

"We might find discarded things there. Furniture. Blankets."

"We might."

Cery moved away from the tree, then looked back and slowly circled it, trying to fix the image of it in his mind. Neither he nor Anyi were used to navigating their way through a forest, and he could see it would be easy to get lost and not find the tunnel opening again. Fortunately the tree did look a little different from the others, thanks to it being half dead, partly sunk into the ground and leaning at an angle.

Turning away, Cery led the way through the trees, counting his steps and noting they were moving downhill. He knew the ground rose up from the Inner Wall to behind and above the Guild buildings, so he guessed he was heading west. After several hundred strides he discovered he was wrong. The slope met another and, in the crease between, a little stream flowed off to the right. *Oh well, at least the stream is something we can follow. It should take us downhill, at least.* He marked the place by moving some stones into a circle and a line pointing back the way they'd come, then headed downstream.

It was not long before they saw signs of habitation ahead. Creeping forward, they made out simple shacks and fences. "Servants quarters?" Anyi murmured.

Cery shook his head. "Too shabby." The ramshackle appearance of the buildings was puzzling. A few large structures appeared to be made from glass, but from the overgrown look of the vegetation inside he guessed they were abandoned. It wasn't until they finally drew close enough to see what the fences surrounded that he worked out where they were.

"The farm."

"Ah. Of course." Anyi pointed. "Is that an orchard over there?"

He looked in the direction she indicated and nodded as he made out rows of carefully pruned trees and arches of berry vines. Next to them were small fenced areas of ground, the earth grooved as if someone had run a very large rake along them.

"The question is: does anybody live here?" he murmured.

Anyi glanced at him. "Let's take a closer look."

They moved closer, hiding behind trees and then the long arched rows of berries. The shacks were spaced along the other side of the crops. Cery's heart sank as he noticed smoke wafting out of a chimney. Further away, a woman in servant's clothing had emerged from one of the shacks. He watched as she disappeared into what looked like a rassook pen.

"Looks occupied to me," Anyi said. "Want to move further along?"

Cery nodded. Retreating to the edge of the forest to take

advantage of the undergrowth, they made their way along the length of the farm. He was right about the rassook pen. At the end of the crops and buildings there were larger open fields where enka, reber and even a few big, lumbering gorin grazed.

Not enough to feed the Guild, he noted, *but they're making use of what space they have.*

"Over there," Anyi said, pointing to the last of the buildings.

He looked, and realised it wasn't the building she was indicating, but a collection of old wooden furniture. Mismatched chairs circled a plank set upon tree stumps. Benches had been constructed out of scrap timber and placed on old barrels.

"We could use some of that straw to make mattresses," Anyi said, pointing toward a shelter under which several bundles had been piled. "I saw it done at the market. You need some old sacks and a needle and thread."

"You can sew?"

"Not very well, but we need mattresses, not ball gowns."

Cery chuckled. "Just as well, eh? I remember your mother couldn't get you to wear a dress. I don't think even the king could get you to wear a ball gown."

"Not a chance," Anyi replied. "Not even if he was the handsomest man in the world."

"Pity," Cery said. "It would be nice to see you all dressed up. Just once."

"I'd settle for a change of clothes." Anyi narrowed her eyes at the huts. "I wonder how many people live here, and what they wear. Probably servant uniforms. I suppose it would be handy to look like servants whenever we sneak out of the tunnels." She pursed her lips. "I'll come back here later and spy on them for a bit, if that's fine with you."

"Good idea. But stay in the forest and don't try to steal anything yet." Cery nodded. "For that we'll come back at night."

Dannyl stared out of the carriage window, not registering the view outside as he braced himself for the morning's dismissal.

Lorkin had been in the palace prison for only three days, but it felt much longer. *Of course, it probably feels even longer to Lorkin.* Ashaki Achati hadn't visited again. Dannyl couldn't decide if he was relieved or regretful about that. Any meeting with Achati was likely to be tense and full of resentment and awkwardness over the situation with Lorkin, but Dannyl missed Achati's company and longed for his advice.

It's a pity he's so close to the king. If only I'd made friends with a Sachakan in a more neutral position. He'd have been able to tell me how best to deal with the situation.

Were *any* of the Ashaki in a neutral position, politically? From what Dannyl had learned, most were either loyal to the king or were allied with Ashaki who would happily seize the reins of power if they had the chance – which they were not likely to get. King Amakira's position was secure, supported by most of the powerful Ashaki.

As the carriage pulled up outside the palace, Dannyl sighed. He waited until the Guild House slave opened the door, then rose and climbed out. Smoothing his robes, he straightened his back and strode toward the entrance.

Nobody stopped him. He had wondered why they'd let him in the previous day, when all they intended to tell him was to go home. Once again he stepped out of the broad passage into the hall, and was told by a slave to wait to one side.

Several people were standing around the hall. The king was present this time. At least Dannyl would be able to give his request directly to Amakira. Not that it would gain him a favourable response. The king finished talking to a pair of men and invited another three to approach.

Time passed. More people arrived. The king saw some of them not long after they arrived – sooner than Dannyl and some of the others waiting for an audience. They must have been more important, or at least the matter to be discussed was. *Or he's deliberately ignoring me to put me in my place.*

Dannyl guessed that a few hours had passed by the time the king looked his way, then beckoned.

"Guild Ambassador Dannyl," he said.

Dannyl approached and knelt. "Your majesty."

"Rise and come closer."

He obeyed. The air vibrated faintly, and Dannyl realised that the king, or someone else, had placed a shield about them to prevent sound escaping.

"You're here, no doubt, to ask me to give Lorkin back," the old man said.

"I am," Dannyl replied.

"The answer is no."

"May I at least see him, your majesty?"

"Of course." The king's stare was cold. "If you promise to order him to tell me everything he knows about the Traitors."

"I cannot give that order," Dannyl replied.

Amakira's stare did not waver. "So you said. I'm sure you could convince him that the order came from those with the authority to give it."

Dannyl opened his mouth to refuse, then paused. *I could agree to try, in order to see Lorkin and confirm he is alive and well.* But what if the king decided that Dannyl had broken his promise? Was that crime enough to be imprisoned for? *Osen made it clear that I should avoid that. And if they take me prisoner, they'll take Osen's ring from me.*

"I cannot do that either, your majesty," Dannyl replied.

The king leaned back in his chair. "Then come back when you can." He made a dismissive gesture. Taking the hint, Dannyl bowed and backed away for an appropriate distance, then turned and left.

Well, at least I got to see the king this time, he thought as he waited for the carriage. *A rejection from the ruler is a slightly better-quality failure than a rejection from one of his lackeys.* He wondered which he'd receive tomorrow, or if they would start refusing him admission to the palace.

When the carriage arrived at the Guild House he opened the door for himself, before any slave could do it. The air outside the house was hot and dry, and it was a relief to escape it into the cooler interior. He headed for his rooms, but before he got there Merria appeared in the corridor ahead.

"How did it go?" she asked.

Dannyl shrugged. "No better, though this time I was given a royal refusal."

She shook her head. "Poor Lorkin. I hope he's all right."

"Any news from your friends?"

"No. They said they're doing what they can to manipulate the Ashaki into objecting to the taking of a Kyralian magician prisoner, but it requires careful timing and can't be hurried."

He nodded. "Well . . . I appreciate their efforts. We all do."

They had reached the entrance to his rooms. She looked up at him, her expression concerned, then patted him on the arm. "You're doing everything you can," she told him. "Everything they'll let you do, anyway."

He frowned. "So you think there's nothing else I could do? Nothing that the Guild is preventing me from doing that I should do? Nothing we haven't thought of yet?"

She looked away. "No . . . nothing that doesn't include a risk of making the situation worse if it fails to work, anyway. Are you hungry? I was going to ask Vai to make me something to eat."

What is this risky idea? he wondered. *Should I ask about it?* "Yes," he said. "But not straightaway. I want to contact the Administrator first."

"I'll arrange something." She headed back down the corridor and disappeared.

The interrogator didn't turn up until some hours after the morning meal. Food had arrived – a slurry of ground grain. A faint symbol drawn with water on the porous wooden tray reassured him it was safe.

Lorkin's stomach stirred unpleasantly as the Ashaki interrogator and his assistant led him in a new direction. The man chose another corridor and stopped at a different doorway, but the room inside was little different from the previous one. Plain, white walls surrounded three worn old stools.

The interrogator sat down and gestured for Lorkin to take one of the other stools, then looked at his assistant and nodded. The man slipped out of the room. Lorkin braced himself for more questions.

None came. The interrogator looked around, then shrugged and began staring at Lorkin with a distant expression. When the assistant returned, he shoved a female slave into the room before him. She threw herself onto the floor before the Ashaki. Lorkin tried to keep his expression neutral, to hide the wave of hatred for slavery he felt at her grovelling and the Ashaki's expectation of it.

"Stand," the interrogator ordered.

She got to her feet, facing the Ashaki with hunched shoulders and keeping her eyes downcast.

"Look at him." The interrogator pointed at Lorkin.

The woman turned to face him, her gaze fixed on the floor. She was beautiful, he realised – or would have been if she hadn't been terrified. Long, glossy hair framed a sculpted jaw and cheek bones that, for a moment, stirred memories of Tyvara that made his heart skip and fill with longing. But this woman's limbs, while as graceful, were trembling, and her dark eyes were wide. At her obvious fear he felt his stomach sink. She expected something bad to happen.

"*Look* at him. Don't look away."

Her gaze flitted up to meet his. Lorkin forced himself not to look away. If he did, he knew the Ashaki would make him regret it somehow. He could not help searching for some hint of resolve in her face, or an effort at communication that might indicate that she was a Traitor. All he saw was fear and resignation.

She expects pain, or worse. The only slaves I've seen down here were carrying things. Why else would she – a beautiful young woman – be down here with no obvious menial purpose?

A slave this beautiful would never be given purely menial tasks.

He felt sick. He could not help thinking of Tyvara again, and what she must have been forced to do as part of her spying. She, too, was too beautiful not to have attracted that kind of attention from her masters.

After all, the first time she met me she expected me to take her to bed.

The interrogator stood up. He took hold of the woman's

arm and pulled her closer to him. One of his hands went to the jewelled sheath that all Ashaki wore at their hip and he slowly drew his knife. Lorkin held his breath as the knife rose toward the slave's throat. The woman shut her eyes tightly, but did not struggle.

Words flooded into Lorkin's throat, but stuck there. He knew exactly what the interrogator intended to do, and why. *If I speak to save her, many, many more will die. If she is a Traitor, she won't want me to betray her people.* He swallowed hard.

The knife did not slice across her throat. Instead the interrogator slid it under one shoulder of her shift and cut through the cloth. He took hold of the other shoulder and pulled, and the slave garment slid away, leaving her naked but for a loin cloth. Her expression didn't change.

The Ashaki sheathed his knife, looked over her shoulder at Lorkin, and smiled.

"Any time you want to talk, go right ahead," he said, flexing his fingers and curling them into a fist. The assistant chuckled.

And then the Ashaki set to work.

CHAPTER 8

COMING TO AN UNDERSTANDING

Putting down the book she had been failing to concentrate on, Lilia looked around Sonea's guest room and sighed.

Though Sonea had been absent or asleep most of the time, her rooms felt strangely empty now that she had left for Sachaka. Lilia was suddenly more conscious of being alone, and that nobody – no magician, at least – was likely to visit.

Well, none except Kallen if I don't turn up to classes on time, but it's not like he makes social visits.

Anyi might still slip in at night via the secret opening in the room's wall panelling but now that she, Cery and Gol were living under the Guild it was safer for Lilia to visit them. There had always been a risk that someone would discover Anyi in Sonea's rooms and realise they hadn't seen her enter or leave by the door.

The only other person who visited Lilia on a regular basis was Jonna, Sonea's servant and aunt. Jonna visited twice a day to deliver meals. *But she must also come here after I've left for classes to clean, too,* Lilia thought, remembering how she usually returned to find everything tidy. While Jonna usually slipped into Sonea's bedroom after the evening meal to change the bed linen and gather robes to wash, that was only because Sonea had worked night shift at the hospices.

Looking over at the open door of her room, Lilia regarded the bag she used to carry textbooks and notes around. It held the food she'd taken from the Foodhall that day, some soap, and clean wash cloths from the Baths, ready to take to her friends. She also had news from Kallen to deliver, but until Jonna arrived with the evening meal, Lilia wouldn't be able to slip away.

In the meantime she tried to study. She looked down at the book in her hands. She'd never really caught up with the lessons she'd missed while a prisoner in the Lookout. Teachers would notice if she slipped even further behind.

Once Cery, Anyi and Gol have settled in, I'll be able to get back to my studies, she told herself. *Maybe I'll study all next Freeday. If my plan works tonight at least there'll be one less thing to worry about.*

Her thought was interrupted by a knock at the door. She stood up in case it was a magician, and opened the door with magic. To her relief, Jonna bustled in. Though burdened with a lacquered box and a large jug, the woman managed to bow before placing it on the table.

"Good evening, Lady Lilia."

"Good . . . evening." Lilia hesitated as she opened the box and saw, to her disappointment, that it held one bowl of a thick soup and a single bread roll, as well as a creamy dessert. *Of course. She won't be bringing more than one person can eat now.* Which made it even more important that Lilia's plan worked.

"What's wrong?" Jonna asked.

"I . . . I was hoping Anyi would visit tonight."

Lilia had been surprised to discover Jonna already knew

Anyi was Cery's daughter, and of the secret entrance to Sonea's rooms, until she learned that Jonna was Sonea's aunt. It certainly explained the way Jonna bossed Sonea around in private, with no fear and little regard for status.

Jonna smiled as she moved the food from the tray to the table. "She drops by a lot these days."

Lilia nodded. "At least she's safe when she's here."

"And she can get a decent meal," Jonna added. She straightened. "I'll go find something for her. Something that will still be nice even if it has gone cold, so she can take it away with her if she has already eaten."

"Could you . . .?" Lilia grimaced. "Could you bring something every night? Even if she doesn't eat it, there are others she'd like to help. *I'd* like to help. And . . . can you bring lamp oil so she doesn't have to find her way here in the dark?"

Jonna looked sympathetic as she nodded. "Of course."

"And . . . I don't suppose . . . if it's not asking too much . . . What does the Guild do with old bedding and broken furniture?"

The servant's eyebrows rose. "Most furniture here doesn't break often. It's so well made it lasts for hundreds of years. If anything does break, we fix it, and if it's no longer good enough for magicians it goes to the servants." She shrugged. "Same with old bedding. When it's too worn for servants it becomes rags." She looked at Lilia. "But there's more old bedding about than furniture. Let me see if I can get my hands on some."

Lilia nodded. "Thank you. I'd buy some things for her, but I'm not allowed to leave the grounds to go shopping."

"I could get them for you," Jonna offered, "if you write down what you want."

"Do you have time? You must be busy."

"Not as busy as you'd think, especially now Sonea's not here. Fetching things for you is part of my job."

"Well . . . thank you. I'd appreciate that."

Jonna gestured at the bowl. "Now, you start on that before it goes cold and I'll go fetch something for Anyi."

As the door closed behind the servant, Lilia sighed in relief and triumph. Her plan had worked, though she felt a little guilty at suggesting that what she had asked for was going to needy people when it was only going to Cery, Gol and Anyi. *But they do need it.*

Looking down at the meal Jonna had brought, she decided to eat it and give the food she'd taken from the Foodhall to Cery and Gol. Soup was much too hard to transport, and the dessert was as likely to spill. At least if Jonna saw evidence that Lilia was eating some of the food she'd brought, she wouldn't worry over Lilia eating enough – or giving it all away.

As she ate, she thought about how such small, everyday things could become so important. Cery and his friend and daughter were safer in the Guild passages, especially with the passage connecting them to the Thieves' Road destroyed, yet something as trivial as getting food to them was a daily difficulty and risk. If Lilia didn't have to constantly find them something to eat, it would be much easier to hide their presence from the Guild.

I want to do better than bring them food, too, she thought. *I want them to be comfortable. I can't ask Jonna to buy anything luxurious, or she'll grow suspicious. Unless . . . I could say it's for me . . .*

Finishing the soup, she got up and gathered paper, pen and ink and began writing a list.

*   *   *

As Sonea blinked awake she marvelled that she had slept at all in the rocking carriage. Looking across at Regin, she saw that he was conscious and watching her. He smiled faintly and politely looked away.

How long was I asleep? She pulled aside the screen covering the window over the carriage door. Green hills surrounded them, tainted with the gold of a late-afternoon sun. *Quite a while. Poor Regin. He's probably been awake and bored for most of the day.*

For the first few hours of their journey the previous night, their conversation had revolved around the arrangements they'd made to take care of things in their absence, Lilia's progress and future, the places they would probably stop along the journey and some of the information they had been given about Sachakan society. When Regin began yawning she insisted he try to sleep. He'd eventually done so, a travel pillow braced between his head and the side of the carriage. The roads nearer the city were smoother than those further into the countryside, so he was not often jostled awake.

She'd spent the night staring out of the window, thinking about the tasks she had been given and worrying about Lorkin. Remembering the last time she had travelled this road, following Akkarin into exile, she felt echoes of emotions from twenty years before. Fear, rejection, hope and love, all softened with time. She let them come, held onto them for a little while, and then released them to fade into the past.

This journey brought some interesting new emotions. Aside from fear and worry over Lorkin, and anxiety at the potential for everything to go badly for herself and Regin, there was a strange elation. After twenty years of being restricted to the Guild grounds, she had suddenly been set free.

Well, not exactly free. I can't just roam about wherever my fancy takes me. I am on a mission.

"What are you thinking?"

Regin's question brought her back to her surroundings. She shrugged.

"About being outside the city. I'd assumed I'd never leave it again."

He made a low noise of disgust. "They should trust you more."

She shook her head. "I don't think trust was the problem. They had no choice but to trust me. I think they feared what would happen if we were invaded again and I wasn't around. Or if Kallen turned on them."

"Do you think Kallen will take advantage of your absence?"

Sonea shook her head, then she remembered the one trait she did not like in Kallen and frowned.

"What is it?"

She sighed. *If Regin can read me this easily, how am I going to fare when I meet with King Amakira and the Traitors? I suppose I'm not fully awake and on my guard yet. Though I wouldn't forgive myself if I failed to free Lorkin or make an alliance just because I was sleepy.*

What to say? Regin had clearly picked up that she had concerns about Kallen, and he would imagine all sorts of reasons if she didn't give him one. She had to tell him something.

The truth. It isn't exactly a big secret, anyway.

"Rot," she said. "Roet. It is his weakness. If I was going to corrupt Kallen, I'd do it by controlling his access to the drug."

Regin's brows knit together. "Do many people know of his weakness?"

"Vinara does. Rothen, too. I suspect many of the Higher

Magicians do, though we've not discussed it. Or, at least, they've not discussed it while I was present."

"Whoever sells it to him knows as well," Regin added.

"Yes."

"Lilia used roet too, didn't she?"

"When she was with Naki. Lilia doesn't appear to have become addicted to it. In fact, she has a distaste for roet and roet users now. I think she blames it for some of the foolish things she and Naki did."

Regin looked thoughtful. "So the Guild has one black magician addicted to roet, and one resistant to it."

"And one who wouldn't go near the stuff if you paid her to," Sonea added, shuddering.

He looked at her and smiled. "You're too smart for that. You don't let anything back you into a corner."

Sonea felt her cheeks warm. "Except the Guild."

"A worthy exception." He looked away. "I wish I'd had your determination and willingness to defy convention when I was younger."

She shook her head. "You? Not determined? I always got the impression you were completely sure of yourself and what you wanted from life."

"Yes . . . but I never had to make any hard decisions. I was told everything had to be a certain way because it kept everyone safe, powerful and wealthy, and I didn't question that. But as I grew older I did begin to question. I saw that my lack of resistance came out of a fear of not being accepted by my peers. I saw that the only people we were keeping safe, powerful and wealthy were my family and House. That the Houses resist change because they fear it will diminish their power and wealth. And still do."

"Kyralia has changed a lot in the last twenty years. The Houses haven't lost power or wealth as a result."

Regin shook his head. "They will. It may take a long time, but it is going to happen. The warning signs are there, if you know what to look for. And you know what I've discovered?" He looked at her and shrugged. "I don't care. Let them fall. They're built on lies and greed."

Sonea felt a pang of sympathy. Since his rather public separation from his wife, Regin had been prone to the occasional sullen and defiant comment about the habits and expectations of the highest class. Part of her approved, another sympathised, yet she wondered how much of his disenchantment would remain once the personal pain faded.

"I'm sure you wouldn't think so if you wound up a beggar on the street," she reminded him gently.

He looked at her and his shoulders sagged a little. "Probably not. But maybe I'd be a better man. Maybe I'd even be a happier man. By taking in lower-class entrants, the Guild has made it possible for people to cross the barriers between classes. I see the newcomers boasting about it, and I want to warn them that there is a cost. Then . . . then I see that the cost doesn't apply to them and I feel, well, *jealous*. Somehow they get to have the wealth and power and magic, but they have no obligations to honour ancient agreements or traditions, or to only associate with the people their House approves of, or marry the woman their family selects."

"They may have to eventually."

Regin shook his head. "No. Look at you." His eyes rose to meet hers. "You were never forced to marry."

"I'm sure if I'd decided to, plenty would have been said about my choice."

116

"Yet nobody would have dared tell you not to."

"That's only because I am the first black magician. I'm an exception. You can't make predictions based on me."

Regin gave her an odd look, opened his mouth to speak, then frowned and closed it again. His gaze slid away from hers. Sonea felt curiosity rising.

"What were you going to say?" she asked.

He glanced at her, his expression uncertain.

"I . . . I was going to ask you why you didn't marry, but I guess it's obvious – and rather rude of me to ask."

She shrugged. "Not rude. Nor is it why you think. It's true I couldn't have entertained the idea for a long time after Akkarin died, but not for *all* of the last twenty years. I might have married Dorrien, if the timing had been better, but he met someone else long before I was ready." *And a good thing that is, too.* "I don't think we would have been well suited. For a start, he loves the countryside and would have had to live in the Guild grounds to be with me, since I could not leave."

Regin watched her now with an almost guilty interest. *It's likely a lot of people have wanted to ask that question*, she thought.

"By the time I was ready, nobody seemed interested," she continued. "Men my own age hadn't quite got over their prejudice toward magicians from the lower classes, and the only magicians from the lower classes were much too young. All were intimidated by black magic. Some of the Higher Magicians hinted to me that they thought a husband would be a weakness that someone might exploit through blackmail – as if Lorkin wasn't that already. Then there was Lorkin. He was always very jealous of other men in my life."

Regin frowned. "What . . .?" He paused and shook his head. "Yes?"

He grimaced. "What will you do if King Amakira threatens Lorkin?"

Not expecting the change of subject, Sonea felt her heart freeze. She paused to draw in a deep breath and let it out slowly, before answering. "I will point out that it is Lorkin who knows about the Traitors, not me. It would be far more sensible to torture me to get Lorkin to speak."

Regin's mouth dropped open, then he swallowed. "Is it wise for you to put the idea of torturing you into the king's mind?"

She shrugged. "I'm sure it will occur to him the moment he learns I'm on my way to meet him. If he's willing to torture *me*, then we must conclude that he has put aside any reluctance to rouse the anger of the Guild and the Allied Lands. There will be no chance of getting Lorkin back, anyway."

She was desperately proud of herself for not letting her voice catch on that last sentence, though it was a close thing. *If I can keep this up, maybe I* will *be able to hide my feelings in front of the Sachakans and Traitors.*

"I hope for all our sakes that it doesn't come to that," Regin said, with feeling.

She nodded in agreement. If King Amakira was willing to torture her, then Regin would not be safe either.

He shifted across the seat so that he was sitting opposite from her, then held out his hands. "It's been a full day since the Meet and my strength has recovered. You should take my power now, before we arrive at the Stayhouse."

She stared at him as reluctance froze her again. *This is ridiculous. I shouldn't hesitate to take power that's willingly offered, when I'm allowed to and may need it.* She hadn't felt this embarrassment during the Meet, she realised. What was it about using black magic on another person in private that felt

118

uncomfortably . . . intimate. *And illicit. Perhaps because the only other time I've done it privately was with Akkarin.*

Regin was watching her, his brow creased with growing puzzlement. Drawing in a deep breath, Sonea took his hands. She felt magic flow from him and began to store it within herself.

"I'm sorry. I can't get used to this," she told him, shaking her head.

He nodded. "That's understandable. You were forbidden to for so long. In fact, I did wonder if you had forgotten how to do it, after all this time." His mouth briefly widened into a teasing grin.

Sonea managed a smile. "If only that was possible."

"It's all clear," Gol said.

Cery nodded. He'd sent Gol ahead to check that their room remained undiscovered. It was hard to give up old habits of caution. They picked up their burdens and carried them through the passages to the room. Cery set down two battered old chairs, Anyi dropped two bales of hay from her shoulders to the floor, and Gol tossed a bundle of sacks next to the box he'd been using as a seat.

Next, they emptied their pockets of the fruit, vegetables and other items they'd picked up around the farm sheds. Cery looked up at Gol as the man set down a reel of coarse thread.

"Where'd you find that?"

Gol shrugged. "In one of the sheds. There was a basket full of them, so I figured nobody would notice if I took one. And this . . ." He turned one side of his coat out to reveal a long, curved needle piercing the lining. "If I'm going to make mattresses, we'll need it."

Cery regarded his friend dubiously. "*You're* going to make mattresses?"

"Anyi said she doesn't know how to sew."

"Oh, did she?" Cery smiled at his daughter's lie. "And you do?"

"Well enough for this. I used to help my da mend his sails." Gol slipped the end of the thread through the eye of the needle with telling dexterity.

"You're a man with hidden depths, Gol," Cery said. Sitting down on one of the chairs, he smiled as he thought back to their raid on the farm. His assumption that servants were living in the sheds had been proven wrong. All were empty of occupants. Though free to move about, he, Gol and Anyi had taken care not to leave signs of their passing and hadn't taken anything that wasn't already there in abundance. Anyi had suggested relocating some of the other chairs around the place as if someone had simply moved them for some purpose and forgotten to return them, to hide the fact that a few were missing.

Anyi was poking at the fruit. "They're not ripe," she said. "A bit too early in the season. It was hard to tell in the dark. How are we going to cook these vegetables?"

"I only picked ones that didn't have to be cooked," Gol said.

Her nose wrinkled in distaste. "Eat them raw? I'm not *that* hungry."

His eyebrows rose. "Some are better raw, especially when they're fresh. Give them a try."

Anyi didn't look convinced. "I'll wait for Lilia. She can cook them with magic."

"She might not always be able to bring us food," Cery reminded his daughter. "The fewer times she has to come see us the less risk of the Guild discovering us here."

"Then I need to find us a secret entrance to the Guild

kitchens." Anyi stood up. "I'm going to see if she needs any help carrying something."

Gol shook his head as she grabbed a lamp and left. "Doesn't know what she's missing," he muttered.

Cery looked at his friend. "I hoped you two would take a lot more than three days before you started getting under each other's skin."

"We might not have any choice about the . . ." Gol stopped as he looked up and saw Cery's expression. His lips twisted into a smile. "Yeah. I'll try not to. She doesn't like being stuck underground, either."

"No," Cery agreed. Hearing a sound, he rose and moved to the room's doorway. High voices reached him, though he could not hear what they said. "Looks like Lilia was already on her way."

Sitting down again, he waited for the girls to arrive. Lilia carried the usual lacquered box, this time full of bread buns stuffed with spiced meat and sticky seed cakes.

"Now that's real food," Anyi said as she seized a bun.

Lilia grinned. "I've made an arrangement with Jonna. She's going to bring something each night for Anyi to eat and give to poor people, and is going to get me lamp oil and blankets. She thinks I'm being charitable."

Cery felt a flash of alarm. "You didn't tell her about us?"

"No." Lilia looked at the chairs, straw and Gol sewing sacks. "All this came from the farm?"

Anyi must have told her about their raid. "Yes."

"They won't miss it?"

"We were careful," Anyi assured her.

Lilia sat down on one of the boxes. "Well, don't go back for a few days. I'll see if I hear anything about trespassers or thieves. Now . . . I have news from Kallen."

Cery's heart skipped a beat. "Yes?"

"He says people in the city are starting to gossip about your absence. Some believe you must be dead. Others think Skellin has you locked up or cornered somewhere."

"That's not far from the truth," Gol muttered.

Lilia glanced at him, then looked again as she noticed what he was doing. Her eyebrows rose but she made no comment on Gol's sewing skills. "Skellin's men have been taking over your . . ." She waved a hand. "Whatever it is that you do."

"Loan money, protect people, run businesses, introduce people, sell—" Cery began.

"Don't tell me," Lilia interrupted. "As Sonea says, it's better I don't know so I can't be accused of being involved in anything."

"I thought I was doing a good job of making it all sound legitimate." Cery looked at Anyi, who rolled her eyes.

"Do any of Skellin's people think Cery's dead?" Gol asked.

Lilia shrugged. "Kallen wasn't that specific. He did want to know if Cery was planning to take back these . . . businesses."

"Tell him I will be in no position to until he gets rid of Skellin. Has he made any progress?"

The young woman shook her head. "He didn't say so. I think he was hoping you'd be as useful to him as you were to Sonea."

Cery sighed and looked away. "You'd better make it clear to him that I'm no use to anybody now."

Anyi made a wordless sound of protest. "You're useful to us."

Cery gave her a disbelieving look. "If it weren't for me, you wouldn't be stuck here. Down here I'm nothing but a problem for Lilia."

Lilia frowned. "You're not a problem. Not a big one, anyway." Anyi put a hand on her shoulder.

He scowled. "The only mark I can make now is to be a

nagging worry at the back of Skellin's mind. People might say I'm dead, but he won't completely believe it because he hasn't seen a corpse. He has to consider I may be alive, and up to something."

He'll be moving in on my territory cautiously, and questioning everyone who might know where I am. Cery felt his heart spasm painfully with guilt. *My people will want to believe I'm dead, because if I'm alive and not fighting Skellin it'll seem as though I've abandoned them. If they find out I was hiding beneath the Guild, they'll think I've been living in luxury with my magician friends, not this.*

If only there was some gain to be had, other than mere survival, from being here under the Guild.

We're isolated from the rest of the city. Magicians are not far away, and one in particular – Lilia – is able to help us. Few people would dare come here, knowing that. Cery frowned. *Would Skellin dare?*

Perhaps if he had a good reason to.

If he did come here, he'd be very *wary. He'd send scouts to make sure it was safe first. Then there would have to be a good reason for him to enter the passages personally rather than send others. No matter where or how he learned about the existence of these tunnels, and how to get to them, he'd have to suspect the information was meant to fall into his hands, and was part of a trap.*

After all, I would.

But if there was something here that Skellin wanted badly enough, perhaps he would take that risk. Cery just had to think of bait powerful enough to lure him into a trap. This time it would have to be something much more tempting than the books on magic.

CHAPTER 9

FRIENDS AND ENEMIES

Lorkin woke in a rush. He blinked up at the ceiling and puzzled at the unfamiliar bare stone, then a heartbeat later he remembered where he was and why.

And that he wasn't alone in the cell.

He turned to see the young woman lying on the floor near the cell's gate. Her skin and the rags that were all that was left of her slave garb were stained with blood. She was staring up at the Ashaki interrogator, who stood in the gate's opening.

As Lorkin got slowly to his feet the Ashaki bent to grab her arm and yanked her upright. She gave a hoarse cry and sagged as if her limbs wouldn't support her, but the man laughed.

"That wouldn't fool a halfwit," he said. He ran his free hand down her arm to her shoulders, then through her hair, then looked at Lorkin and grinned.

"Nice bit of Healing. Considering how much was broken, it must have worn you out."

Lorkin met the man's eyes and shrugged. "Hardly."

The interrogator chuckled. "We'll see." He looked at the slave girl. "Walk or be dragged."

She gave up on pretending to be wounded. Bracing her feet, she stood properly, then looked down at herself in amazement before her wonder at being whole evaporated as the Ashaki pulled her toward the gate.

"Come with me, Kyralian," the Ashaki said. "We have more to discuss."

Lorkin considered refusing to leave the cell, but he couldn't see how it would gain him anything. It would force the Ashaki to use magic to drag him out, but very little magic and nothing that couldn't be replaced by taking strength from a slave. He doubted the Ashaki would hesitate to torture the girl here instead. Saying nothing, he followed the interrogator out of the cell. The man's assistant, as always, fell into step behind him.

The slave girl walked with slumped shoulders. Lorkin could not stop images and sounds from the day before running through his memory. The Ashaki's torturing had been slow and brutal, calculated to cause as much pain and damage as possible without killing her.

It had taken all Lorkin's determination to stay silent. He could not help trying to think of other ways to stop what was happening, even if temporarily, but none would work for long. These ideas kept taunting him, though. Lying to the Ashaki. Telling him things about the Traitors that were true but irrelevant. Even offering his own life in exchange for the woman's.

Eventually he managed an unpleasant detachment from it all. He gave up on any notion that he could do anything to help the woman or himself. Later he shuddered at what he had done, and worried that accepting that he couldn't help the slave might eventually shift into giving up on protecting the Traitors.

He tried to keep Tyvara in his thoughts to bolster his determination, but that only led to him thinking about what she must have suffered at the hands of Ashaki while pretending to be a slave. *Beatings. Being used as a pleasure slave.* Lorkin's dislike of slavery had deepened into hatred.

The previous day he had been sure the Ashaki would eventually kill the slave woman. He certainly hadn't expected the man to toss her into the cell with him. As time passed his detachment had faded. He'd found it harder and harder to bear listening to the woman whimpering and gasping in pain.

Did they simply hope to wear me down with guilt? Or were they only hoping I'd weaken myself by Healing her? Or see if I'd kill her myself to end her pain.

Using the extra power Tyvara had given him to Heal the slave would not cost him a lot, he'd decided. It would never be enough to protect him for long, if the interrogator decided to torture or kill him. Only afterwards did it occur to him that Healing her meant the Ashaki would be able to torture her all over again.

She had thanked him, which only made him feel worse. He lay awake for a long time, trying to convince himself that the interrogator had achieved his aim. The purpose in using her had been to force him to use up his power. Lorkin had shown that he would not be persuaded by her torture to speak. She was no longer needed.

Now it seemed like a foolish delusion.

The Ashaki led them to the same room. It had been cleaned. The slave girl was shoved into a corner where she threw herself into a submissive, defensive crouch.

As before, Lorkin was directed to a stool. The interrogator leaned against the wall and crossed his arms. The assistant perched on another stool.

"So, have you anything to tell me?" the Ashaki asked. "Anything relating to the Traitors, that is."

"Nothing you don't already know."

"Are you sure about that? Why don't you tell me what you think I know about the Traitors?"

"And see if our knowledge matches?" Lorkin sighed. "As if I'd fall for that trick. When are you going to accept that I'm not going to tell you anything?"

The interrogator shrugged. "It's not up to me. It's up to the king. I'm merely his . . ." he pursed his lips in thought, "his researcher. Only I extract information from people, not dusty old books and scrolls, or by exploring distant places, or spying on foreign lands."

"Torture must be the least reliable kind of research."

"It takes a certain skill." The Ashaki uncrossed his arms and pushed away from the wall. "One that I don't get to practise often, so I'm happy to have the opportunity now. Unless, of course, you distract me with something more interesting."

Lorkin made himself meet and hold the man's gaze and keep his voice level, though his stomach churned as he spoke.

"Has it occurred to you that the means you're using to convince me to talk might make me even more determined to stay silent?"

The Ashaki's smile was unconcerned. "Does it really? Well, then. Let's put that theory to the test."

As he turned to look at the slave she whimpered. Lorkin felt his resolve weaken. *But if I tell them about the Traitors, thousands could end up like this woman. And if she is a Traitor, she knows this and would not want me to betray them.*

He clung to that thought, and tried to put out of his mind

that she might not even be a Traitor, as the interrogator set about undoing everything Lorkin had mended the night before.

Like most novices, Lilia had learned early on that a complex of inner passages and rooms lay within the University building, reached through short passages made to look like small storage rooms. They weren't forbidden to novices, however. Hundreds of years ago the Guild had grown so large that the need for teaching space outweighed whatever purpose the inner rooms had been designed for. Now, specialised or private classes were held in them.

The passages under the Guild were no great secret either. Everybody knew they'd been used during the Ichani Invasion. Though they were forbidden to both novices and magicians because they were deemed unsafe, the threat of cave-ins was never going to deter the more adventurous of them, so all of the passage entrances in the University had been sealed not long after the war.

Lilia wasn't the only novice who suspected the Guild might have kept a few open, just in case. Anyi's explorations had revealed that the Guild had been telling the truth, however. All of the passage entrances had been bricked up. Lilia had been hoping that her friend would find at least one access point into the University. It would be a lot easier than climbing down the narrow gap inside the Magicians' Quarters wall.

Not to be deterred, Anyi had been working on making a new entrance. The night before, she had announced that she had broken through the brickwork at one entrance. Lilia had gone to inspect it. The hidden door in the panelling beyond had needed a little oiling before it would open smoothly.

Beyond it was one of the inner passages of the University. When it was time to leave her friends, she'd used the door and then made her way back to Sonea's rooms.

Now she was heading back to the hidden door, hoping it was too early for other novices to be in the inner passages. Jonna had brought a large bottle of lamp oil with the morning meal. Lilia was all too conscious that her friends were fast running out of sources of light – especially since Anyi had used lamp oil to loosen the secret door's hinges. The new route into the passages would be much faster, since she didn't have an awkward climb up to Sonea's rooms, and when she returned she would be closer to her first class of the day.

Entering the University, she turned into one of the narrow corridors between the classrooms, and headed for the small room at its end that led to the inner passages. Somewhere behind her Lilia heard the sound of echoing footsteps following her. Probably a novice heading for a private class. The inner passages were usually quieter than the main part of the University, but she'd have to be careful nobody saw her slip through the secret door.

The odd little room that divided the main and inner parts of the University contained a wall of locked cabinets. Apparently these rooms had been bare until the former University Director had died, and his replacement had decided that no storage space should be wasted. Lilia pushed through the door opposite and entered the inner passages.

She had taken ten or so steps when she heard the door to the other side of the little room open and close, muffled by the door behind her. Whoever followed was gaining on her. She lengthened her stride in the hope that she would turn a corner before this other person would emerge and see her, but the distance was too great. She heard the door open behind her, then a laugh.

"Hey, Lilia," a voice called. "Where you going?"

Her heart sank. *Bokkin.* From the menace in his tone she knew he had been tailing her. She stopped and turned to regard him. *How stupid can this boy get? He doesn't know how strong or weak I am. He doesn't even have any friends with him to gang up on me. If he's hoping I'm up to something that he could turn me in for, he shouldn't have called out to me before he found out what it was.*

Even so, he had messed up her plans. Perhaps that was all he was aiming for.

"Come to offer me your powers, Bokkin?" she asked.

He sauntered toward her. "You've got big ideas about yourself now, haven't you? Think you're better than anyone because you know black magic. It's the other way around, you know. You're the lowest scum of the Guild and everyone hates you. That's why you've got no friends. Everyone knows Naki's death was your fault."

She felt something shrivel inside her, but instead of it making her cringe away from him it left a void that quickly filled with anger.

Be careful, she warned herself. *Show anger and he'll know he's got to you, and accidentally injuring another novice will only add to the reasons people don't like you.*

She smiled. "Glad you got that off your chest, Bokkin?"

He moved closer, trying again to intimidate her with his bulk and height. "Yes. But I'm not done with you. I want you to apologise – no, I want you to beg me . . ."

The door behind them opened and he quickly stepped back. "Lady Lilia."

Confusion and relief rose as Lilia recognised Jonna's voice.

She peered past Bokkin to see the servant approaching. The woman bowed briskly at them both.

"A message came for you," Jonna said. She pushed past Bokkin. "Excuse me, my Lord."

Jonna placed a hand on Lilia's arm and guided her along the passage, away from Bokkin. The novice remained silent, and Lilia didn't dignify him with a backwards glance. She and Jonna turned a corner. When they had continued far enough Jonna glanced back.

"He's not following us. Was he bothering you?"

Lilia shrugged. "He's a troublemaker, but a pretty thick-headed one."

"Don't dismiss him too quickly. He may come back with others. Sonea had enemies among the novices when she was learning here, and they made her life here a torment."

"Really? Who was the leader?" *How humiliating to live your life known as the novice stupid enough to have picked on the famous Black Magician Sonea.*

Jonna looked amused. "Lord Regin."

Lilia stared at her in astonishment. "*Really?* He's not dumb."

"No."

"I guess novice bullies were smarter in those days."

Jonna patted her arm firmly. "What I want to know is, where are you going with a bottle of lamp oil in your bag?"

Lilia looked down at her bag then back up at Jonna. "What bottle? I left it in the room."

"You most certainly did not, and it's obvious from the way that bag is bulging and swinging that you have it in there." Jonna frowned in a motherly, disapproving way. "I told Sonea I'd keep an eye on you. I helped raise Sonea's son, Lorkin, so I know how to spot when a novice is up to something."

Lilia gazed at the servant in dismay. It wasn't that she didn't want to tell Jonna about Cery, Gol and Anyi living under the Guild, but she had agreed not to. *But if I don't, Jonna won't get me the things they need.*

Jonna had lived in the slums before she became Sonea's servant. She would surely empathise with Cery's situation. Even if she didn't, perhaps she would help out of sympathy for Anyi.

But am I being too trusting?

"Tell me, Lilia," Jonna said. "I may not like it, but I promise I won't report it to the Guild." She frowned. "Well, unless you're teaching someone black magic. Though I suppose I wouldn't have turned Sonea and Akkarin in, if I'd known what was really going on."

"I'm not teaching anyone black magic," Lilia told her, and winced at the sound of protest in her voice. She drew in a deep breath, lowered her tone to a whisper. "Anyi is living under the Guild."

Jonna looked thoughtful. "I see. I guessed that she'd been travelling that way to visit you for a while already. Is it safe?"

"We've been making it safer," Lilia assured her.

"So . . . why is she there?"

Lilia shook her head. "It wasn't safe in the city. Skellin's people nearly killed Cery—"

"You mean Cery is down there as well?"

Jonna's eyes narrowed. Lilia sighed and nodded.

"How many people are down there?"

"Just them."

The servant looked relieved. *I expect she was imagining what the Guild would think of a Thief setting up his business down there,* Lilia thought, *with numerous criminals coming and going all the time.*

Jonna gestured to the corridor. "So why come here?"

"We opened one of the old entrances."

Jonna frowned and shook her head. "Now, that's too dangerous," she decided. "And I don't mean being below, I mean up here. Someone will see you. You must only use the passage in Sonea's rooms."

Lilia smiled, relieved that she had been right to trust Jonna. "Haven't you noticed how scuffed and dirty my robes have been lately."

"I haven't failed to note their condition." Jonna lifted her chin and gave Lilia a haughty look. "We shall have to do something about that. Like get you alternative clothing, for instance. In the meantime," she reached down and opened Lilia's bag. "I'm taking the bottle and you are going straight to class. Tonight we will discuss more effective strategies for dealing with our guests."

Hefting the bottle of lamp oil, she gave Lilia a stern look, then turned and strode back down the corridor. A faint whiff of her perfume lingered, something Lilia hadn't noticed about her before.

Closing her bag, Lilia shook her head. *I had no choice but to tell her*, she reasoned. *And she's not going to tell anyone. In fact, having her know everything could be useful.* Then she sighed. *In the meantime, I hope Cery, Gol and Anyi don't end up sitting in the dark.*

Dannyl dipped his pen into the ink pot then continued writing, but the nib soon began to scratch the paper ineffectually. He dipped the pen once more, then sighed as he saw that the reservoir was nearly empty. *Run out again*, he thought. Straightening, he groaned as his back protested. *How long have I been working at this?*

A day after Lorkin had been imprisoned, Dannyl had brought all of his research notes together and begun transcribing everything into a large notebook. His discussion with Tayend on the possible intentions of the Traitors had led to him worrying that, if the more dramatic situations they'd considered should eventuate, he might not get the chance to write down everything in a form others could comprehend. He had plenty of time to fill, and he was not making any progress in his research anyway, so he was writing sections of text and noting where they were to be slotted into his history of magic.

The work had proven to be a calming, welcome distraction. It reassured him that he had made some important discoveries about the history of magic, and hadn't wasted his time in Sachaka. He would make substantial additions to his history of magic once he returned to Kyralia. *If I live to finish it.* He shook his head. *No, don't be silly. Tayend agreed that the worse scenarios we imagined are the least likely to come about.*

Even so, he'd decided to make an extra copy to be stored in a safe place somewhere outside the Guild House, so that if this building was attacked his work wouldn't be lost. Ideally, it should go to the Guild, but he couldn't be sure it would arrive there. No doubt King Amakira had people in place to intercept and examine anything leaving and arriving at the Guild House.

In case his work was read by Sachakans, Dannyl had been careful to leave out any mention of gemstones with magical properties, apart from the famous Storestone that had created the wastelands. He'd had to come up with a way to hide references to them when writing out his notes on the Duna tribes' legends, so that he wouldn't be betraying the Duna's trust if someone happened upon the copy. The stones were now people – powerful magicians referred to by their title. Dannyl would have to change all mentions of these fictional characters back to gemstones when he came to write his book.

After making his first coded version of his notes, he'd destroyed his original notebook. *If I die and somebody finds the new version, I'm going to be the perpetrator of some very big lies in our history.* After all the effort he'd put into digging up the truth about some of Kyralia's hidden past, it would be a sad irony.

Now he was near to finishing the copy – well, he *had* been until he'd run out of ink. A movement in the doorway drew his attention away, and he looked up to see Kai throw himself on the floor.

"Ashaki Achati has arrived, master."

Dannyl cursed silently at the conflicting eagerness and dread the news stirred. He pushed himself to his feet. *Is Achati angry at me for breaking my promise to tell him of anything that might threaten Sachaka? Will I be able to forgive him for condoning the king's imprisonment of Lorkin? Is any chance of us becoming lovers gone?*

The slave scampered out of the room as Dannyl took the first step toward the door. Taking a deep breath, Dannyl walked down the corridor and found Achati waiting in the Master's Room, looking dignified in a black version of the typical Ashaki trousers and short jacket.

"Ambassador Dannyl," he said.

"Ashaki Achati," Dannyl replied. He decided not to sit down, or invite Achati to. He suspected he would slip into being inappropriately friendly if he didn't remain standing.

Achati hesitated, looked away, then raised his gaze to meet Dannyl's again.

"You turned down my invitation to dinner," he observed.

Dannyl nodded. "It would not have been appropriate to accept."

"In your eyes or in the eyes of the Guild and Allied Lands?"

"Both."

Achati looked away again, frowning and shifting his weight slowly from one leg to the other. He looked as if he was considering his words carefully.

"I've persuaded the king that I should maintain our friendship," he began.

"So you can keep trying to persuade me to order Lorkin to speak?" Dannyl finished.

"No." Achati winced. "Well, yes, as far as he is concerned that is the reason, but I have no intention of doing that."

"What *do* you intend to do?"

The man's mouth twitched and his eyes crinkled with amusement. Which made Dannyl miss their former banter.

"Try to rescue what remains of our friendship," he said. "Even if it means pretending none of this unfortunate business is happening."

"But it *is* happening," Dannyl said. "You would be as incapable of pretending otherwise if . . . if your cousin or . . ." A memory of the slave that Achati had cared for slipped into his mind. "Varn . . . maybe not Varn, since he's a slave."

"It would be upsetting if Varn was unjustly treated," Achati admitted.

"So you admit that Lorkin's imprisonment is unjust?"

Achati smiled. "No. How would you feel if . . . if the Elyne Ambassador in Kyralia was protecting a rogue magician?"

"To be a fair comparison, we'd not know if the man was a rogue or not. You don't know if Lorkin has useful information and we're not refusing to pass that information on to you, just asking that we have the opportunity to question our own man first. And if there was a rogue, well, the alliance states that all rogues are the Guild's concern."

Achati sighed. "Yes, that last is the key difference. Kyralia and Elyne are allies. You trust them. Kyralia and Sachaka are not allies. You ask for more trust than we can give."

Dannyl nodded. "You'll have to learn to trust us, if we are to become allies in the future."

"Then don't you have to trust us, in return?"

"You've got more convincing to do," Dannyl pointed out. "We have more recent aggressive acts to forgive, before we trust Sachakans."

Achati sighed. He looked at Dannyl, saying nothing, before finally ending the pause in their conversation with a shake of his head.

"I hoped we could talk as friends, but instead we speak as if we are our nations. I should go." But he didn't move away. He chewed his lip. "I can at least assure you that Lorkin is fine. The king won't dare to harm him. Don't stop trying to see him, though. Goodbye, for now."

"Good night." Dannyl watched the Ashaki walk to the entrance corridor and disappear. He waited until he heard the front door open and close, then moved to the chairs, sat down and let out a long breath.

"I know you won't like me saying so, but I don't buy any of that."

Looking up at the voice, Dannyl frowned as Tayend moved into the room.

"How long were you spying for?"

"Long enough." Tayend moved to a chair and sat down. "You don't believe him, do you?"

Dannyl considered. "Which part?"

"That he wants to be your friend only for the sake of being friends."

"I don't know."

"Surely you don't trust him?"

Dannyl spread his hands. "Trust was never part of it."

The Elyne's eyebrows rose. "Well, then. Perhaps I should have asked if you still *like* him?"

Looking away, Dannyl shrugged. "I haven't made up my mind. However I decide, it won't stop me obeying orders or helping Lorkin."

Tayend nodded. "I know it won't. I admit I was worried about you, but you are still your old self, underneath."

Dannyl straightened in protest. "Underneath *what*?"

The Elyne stood up, waving one hand in Dannyl's direction. "All . . . *that*."

"I'm reeling at your descriptive clarity," Dannyl told him.

Tayend opened his mouth to say more, then closed it again and shook his head. "Never mind. I'm going back to my room. I have a trade agreement to negotiate. Are you still copying your notes?"

"Yes. No. I've run out of ink again. The slaves mustn't have refilled the bottle this morning."

"Actually, they put the last of the House's supply in my pot last night. I sent one off to buy more this morning but he came back empty-handed." Tayend's expression became serious. "It was hard to get any sense out of him. Seems someone took it off him, but he claimed he didn't know who in that way people do when they're lying and they want you to know it."

Dannyl frowned. "Someone *took* it from him? A thief?"

"Or someone working for the king. Maybe they don't want us writing-up documents."

A chill ran down Dannyl's spine. "Or making copies of research notes."

"Surely not. How would they know you were doing that?"

"The slaves," Dannyl replied.

Tayend's eyes narrowed. "Who won't know you're only writing about your research, not about Lorkin's discoveries."

Dannyl sighed. "I'm not going to be able to get that second copy to the Guild safely, am I?"

"I could be wrong about the king's men taking the ink," Tayend said. He looked at Dannyl thoughtfully. "Or not. Maybe you had better lock those notes up with magic in case the slaves are ordered to steal them from you." He took a step toward the corridor, then stopped and looked back. "I'll bring my ink pot over for you. Maybe Merria or I can get more ink from our Sachakan friends."

CHAPTER 10

NO GOOD CHOICES

Lorkin lay on the hard, cold floor of the cell and tried not to listen to the slave woman struggling to breathe.

I don't even know her name, he thought. Surely he should at least know the name of the woman who was suffering so much pain because of him. *Because of the Traitors as much as me*, he reminded himself. But he couldn't bring himself to ask her. Not when he was deliberately avoiding Healing her.

If he did, the interrogator would hurt her all over again.

If he didn't, she might die. Then the interrogator would find another slave to hurt. At first Lorkin had reasoned that it was better for fewer people to be hurt and killed than more, but she had hissed at him to stay away when he'd approached her, and again when he'd tried to explain that he could at least stop the pain. Though she could not have stopped him Healing her, if she wanted to escape her predicament by dying he felt he ought to respect her wishes. Or perhaps, eventually, the pain would be too much and she would ask him to help her.

It had been a very long day. One horrible moment was followed by another, and another. Time stretched out beyond his ability to judge its passing. At times he felt as if he was trapped in a nightmare that would never end. The interrogator didn't appear to tire of his work, or run out of ways to cause a human as much pain as possible while causing minimal damage. Lorkin had seen things he would never forget. He had heard sounds that would haunt him for the rest of his life. He had smelled aromas no civilized person should ever smell.

He knew sleep was beyond possible, but he tried. When he gave up on trying, he pretended he was asleep.

A contorted hiss came from the slave and he was instantly alert, heart beating fast. He told himself she was just voicing the pain, not calling for attention, but the same pattern of sounds came again. Slowly, reluctantly, he turned to look at her.

She was lying on her side, curled up and cradling her broken arm. Her eyes were wide open and staring at him. As he met her gaze her lips moved and though no sound came the words were clear, as if she'd spoken in his mind. He went cold all over at their meaning.

Kill me.

He stared back at her in disbelief. *No, not disbelief. Death is the only escape she is going to get. I can stop the pain, if she'll let me, but that is only the physical part of torture. I can't stop the horror, humiliation and fear.*

But . . .

His insides twisted. *I can't kill her.* He felt guilt deepen and turned away. *It's all my fault.* He shook his head. *No. It isn't. But I can't pretend I'm not partly responsible for what's happening to her. If there's anything I can do . . .*

Anything? *But I've never killed anybody. It's not that I wouldn't if I had to defend myself or someone else, but to kill someone who isn't trying to hurt anyone is* wrong.

Her lips shaped the plea again.

He remembered his mother's words, from long ago: *"As Healers we can do much to prevent death, but the limits of what we can do sometimes clash with what we should do. When a person is beyond saving and only wishes to die, keeping them alive is a kind of cruelty."*

Listening to the slave's shuddering breaths, he knew it was cruel to let her suffer with no hope of escape.

How would I even do it? The Ashaki guard was sitting outside the cell, watching them. Whatever Lorkin did, it would have to be gentle and subtle enough that it didn't attract attention.

I can't believe I am actually contemplating it.

Eventually the slave's death would be noticed. What would they do once they knew Lorkin had killed her? He felt a traitorous relief as the answer came to him. *She is the king's property — or somebody's. I don't know how bad a crime it is to destroy someone's property, but it would definitely be something they'd hold against me.*

Perhaps they were hoping he'd kill her. Perhaps it would give them the excuse they needed to read his mind, or worse. Once he was officially a criminal they could do anything to him.

The more he thought about it, the more convinced he was that this was their plan. Why else were they locking her in the cell with him every night? If he went on Healing her he would soon use up all the power Tyvara had given him. But that couldn't be their only aim. There were plenty of other ways they could sap his strength, if that was what they wanted. If they only intended to break his resolve by torturing others, why leave the slave woman in his cell? They could always lock her up close by, just out of reach, so he witnessed her suffering but couldn't help her.

Suddenly he wanted to kill her, just to spite them.

No, I don't, he told himself quickly, shuddering at the thought he might be turned into a murderer so easily.

"*Kill me*," came the whisper again. It sent a shiver down his spine.

Was there a way he could kill her that would leave no evidence he had done it? *If the injuries the interrogator gave her are bad enough . . . No, he would have made sure they weren't.* Yet from the sound of her breathing something inside her chest was damaged. Perhaps a rib was cracked or broken. If he could manipulate it . . .

But that would be using Healing power to kill. Healers were supposed to heal, not harm.

Well, that's always been a complicated philosophy. Cutting open a body to remove a tumour involves harming in order to heal. And then there's the argument for helping people die. And my mother used Healing in defence, to kill some of the Ichani invaders.

"Www . . ."

A soft scraping noise came from the girl, and he reluctantly turned his head to look at her again. She was reaching toward him. *No*, he corrected himself, *she's reaching toward my legs.*

"Wwwater," she gasped.

Relief came as he realised that now she was only asking for something to drink. He pushed himself up into a sitting position. The food-bearing slave had brought a meal. Lorkin had tried to share it with the slave woman but she'd refused to eat. He reached for the jar of water and froze, remembering the warning glyphs that had indicated it was unsafe.

I wonder how unsafe . . .

He shrank from the thought, but it sprang straight back into his mind. If the water was poisoned and she drank it, she

143

might gain the death she wanted without anyone but him knowing it was his fault. *Well, except for the Traitors who left the warning.* He felt a shiver go up his spine.

If the slave woman was a Traitor, she might know about the warnings. She might know the water would kill her. He turned to look at her. She gazed back at him, her eyes seeming to say, *Yes. Free me.*

If she was a Traitor, they must know she was here. Had they provided her with a means to kill herself?

But would the water kill her? He dropped his arm. The Ashaki must be the one adulterating Lorkin's food. Surely they weren't trying to kill him? He was of no use to them dead. Most likely the poison in the water was meant to make him sick, or force him to use up more strength by Healing himself. Still, they might reason that the stronger the toxin, the more magic he would be forced to use. It could be a lethal dose.

The woman made a low noise and stretched her unbroken arm toward the bottle. Outside the cell, the watcher eyed them both.

Kill me. Free me.

Lorkin looked from her to the water. He had to make a choice. And there was no right one. No matter what he decided, the consequences would be shocking. No matter what he decided, afterwards he would never be the same person again.

By the way Lilia had admitted to telling Sonea's aunt that Cery, Gol and Anyi were living under the Guild, it was clear she thought they would be angry. *Which is amusing and endearing, considering that she is a magician and we are mere commoners*, Cery thought. She had paced a little as she explained how the servant had followed her and the discussion it had led to. Now she looked surprised that nobody was concerned by the news.

"Better that Jonna knows, than anybody else up there," Anyi said. "In fact, she could be useful."

"Jonna never liked me," Cery told them. "But that was back when I was a youngster and she thought I was leading Sonea astray. She knew I was slipping into Sonea's room now and then these last twenty years, but she never told anybody about it. Good odds she can be trusted."

"If Sonea trusts her, I reckon she's all right," Gol agreed.

Lilia's eyes had lit up with a peculiar light. "You've been seeing Sonea for the last twenty years?" she asked Cery.

He shrugged. "Of course. You didn't think some rule about associating with criminals would stop her talking to her old friends, did you?"

"No, I can't see that stopping either of you. I wonder what people would say if they knew. It would be a scandal, I'm sure." Lilia smiled and sat down next to Anyi. "They'd also finally know why Sonea never got married."

Cery frowned as he realised she had assumed his visits had been romantic. "Wait. I didn't . . . that's not what I was visiting her for."

Gol began to laugh. "You certainly made it sound like it was. For a moment there I thought you'd managed to hide something from me all this time."

Anyi shook her finger at Lilia. "My father was happily married for most of the last twenty years," she said indignantly. Then she grimaced. "Well, during the second marriage, anyway – but he *was* married to my mother before that, even if it wasn't exactly what you'd call 'happily' married."

"I'm sorry. I didn't mean to suggest he was unfaithful," Lilia apologised.

Gol chuckled in a knowing way.

It was time to change the subject, Cery decided. "I've been thinking about what we should do next," he said. Immediately all eyes turned to him. Anyi looked eager, Lilia relieved and Gol narrowed his eyes, no doubt ready to find the holes in whatever schemes Cery thought up. "What we should do is obvious, once I started thinking less about how we are stuck here and more about how we can turn being here to our advantage."

Now Lilia was looking a little worried.

"We're safe here – not because Skellin won't have guessed we sought the Guild's protection but because he won't risk coming here," he continued. "He'll assume if we're here we're in one of the Guild buildings, under magical protection. If he learned that we were under the Guild, and that the magicians don't know we're here, he'd would slip in and kill us all – and feel smug that he did it without the Guild noticing."

"But the Guild *would* notice," Anyi pointed out. "Lilia knows we're here and will stop him, or if she can't then she'd get help."

"Yes, but *Skellin* doesn't know that," Cery pointed out.

Gol gave a low growl. "No," he said.

Cery turned to his friend, amused by the one-word disapproval. "Why not?"

"This is our last and only safe place," Gol said. "We can't risk losing it."

"We do have one more safe place." Cery pointed upwards. "The protection Skellin thinks we're enjoying." He gestured around them. "This, here, is our last and only chance to lure him into a trap."

"A trap that, if it goes wrong, will see you dead," Gol said.

"Lilia will protect him," Anyi said, her eyes bright with the prospect of finally doing something.

Lilia nodded. "And Kallen. You are planning to tell Kallen, aren't you?"

"Yes," Cery replied. "It's a bit much to ask Lilia to shoulder all the burden of magical protection or to confront two rogue magicians, if Skellin brings his mother along."

Anyi rubbed her hands together eagerly. "So what will we use as bait?"

Gol snorted. "It's obvious. Your father intends to lure Skellin here with something he wants more than anything else."

Lilia's face went a little pale. "Black magic?"

"No," Gol said. "Skellin wants to know he has full control of the entire underworld. If he finds out Cery is alive, he'll know there's always the danger Cery will try to get it back – with Guild help. He'll risk a lot to kill him."

Anyi's eager grin vanished. She stared at Cery, searching his face as if hoping for a sign he was joking. When he nodded she scowled and crossed her arms. "Gol's right. That is too much of a risk."

"What else do you suggest? What else would tempt him to risk coming this close to the Guild?"

Anyi looked at Lilia. "Black magic—"

"He won't risk trying to capture her. She could be many times stronger than him. In fact, for this to work it has to be obvious that Lilia isn't here. He might believe the Guild doesn't know I'm here, but he won't as easily believe *she* doesn't. Lilia will have to be seen somewhere else before he'll come looking for me."

"But you'll need a magician here," Lilia pointed out. "Or you won't be able to stop him killing you all."

He nodded. "Yes. Kallen. Tell him that we have a plan to trap Skellin and ask how we should contact him when we're ready. Don't tell him where the trap will be sprung of course. I have a feeling he'd decide keeping people out of these passages is more important than catching Skellin."

Lilia nodded. Anyi was shaking her head. "I don't like it," she said.

Cery crossed his arms. "Why?"

"I . . ." She looked away and scowled. Abruptly she got up, grabbed a lamp and stalked out of the room.

The room was silent for several heartbeats. Lilia glanced at Cery and Gol, then hurried after her.

Cery stared at the empty doorway. His heart twisted in a way that was both painful and pleasant. He did not want to risk anybody's life. Certainly not his own. But they could not stay here forever.

Thinking back, he remembered the angry, defiant young woman he had tried to keep in contact with after parting from her mother. Anyi had hated him – or at least she had behaved as if she did. Knowing that he had somehow won her over was a bittersweet pleasure. It had come at the price of her safety.

But then, being related to him was all it took to make life dangerous, especially while a rogue magician Thief ruled the underworld, and that rogue hated Cery.

"For once your daughter and I agree," Gol said in a low voice. "It is too dangerous."

"Let's see what Kallen says to that," Cery replied.

*   *   *

Within a few paces, Anyi slowed down to let Lilia catch up, but did not stop walking.

"Are you all right?" Lilia asked.

Anyi shook her head. "No. Yes. I . . . I need to think."

Her tone suggested that she wasn't in the mood for talking, so Lilia stayed silent. She drew magic to create a globe light, and Anyi wordlessly turned her lamp's flame down low to conserve oil. They didn't travel far. After a few hundred paces Anyi's stride became purposeful and soon it became clear she was leading Lilia to some rooms nearer to the University that she'd recently discovered.

Anyi chose one room at random, then, since there were no chairs, sat down on the floor with her back to a wall. Lilia sat down beside her, disturbing a dust-covered broken plate. She wiped the surface clean, uncovering a Guild symbol imprinted into the underside. *This isn't very old. I wonder how it got here.*

"I shouldn't care," Anyi said.

Lilia turned to look at her. "Of course you should. He's your father."

Anyi's mouth twisted into a bitter smile. "Not much of one. For most of my life he ignored me. It was only when his other family was murdered that he paid any attention to me."

Not sure what to say, Lilia said nothing.

"That's not really fair, though," Anyi added, her voice quieter and softer. "Mother left him. She said it wasn't safe being the wife of a Thief, and that she couldn't stand being hidden away all the time. I don't think two people should be forced to be together if they don't want to be."

"How did Cery come to marry again?" Lilia asked. Divorce was something only the king could grant. She couldn't imagine a Thief asking the king to end his marriage.

Anyi shrugged. "He just did."

"But that's . . ."

"Bigamy?" Anyi looked at Lilia and shrugged. "Not really. Nobody in the underworld can afford a legal marriage. I suppose Cery could, but why pay attention to one of the king's laws when you don't pay much to the rest of them? We have our own ways of declaring ourselves married — or unmarried."

Lilia shook her head in wonder. "It's a whole other world." She shrugged. "Though I could say that about the family my parents were servants for. We might have been a part of their world, but we weren't *in* their world. It would have been nice to be that rich, and to be able to order people around, but sometimes they had even less choice about their lives than we did. They don't get to decide who they marry, and they *do* have to ask the king for a divorce — and hope he grants it."

"Perhaps that's why Sonea never got married. She's not from the Houses so she doesn't have a family deciding who she marries, but she'd have to have a legal marriage if she did and then if she wanted to end it she'd have to hope the king let her."

Lilia chuckled. "I can't imagine some man ordering her about."

Anyi grinned. "No. More likely it'd be the other way around." But as she met Lilia's gaze she grew serious again. She looked away and sighed.

"He's going to get himself killed. He finally lets me into his world and now I'm going to lose him."

"Only if things go wrong — and we'll make sure that won't happen."

Anyi gave her an accusing look. "You think he's right."

"No." Lilia shook her head. "But I suspect we won't have much say in it."

The other girl scowled, then her expression became thoughtful. "You could tell him Kallen doesn't want to do it. Put Cery off for a while."

Lilia nodded. "I could. But then he might try to do it without Kallen." She thought back to what Cery had said. "I can't help thinking he is right about one thing: Skellin will guess you all came here. Where else would you go? He probably knows there are tunnels. It's not a secret in the Guild, so I doubt it is outside of it. He'll come to have a look eventually. When he does, he'll find you here. And if I'm away in lessons, I won't be able to stop him killing you all."

Anyi turned to look at Lilia, her brow creased with worry.

"Perhaps the only way you can be safe is under the Guild's protection," Lilia continued. "I know none of you like that idea, but if Cery's trap fails, that's where you'll end up anyway. I suspect the Guild won't like it either, but they'll be more willing to protect you if there's evidence Skellin actually entered the Guild's underground passages."

Anyi groaned and rubbed her face with her hands. "You're making sense, and I don't like it."

"I don't either," Lilia admitted. "But I know I can't be the protector you need. Mostly because I'm not here that much, but also because I don't know how powerful Skellin is. If he comes here with Lorandra I doubt I'll be able to protect myself, let alone the rest of you. Even if he doesn't, how are you going to let me know you need my help? What if I don't get here in time?"

"We'll use an escape route."

"What if you don't make it? Even if you do, you'll come

up in the Guild's grounds and if he's still following you then you'll have to seek the help of the Guild anyway." Lilia sighed and felt the frustration and worry of the last few weeks gather up behind her words. "It's not safe down here, and you could be living more comfortably, and it's so hard getting food to you, and . . . I miss you."

At that last admission, the flood of words that had been pouring out of her ran out. She felt her face heat and looked at Anyi sheepishly. The other girl had an odd, surprised expression.

"I mean I miss being alone with you. Maybe that's a little selfish," she began. "I—"

But she got no apology out, because Anyi leaned forward, caught hold of her jaw and kissed her.

"I miss you, too," she said quietly and fiercely.

Then she drew Lilia into her arms. For a time they simply held each other, taking comfort in physical warmth and closeness. Too soon Anyi sighed and pulled away.

"Cery will be wondering where we've got to," she murmured.

Standing up, she held out a hand to Lilia. As Lilia took it Anyi hauled her to her feet, but in the same movement she pulled Lilia close and kissed her again. This time it was a lingering kiss, as if she had forgotten her last words.

A footfall, followed by a sharply indrawn breath, jolted Lilia back to her surroundings. She and Anyi sprang apart and whirled towards the door, Anyi bracing in a fighting stance. Lilia had drawn magic and formed a shield before she saw that it was only Cery standing in the doorway.

His face was frozen in surprise. As Anyi uttered a curse, Cery's expression changed to a mix of embarrassment and amusement.

"Didn't mean to interrupt," he said, taking a step backwards. "Come back when you're ready."

Then with a barely suppressed smile, he turned and hurried away.

Covering her face with her hands, Anyi groaned. Lilia placed a hand on her friend's shoulder in sympathy. *I wouldn't want my father walking in on me kissing another woman.* As Anyi's shoulders started to shake and she began to make choking noises, she felt her heart twist, until she saw her friend's hands shift to her mouth and she realised Anyi was laughing.

"Well," Lilia said as she waited for Anyi to stop. "That's not the reaction I was expecting."

Anyi shook her head. "No. Guess it wouldn't be." She took a couple of deep breaths, only breaking into spluttering once. "I've been worrying about how to tell him for months. Now I don't have to."

"You were going to tell him about us?"

"Of course."

"But . . . won't he be angry?"

"No. A bit dismayed, maybe. Did I ever tell you where he was born and grew up?"

Lilia shook her head.

"Well, it's really his story to tell — many stories, actually. It was a place you meet people with all kinds of tastes and ideas." Anyi took Lilia's hand. "Come on. We really should go back. He'll be worrying that we're too annoyed or embarrassed to return. And I want to make sure this fool's plan is as fool-proof as possible."

CHAPTER 11

A CHANGE OF PLAN

The words on the page before Dannyl were as grey as an overcast sky. Tayend had given Dannyl his meagre supply of remaining ink and, since neither the slaves nor Merria had managed to bring any more into the Guild House, Dannyl had to thin out what was left with water. Following Tayend's advice, he now locked his research notes away with magic whenever he was done working on them.

A movement drew his attention to the doorway in time to see Kai throw himself on the floor.

"A carriage from the palace has arrived, master," the slave said.

Achati again. He sighed and closed his eyes for a moment. *This doesn't get easier.* Opening his eyes, he dried the ink on the page, cleaned his pen, stowed everything away in a drawer and protected it all with magic. Dismissing Kai, he straightened his back and made his way to the Master's Room.

The door slave was literally hopping from one foot to another, until he saw Dannyl and dove face-first onto the floor.

"Lord Lorkin has returned, master!" he declared.

Dannyl's heart skipped a beat. "Lorkin?"

He hurried forward, but Sonea's son was already emerging from the entrance corridor. As the young man entered the room

Dannyl felt a chill run down his spine. *Something has happened to him*, he thought, though he wasn't sure how he knew. Dannyl looked Lorkin over. There was no sign of injury, though it was hard to tell when Guild robes concealed so much. Other than dark shadows under his eyes suggesting a lack of sleep, Lorkin looked well.

"Ambassador Dannyl," he said.

"You're free!" Dannyl had to resist an urge to hug the young man, instead grasping Lorkin's arm in the usual gesture of Kyralian greeting. "What happened? King Amakira let you go?"

"Yes," Lorkin replied.

"Do you know why?"

Lorkin looked away. "He didn't say."

Dannyl stepped back. Lorkin's voice was flat and expressionless. *He should be relieved. Puzzled by his unexpected release. Angry that he'd been imprisoned in the first place.*

"Come sit down." Dannyl ushered Lorkin to the seats, but the young magician didn't sit down. "Are you hurt?"

"No."

"Did they read your mind? Or attempt to?"

"No."

"Lord Lorkin! I thought I heard your name."

They both looked up to see Tayend standing in the doorway. The Elyne hurried forward, reaching out toward the young magician as if to hug him but, Dannyl was amused to see, letting his arms drop to his sides at the last moment. He gave Lorkin a critical look.

"You don't look too bad, for someone who has been locked up in a prison," he observed. "But they wouldn't have dared harm you physically. How are you feeling?"

Lorkin shrugged, but his eyes betrayed the same wary evasiveness Dannyl had noted earlier. "Tired. Hungry. I could do with a bath."

Tayend sniffed and smiled. "You're right about that. I don't imagine the palace prison contains hot tubs. Let's get you to our perfectly civilized Guild House ones. I'll have the slaves prepare you something nourishing and fetch you some clean robes."

Lorkin nodded, but before he succumbed to the Elyne's attempts to usher him out of the room he reached into his robes and turned to Dannyl. Wordlessly, he drew out a scroll. Dannyl noted King Amakira's seal before looking up at the young man again. Lorkin's eyes were hard and knowing.

Then he turned away and left.

Dannyl sat down and broke the seal. It was an official order from the king and simply declared that Lorkin was forbidden to leave the Guild House. No reason was given for his release from the palace prison. No mention was made at all of his incarceration. *What did I expect? An apology?*

Tayend returned to the room and sat down next to Dannyl.

"He's not all right," the Elyne murmured.

"No," Dannyl agreed.

"Whatever they did to him – or forced him to do – he is not ready to talk about it. I will keep an eye on him and let you know if he tells me about it – if he doesn't make me promise to keep it a secret, of course."

"Of course."

"So what does it say?" Tayend nodded at the scroll.

"Lorkin is forbidden to leave the Guild House."

Tayend nodded. "He's not completely free, then." He reached out and patted Dannyl's arm. "He's out of that place. That, at least, is a good thing." He stood up. "I have to report this. You had better tell Administrator Osen."

Dannyl watched Tayend hurry away, and managed a sad smile. If Lorkin did prove reluctant to talk about what had been done to him in the prison, or had some guilty secret to admit to, Tayend was the one most likely to coax it out of him. He could be uncannily perceptive when it came to other people's troubles. *Except when it came to our troubles*, Dannyl reminded himself.

I hate to think it, but I hope Lorkin isn't here because they forced him to betray the Traitors. It could be very bad for them — and might be for us, if whatever Lorkin and Osen were communicating about involved us working with the them.

Osen. As Tayend had pointed out, the Administrator would want to know Lorkin had returned. Reaching into his robes, he drew out Osen's blood ring, took a deep breath, then slipped it on his finger.

"You have got to be kidding me," Sonea exclaimed under her breath as she looked up at the Stayhouse sign.

"What is it?" Regin asked.

She said nothing, because a stocky man had appeared in the doorway.

He bowed. "My Lord and Lady! Come in! Come in!" the man said. "I am Fondin. Welcome to Fergun's Rest, the finest Stayhouse in Kyralia."

She heard Regin chuckle, but he said nothing as she moved through the doorway. As always, the ground floor was a dining and drinking area. It was busy despite the late hour, the room echoing with many voices. The clothing of the customers suggested they were locals and had dressed up for an occasion.

A few looked up at her and Regin, and their eyes went wide with surprise.

"Please sit a moment and rest," Fondin invited them, gesturing toward a quieter corner. "Do you need one room or two?"

"You're busy tonight," Sonea observed.

"Yes. We're hosting a celebration and there are many who have come from afar," Fondin said. "But don't worry about the noise. We'll finish up at a decent hour and then it'll be nice and quiet here."

As if on cue, the room began to quieten. Sonea heard hissed whispers. Fondin turned back to them, then his eyes dropped to Sonea's robes and widened. He'd obviously not noticed the colour in the dim light outside. Even in the subdued lamplight, she could see his face grow pale.

"What is the reason for the celebration?" she asked.

"W-w-w-wedding," Fondin stuttered.

"Then pass on my congratulations to the bride and groom." Sonea smiled. "Are they staying here tonight?"

"N-n-n . . ." Fondin took a deep breath and straightened. "No, they'll be off to their new house tonight."

But many of the wedding guests would be staying here, she guessed.

"A new home as well. Well, we won't take up much more of your time. I'm sure we can manage in one room," Sonea told him. "With separate beds and a privacy screen, of course. We'll eat there so you can keep your full attention on your guests. Could you show us straight to the room?"

Fondin nodded, then, for good measure, bowed deeply before whirling around and leading them upstairs. He paused at several doors, wringing his hands, then with obvious reluctance led them to a room at the end of the corridor. As he opened the door Sonea was pleased to see it was a rather plain room, with a single one-person bed, but no signs of current occupants. She had been worried he'd throw guests out of one of their rooms, or that none of the rooms were empty. Stayhouses along major routes were paid by the Guild to keep one room free at all times, and everyone expected it would be their best room, but it must be tempting to put guests in there on busy nights, especially on lesser-used routes like this one.

"This will do," she told him.

"I'll have another bed and a screen brought in, my Lady," he said, then hurried away.

She entered the room, and Regin followed.

"Should I offer to sleep on the floor?" Regin asked.

Sonea turned to see him smiling. "I won't spoil anybody's night by insisting on having the best room, or two rooms, but sleeping on the floor is going a bit too far."

Before long the arrangements had been made. A generous meal and a bottle of wine were laid out on a small table. The wine was very good. Too expensive even for a local wedding, Sonea suspected. More likely the Guild had ensured a supply of decent wine was kept here for its members.

"Do you have more of this wine?" she asked the young woman when she returned to collect the dishes.

"Yes, Lady."

"Are the newly-weds still here?"

"About to leave, Lady."

"Give them a bottle as a wedding gift."

The young woman's eyes widened. "Yes, Lady."

Regin's pursed his lips, then to Sonea's surprise he slipped out of his chair and quietly followed the woman downstairs. When he returned, Sonea raised an eyebrow at him.

"Just making sure the gift reached the recipients," he said. He sat down. "So. Fergun's Rest." Regin frowned. "Didn't he run away when the Fort was attacked by the Ichani?"

"He hid. Which was the only sensible thing to do."

"And cowardly." Regin shrugged. "Still, nobody knows how they'll react when confronted by a real battle. Naming a Stayhouse after him?" He shook his head. "Tell me there are Stayhouses all over Kyralia named after magicians who died in the war, not just Fergun."

"I don't know. I hope so." She grimaced. "It irks me more that a man who locked up my friend so that he could blackmail me has anything named after him, but that's too personal a grudge to justify not honouring him among the rest of the dead."

Regin looked at her. "Ah, that's right. He wanted you dishonoured and thrown out of the Guild to ensure no lower-class people would join the Guild again."

"Yes. He'd be horrified, if he were alive today, at the changes in the Guild."

"You never know. He may have changed his mind, after the invasion. Lots of people did, you know."

She looked up at him. He held her gaze for a moment. In his eyes was a hint of expectation. *For what? For me to acknowledge he is a much better person now? Reassurance that I don't hold a grudge still? Or to admit I have come to trust even him? Perhaps even like him? Well, maybe I shouldn't go* that *far.* She drew in a breath to speak.

—*Sonea?*

Administrator Osen's voice in her mind made her jump. She let out the breath in a startled gasp. It was always surprising to be contacted through one of her blood rings, since she never knew when the other person was about to put it on.

160

—Osen!

—I have good news, Osen sent. *King Amakira has released Lorkin.*

Relief rushed through her, followed by a new anxiety.

—Is he all right?

—Yes. We don't think he was tortured or harmed, though Dannyl suspects the experience was harrowing.

—Will he be leaving for home soon? Should I meet and escort him?

—Amakira has forbidden him from leaving the Guild House.

—Oh.

Anger flared inside her, then a quieter puzzlement. Why release Lorkin then force him to stay in the country?

—At least he is one step closer to coming home. We will continue to insist Lorkin be allowed to return, through Dannyl.

—And myself?

—Yes. There is no need to change plans and you still have the other matter to attend to.

—Of course.

—Good luck. I will contact you if I learn more.

—Thank you.

A feeling of silence where his voice had been told her he had taken off the ring. She blinked as her eyes registered her surroundings again. Regin was watching her closely.

"Was it Lorkin or Osen?"

She stared at him. "How did you know Lorkin had one of my blood rings?"

His smile was lopsided. "As if you'd let him out of your sight without one."

She nodded. "Yes, it wouldn't be hard to guess that one correctly. It was Osen. Lorkin has been released, but the Sachakan king has forbidden him to leave the Guild House."

161

Regin straightened. "That's good news. Are we still travel-ling to Arvice, then?"

"Yes."

His eyes narrowed. "Not simply because you want to make sure he gets home?"

Sonea crossed her arms. "You think I'd disobey the Guild?"

"Yes." He held her gaze, but was smiling. "But only for Lorkin's sake."

"I didn't run off to save him when he first disappeared," she reminded him. "Anyway, Osen's orders were to continue with our plans."

Regin nodded. "All of them?"

"Yes. What plans did you think we might abandon, at this point?"

He shrugged and looked away. "I don't know. You said 'plans' not 'plan'. We have only one official reason to be going to Sachaka."

"With multiple possible outcomes to deal with." Sonea rolled her eyes in exasperation. "Are you going to spend the entire journey looking for hidden objectives and secret motives in everything I say?"

"Probably." Regin grinned. "I can't help it. It's a habit. It could be considered a talent. An annoying one, perhaps, but I do try to use it for good."

Sonea sighed. "Well, don't annoy me without good reason. That would not be good."

"No." He shook his head in emphatic, exaggerated agreement, his eyes bright with humour. She felt a smile pulling at the corners of her mouth, until she recalled that he was right: there was another reason for their journey. She felt a brief but powerful urge to tell him about the meeting with the Traitors.

Not yet.

She sighed and finished her glass of wine. "Then I hope you don't snore, because I'm used to working night shifts and wake up easily. If I don't get a full night's sleep I'm going to be cranky."

He rose and started toward the bed on the other side of the screen. "Ah, Sonea. You ask for the one thing I can't promise."

Later that night she did find herself awake and listening to the sound of his breathing. It was not loud, but it was strange to be hearing someone else sleeping nearby.

And unexpectedly soothing, she realised.

Ever since the first time she had climbed down the hidden chimney between the panelling of Sonea's main room and the outer wall of the Magicians' Quarters, Lilia had wondered what its original purpose had been. All of the rooms had them, though she suspected none of the occupants knew of their existence. Bricks protruded at regular intervals up the narrow space, too convenient not to be intended as a kind of ladder.

Cery's guesses included garbage chutes and latrine outlets. Fortunately, there was no sign that the gap had been used for either purpose for a long time, if ever. Lilia thought of them as chimneys, despite there being no sign of soot on the bricks or mortar.

Reaching the top, she peered through the spy hole Cery had drilled long ago. Sonea's main room was unoccupied.

Where is Jonna?

Perhaps the servant had gone into one of the other rooms. Perhaps she had been called away. Lilia reached out to the latch, then hesitated. It was still possible that Jonna was in one of the bedrooms with a visitor, though Lilia could not think of any good reason a stranger would be in there with her . . . except a few scandalous ones that Lilia could not imagine Jonna indulging in.

She tapped on the panelling lightly, in a random pattern that anyone who didn't know there was gap behind the wood might think was a bug scuttling across the surface. A moment later, Jonna hurried into the room, her eyes focusing on the hatch. Though she couldn't see Lilia, she nodded and beckoned with one hand.

The latch slid open without a sound, then the door swung inward silently. Jonna stepped forward to help Lilia out. The hatch was slightly higher in the wall than was comfortable to step down from, not helped by the fact that she had to fold double to get through it.

"How are they all?" Jonna asked.

"Fine," Lilia told her. "Grateful for your help. Is Black Magician Kallen back yet?"

"Yes, about ten minutes ago."

Lilia headed for her bedroom to change back into her robes. "I'd better hurry up, then, or I'll catch him in his bedclothes."

Jonna made a small noise of amusement. "That would be an odd sight."

Lilia grinned. "It sure would be."

The simple trousers and shirt Jonna had found for her to wear when visiting Cery and Anyi were much easier to climb in, and she felt a wave of gratitude as she saw the scuffs and stains she'd gained that night. Better she spoil these than her robes.

Changing quickly, she returned to the main room.

"Thanks for waiting for me," she said to Jonna. "You don't have to hang around now. I'll come straight back after talking to Kallen."

Jonna shrugged. "I don't mind staying." She straightened and placed her hands on her hips. "I promised Sonea I'd keep an eye on you, and I won't sleep right unless I know you're back here in your bed at a decent hour."

Lilia rolled her eyes and sighed. "Nobody ever worried about that when I was staying in the Novices' Quarters." But she didn't mind. It was nice that someone cared enough to look out for her. *I don't want to take any longer with Kallen than I need to, anyway.*

Slipping out of the main door into the corridor, she walked to Kallen's rooms and knocked. A short pause later the door swung inward. At once she smelled the faint scent of roet smoke, but it was stale and faded as if emanating from the furnishings. Kallen was sitting in a large chair, a book in his hand and a look of mild surprise on his face.

"Lady Lilia," he said. "Come in."

She stepped inside, pushed the door closed and bowed. "Black Magician Kallen."

"How can I help you?" he asked.

He had the patient expression of a teacher interrupted at a bad time by a novice. She resisted a smile. She was acting as messenger, not a novice, and the content was far more important than mere lessons.

"You know I occasionally meet Anyi, my friend and body-guard of the Thief Cery," she began, sitting down on another chair. "Without leaving Guild grounds," she added quickly.

He nodded. "Yes."

"I've already told you that Cery is in hiding, and can't maintain his . . ." She waved a hand, searching for the right term. "Business arrangements and . . . contacts."

"Everyone in the city thinks he is dead."

165

"It's likely Skellin won't believe Cery is dead unless he sees a body."

Kallen nodded. "Or sufficient time passes."

"This makes Cery the ideal bait to lure Skellin with. Which is his own idea," she reassured him. "He said to tell you he is prepared to do it and proposes you meet with him to work out a place and time."

"Hmm." Kallen frowned and looked away. "That is a very generous and brave offer. One that I admire and appreciate and I'm sure the rest of the Guild would too, if they knew of it. One that we might take up." He shook his head. "But not right now. We're exploring another avenue. I can't tell you the details yet, but if it succeeds we will not need to risk Cery's life at all."

Lilia felt a brief disappointment, then relief, followed by anxiety. "How long until you know? Cery's hiding place is . . . well, it's his last safe place. If Skellin discovers it, Cery won't have anywhere else to go."

"What we're doing can't be hurried. It may take weeks, or months. How long does Cery believe he can remain hidden?" Kallen asked.

Weeks! Months! Anger flared inside her, but when she looked at Kallen she saw genuine concern in his eyes. The anger ebbed away.

"I don't know. He doesn't know. Skellin could find him tonight, he could find him in a few weeks. Getting food without being seen is difficult. Each time they go out it's a risk."

Kallen reached out and placed a hand on her shoulder briefly.

"I understand. We are doing everything we can, Lilia. Tell Cery we appreciate his offer, and may take it up if our other plans fail. In the meantime, he should do all he can to stay hidden."

Lilia nodded, and sighed. "I'll tell him. He won't like it, though."

"I don't expect he will." He gave her a sympathetic look, but it suddenly changed to a frown. "He won't do anything foolish out of impatience, will he?"

She swallowed a bitter laugh. "I don't think so, but he's a Thief. He's used to being in charge of his life." Seeing Kallen's eyebrows lower further, she shook her head. "Anyi and I will do all we can to talk him out of it, if he tries. And Gol is used to talking sense to Cery, I suspect."

Kallen nodded. "Good."

Getting to her feet, Lilia smoothed her robes. "I had better be going. Goodnight, Black Magician Kallen. I hope your plans are successful."

He nodded. "Thank you. Goodnight Lady Lilia."

As she turned toward the door it swung open. Stepping out into the corridor, she breathed the cleaner air outside with relief. Then her mood darkened again.

Cery isn't going to like this. But I think he trusts . . . no, it's more that he respects Kallen than trusts him . . . enough to wait and see if these other plans work. That wasn't the main problem, though. *How am I going to keep them fed and undiscovered for weeks — perhaps even months? Someone's bound to notice something eventually.*

She could only hope that, with Jonna's help, they could prevent that, or for Kallen's "other avenue" to succeed.

CHAPTER 12

SPIES

"Do you think we should wait until Lilia is with us?" Anyi said as she eyed the roof of the tunnel.

Cery lifted his lamp. "It doesn't look like it's about to cave in this very moment." The tunnel was long and Anyi had set a brisk pace. Too brisk. He'd taken advantage of the sagging roof to pause and catch his breath, hoping the others would think he was being cautious. "But then, how do you tell?"

"I don't know," Anyi admitted. "I figure it won't collapse so long as we don't touch anything. But we shouldn't hang about."

Gol made a low noise that suggested they were both crazy. He was regarding the tree roots hanging from the ceiling and matted over the sides of the tunnel with a frown. As he took a step toward it, Cery realised it wasn't a frown of disapproval but of interest.

Then he saw what Gol had noticed. Light didn't penetrate beyond some of the roots as it should have. Behind lurked a stubborn darkness. He moved closer then hooked his fingers in the cascade of white roots and pulled gently. They swung forward with no resistance.

They're not attached to anything. There's a hole behind here.

"Remember what I said about not touching any . . ." Anyi began as he pulled the roots aside. "Oh."

The entrance to another tunnel opened before them. The same deteriorated brickwork held back the earth and supported the roof. He glanced at her and smiled as she came closer and peered inside, eyes bright.

"Now that's a bit of luck," she remarked. "If we have to make a run for it, we can slip through here. So long as whoever was chasing us didn't see us do it they'd never know where we'd gone."

"Want to explore?" Cery asked.

"Of course."

Cery looked back at Gol. "Stay here. You hear anything like a cave-in, go get Lilia."

Gol looked like he was about to argue, but then heaved a heavy sigh and nodded. Cery held back the roots so that Anyi could slip through. She moved slowly, lifting her lamp to examine the walls, roof and floor. The passage was in no worse condition than the one they had been following. Parts had deteriorated, but most still looked solid.

As they made their way along it, Cery wondered how Lilia's conversation with Kallen had gone. They wouldn't hear from her until the morning. Cery had decided that they should spend the night exploring the passages and considering where they might set their trap for Skellin. Anyi believed they should lure Skellin to the underground rooms near the University, so they could escape to the building. The rooms were the ones Cery had found Anyi and Lilia in. He felt his face warm as he remembered. In the whorehouse he'd grown up in, he'd known women who sought other women's affections, some forming bonds that lasted many years. It had been one more of many ways that he'd seen people seek pleasure, companionship and love. Yet he also came to realise that he was living in a particularly tolerant world. Outside it were people who did not approve of anything different from their own experience and tastes. And not just people from the higher classes. The underworld was no better or worse.

I wonder if her mother knows. Vesta always enjoyed feeling that she was better than others. She was always looking for something to disapprove of in other people. Sometimes I think the only reason she wanted me was because I was a Thief. It made her feel more important than most other people. Well, it did for a while.

The last thing he wanted Anyi to feel was disapproved of. He certainly didn't mind her being with Lilia but . . . He felt a small pang of envy. *I once loved a Guild magician, but the only kind of love I got in return was friendship.* He shook his head. *That sounds peevish. Sonea's friendship is no small thing, and I did find love elsewhere.*

He wondered if Anyi had had many previous lovers, then remembered her story of the one who had betrayed her. *Aha. That must be why I never found him. It wasn't a "him", it was a "her".*

Anyi gave a little gasp. "Look!" she whispered.

The tunnel ended at a brick wall, but it was no ordinary wall. A familiar mechanism had been attached to the brickwork – the workings of a hidden door. Cery located a brass spy hole cover. It was stiff and green with age, but he was able to force it open. Looking through, he saw only darkness.

"Can't see anything," he said.

"Do you want to try opening it?" Anyi asked.

Cery considered. If he let his imagination go where it pleased, it conjured up dangerous prisoners or incarcerated monsters waiting for the chance to be free – killing anything that stood in their path.

More likely it's another old storeroom. Besides, there's no lock preventing anyone opening the door from the other side, as far as I can see.

He nodded.

Anyi took the lever and hauled on it, but the door did not budge. Looking closely at the mechanism, Cery saw that it wasn't rusted. There were black lumps around the joins. He poked at them. They were soft. Probably old oil or grease grown thick with time and dust. Cery took a turn pulling the lever, then they both put their strength into it, but with no effect.

"Go fetch Gol," Cery said.

He peered through the spy hole again – even tried holding up the lamp and looking through at the same time, but saw nothing but darkness beyond the door. It occurred to him then that maybe the hole was blocked. Digging a pick out of his coat, he poked it through and confirmed there was a void on the other side.

Maybe it's a trap, set up by Akkarin or someone else long ago. Perhaps for the same reason we want to set traps: to fool and stop pursuers. Who knows what reasons the Guild had, in the past, to dig these tunnels.

The sound of two sets of footsteps approached behind him and he turned. Gol rolled his eyes as he saw the door.

"Can't leave a mystery unsolved, can you?" he rumbled.

Cery shrugged. With a roll of his eyes, Gol moved to the door and grasped the handle. He pulled once, paused to examine the mechanism, then took the handle again.

"Be careful: you don't want to pull that wound open," Anyi said.

Gol stepped back from the lever, then cast about. He moved back down the passage for a short distance and picked something up. As he returned, Cery saw that it was a brick.

"That'll make a lot of—"

The clang that filled the passage as Gol struck the mechanism was painfully loud.

"—noise," Anyi finished.

But the shock appeared to have done what Gol intended: break the seal of the old oil. The lever now flexed under his hand. Cery felt his heart beat a little faster as the door swung open. It was heavy: the other side was covered with thin bricks and mortar. The door formed the back of an alcove.

As the light of the lamps penetrated the darkness it illuminated old wooden cupboards and tables. Cery felt his heart sink with disappointment. He wasn't sure what he had been hoping to see. Hidden treasure, maybe? A better place to hide?

They moved inside the room. As the light of all three lamps filled the space, Cery felt apprehension replace his earlier anticipation. The room was clean. There was no dust or rubble. He moved to one of the tables. It was covered in small pots. Each contained earth and a tiny plant.

"Are we at the fa—" Gol began.

"Quiet!" Anyi gasped.

Cery and Gol turned to see that she was peering up a narrow staircase, holding her lamp away from the well so that its light wouldn't penetrate. They moved closer and, as they joined her, heard voices above. There was the creak of a handle being turned.

Without another word, they fled into the tunnel, Gol pulling the door closed behind him. Cery's heart was beating so quickly his chest hurt. Anyi put her eye to the spy hole and Gol set his ear to the door. Amused, Cery gently pulled a silently protesting Anyi aside and took her place at the spy hole.

The room beyond was no longer dark. Something bright was moving down the stairwell. He felt a wry relief as he saw a magical globe of light appear, then two magicians descend into view. One was an old woman, the other a young man.

"What's happening," Anyi murmured.

"Magicians. They're looking around the room. Can you hear them, Gol?"

"Faintly." The big man replied. "One said he thought he heard something. The other agreed."

The two magicians shook their heads and walked toward the tables. The male one picked up a plant, then put it down with obvious careless anger.

"The old woman asked something. The young one says he's sure," Gol reported. He paused, and Cery could hear the faint sound of voices. He signalled for silence, then pressed his ear to the door.

"So we've been tricked," the woman said. She didn't sound surprised.

"Yes, as you suspected we would be," the younger magician replied. "If you smoked this . . . this common garden weed, you'd get nothing but a headache."

"Well, we knew getting hold of roet would not be easy."

Roet? Cery felt something hot race through his veins. *The Guild wants to grow roet?*

"We'll just have to keep trying," the woman continued. "Skellin must be growing it somewhere – and growing a lot. Eventually someone will betray him, if we offer enough money."

"All we need are a few seeds."

"I wish that we didn't need any."

The voices were growing quieter. Cery put his eye to the spy hole again and watched them ascend the stairs, the magic light rising ahead of them. When all light disappeared abruptly, he guessed that the door above the stairs had been closed. He pulled away from the spy hole, closing its cover, and described what he'd heard to Anyi and Gol.

"What does the Guild want roet for?" Anyi asked, scowling at the door.

"Maybe it has potential as a cure," Gol suggested.

"Maybe," Cery echoed. "Maybe more than a few Guild magicians are addicted to it now, and they want to take control of their supply out of Skellin's hands."

"Perhaps they want to put Skellin out of business," Gol said. "Then when they control all trade, stop growing it."

Anyi turned to stare at him, horrified. "What about all the common people who are addicted to it? It would be . . . people would go mad!"

"The Guild has never stopped the underworld acquiring anything it wanted," Cery reminded her.

His daughter did not look reassured. "It's never going away, is it?" she said, her eyes wide with realisation. "We're stuck with roet forever."

"Probably," Cery agreed.

Gol nodded. "But maybe if the Guild gets hold of some, and studies it, they'll find a way to stop it being so addictive."

Anyi still looked glum. "I guess, as an escape route, this is no better than fleeing into the University"

Cery looked at the door. "We don't know if whatever is above that cellar is occupied by magicians all the time. It will probably be guarded by someone, if they get more seeds and try again, but that could be just a servant or two."

"Skellin is more likely to follow us through there than into the University," Gol added. "So it might be a good play to lay our trap."

"Might be. But let's not tell the Guild we know they're trying to grow rot until we have to."

"Bad memories?"

Sonea looked at Regin in surprise. *Was it that obvious?* Since the carriage had begun its slow ascent into the mountains she had been pushing aside dark and gloomy feelings. At first she'd dismissed it as weariness and worry, but then she would see some feature – a tree or rock – and feel sure she'd noticed it the last time she had travelled this road. But surely her mind was playing tricks on her. *My memory can't be* that *good.*

Not sure how to answer Regin's question, she shrugged. He nodded and looked away. She'd thought at first that their conversations had dwindled to silence because he was distracted by the view outside. Unlike her, he had never travelled this road before. Now she wondered if the silence was her fault. She hadn't felt like talking for some time now.

Is that the place we stopped? A gap had opened in the trees, revealing fields and roads stretching into the distance, divided by rivers, roads and other human-made boundaries. The trees seemed small, however. Surely they would have grown taller in the last twenty years. *But objects tend to be larger in our memories. Though . . . I thought that only applied to objects remembered from childhood, because we were smaller then.*

"What is it?" Regin asked.

She realised she had been leaning forward, craning her neck to better see the outside. Leaning back in her seat, she shrugged.

"I thought I recognised something." She shook her head. "A place we stopped, last time."

"Did . . . something happen there?"

"Not really. Nobody said much during that journey." She couldn't help a smile. "Akkarin wouldn't talk to me." *But I kept finding him looking at me.* "He was angry with me."

Regin's eyebrows rose. "For what?"

"For making sure they sent me into exile with him."

"Why would he be angry at that?"

"His plan – or so I thought at the time – was to get himself captured by Ichani and communicate the result to all magicians."

Regin's eyes widened slightly. "A brave decision."

"Oh, very honourable," she said drily. "Shock the Guild into realising the danger it faced while sacrificing the only person who could do anything about it."

His eyebrows rose. "But he wasn't. There was you."

She shook her head. "I didn't know enough. I didn't even know how to make blood rings. We wouldn't have beaten the Ichani if he hadn't survived." *But that wasn't why you followed him*, she reminded herself. *You did so because you couldn't let Akkarin die. Love is selfish.* "By forcing him to keep me alive, I forced him to keep himself alive."

"Those weeks must have been terrifying."

She nodded, but her thoughts suddenly shifted to the Traitors. She'd always suspected there was more to Akkarin's time in Sachaka than he'd told her. Once, when checking facts for his book, Lord Dannyl had asked her if there was any truth to the rumour that Akkarin had been able to read a person's surface thoughts, without touching them. She could not remember Akkarin speaking of it. People had believed Akkarin had all kinds of extraordinary abilities, even before it had been revealed that he'd learned black magic.

Perhaps he had been able to, but kept it a secret. Like his deal with the Traitors. Made with the Traitor Queen, no less, though maybe she hadn't yet become queen. I'm sure he told me the person who taught him black magic was a man. Was it a deliberate lie, to help conceal the Traitors' existence? I can't help feeling a little hurt that he didn't trust me with the truth, but then I wouldn't have wanted him to break a promise made to somebody who saved his life.

Sighing, she looked out of the window at the sun, which hung low in the sky. Her memory of the end of the climb to the Fort was of exposed rock and little vegetation. While stretches of rock were visible here and there, the trees had not yet thinned to the degree she recalled. *We're going to arrive later than I planned — maybe even after dark.*

A sharp turn to the side forced her to brace herself. Surprised, she leaned close to the window, wondering why the carriage had changed direction, and blinked at the unexpected brightness of a tall, curved wall blazing yellow in the late sun ahead of them.

Not late after all, she thought. *Trees must have grown over all that bare land I remembered.*

"We're here," she told Regin. He moved to sit beside her so that he could look out of the window on the other side.

She watched his face, glimpsing echoes of the awe she'd felt as a young woman on seeing the Fort for the first time. The building was a huge cylinder carved out of solid rock, encompassing the gap between two high, near-vertical rock walls. Turning back to the window, she saw that the facing wall was not the flawless smooth surface that she remembered. A different-colour stone had been used to fill large cracks and holes. They must be repairs of damage done during the Ichani Invasion. She shivered, remembering the battle here, seen by all magicians as the Warrior leading the Fort's reinforcements, Lord Makin, had broadcast it mentally, until he died at the hands of the invaders.

The carriage rolled to a halt before the tower. A red-robed magician and the captain of the Fort's unit of Guard walked forward to meet them. Sonea unlatched and opened the door with magic, then paused to look at Regin. The excitement in his face made him look younger – almost boyish. It brought a flash of memory of him as a smiling young man, but she didn't entirely believe that memory was real. In her recollections of him at that age, his smile had been always full of malicious triumph or glee.

Not for a long time, though, she thought as she climbed out of the carriage. *Actually, I don't remember him smiling much this last year. Unless with forced politeness, or maybe in sympathy.* To her surprise, she felt sad. *He's a very unhappy man*, she realised.

"Greetings, Black Magician Sonea," the red-robed magician said. "I am Watcher Orton. This is Captain Pettur."

The captain bowed. "Welcome to the Fort."

"Watcher Orton." Sonea inclined her head. "Captain Pettur. Thank you for the warm welcome."

"Are you still planning to stay for the night?" Orton asked.

"Yes." The title of Watcher had been created for the leader of the magicians who now guarded the Fort along with their non-magician counterparts. The Guild had been worried that no magician would volunteer for the role, so they had given it extra benefits of both influence and wealth. They hadn't needed to. Watcher Orton and his predecessor were both men who had fought the Sachakan invaders and were determined to ensure none would enter Kyralia again without a decent effort at resistance.

"Come this way," Orton invited, waving toward the open gates at the base of the tower.

Sonea felt a shiver of recognition as she saw the tunnel beyond. They walked into the shadows of the interior. Lamps kept the way illuminated, revealing more repair work, and the traps and barriers that had been added.

"We have a memorial to those who died here at the beginning of the invasion," Orton told her. He pointed to a section of wall ahead, and as they drew closer Sonea saw that it was a list of names.

Reaching them, she stopped to read. She saw Lord Makin's name but the rest were unfamiliar. Many of the victims had been common Guard. At the top of the list were longer names that included House and family – men from the highest class who had sought a career in the Guard and were guaranteed a position of power and respect. The men working at the Fort in those days, however, had often been failures or troublemakers, sent to where it was believed they could do no harm – or, if they did, it was well out of the sight of anyone who cared.

Above those were the magicians. The family and House names were familiar, but she had been too young and new to the Guild to have known any of the magicians personally. Except one.

Fergun's name drew her eyes. She felt an uncomfortable mix of dislike, pity and guilt. He had been a victim of the war. For all that he had done, he hadn't deserved to die by having all the energy within him ripped out by a Sachakan magician.

But that still doesn't change the fact that he wasn't a good person.

At that thought, the conflicting emotions faded away. She

understood it was possible to feel sadness at the injustice of a person's death without having to convince herself that they were a better person than she'd known them to be.

And he got a Stayhouse named after him. She turned away. *Which I'm sure would have appalled him for entirely different reasons than it appalled me.*

Watcher Orton led them to a dark, narrow door. A complicated procedure followed, in which he identified himself, the captain and their visitors, and then all kinds of sounds followed as a locking mechanism was worked. When the door opened, she was amused to see it was a hand-span thick and made of iron. They entered a room, then went through the same procedure to pass through another, equally robust door. The occupants of the Fort were not taking any chances.

A narrow, curved passage with a sloped floor led steeply upwards. The ends of pipes protruding on either side suggested that something could be poured into the space. *Water, or something less pleasant?* Physical defences wouldn't necessarily stop a magician, but they could use up power, trick a magician into lowering his guard, or surprise one before he or she could find an appropriate way to counter it. The passages were designed as a labyrinth to confuse and disorientate, and allow fleeing occupants time to escape.

When they had reached the end of the passage, Orton paused to look at her.

"I hope you weren't relying on the Sachakans being unaware of your arrival here."

She looked at him and felt a shiver run down her spine.

"Why?"

"We're sure the road is being watched. Patrols have found tracks and other evidence on the Kyralian side of the mountains.

Of course, we can only observe the Sachakan side from afar, but our watchers have seen small groups of men moving about."

"Ichani?"

Orton frowned. "I suspect not. Ichani don't carry good-quality rations. Whoever it is, they aren't concerned about hiding their tracks when they do venture over our side. I suspect because they don't realise they have. It's not as though we have painted a line where the border lies."

The thought that the Ichani made a habit of wandering into Kyralia was not a comforting one. But the outcasts who inhabited the mountains had always been a disorganised rabble, preying on each other more often than the occasional unfortunate traveller. The humbling fact was, the invaders who had nearly overtaken Kyralia had only done so because one of them had the strength of will to unite a handful of them – and it had taken him years to do so.

An organised Sachakan army would have been unstoppable. Might still be. And here she was, one of Kyralia's few weapons of defence, heading into Sachaka itself to rescue her son. *I have to hope that Kallen and Lilia are defence enough, if the Sachakans take advantage of my absence. One a roet addict. One a naïve young woman.* Suddenly she felt light-headed and nauseous.

Time to stop thinking about that, she told herself.

"Who do you think these people are, then?" she asked.

"Spies."

"Of the Sachakan king?"

Orton nodded. "Who else could they be?"

Who else, indeed.

Several twisting passages later, they arrived at a dining room large enough to seat ten people. It was laid out with impressively fine tableware. Three women and two men stood waiting to be introduced. Two minor captains and their wives, and the wife of an absent captain. Orton invited them all to sit, took his place and asked a servant to bring the meal.

The food was surprisingly good. Orton explained that he believed good food did wonders for the morale of the people here, who must always live far from Imardin and with the threat of possible invasion. Local farmers and hunters benefited from the trade, too. Yet the meal was not an entirely relaxed one. They were interrupted several times by guards bringing messages or making reports. At first Sonea listened attentively, assuming that something important must have happened, but it became clear that this was simply a routine that was never abandoned – not even during dinner with a high-ranking magician.

The other guests were used to this, and barely paused in their conversation. Sonea only realised that she had stopped paying attention to the reports when Orton interrupted a conversation she was having with Captain Pettur.

"Black Magician Sonea," he said, his tone grave and formal.

She turned to see that, despite his calm expression, his eyes betrayed anxiety.

"Yes, Watcher Orton?"

"A strange message just arrived." He handed her a piece of paper, folded in odd, converging lines. "The guards on duty who received it said it glided through the air like a bird, and landed at their feet."

She looked at the neat writing and her heart skipped a beat, though whether in excitement or trepidation she couldn't decide.

We advise Black Magician Sonea to remain at the Fort until safe passage can be arranged. Instructions will follow soon.

182

A symbol had been drawn underneath the writing: a circle with a spiral scrawled within. Lorkin had described it to Administrator Osen, saying that it was one the Traitors had told him they would use to identify themselves. She felt a thrill of excitement. Soon she would be judging for herself the people who had impressed Lorkin so much, and who had helped Akkarin escape slavery all those years ago.

Sonea suspended the paper in the air with magic and set it alight. The other guests murmured in surprise as it quickly turned to ash. She turned to Orton and smiled. "I don't think those spies are going to be a problem for much longer, Watcher Orton."

After several nights lying on a cold stone floor I ought to have no trouble sleeping now that I'm in a proper bed. What is wrong with me?

Lorkin could feel that his body was tense. No matter how much he stretched, practised breathing exercises and tried to relax into the soft bedding, he could not settle. It did not help that every time his mind entered that period of wandering just before sleep, memories of the slave girl returned.

He did not want to think about her.

But he did.

She had taken the water so eagerly, as if she knew what it contained. Perhaps she had been a Traitor after all. She'd struggled to conceal the poison's effects in the beginning. Surely that meant she'd known what she was taking. Eventually she hadn't been able to stay quiet. If it had not been for the watcher intervening and dragging her out of the cell, Lorkin would have given in and Healed her. In an outburst of frustration and self-loathing, Lorkin had thrown the water jar at the man, but it had struck the bars and shattered.

Afterwards, the Ashaki interrogator had arrived. Lorkin had expected him to gloat and reveal that her death was his intention all long, but he examined the dead girl silently, said nothing to Lorkin and left wearing a frown of worry.

The next morning, men Lorkin had never seen before had taken him from the cell and to a small courtyard. When the carriage they put him in arrived at the Guild House, Lorkin had wondered if he was having a particularly vivid dream.

It wasn't a dream. The king had released him. No explanation had been given. No apology for his imprisonment. Just the order for him to stay there.

Why?

Lorkin rolled onto his side. His globe light burned softly above, and he'd placed a barrier across the doorway, both slowly using up what was left of the magic that Tyvara had given him. Though he was now sleeping in a different room to the one in which Riva had died, the memory of someone crawling onto his bed in the darkness was surprisingly vivid and unpleasant, despite the fact that the original experience had been rather pleasant to begin with. He could not help imagining someone was lurking in the darkness, or that he was lying next to a corpse.

Eyes staring at the ceiling, seeing nothing. Like the slave in the prison.

He stared up at the glowing sphere and gave up on any hope of sleeping.

Then he opened his eyes and, though nothing had changed, knew that time had passed. He had fallen asleep after giving up on falling asleep. But why had he woken up? He could remember no dream or nightmare.

A thump from the central room sent a chill through his

blood and he froze. Forcing his head to turn, he looked beyond the bedroom door and saw light in the room beyond.

Someone is in there . . .

He dropped the barrier over the doorway and created one around himself, then rose and approached the other room cautiously. Two slaves were in the centre of the room. A young man lay on the floor, a middle-aged woman crouched over him, one hand pressed to his head, the other holding a knife.

Oh, no. Not again.

But then the man blinked. He was alive. *She's reading his mind*, Lorkin realised. She looked up at him and he recognised her as one of the kitchen slaves. "Lorkin," she said. Removing her hands from the man's brow, she rose to her feet. "I am Savi. The queen sends her regards."

Lorkin nodded. "How is she?" he asked automatically, then realised he ought to thank her first, since the man she had tackled had probably meant to kill him.

"Dead." She grimaced. "Two days ago."

"Oh." He thought of Zarala's mischievous eyes and sense of humour and felt a wave of sadness. "I am sorry to hear that. She was nice." Then something occurred to him. "She wasn't . . . ? How did she . . .?"

"She came to the natural end of a long life." Savi straightened. "Savara was elected in her place."

Lorkin nodded again, not sure if it was polite to express pleasure at the news of a new queen when the old one had so recently died. The spy had told him in a matter-of-fact way that suggested she didn't expect him to comment. He was glad to hear Savara had been chosen as the new queen. Not just because she had helped him many times and was Tyvara's superior, but because she was smart, open-minded and fair.

185

The spy turned to face the main door to the room. The reason for her distractedness came a moment later when Dannyl and another slave stepped into the room.

Dannyl looked at the man on the floor who, despite being awake and staring at them all, wasn't moving, then at Savi and Lorkin.

"What happened?" he asked.

Lorkin shrugged. "I'm not entirely sure." He turned to Savi.

"There have been some additions and removals of slaves here lately that were suspicious," she told them. "This one," she pointed to the man on the floor, "is no slave. He is a magician of low status. He was offered land and Ashaki status if he posed as a slave and helped abduct Lorkin."

"Abduct him?" Dannyl repeated. "Again?"

Her eyes warmed with amusement. "Not by us. He received the offer through a friend. He believes it came from the king, though he has no proof of that."

"Of course not." Dannyl looked around the room, his gaze settling on the slave who had brought him to the room. "Is she . . .?"

"Trustworthy? Yes," the Traitor replied.

"Good." Dannyl looked at the younger woman. "Could you wake Ambassador Tayend and bring him here?"

The slave nodded and hurried away. She had not thrown herself to the floor, or even bowed, Lorkin realised. Dannyl was too lost in thought to notice. He walked over to the man and stared down at him. "Not restrained," he murmured.

"I have taken his strength," Savi replied. "Would you like me to kill him?"

"No. Not yet, anyway. We should not discuss anything within his hearing or sight, though."

The woman shrugged. A dome of white light covered the man's face. "He won't hear or see you. I am Savi, by the way."

"Thank you for intervening, Savi," Dannyl said. "So he thinks the king is behind this?"

She nodded. "Amakira probably intended to blame Lorkin's abduction on Traitors."

"After which he'd read Lorkin's mind—"

"Attempt to," the spy corrected.

"—torture the information out of him, and then kill him and make it look like the Traitors did it."

Lorkin felt a chill run down his spine. Images of the tortured slave flashed through his memory. *I'm not sure I could endure as long as she did.*

A movement in the doorway caught everyone's attention. Tayend entered, the young slave woman following. He took in the prone man, Savi, Lorkin and Dannyl, then listened silently as all that had been discussed was repeated to him.

"What matters now is what the king will do when he realises his plan has failed," he said. "We have no proof he arranged this. To suggest it would be an insult. He may also decide he must remove Lorkin from the Guild House for his own protection." He looked at Lorkin. "Somewhere nobody will find him."

Lorkin winced. "Can we pretend nothing happened?"

Dannyl and Tayend exchanged looks.

"We could," Tayend said, "if it weren't for this man. We can't kill him. He's meant to be the king's property."

Dannyl narrowed his eyes at the prone man. "Well, if we're all pretending that he's just a slave . . . we could say that we caught him using magic, and demand he be removed. We'd have to wait until he regained his strength, or they'll have to wonder how any of us managed to strip him of power."

"We can't send him away. He knows Savi is a Traitor," Lorkin protested. "If he tells the king that, she'll be in danger."

Dannyl looked at Savi. "Can you leave?"

She shook her head. "This House is being watched closely, day and night. Food and supplies are brought here. The slaves who attempted to go out for other items have been stopped." She looked down at the spy. "The king may still use his presence here as reason to remove Lorkin to some-where safer. I suspect there are other slaves here who may be Amakira's spies, too."

They exchanged silent, worried looks. Dannyl sighed and looked at Lorkin.

"We have got to get you out of Sachaka."

"I couldn't agree more," Tayend murmured. He looked at Savi. "I suppose this restriction of slave movement means your people can't arrange that?"

"If we could have, we'd have done it already."

Dannyl shook his head. "I wish I'd known about this. I don't expect to know everything, but the more I do the easier it is to make decisions."

"To tell you would reveal who I was," Savi pointed out.

Dannyl turned to the Traitor woman. "Well, you have now and that could be to our advantage. Could you read the minds of all the slaves here? Find out which are Amakira's spies – and if any are magicians?"

She nodded slowly. "Yes," she said, but with reluctance.

Lorkin frowned. *But that would reveal who she was to all the slaves. Yet how else do we find out which slaves are spies or potential abductors?* A chill ran down his spine as another option came to him.

She was not the only person in the Guild House who could read minds.

But if he revealed that he could, he would reveal much, much more. *I'm going to have to eventually, and I'm not letting another woman be tortured and killed because of me.*

"I'll do it," he said.

Dannyl and Tayend turned to stare at him.

"You know how to . . .?" Tayend's eyebrows shot upward. "Oh!"

Lorkin saw Dannyl frown and braced himself for the man's disapproval, but the man only shook his head.

"Don't jump to conclusions, Tayend," he said. "Sonea learned to read minds before she learned black magic."

Tayend looked relieved. "Really? I thought reading the mind of an unwilling person was something only the black magicians could do."

Dannyl's lips pressed into a grim smile. "We let people believe that. Like black magic, it's a skill that would be too easily abused."

Tayend turned to regard Lorkin, his gaze sharp and thoughtful. *He's wondering what else I've learned. Should I tell them the truth now? It might be seen as suspicious if I conceal it too long.*

"Another piece of information you didn't tell me so I can't reveal it if I'm interrogated?" Dannyl asked.

Lorkin nodded. *He's right. I can't tell him yet.*

"Well . . ." Dannyl turned to Savi. "I'll block all of the House's exits to make sure nobody attempts to leave. In the meantime, rouse the head slave and send him to the Master's Room, where Lorkin will order him to bring all of the slaves to them to have their minds read." He looked at the failed abductor. "We should lock him up somewhere out of sight, too." He sighed. "This barely qualifies for the term 'plan', but it'll gain us some time to think of a better one."

189

CHAPTER 13

UNEXPECTED HELP

"I'm a bit . . . new at this," Lorkin said, his expression apologetic as Dannyl sat beside him. "It may take a while."

Dannyl shrugged. "Don't hurry it. I have plenty to think about. Like a way to get you out of this mess."

"Let's hope we have time enough for both tasks." Lorkin called one of the slaves over. The man threw himself to the floor. Lorkin instructed the slave to kneel before him, then placed his hands on either side of the man's head and closed his eyes.

Dannyl examined the rest of the waiting slaves. Aside from a few eyebrows rising in surprise, they showed no expression that might indicate which were the king's spies. He looked across at Tayend, sitting on the other side of Lorkin. The Elyne met Dannyl's eyes and nodded, perhaps indicating that he was keeping an eye on the slaves, too.

The Traitor woman, Savi, had assured him other Traitor spies would be among the slaves and would help should a fake slave react to imminent discovery by attacking them. It would be better if they were not forced to reveal their identities, however. As for the failed abductor, he had been locked in a stone-walled storeroom under the kitchen, watched over by Savi and Merria.

So. Time to get thinking, Dannyl told himself. *If the king did arrange this, then he will know his plan has failed when his abductor doesn't turn up with Lorkin. He may already know it's failed, if the man was supposed to deliver Lorkin by now. So what will he do?*

He can't do anything unless we reveal something happened, unless he had another spy in place ready to slip away and call for "help". So what if he did? If we claim Lorkin read the abductor's mind and found out the truth, the king will insist on taking the man away to check. The man will suffer some kind of accident so when Amakira claims the man was tricked into thinking he worked for the king, nobody will be able to prove otherwise. He'll then use the attempted abduction as an excuse to take Lorkin away.

If we pretend nothing happened, the king will know we're lying. The abductor can prove otherwise. Dannyl did not want to kill the man. Not just because he'd rather not have to murder anybody, but if evidence was found that a Kyralian had killed a Sachakan — especially a free Sachakan — it would weaken the already shaky peace between their countries. *And I'd end up in the palace prison for having destroyed the king's property.*

What else could he do with the man? Smuggle him away? With the House being watched so closely that even a Traitor didn't think she could sneak out, he doubted they'd succeed. *If we kill him we'll have to destroy the body completely or make sure someone else is blamed. I'm not sure how to do the former, but it has to be less risky than the latter.* He shook his head. *I can't believe I'm contemplating this.*

A faint hammering noise brought his attention back to his surroundings. Lorkin had sent the first slave away to the other side of the room. He looked at Dannyl.

"I think someone's knocking on the front door."

With all slaves in the Master's Room, there was nobody outside to greet anyone. "Well, that didn't take long." Dannyl muttered.

"It's not too late for social visits," Tayend pointed out. "According to Sachakan customs."

Dannyl sighed and stood up. "I'll go see who it is."

Lorkin didn't look reassured. "Should I . . . clear the room?"

"Yes, but . . ." *Where to put the slaves?*

"Take them to my rooms," Tayend offered. "You can continue the mind-reading there."

Dannyl looked at the lone slave who had been read. "Is he trustworthy?"

Lorkin shrugged. "He's not a spy, if that's what you mean."

"Good enough," Dannyl beckoned to the man, who hurried forward and threw himself on the floor. "Wait until everyone but me has left the room, then go bring our visitor here," Dannyl ordered.

Within a surprisingly short time, Dannyl found himself alone in the Master's Room. He drew in a deep breath, let it out slowly and braced himself for a troupe of Sachakan magicians to emerge from the corridor. Only one set of footsteps reached his ears, though, then a lone man appeared and hesitated at the threshold of the room.

"Achati!" The name leapt out of Dannyl's mouth. "Aşhaki Achati," he quickly added, as proper formality dictated.

Achati's forehead was deeply wrinkled. He searched Dannyl's face as he hurried forward. *He looks anxious*, Dannyl thought. *He's actually wringing his hands.*

"Ambassador. Dannyl." Achati paused two steps away, once again gazing at Dannyl searchingly. "I must warn you of a plot. I expect that you won't believe me, but I had to at least try to warn you. The king has a spy among your slaves. Probably a man, since we have few woman magicians and they aren't trusted. He will try, some time in the next few days, to abduct Lorkin. You need to keep a watch and limit the slaves' access to Lorkin. And perhaps, to weed out the spy, you could use those interrogation skills you put to use when we were looking for Lorkin."

Dannyl stared at Achati in amusement and suspicion. *What is he up to? Why warn us when it's already happened? Does he mean to trick us into trusting him? Has the king sent him to check if his abductor has acted yet? Hmm. I guess I'll have to play along and see where this leads.*

"When we thwart this abduction, what should we do then?" he asked. "Kill the spy?"

Achati shook his head. "No, you would be destroying the king's property."

"Only if the spy *is* a slave, and the king admits he owns the man."

"Oh, he won't admit to anything. He'll claim to have no knowledge of the plot, and say the man was bribed by the Traitors. When the man is revealed to be a magician, not a slave, you'll be charged with murder."

"Despite the fact that I didn't know this?" Dannyl shook his head. "So he's setting me up, then?"

Achati shook his head. "Not specifically, but if you were foolish enough to kill the man, it would give him the perfect excuse to send you back to Kyralia."

"Then what is the king's aim? Ah. It's to manufacture a good reason to claim Lorkin isn't safe here and take him away."

Achati's mouth twisted into a grim but approving smile. "I knew you'd see the danger."

"So what do we do? We won't be able to pretend nothing

happened. The spy will inform the king of his failure. He'll try again, or the king will send another spy to abduct Lorkin. There may already be others here already, in case the first attempt fails."

Achati grimaced. "If Lorkin can be smuggled back to Kyralia, you should arrange it."

Disobey the king? That's not what I expected. "How?"

Pinching his lower lip between two fingers, Achati frowned. "If there are any Traitors among the slaves, they might be able to arrange it."

"With the House being watched so closely? I doubt it. Is this all a ploy to capture some Traitors?"

Achati opened his mouth to reply, but another voice cut him off.

"Well, well. Ashaki Achati. What brings you to the Guild House at this late hour?"

Dannyl and Achati turned to see Tayend stroll into the room. The Elyne's lips thinned in apology as he approached Achati. He glanced at Dannyl. "Merria is helping out," he added quietly, reassuring Dannyl that Lorkin wasn't dealing with the slaves alone.

Achati nodded. "I was sent to make another attempt to persuade Lorkin to talk tomorrow, but . . ." He repeated his warning about the abductor. "That is my true reason for visiting."

"You think Dannyl should interrogate the slaves?"

"Yes, to find out which is the spy."

"Wouldn't that be dangerous? You said this spy is a magician? How strong is he? Is he a higher magician?"

"I don't know," Achati admitted. "Probably. He has been ordered not to kill anybody. He . . ." His gaze shifted to the doorway Tayend had entered through. Dannyl followed his gaze and felt a shock of surprise as Lorkin walked into the room.

The young man's gaze met Dannyl's, then slid away. His eyes were very dark and his face pale. Straightening his back, he gave Achati a forced smile.

"Ashaki Achati. What brings you here so late at night?" Lorkin asked, his tone jovial but strained. "Come to take me back to the palace prison?"

A strange, pained look crossed Achati's face, then the man's expression smoothed. "No, no. I am trying to prevent that."

What was that expression? Dannyl asked himself. Then he felt a jolt as he recognised what he had glimpsed: sympathy and sorrow. He felt his recent doubts about Achati weaken a little.

"Achati has warned us that a spy among the slaves is going to attempt to abduct you soon," Tayend said.

Lorkin's eyes widened and he looked from Tayend to Dannyl. "Really?"

"Yes," Dannyl replied. "Tomorrow night, or a following night."

Dannyl was relieved to see Lorkin's eyes narrow as he considered the implications. He looked at Achati again.

"Why are you helping us?" he asked bluntly.

"I . . ." Achati sighed and looked down, then lifted his head to regard Tayend, Lorkin and Dannyl in turn. "I don't like how the king is treating you. Sachaka may not need Kyralia as an ally, but it also doesn't need another enemy. We received news a few months ago that has divided our opinion. The . . ." Achati paused and frowned, then shook his head. "I see no way to explain this without telling you: our spy among the Duna revealed that the Traitors proposed they join forces and attempt to take over Sachaka."

195

Dannyl felt a chill run down his spine. *I wonder . . .*

"Unh?" he asked.

Achati smiled. "I'm hardly going to tell you who our spies are, Dannyl."

"No," Dannyl agreed. "But Unh's name did spark some interesting reactions from his people when I mentioned it. If it is him, then I suspect they know he is a spy."

"The Duna turned down the Traitors. Many of the Ashaki have concluded that the Traitors would not approach the Duna unless they needed them, and they feel confident the Traitors would not win a confrontation with us."

Was this why the Traitors had destroyed the Duna's stone caves? Was it punishment for refusing to help? Dannyl wondered.

"The king agrees," Achati continued. "He does not believe the Guild is to be feared. He says you are a Guild of only two magicians. It is more important to rid Sachaka of the Traitor threat before they become strong enough to beat us than to avoid offending Kyralia and the Allied Lands. Only the voices of Ashaki who do not want to lose trade and peace with the Allied Lands, like myself, prevent him taking the information from Lorkin by force."

A tense silence followed Achati's words. Lorkin was staring at the floor. The young magician sighed and narrowed his eyes at Achati.

"You wouldn't have come here if you weren't willing to work against your king's orders and wishes," he said. "How far are you willing to go?"

The Sachakan stared back at Lorkin. He looked uncertain. "I don't know," he admitted. "There's a big difference between preventing my king doing something foolish, and outright betrayal. What do you have in mind?"

Lorkin opened his mouth to reply, but did not get to speak. "Take the spy away," Tayend injected. "Make him disappear."

Dannyl frowned. Though it was a test of Achati's trustworthiness, it was not a good one. If Achati took the spy to the king instead, the king would still claim that Lorkin wasn't safe in the Guild House – and he would find out Savi was a Traitor, too.

"No," Lorkin said. "Take me."

Dannyl blinked in surprise. *Maybe he hasn't realised this could all be a trick to get us to trust Achati.* Tayend shook his head and laid a hand on Lorkin's arm, but before anyone could speak, Lorkin raised his hands to stall their protests.

"I'm not stupid. I know it's a risk." He looked at Achati levelly. "He could hand me over to the king, but judging by the number of slaves here that aren't slaves – and I don't mean they're Traitors – I'm going to end up back at the palace soon anyway."

This time the shiver that travelled down Dannyl's back sent cold through his whole body. *Just how many spies are there? How many of them are magicians?*

"All you need to do is smuggle me out of the Guild House and take me to your mansion," Lorkin told Achati. "The Traitors will arrange the rest. They will ensure the king does not know your part in my escape. In return, and not until I am sure of my safety and freedom . . ." Lorkin sighed, then his expression hardened ". . . I will answer the question your king most wants to ask me. I will tell you where the Traitors' home is."

Achati stared back at Lorkin, his surprise changing to thoughtfulness, then approval. He nodded. "I can do that. It won't be easy getting you into the carriage unseen but—"

"Lorkin," Dannyl interrupted. "You don't have to betray the trust of—"

"Let him go," Tayend said. He met Dannyl's eyes, his gaze sharp and unwavering, and nodded. Dannyl felt a stab of anger, but it quickly faded.

Tayend wouldn't do anything to risk Lorkin's life unnecessarily. He must think this will work. Or that it is the only chance Lorkin has. Which meant that Tayend thought Achati was telling the truth. *How strange that it is Tayend who trusts Achati now, when I'm no longer sure of him.*

Dannyl could believe that Achati didn't approve of the king's actions, but it would take a lot to convince him that the man was willing to go against his ruler's orders, and risk that his actions would be discovered and considered treachery. He would lose not just the king's trust, but his position, reputation and wealth. And possibly his life.

But Dannyl couldn't think of an alternative, so he watched in silence as Achati and Lorkin sealed their agreement with vows. When they were done, Tayend beamed at them all.

"Perfect! Now all we have to do is figure out how to get Lorkin into Achati's carriage without any of those pesky watchers noticing."

Finishing her cup of raka, Lilia sighed with relief. In the last day or so she had begun to feel a bit worn around the edges – like the old clothes Jonna had given her to wear when she visited Anyi, Cery and Gol. Late nights spent underground and early morning lessons with Kallen were starting to take a toll.

She suppressed a groan at the thought of facing Kallen this morning. Anyi had told her about the cellar she, Cery and Gol had found under the Guild, and the conversation they'd over-heard. From the descriptions, she suspected the two magicians were Lady Vinara and the Healer in charge of growing cure ingredients.

The news that they wanted to grow roet had shocked her at first, but it made sense. She didn't agree with Cery's theory that the Guild wanted to grow roet in order to put Skellin out of business – or at least prevent him being the sole supplier of the drug to magicians. It was far more likely that the Guild wanted it to help them find a cure for roet addiction, as well as to explore the plant's potential as a cure for other maladies. After all, cures for the ill effects of plants were often found in the very plant that caused them.

But the news that the Guild was seeking roet seeds roused other suspicions, and for that reason she was not looking forward to meeting Kallen. Part of her wanted to confront him with what she'd learned. *Is this why he won't help Cery set a trap for Skellin? Are he, and the other magicians addicted to roet, afraid of removing Skellin in case it cuts off the roet supply?*

Cery had told her to keep what she knew to herself, unless she had good reason to reveal it. She would have to pretend not to know anything while around Kallen, and somehow act as if she didn't suspect him of having selfish motives for failing to help her friends.

"You're lost in thought today," Jonna noted. She moved to the table and leaned down to pick up the empty dishes from the morning meal. As she did, Lilia caught a strange but pleasant fragrance.

"Are you wearing perfume, Jonna?" she asked.

Jonna hesitated and looked a little guilty. "Yes."

"What's wrong?" Lilia frowned. "You don't usually wear perfume. Are servants not supposed to?"

"Oh, nobody would be that fussy," Jonna waved a hand, "but . . . Sonea doesn't like this one. It was hers, but after she found out what it was made from she told me to throw it out. I like it and . . . well you can't blame the plant for what it is. I don't wear it when I'll be around her, of course."

"Which is why I haven't noticed it before." Lilia nodded. "It is lovely. What's it made from?"

Once again, Jonna looked sheepish. "Roet flowers."

Surprised, Lilia sniffed the air and tried to find some link between the odour and the smell of roet smoke. "It's hard to believe the scent comes from the same plant." Then something else occurred to her. "Where do the perfume makers get roet flowers from?"

Jonna shrugged. "I suppose from the people who grow it for the drug."

Thinking back to Healing lessons on the sources of the Guild's cures, Lilia considered what she knew about plants. Flowers usually contained a plant's seeds. The Guild wanted roet seeds. From what Anyi had said, the plants the Guild had grown were not roet. They'd been tricked. Cery didn't think any roet grower would dare sell seeds to the Guild – though they weren't averse to cheating the Guild for what would have been a huge profit by substituting some other plant seed. If Skellin found out they had sold anyone roet seed, they wouldn't live long.

Cery didn't think roet was grown in Kyralia at all. He suspected it was cultivated elsewhere, harvested and dried before it was shipped to Imardin. Was the same true of the perfume? Most perfume makers were based in Elyne. Did they need fresh plants, or would dried ones do for making perfume?

Lilia stood up. "I had better go. Don't want to be late and make Kallen nervous."

Jonna smiled. "See you tonight."

As she walked to the Arena, Lilia considered everything she knew and how little she could reveal in order to get answers to her questions. In brief moments of rest during Kallen's lesson she weighed the risks and benefits. *The sooner the Guild gets roet seeds, the sooner Kallen will help Cery. I just need to work out how to tell Kallen that I know the Guild is trying to grow it without revealing how I know . . .*

She did not head to the University as soon as Kallen said they were done. He already had that distant, distracted manner where he didn't meet her eyes but gazed into the distance when she approached him. As he saw she wasn't leaving, he frowned and then his lips thinned.

"You can go now," he told her again.

"I know, but I thought you'd like to know something: word on the street is that the Guild tried to buy roet seeds. Is it true?"

His gaze snapped to hers. His pupils widened. *That got your attention*, she thought.

"You shouldn't believe everything you hear from your friends," he told her.

"But it's true, isn't it?" She narrowed her eyes at him. "Is this why you won't help Cery? Afraid the supply will run out if the supplier is captured?"

Kallen's eyes flashed with anger and his jaw tightened. "You have no idea how lucky you are," he told her.

She blinked in surprise then felt a flash of anger. "Lucky? *Me?* My closest friend tricked me into learning black magic

201

to set me up for murdering her father, then tried to kill me. The only people who care about me are far away, or likely to die any day now."

His eyes widened, then his expression softened. "I apologise. I only meant . . ." He looked away, grimacing as if in pain. "You are fortunate to avoid being trapped by roet. There are many, many magicians who wish they had your resistance."

Like yourself, she thought. But she found she couldn't sustain her disgust at him. His reputation as a man whose integrity was infallible was essential to his role as a black magician. To lose his will to a mere pleasure drug must be humiliating, and would have shaken his confidence. The fact that he was a black magician must be making the other magicians who knew of his affliction nervous. Though, it was as frightening to contemplate what could happen if high numbers of ordinary magicians were held hostage by Skellin.

"How many?" she asked, unable to keep the concern from her voice.

He frowned. "I can't tell you that. But . . . we are doing something about helping them."

"By trying to grow it?"

"To take control of the supply at least. To find a cure or breed a less damaging drug if we can." Kallen sighed. "You are partly right. We may reduce our chances to acquire seeds if Skellin is killed. We can't risk attempting to catch him. Yet." He met her gaze levelly and a fierce determination entered his gaze. "I promise once we have what we need we will find and remove Skellin. That may include accepting your friend's offer, if he is still willing to take the risk."

Lilia nodded. She considered what he had told her. It made

sense, and she could see no hint that he was lying. There was no advantage in holding back from telling him her idea.

"Did you know there's a new perfume being sold in the city that is made from roet flowers?"

His eyebrows rose and the spark of interest she had expected flared in his eyes. "No."

"They have to get the flowers from somewhere." She smiled. "Maybe the Guild should investigate. Anyway, I should be getting to the next class."

"Yes. Don't be late . . ." he said distractedly.

She left him standing there. When she looked back she saw that, as always, his gaze had fixed on the distance again, but this time he wore an expression of startled realisation.

It was almost unbearably stuffy and hot in the cart, and Lorkin had lost count of the times he'd had to grab his nose to stop sneezing. Like the other slaves in the vehicle, he was covered in a grey powder meant to kill off body lice. For the same reason, his hair had been shaved off. His ankles were chained together and to a metal loop in the centre of the cart's floor.

His back itched and burned where he'd been whipped, and he had to resist the constant urge to Heal the welts. There had been no reason for the punishment other than the driver establishing his superiority, after Ashaki Achati's slave master had warned that "this one is trouble". He resisted gazing in horror at his fellow passengers and tried to hide the anger he felt at their fate. They were the rejects of the city's slaves, too old, damaged, ugly or disobedient to be of use to their former owners. As far as they knew, they were being shipped off to work in a mine in the south of the Steelbelt mountains.

Bartering had been quick and few questions had been asked, to hasten the sale. Apparently some Sachakans believed that a slave who had been born into a household ought to be cared for by that household if he or she had worked hard for their master, or was crippled in their service. Sometimes they followed the mine cart around, calling shame upon owners who sold slaves to it. None of these protestors had pursued the cart today. It had trundled to the edge of the city without attracting any attention.

Now it was rolling slowly out into the countryside. Lorkin closed his eyes and thought back to his escape from the Guild House.

Tayend had come up with the solution to getting Lorkin out without the watchers noticing. They knew it was likely that the watchers had counted how many slaves Achati had brought with him, so he had gone out to the carriage and told one that he was being loaned to the Guild House to help keep an eye on Lorkin, but in truth to spy on the magicians.

Once the slave had been accepted with thanks and sent off to join the rest, Lorkin had donned Achati's clothing, padding his torso by stuffing his clothes with clean rags. Achati had put on a slave's wrap. It would have been amusing to watch Tayend instructing the dignified Ashaki how to walk with a slave's hunch, if they hadn't all been so worried that their plan would fail.

As always, the courtyard of the Guild House had been lit by one lamp and they had both kept their faces turned from it. At Tayend's suggestion they had kept their actions simple: Lorkin strode out of the House and into the carriage, Achati had hurried after and climbed onto the back of the carriage. They'd left the Guild House without any interference. All the way to Achati's home, Lorkin had sat rigid in the carriage, waiting for a call for them to halt, but none came. Once the carriage passed through the gate of Achati's mansion, the Ashaki climbed inside the carriage and they'd quickly exchanged clothing.

Lorkin's rescuer had told him to stay put, then left to have a quiet conversation with a man Lorkin learned later was the household's slave master. Achati had returned to explain his plan. Once again Lorkin would be disguised as a slave, only this time he must be prepared to endure much harsher treatment – and hope that there were Traitors among Achati's all-male slaves.

I also have to hope that they saw and recognised me, found out I'd been put on the cart, were able to pass on messages to other Traitors, and that the Traitors are actually able to catch up with the cart, stop it and free me without revealing their, and my, identities.

Thinking about it like that, it sounded a crazy scheme with far too many ways it could all go wrong.

What's the worst that could happen? I might have to go all the way to the mine. The Steelbelt Ranges run along the border between Sachaka and Kyralia. How hard would it be to free myself with magic, and travel the rest of the way to Kyralia?

How hard depended on whether Sachakan magicians ran the mine. Or if Ichani lurked in the mountains.

I should leave the cart before I get there, when there are no Sachakan magicians around, but we are close to the mountains. If only I knew what Sachaka was like down in the southern corner. Does the wasteland extend as far as the sea? Do the Ichani roam that far?

The cart began to slow. Opening his eyes, Lorkin glanced around to see both fear and hope in the faces of the other slaves. He heard the sound of a stomach growling. Perhaps they were going to be given food and water.

The cart stopped and he heard voices outside.

"The well's likely to collapse. I don't want to risk one of mine. They're healthy and useful," a haughty voice said.

The driver replied in a low, wheedling voice. Lorkin could not make out the words.

"Name the price," the haughty one commanded.

A pause, then the cart shifted and two sets of footsteps moved around to the rear. The lock rattled, then the doors opened. Bright light flooded in, blinding Lorkin.

"That one will do."

"He's trouble."

"Then you'll be glad to be rid of him. If he survives and is troublesome, I'll sell him back to you. Here."

The clink of coins followed. Lorkin's eyes had begun to adjust to the light. He could see an Ashaki standing next to the driver, who was leaning in to unlock the chains of one of the slaves.

Lorkin's heart stopped as he realised those chains were his own.

For a wild moment he considered blasting his way out of the cart with magic, but stopped himself with an effort. *Wherever you end up, there will be Traitors*, he told himself. *They will find you. They will free you.*

Whatever work this Ashaki planned for him sounded dangerous, but at least Lorkin could use magic to protect himself. *At least none of these other poor slaves will have to risk their lives doing it.*

"Come on," the driver said, grabbing Lorkin's leg and pulling. Lorkin hauled himself to his feet, stepping over the legs of other slaves between him and the open doors. He had to jump to the ground, and the restraining chains prevented him keeping his balance. He fell face first on the ground.

Well, at least that saves me the humiliation of throwing myself on the ground before my new owner.

"Stay there," the haughty voice said.

The man waited until the cart had driven away before he spoke again. By then Lorkin had stolen enough glances to either side to see there were two burly male slaves standing alongside him and the Ashaki.

"Get up. Follow me."

Lorkin obeyed. The chains rattled and shortened his stride as he followed the Ashaki and his two slaves through a small gate and into a courtyard. Another slave waited with a large hammer.

"Get rid of those," the Ashaki ordered.

The slave pointed to a bench. Lorkin sat down and obediently positioned the leg chains where the man directed. After a few nerve-wracking but accurate blows, the chains fell from Lorkin's ankles.

The Ashaki watched it all, looking bored. He then gestured for Lorkin to follow and led the way into the building. Damp, freshly scented air surrounded them as they entered a bathhouse. The Ashaki gestured to a pile of cloth on a wooden seat.

"Clean yourself and put those on. Don't take too long. We don't have much time."

Lorkin glanced behind to find that the two burly slaves hadn't followed them into the building. The Ashaki smiled, all haughtiness gone, then left the room. Alone, Lorkin stared after the man.

Something isn't right about this.

Moving over to the seat, Lorkin lifted the topmost piece from the pile of cloth. His heart skipped, then soared, and he found himself grinning.

They were the simple, comfortable clothes of a Traitor.

CHAPTER 14

ANOTHER CHANGE OF PLAN

"Safe journey," Watcher Orton said, as the carriage pulled away from the Fort. Above him, an array of small windows looked out from the Sachakan side of the building, some bright squares of light, some dark and near-invisible. Sonea gazed back at the building until it was swallowed by darkness.

Then she extinguished the small globe light she'd set hovering inside the carriage. The darkness in the cabin felt appropriate for discussing secrets, yet she hesitated. "It's a relief to hear Lorkin has escaped the city," Regin said.

"Yes," Sonea replied, seizing the opportunity to delay. "Dannyl will be pleased, too. I don't know how he arranged it, exactly, but it involved taking a big risk. Though . . . we have to trust that the message did come from the Traitors, and is true."

"Do you think it might be a lie?"

Sonea shook her head. "Not if it came from the Traitors. I can't help worrying that this whole thing is some elaborate ruse set up by King Amakira. Lorkin would have to have been deceived as well, as I detected no feeling of deceit from him when we spoke via the blood ring." She frowned. *In fact, I didn't detect anything of his thoughts and feelings. That's odd. The*

ring should have allowed me to do so. It's as if . . . aah, of course.
Lorkin's thoughts were being protected somehow. Possibly the
same way hers were protected by Naki's ring. Was he carrying
a similar gemstone? *Did Naki's ring originally come from the
Traitors? If it had, how did it get to Kyralia? She said it had been
passed down through the women in her family. Was one of them a
Traitor?*

"He has the ring now?"

She turned her thoughts back to the conversation. "Yes."

"So that's how you knew the messages were from the Traitors,"
Regin said, more to himself than her.

She looked at him, or rather, what she could see of him
in the dark. They had a couple of hours before they had to
leave the carriage. She considered her hesitation to tell Regin
what their other purpose was in Sachaka. The Traitors had
assured her the pass was safe, though they'd recommended she
travel at night and as quietly as possible. Once she told Regin,
he would have questions. If she didn't tell him until it was
time to leave the carriage, she might not have time enough
to answer them before they would be forced to stay silent. *Yes,
I think it has to be now.*

"Lord Regin," she began, and in the near-darkness she saw
his head turn quickly toward her. "Freeing Lorkin isn't the
only task we are undertaking. There is another."

He hesitated before answering. "I thought there must be.
So. What is this other task?"

"We're to meet with the Traitors. They want to discuss the
possibility of an alliance and trade."

Over the rattle of the carriage, she heard him exhale.
"Ah."

"The driver will stop in an hour or two. We'll get out

and walk from there, north of the road. The Traitors left me instructions on where to go. In a few days they'll meet us, and Lorkin will be with them."

"You left this to the last moment to tell me."

"Yes, and I would have waited longer if I could have. You couldn't be told before now in case we were waylaid by King Amakira's men and your mind was read."

"And your mind?"

"Is protected."

She waited for him to ask how, but the question never came. He did not speak at all. The silence in the cabin felt a little reproachful.

"It isn't that we – the Guild – didn't trust you with the information," she began. "We—"

"I know," he interrupted. "It doesn't matter." He sighed. "Well, one thing does. Do *you* trust me?"

She paused, not sure how to read the tone of his voice. It wasn't accusing, but it did hold a hint of demand. To avoid answering could make matters unnecessarily strained between them.

"I do," she told him, and felt the truth of it. At the same time she realised he had cornered her somewhat, and it was only fair to do the same in return. "Do you trust me?"

Again she heard him exhale, but slowly this time.

"Not completely," he admitted. "Not because I regard you as untrustworthy, but . . . I know you do not like me."

She felt her heart skip. "That's not true," she told him quickly, before old memories rose to argue their case and make saying it awkward. "I haven't always. You know why. We don't need to go over that again. It's in the past."

He was quiet for a short space of time. "I apologise. I should not have brought it up again. Sometimes I find it hard to believe you have forgiven me, or could even like me."

"Well . . . I have. And I do. You are . . . a good person."

"You made me that person." His tone was warmer, now. "That day, during the invasion."

Sonea caught her breath as a wave of sadness washed over her. *And another good person died that day.* Suddenly she could not speak, and dread rose — not for the first time — at the memories she knew would return when she walked in the darkness over the bare rock of the mountains. *But with a different companion. A different man.*

"What's wrong?"

She blinked in surprise. How had he even known she was upset? Then she realised that the rock wall on one side of the carriage was gone and the faint light of a crescent moon filtered into the cabin. She drew in a deep breath and let it out slowly, gathering all her self-control.

"We both changed that day. You for the better, me for the worse."

"Only a fool would think that of you," he told her, misunderstanding her meaning. "You saved us and the Guild. I have admired you ever since."

She looked at him, but his face was mostly in shadow. How could he understand the bitterness and self-loathing that had come after Akkarin's death? *No matter how much my mind knows it wasn't my fault, my heart never quite believes it.*

The moonlight reached his face and revealed an expression she had rarely seen before. There had been a hint of a smile in his voice, she realised. What had he said? *'I have admired you ever since.'*

She looked away. All his rivalry and hatred of her and what

211

she represented had changed to something almost completely opposite. *And just as undeserved. But it would be unkind and ungrateful to say so. I'll take admiration over distrust and contempt any day.*

Admiration and friendship were very different. As different as friendship and love. *I've seen novices who hated each other become friends after graduation. That didn't happen with us. I've also seen people who hate each other skip the friendship bit in the middle and fall in love.* Her heart skipped a beat. *Wait . . . Surely not. No, he doesn't mean* that *sort of admiration.*

Glancing at him again, she did not have a chance to search his expression. Regin's attention had fixed somewhere outside the carriage. He shifted across his seat and leaned forward.

"So that's the wasteland," he said in a hushed voice.

She peered out the window. The faint moonlight touched the edges of the landscape below, the ridges of many, many dunes creating eerie patterns.

"Yes," she explained. "It goes all the way to the horizon."

"So far. How did we do it?" Regin wondered. "Where has that knowledge gone?"

"Ambassador Dannyl has unearthed some interesting records, from what Osen had told me."

"Any ideas on how to restore the land?"

She shook her head. "If a magician ever manages to return this to fertile land, it will be the greatest act of healing anyone has ever achieved."

Regin gazed a little longer at the view, then leaned back in his seat again. "A few hours, you say?"

"Yes. The driver knows the landmark to look for. He'll drop us there, then continue on to Arvice and the Guild House with the mail and supplies. I told him we didn't need to go to Sachaka now that Lorkin was free, but we wanted to see the sun rise over the wasteland and would walk back to the Fort."

"Brave man, travelling without magicians on board," Regin said. "I suppose none of us would be safe if the Sachakan king decided to attack us. Or the Ichani. Or the Traitors."

"No, but we have to hope that the Traitors are on our side. They've assured us they'll keep the Ichani and the king's spies out of our way."

"Really? I'm looking forward to meeting them."

She nodded. *I am, too. Not only because I'll finally get to see Lorkin, and ensure he gets home safely, but I want to meet these people who impressed him so much that he agreed to go to their secret city, despite knowing he might never leave it again.*

With Anyi and Lilia gone, the underground room was silent but for the sound of breathing. Gol was sitting on one of the mattresses he'd made, his back to the wall. Cery remained on one of the stolen chairs. He considered what Lilia had told him about Kallen and the Guild's reason for seeking roet seeds.

"He said he would get rid of Skellin after they had seeds, and that they might accept your help then, if you're still prepared to give it," she'd told him.

"Can we trust them?" Cery asked aloud.

Gol grunted. "I should ask *you* that. You're the expert on the Guild. What do you think?"

Cery drew in a deep breath and sighed. "They'll look after themselves and the Houses first, and their notion of 'the Kyralian people' second."

"Which doesn't include Thieves and criminal types."

"Not unless those Thieves have helped them, and then only in ways the public doesn't get to hear about."

"They'll feel obliged to help us." The bodyguard looked at Cery. "Even though we aren't helping them now, and Sonea's gone. Because we helped them in the past."

"I hope so." Cery sighed. "The sooner Sonea gets back, the better," he muttered, mostly to himself. "I don't like having to trust Kallen if he's as addicted to roet as Lilia says."

"Hmm," Gol nodded. "If he wanted to sell us out to Skellin he'd have agreed to your plan and said nothing about waiting. He'd have arranged a meeting and Skellin would have arrived instead."

"That's true. Even so, I'd rather be here, where we can leave if we have to, than stuck in a room in the Guild."

God nodded. "At least we can keep an eye on that cellar so we know when they've got roet seeds. We should wait until the plants get to the same size as the ones we saw, which was big enough for the magicians to tell they weren't roet."

"Do you know what roet plants look like?"

Gol frowned and shook his head. "Anyi might. Didn't her boyfriend smoke it?"

"Or girlfriend. She never did say."

The bodyguard's face darkened in the dim light and he looked away. *Is he blushing?* Cery couldn't help smiling.

"They might try other ways to find Skellin before they consider our plan." Gol drummed his fingers on the sides of the chair. "If they're reluctant to work with a Thief."

"If they don't like working with a Thief, I doubt they'll be reluctant to use a Thief as bait," Cery pointed out.

Gol chuckled. "True."

"If they do want to try our plan . . ." Cery considered. "I

guess we ought to make sure we're ready for them. We should have a trap all set up, ready to go."

"It'll be a waste of effort if they decide not to work with us?"

"What else are we going to do?" Cery sighed. "We're right underneath the Guild. Surely that's to our advantage. I wish . . . I wish there was a way to trick Skellin into walking right into their hands, whether the Guild wants it or not."

"A trap that's as much for them as for Skellin."

"A trap that will get their attention when – and only when – Skellin comes snooping."

The bodyguard's eyes brightened. "I know just the thing. It'll get the magicians' attention for sure." He looked thoughtful. "I'll have to go into the city to get supplies. And we'll have to set it up somewhere strong, so we don't accidentally bury ourselves. What's the sturdiest area down here?"

"I think I know just the place." Cery picked up a lamp. "Come with me."

Getting to his feet without even a grunt of effort, Gol followed Cery out of the room. *Good to see he's healed up so well,* Cery thought. *Between him and Anyi, I feel twice as old as I am. If I ever get my former life back I'm going to keep some grizzled old men around to make me feel younger.*

He led Gol out of the room. Soon they arrived at the cluster of rooms where Cery had run into Lilia and Anyi. Gol took the lamp from him and entered the first one, lifting it to illuminate the sturdy brick walls and vaulted ceiling.

"This is in much better shape than the room we're living in," the bodyguard said. "Why haven't we been staying here?"

"Anyi only found the rooms recently." And there was something about this one that bothered Cery. It set his heart beating a little too fast. As Gol lowered the lamp, a dusty, broken plate caught the light. Cery picked up one of the pieces. A Guild symbol marked the glaze. He shivered as memories wafted up like smoke. *Is this the room Fergun locked me in all those years ago? I didn't get to see it much. I was stuck in the dark for days.*

"This is closer to the Guild buildings. A shorter run to escape, if we need to, and not so far for Lilia to travel to see us. Let's move our stuff in here," Gol said.

Sighing, Cery pushed away the memories and his discomfort and nodded. "Yes, but let's choose another room. This is the first one anyone comes to. We'll want a little bit more warning when someone is approaching."

As the last of the food-bearing slaves left the Master's Room, Tayend looked at Dannyl.

"Now that Lorkin is safely away, what are you going to do with our unwanted guest?"

Dannyl looked at his meal and sighed as his appetite faltered. He drew magic and surrounded himself, Merria and Tayend with a shield to prevent anyone overhearing their conversation.

"What do you suggest?" he asked in reply.

A whole day had passed since the failed abduction. Savi was keeping the spy regularly drained of strength. Since she was the head kitchen slave, none of the other slaves thought it odd that she was the only one allowed to see something in one of the kitchen storerooms.

"I can see only two choices: either he dies or Savi leaves."

The last of Dannyl's appetite vanished. "Since the latter isn't possible, that leaves us only one choice."

Merria frowned. "But whether the king pretends his spy is a slave or admits he's not, you'll be breaking a law."

Tayend nodded. "Better to be charged for destruction of the king's property than murder. Perhaps you could make it look like an accident."

Why must I be the one to do it? Dannyl thought. *Because I'm the highest-ranking person in the house.* Then he felt a traitorous hope. *Does Tayend outrank me, as an Ambassador to a country rather than just the Guild?*

"If Savi kills the man using black magic it'll be clear none of us did it," Merria suggested.

"But it'll also be clear there's a Traitor here somewhere," Tayend pointed out.

"She can block a mind-read, can't she?"

"If the king knows no slave has entered or left the House, and is determined to find which is the Traitor, he could have them tortured."

"Or kill them all," Tayend added.

A slave appeared. Dannyl realised it was Tav, the door slave. The man dropped to the floor.

"Mind what you say," Dannyl warned, then let the shield fall. "What is it, Tav?"

"Someone at the door," the man gasped.

"Go find out who it is."

The slave hurried away. The Master's Room was quiet as they waited for him to return. The rapid, soft thud of footsteps growing louder preceded the slave's return.

"A message," he said.

"Bring it here," Dannyl ordered before the man could abase himself again. The slave quickly padded forward, a scroll held out in both hands. Dannyl took it and waved a hand. "Leave us."

He unrolled the message. Tayend and Merria leaned in on either side to read it.

"A summons to the palace," Merria murmured.

"'Immediately'," Tayend read.

Dannyl let the scroll snap back into a roll. "Whatever we do, we have to do it now. Kai!"

His personal slave appeared in the corridor.

"Fetch Savi." As the man disappeared, Dannyl spoke quietly, "Only reasonable to ask her what she'd prefer us to do."

They did not wait long. The woman entered and threw herself onto the floor as quickly and unselfconsciously as any ordinary slave.

"Is the meal not to your liking, master?" she asked.

Dannyl glanced at the plate in his hands, the food barely touched. He sighed and raised the barrier of silence again.

"I've been summoned to the palace," he told her. "We have to come to a decision about the fate of the king's spy. What would you have us do?"

She grimaced. "Well . . . swapping clothes is definitely not going to work this time."

Tayend straightened abruptly. "Ah!"

All eyes turned to him. "What?" Dannyl asked.

The Elyne raised a hand, palm-outward. "Wait. Give me a moment. I have an idea . . ." He closed his eyes and his lips moved, then he nodded. He looked around at them, then at Savi. "Tell me if this will work: could you get away with being one of the carriage slaves, despite it not being your usual work, and that you're a woman?"

She frowned. "If it worked for Ashaki Achati, it might for me."

"Is there a safe place on the way to the palace that Dannyl could drop you off?"

Her eyes brightened. "Yes."

Tayend looked at Dannyl. "I think this is our best option. If we can get Savi out of harm's way, there's no need to kill the abductor."

Dannyl nodded, his heart lightening with relief until he remembered that a live abductor was also going to reveal more than that Savi was a Traitor. *The king isn't going to admit publicly the man was his spy, though. Which will be very, very annoying after all we've been through. Unless . . .*

"We'll take him with us," he decided.

Merria's eyes widened, but Tayend only chuckled. "You're going to tell the king everything."

"Except how Lorkin got away."

"Then I'm coming too. I have to see this."

"Tayend—"

"No, Dannyl. I *have* to see this. My king would be *most* disappointed if I didn't."

Dannyl could not argue against that. *It will be better if there are witnesses other than myself, Osen and the Sachakan court, too.* He dropped the barrier of silence.

"Merria, go with Savi and fetch the spy. Kai!" The man dashed into the room. "Have the carriage brought to the front."

As Savi and Merria hurried away and Kai disappeared, Dannyl restored the shield again. Tayend rubbed his hands together. Then he stopped and his grin faded. "I hope Achati's involvement won't be discovered."

Something inside Dannyl swooped downwards. He sighed and set his plate on the floor. The previous night he'd lain awake, either worrying that Achati would turn Lorkin over or anxious at the risk Achati was taking by helping Lorkin escape.

Tayend's spoke in low tones, despite the barrier of silence.

"It occurred to me last night . . . What if the king orders Achati to wear one of his blood rings? They allow the creator to read the thoughts of the wearer, right? I'm sure Achati was communicating with the king during their journey to Duna. I doubt the king would wear anyone else's blood ring and risk them reading his mind, so Achati must have been wearing one of his. Will Achati now refuse to wear a ring?"

"I don't know." Dannyl shook his head. "Achati knew what he was doing."

"Well . . . I hope it wasn't sacrificing himself for us. He turned out better than I expected. I like him."

Dannyl looked at Tayend in surprise and gratitude. *Tayend liking Achati makes me like Tayend better*, he realised. *Tayend's good opinion also makes me like Achati better, too.* All because Achati had helped Lorkin. *But at what cost?*

Footsteps heralded the return of Savi. She was pushing the spy, bound and gagged, before her. The man was staggering as if exhausted, Dannyl noted. No doubt she'd drained his power again.

A grim silence fell between them all as they filed down the corridor to the front entrance. The carriage was not waiting, but before long the doors to the stable swung open and the horses and vehicle emerged. Dannyl ordered Savi to climb up onto the back to cling on beside the usual carriage slave, then hauled the spy up into the cabin. He climbed in after, and Tayend followed.

"Good luck," Merria said quietly, then pushed the door closed.

At Dannyl's order, the carriage left the Guild House. He did not speak and Tayend stayed silent. They couldn't discuss what they were planning to do in front of the spy, and it was hardly a situation for small talk. The spy huddled opposite

220

Tayend and Dannyl, his frightened gaze flickering from one to the other, which was disconcerting enough. When the driver suddenly shouted they all jumped.

The carriage began to slow. Dannyl opened the window and leaned out.

"What is it?"

"The slave, master. She jumped off and ran."

Dannyl paused and looked behind, but Savi had already disappeared.

"We can't stop," he told the man. "Continue to the palace."

Perhaps it was the mention of the palace, but the abductor had stopped staring at them. Relieved, Dannyl spent the rest of the journey considering and refining his plan, and gathering his courage. When they arrived, he dragged the man out after him. Leaving Tayend to hurry after, he forced the spy before him and marched into the palace.

The guards watched intently, but didn't stop him. Once in the hall, Dannyl was pleased to see the king had arranged for a large audience of Ashaki to watch the meeting, including a few who, Merria had learned, disagreed with Lorkin's treatment. *Perfect.* Achati stood near the throne, to Dannyl's relief looking unconcerned.

The monarch's eyebrows rose as Dannyl pushed the spy to the floor. Following protocol, Dannyl knelt and Tayend, hurrying up beside him, bowed.

"Rise Ambassador Dannyl." The king looked at the spy. "What is this?"

"Just returning what I am told is your spy, your majesty," Dannyl replied as he straightened.

The king's gaze snapped to his. "*My* spy."

"Yes, your majesty. Last night this man tried to abduct my

221

former assistant, Lord Lorkin. A Traitor prevented it. She also read his mind and learned that the man was hired by you." Dannyl looked around at the Ashaki, who looked amused but not shocked. "I request that someone here read his mind to confirm it."

Heads turned back and forth. Glances were exchanged. A few words were muttered. The king ignored everyone and continued to regard Dannyl.

"Very well. Ashaki Rokaro, would you grant Ambassador Dannyl's request and tell us if this accusation is true."

No protest came from the gathering as a man with grey in his hair stepped forward. All watched as the spy's mind was read. The Ashaki appeared to be doing a thorough and careful mind-read, as it was taking longer than Dannyl had seen one take before. When he let the spy go, the man sagged to the floor again, reaching out to the king like a slave pleading for forgiveness.

"Well, Ashaki Rokaro?" the king prompted.

The Ashaki looked from the spy, to Dannyl, then to the assembled Ashaki.

"It is true," he said.

Dannyl felt a mild surprise. He'd expected the Ashaki to deny it, or say that the man believed it but had no proof his orders had come from the king. Looking up at the king, Dannyl saw no concern or guilt and felt his stomach sink.

"You say a Traitor helped you," the king asked.

Dannyl hesitated, a warning chill going through him. "We could hardly refuse."

"Where is she now?"

"I don't know. Not in the Guild House."

"And Lorkin?"

"Gone."

"Where?"

"I don't know. With the Traitors, I imagine."

"They seem to be his preferred companions these days." He turned and smiled at Achati with obvious approval. "But at least we have gained what we all desired: freedom for Lorkin in exchange for information."

Information? Abruptly Dannyl remembered Lorkin's promise to Achati. *"I will answer the question your king most wants to ask me. I will tell you where the Traitors' home is."*

Dannyl had not believed Lorkin would carry out his promise. He'd assumed Lorkin had some deception in mind. But what if he *had* given Achati the location of Sanctuary? What if Achati had turned Lorkin over to the king, not helped him escape? Were the Traitors lying about rescuing him in order to take revenge for Lorkin revealing their home? Or did they not know what Lorkin had done yet?

The king glanced at the spy. "I guess I should thank you for returning my spy to me, though he has hardly earned the title." The king looked up at Dannyl and Tayend. "You may return to the Guild House, Ambassadors."

CHAPTER 15

INTO THE WASTELAND

The night air was surprisingly cold, considering how hot it was in the wasteland during the day. Lorkin pulled on the reins, yet again discouraging the hardy little mount he was riding from trying to catch up with the horse in front. She tossed her head in protest, and he heard the water sloshing about in the barrels lashed to her side.

They'd been riding since dusk the day before. The Traitors' fake Ashaki had taken Lorkin to the edge of the wasteland in his carriage and left him with two male slaves from a nearby estate. The slaves had told Lorkin that they could only take him as far as the hills, where a group of Traitors would meet them. Though they had a spare horse to help carry water and food, they couldn't carry enough to last them to the mountains and back without raising suspicion.

Looking over his shoulder to the east, Lorkin saw that the sky was beginning to brighten. He hadn't slept in more than a day, and during the previous two nights he'd had to curl up on a cramped carriage seat. Though he could ease the weariness with Healing magic, the constant travel and fear of discovery was exhausting. Just to sit still for a while would have been welcome, but he doubted he'd be enjoying that for some time.

The hope that Tyvara would be among the Traitors waiting for him gave him a boost of energy every time he thought of her, which he did whenever weariness had him sagging in the saddle. Thought of her warm smile, the sound of her voice, the touch of her bare skin. *Soon*, he told himself.

He was going to be very disappointed if she wasn't among them, but not surprised. Tyvara had been forbidden to leave the city for three years, as punishment for killing Riva. *But at least she's safe there, and if she isn't with them the thought of her will sustain me until I do see her again*, he reasoned.

The sound of teeth snapping brought his attention back to his mount again. He saw that she had crept close enough to the horse in front to attempt another bite, and quickly hauled on the reins. *Mad, spiteful little beast*, he thought, muttering a curse. *I'm glad she doesn't try this on humans.*

Though she obediently slowed, the horse in front followed suit. Lorkin opened his mouth to warn the slave, then closed it again as the man gestured for silence. They came to a halt. Even Lorkin's mount stilled and pricked up her ears.

Lorkin could hear nothing, but one of the slaves slid off his horse and ran up the side of a nearby dune. After crouching for a short time, a dark shape against the paler sand, he hurried back to them.

"A group of eight," he murmured.

The other slave nodded, then turned to Lorkin. "Probably Traitors. Ichani travel alone, with only a few slaves."

Lorkin nodded. His heart was racing. He began to dismount, but the slave frowned and shook his head. "Stay put. Just in case we're wrong."

The other slave mounted his horse again. They moved into the long, low shadow of a dune, which only half

225

concealed them, but with the brightening sky behind them they would be a little harder to make out.

What if it is an Ichani? Lorkin felt the night's chill seep into his clothing. *What if it is more than one? We can run, but would we get far? Could I stop their attempts to hold us with magic for long enough to escape? I doubt much of Tyvara's magic is left, and even if I had it all I couldn't beat several Ichani.*

Figures appeared in the valley between the dunes ahead. The glow of the sky had grown warmer, and now bathed the newcomers with gold. Though all wore trousers and tunics, it was easy to distinguish woman from man. Each wore a belt over their tunic, and on each belt was a sheath. Unlike the Ashaki's blades, the knife handles were undecorated and the sheaths were straight, not curved. As Lorkin recognised the lead figure, he breathed a sigh of relief.

Savara.

She strode toward them, unhurried but purposeful. Looking past her, Lorkin searched for the face he most wanted to see, his pulse speeding even as he braced himself for disappointment. When his eyes found hers, he thought he must be mistaken. Then she smiled, and he felt his heart leap, and an intense longing to draw her into his arms and feel her body against his. He dismounted, as did the slaves, but forced himself to stay still and face the Traitors' new queen.

"Gal. Tika. Right where you were supposed to be," Savara said, smiling as she reached the slaves. She turned to Lorkin. "It is good to see you again, Lord Lorkin. We were worried we might have to break into the palace to get you. We haven't had to do that in centuries."

Placing a hand on his heart, he waited. She smiled sadly, then nodded.

"It is good to see you, too, your majesty" he told her. Still unsure of Traitor protocol when a monarch had died, he decided to err on the side of speaking plainly. "I was saddened to hear of Queen Zarala's passing, but glad to hear of your election."

She looked down. "She will be remembered." Her lips pressed together, then she turned to the slaves. As she thanked them, Lorkin looked at Tyvara again and drank in the sight of her, resisting a wave of impatience. *It feels like months since I last saw her.*

The slaves mounted their horses again, one taking the reins of Lorkin's horse, and set off toward the east. They disappeared around a dune, toward an orange sun that hinted at the coming daytime onslaught of heat.

"Now, we must travel as quickly as we can manage," Savara said, turning back to the group and ushering him toward them with an outstretched arm. "Your mother awaits us in the mountains."

He felt a twinge of apprehension and eagerness, but forgot both as Tyvara stepped forward to meet him. She was smiling broadly.

"I'm so relieved the king let you go. Savara said the king wouldn't dare harm you, but that didn't stop me worrying." She took his hands. Stepping close, she kissed him quickly, but pulled away when he tried to draw her closer, her eyes flickering to the others and giving him a warning look that plainly said "not now". He felt a petulant disappointment, but put it aside. She was here. That was enough for now.

"I'm not the only one who's been let out," he said.

She shrugged. "I have more important things to do than running the sewer. And I'm sure the punishment will resume once we're done."

As one the group turned and started in the direction they had come. Someone passed Lorkin a pack, murmuring that he'd find a water bottle inside. He shouldered it and looked across at Tyvara. She was frowning at him.

"What is it?"

She lowered her voice. "Was it bad, in the king's prison?"

His stomach lurched at the question. Suddenly the lightness in his heart was gone, and weariness returned. He looked away.

"It wasn't fun," he replied, shrugging. *Should I tell her about the slave girl? What will she think of me, for helping the girl die? Maybe if the girl hadn't been a Traitor . . . no, I don't think that would make much difference. Still, Tyvara must have had to make some difficult choices as a spy.* He drew in a deep breath. "You must have been through worse, as a slave."

She said nothing. He made himself look up at her. She met his gaze reluctantly, then her eyes dropped to the ground.

"Would that be a problem for you, if I had?" she asked.

It was an odd way to phrase her answer, but as her meaning came to him he felt both dismay and affection.

"No," he said. "I'm . . . I know what . . . what pretending to be a slave would have involved. It's not like you had a choice."

"But I did have a choice – whether to be a spy or not."

"For the good of your people. And to help others." *Whereas there was nothing noble about me helping the slave girl die.* And yet he hadn't chosen to be put in that situation.

"Enough talking," Savara said, glancing back at Lorkin and Tyvara. "The Ichani were far away last time we checked, but they can be unpredictable. We should travel in silence."

Tyvara frowned and bit her lip. As they strode onward, she glanced at him from time to time. On each occasion, he only caught sight of her expression briefly, since her back was to the rising sun. Clearly she wanted to say something to him. Frustrated by the necessity for silence, he concentrated until he could detect her presence. He imagined he could hear her thoughts like a buzz at the edge of his senses, not quite loud or clear enough to be audible.

Finally he could not stand it any more. He moved closer and grabbed her hand.

—*What is it? What is bothering you?*

She looked surprised, then smiled and squeezed his hand.

—*You know where we're going?*

—*To the mountains. To meet my mother. I'm assuming to discuss trade or an alliance.*

—*Yes.*

She looked at him questioningly, and he heard, somehow, faint words that she perhaps hadn't intended to send to him.

What will he do then?

He frowned. He'd been putting off asking himself the same question. What *would* he do once negotiations were over? Go back to Kyralia with his mother? Stay in Sachaka with Tyvara? The answer was even more important if the negotiations failed to bring about any kind of agreement between the Allied Lands and the Traitors.

The Guild would want him to come home. His mother would want him to come home. But that might mean he'd never see Tyvara again.

What does he want? came Tyvara's badly hidden thought.

—*I want to be with you*, he told her.

She blinked in surprise and turned to stare at him. He sensed puzzlement, and a little embarrassment. Her grip loosened as if she was about to pull away. Then it tightened again,

—*Will the Guild let you stay with us?*

—They won't like it, but they'll have to accept it.

She nodded and looked way, pulling her hand free. He focused closely on her, trying to judge her expression, and heard words at the very edge of his senses again.

He'll change his mind once he knows we're about to go to war.

Lorkin felt his muscles go rigid with shock and nearly stumbled. He shook his head. He must have imagined it. It was not possible to hear someone else's thoughts without touching them. Unless that person had deliberately sent them. Looking around, he saw that none of the other Traitors looked alarmed or were watching him, as they would have been if they'd known Tyvara had revealed their plans to him.

No. I must have imagined it. After all, he'd seen hints in Sanctuary that the Traitors might be planning to attack the Ashaki. His mind was merely pointing out, in an unexpected way, that war *would* make his choice much more difficult. Tyvara had to be wondering if he wanted to avoid being caught up in a war. *Of course I would. People die in wars. Tyvara might die. Unless . . . could I find a reason to take her to Kyralia with me? Perhaps I could persuade Savara that the Allied Lands need a Traitor Ambassador. But would Tyvara go? I doubt it.*

So now he had to decide whether he'd stay with Tyvara or go to Kyralia and pass on stone-making knowledge, how to tell his mother that he'd learned black magic, whether to tell Tyvara about the poisoned slave girl, and what he'd do if the Traitors went to war. Fortunately he had hours of trudging through the wasteland to the mountains ahead of him. Plenty of time to think.

Though it was still early spring, buds on the trees within the Guild gardens were already bursting open and the scent hinted at warmer days to come. Lilia breathed it in, enjoying a brief moment of peace and promise. She was alive, not in prison, accepted by the Guild, and Cery, Gol and Anyi were still safe and undiscovered.

Of course, the moment could not last long. Her friends were not all that safe, the Guild's acceptance of her involved conditions that would restrict her for the rest of her life, and she was heading for another lesson with Black Magician Kallen. But her mood soured sooner than usual as she saw a trio of novices standing outside the Novice's Quarters, watching her. One was Bokkin.

She spared them the briefest of glances, but though she kept her gaze on the path ahead she paid attention to their shadows in the corner of her eye. For good measure, she threw up a weak shield against any pranks.

Nothing happened, though she was so alert for trouble that she didn't notice, at first, that no other novices were waiting with Kallen by the Arena. He always wore the same slightly distracted frown, yet it was a little deeper than usual. And his gaze was a little more alert.

"Black Magician Kallen," she said, bowing as she reached him.

"Lady Lilia," Kallen said. "Today's lesson will be held within the University."

Her heart skipped a beat and she had to smother the urge to cheer.

"So . . . no fighting practice today?"

"No."

He indicated that she should walk beside him and started toward the University. Bokkin, she saw with relief, was gone. She considered whether to ask Kallen what she'd be learning,

231

but experience had taught her that if he didn't offer information she was not likely to get useful answers. Once they were
inside, she heard him draw in a deep breath, then sigh. Sneaking
a quick glance, she noted that his mouth was pressed into a
thin line.

He's not happy about something, she thought. *Well, more unhappy
than he usually is, anyway.*

He led her through to the inner passages of the building
and into one of the small rooms reserved for private lessons.
Indicating she should take one of the two chairs, he sat on the
other and regarded her across the sole table.

"The Guild has decided it is time you learned to use black
magic."

She felt a jolt of fear and guilt, but they quickly faded into
amusement. "But I already know how to use black magic."

"You know how it is used," he corrected. "Aside from your
single experiment, you have not consciously and deliberately
used it, and you've never needed to store power. There are also
other tasks that black magicians are required to perform that
do not involve the acquisition of magic."

"Like?"

"Reading minds. Making blood rings."

Lilia's heartbeat quickened. She had assumed she wouldn't
be taught either skill until she had graduated and taken up
the official role of black magician.

"Why now?"

Kallen's brows lowered still further. "While Sonea is absent,
many would rather that you were taught to use black magic
than we have only one fully trained black magician in Imardin."

*No wonder he's grumpy. The implication of that is that he needs
watching. That he can't be trusted.* She felt a small surge of

triumph that he experienced the same suspicion and distrust that she did. *Though people distrust me because I broke a rule when I learned black magic, even though I thought I couldn't succeed. But I suppose they distrust Kallen because he's a roet addict.* She felt triumph fade. It was replaced with sympathy. *And he probably didn't think that could happen, either.*

She nodded. "So . . . what first?"

He straightened and took something from within his robe. Light reflected from the polished surface of a small, slim knife. Kallen lifted his other hand so that the sleeve fell back, then placed his arm on the table. He looked at her.

"I will cut myself. Place your hand over the wound and try to recall what you did to . . . Take enough that you can sense your own strength has increased."

To Naki, Lilia finished. She pushed away a memory of a library, and the words that had seduced her into learning what was forbidden. *"I'd do anything for you."* Kallen ran the blade across the back of his arm. She obediently placed her palm over the shallow cut, and closed her eyes.

The trick was to see that my own magic is contained within my skin, she remembered. The awareness came back to her slowly, but once her mind recalled it the sense of magic within her body was suddenly clear. She paused to marvel a little at it, but the call of an *otherness* nearby drew her attention. Shifting her focus to her hand, she detected Kallen's presence and saw the gap in his defences.

She hesitated. To draw magic from Kallen, whom she had half feared most of her life and who was one of the Higher Magicians, seemed presumptuous. But he'd told her to, so she gathered her will and *drew*.

Magic flooded into her body. Immediately she slowed the

pull. He would be able to sense it, she guessed, and know if she was overdoing it. He'd said to take magic until she could feel it had added to her own strength. Concentrating, she realised that she was already aware of being stronger. Halting the draw of power, she opened her eyes and withdrew her hand.

Kallen stared at her intently. "Take more."

This time she was immediately aware of the break in his barrier, and she found that she didn't need to sense the containment of her own power to do so. She forgot to close her eyes and realised she didn't need to. Kallen's face had gone strangely slack, she noted. He looked sad and tired.

When she stopped, expression returned to his face. He looked at her again, and this time he nodded.

"Good. I can sense that you are storing power now." His lips thinned in grim approval. "Whenever we hold more power than we naturally possess, a little of it escapes our barrier. Focus on the natural containment at your skin until you sense this leakage, then send a little magic to reinforce your barrier."

This time she did close her eyes. Drawing her attention within, she noted that she could feel that her power was enhanced. She concentrated on the barrier at her skin, which was the border of her control. Sure enough, magic was seeping through it, more in some places than others.

Exerting her will, she tapped a little of her magic and sent a steady trickle of it to thicken and harden the barrier. At once the leakage stopped.

Kallen nodded when she opened her eyes.

"I can't sense it any more." He almost smiled. "Now, it is also possible for another magician to sense the taking of magic. This is a similar problem of leakage, but it happens at the site of the wound. You need to extend your barrier a little to overlap that of the, ah, donor of magic."

Following his instructions, Lilia managed to succeed in this lesson after a few attempts. After that, Kallen had her attempt to take magic so slowly that he barely noticed, then as quickly as she could. He was able, haltingly, to speak to her during the first, but obviously had trouble staying upright during the second.

"You should experience the weakening effect of being drained," he told her. "Black Magician Sonea was not careful enough to avoid being cut during one fight with the Ichani because she hadn't appreciated how disabling it was to be subjected to black magic. It is something you certainly don't want to experience again, once you've felt it." He waved a hand. "But it can wait until another lesson."

"I remember something like that, from when Naki tried it on me," Lilia told him. "She said it didn't work, but I think she was lying."

Kallen's expression darkened, but then his lips thinned in sympathy. "In descriptions of the higher-magic rite between magicians and apprentices of old, the apprentices would kneel before their masters. They must have been able to remain upright. Perhaps the apprentices grew immune to the weakening effect."

"Or the masters knew how to draw power without it affecting them."

He nodded. "We could experiment, if you are willing. There is much about black magic we don't understand, and I fear that our counterparts in Sachaka could use that against us."

Lilia smothered a shudder of reluctance. Though experimenting with black magic with Kallen didn't sound like much fun, she had to agree that the Guild couldn't allow any holes in its knowledge of magic to remain unexplored.

Kallen ran a hand over the cut, which had now closed to a pink line. "Of course, you'll only have to acquire magic this way from non-magicians or an enemy magician. Normal transferral of power can be done without cutting the skin. The weakening effect is also an advantage in battle. I can't see many situations where taking power forcibly while avoiding the weakening effect will be of much use."

"Perhaps . . . if you have to take power from an old magician who is dying but for some reason – perhaps they're unconscious or senile – they can't will their power to you."

Kallen grimaced. "Yes. It would be kinder if they didn't have to experience the weakening."

She looked at the knife. "What do you do if you don't have a knife? Could you use magic to make the cut?"

He shook his head. "Even if a magician is too weak to shield, so long as they are alive they still contain some energy and a barrier at their skin. At its most basic, that barrier is a shield against another's will and must be broken."

"But if you shaped magic into a sliver of force and send it out from yourself like a strike, overcoming the barrier, would it work?"

His eyebrows rose. "Perhaps. I guess if a strike is strong enough . . ." He frowned. "It would be difficult to test. The subject would have to be willing to be harmed, perhaps quite badly . . . though if you first gained some skill in forming a small, stabbing strike that only penetrated a tiny distance it would be no worse than a small cut." His eyes narrowed in thought, then he looked at her appraisingly. "It is an interesting idea. We should explore it."

She nodded, before the idea of letting him stab her could overcome her satisfaction at thinking of something that hadn't occurred to him before.

"Well . . . that will do for today," he said. "Tomorrow I will begin your training in mind-reading. We will need a volunteer for you to practise on. Once you have satisfactorily achieved that skill, I'll teach you how to make a blood gem."

A blood gem! Lilia resisted a smile, not wanting to seem too eager to learn more about what had once been forbidden magic. She rose as Kallen stood up and followed him to the door.

"Should I meet you here?" she asked.

He nodded, then gestured to the corridor. "Yes. Until tomorrow, then."

She bowed and set off toward the outer rooms of the University, and her next class, unable to help feeling a thrill of excitement.

For the first time, knowing black magic doesn't feel like a . . . a punishment – or a disease. The Guild wants me to learn it. And it's actually interesting.

As the morning sun rose higher and brighter, the colours of the wasteland began to bleach away. Sonea clasped her hands together around her knees, wistfully remembering how she had once been able to hug her knees to her chest. It had been a long time since she'd been that flexible. Life as a magician – and wearing full robes – tended to demand more dignified sitting. It was little losses like these that told her she was getting older.

Regin rose and moved to their packs, which were looking somewhat emptier than they'd been two evening ago when they'd arrived at the Traitors' meeting place.

I followed the instructions strictly, she told herself. *They'd made perfect sense. Regin agrees with me. We must be where we're supposed to be.*

And yet, no Traitors had appeared.

She looked to the right, where the mountains curved away to the south-east. When she and Akkarin had entered Sachaka twenty years before, they'd travelled that way. Across the slopes of the mountains with no supplies, no home and with Ichani hunting them. This time she and Regin had travelled north-west, still across the harsh mountainside, but with plenty of food, no Ichani to worry about and a Guild waiting to welcome them home.

Amazing the difference some basic necessities and not fearing for your life can make.

Still, the wasteland was a harsh place. Below, the rocky slopes plunged into dunes stretching off toward the horizon. The first day they'd waited here, they'd watched a sandstorm move across the land to the north, obscuring all in its path. They'd been worried that they would have to endure the storm, but it died out when it hit the northern mountains. Turning to the left, Sonea considered the peaks extending into the distance, each crouching behind the other, growing paler the further away they were.

Somewhere beyond them lies Sanctuary, the Traitors' home. From what Lorkin says, they were much kinder captors than King Amakira.

Not that anybody had described what Lorkin's imprisonment in the palace had been like. She was almost glad that she had not been able to read his mind through her blood gem. She swung from wanting to know to thinking perhaps it would be better if she never did. If he'd suffered, she was not sure what she would feel or want to do, but she was sure neither would be good.

He's free now. Free and alive. I must take care that nothing I do changes that.

"Sonea."

She dragged her eyes away from the view and turned to regard Regin. "Yes?"

He gestured to the bags. "Should we keep rationing?"

She nodded. He was asking more than that, she knew. He was asking if they would stay here or give up and return to the Fort soon. *We could hunt for food, like Akkarin and I did.* Memories rose of a meal gathered, cooked and eaten in a little hidden valley. She smiled as she remembered what else had happened in that place.

"At least we have plenty of water," Regin said, turning to look at the spring. "And it's clean now."

She followed his gaze. The trickle of water seeped through a crack in the rocky ground and gathered in a small, smooth pool before brimming over into a tiny stream. The water had obviously been attracting animals. When they'd arrived they'd had to wash away accumulated bird droppings. The stream did not continue for long, swallowed up by a crevasse in the rocky ground.

If we hide, maybe birds will come to drink. We can catch and eat them.

Standing up, she walked to the pool and regarded it. Clearly the wasteland had some water, but even here, right by the spring, there was no life. She crouched beside it and dipped her hand in the pool. Concentrating, she sought the scattered sense of energy within water that came from ever-present tiny life forms in it.

Nothing.

She frowned. When they'd arrived she'd checked if the water was safe to drink. Despite the bird droppings, the water had been pure. Which was . . . odd.

Perhaps a Traitor came by just before we arrived and drew all the energy out. The smaller and less sophisticated a living thing was, the weaker the natural barrier against magical interference. Even trees could be drained of magic without their bark being cut, though the magic came slowly and there was never as much as in an animal or person.

Killing the little life forms makes the existing water safe to drink, but the fresh water should quickly add more tiny life forms. She reached up to the trickle that fed the pool. Cupping her hand to collect some water, she concentrated again.

There. Like tiny pinpoints of light.

She let the gathered water drop into the pool. There could be only one explanation. Something was killing off all life once it entered the pool.

Her stomach clenched in sudden apprehension. Was the pool poisoned? They had been drinking from it for a few days. What could kill off small life forms instantly but not affect people?

The bowl was smooth. It could have been shaped by time or man or magic. Reaching into the water again, she ran her hand slowly over the surface of the stone. She did not expect to sense anything. Detecting a poison within a body was more a matter of detecting its effect. Her fingers encountered a bump in the surface. She explored it with her fingertips, then sent her mind out.

Something tugged at her senses. She drew a little magic and let it seep from her fingers. It was drawn away immediately.

Her blood went cold.

240

Sitting up, she stared at the little bump in the bowl's otherwise smooth surface. *It is not a part of the rock. If it does what I think it does, it has been placed there to clean the water. But if it does what I think it does . . .*

"Regin."

She felt the coolness of his shadow on her back.

"Yes?"

"Could you get me a knife or something good for gouging?"

"Why not use magic? Oh . . . of course. You won't want to use it up."

He moved to the packs. While he was busy, she drew magic and used it to channel the trickle of water away from the pool. Then she emptied the pool with a sweep of force. The surface began to dry immediately and by the time Regin returned the bump was visible as a darker patch in the stone.

He held out a silver pen.

"Is that all we have?"

"I'm afraid so. Nobody expects magicians to need knives."

Sonea sighed as she took the pen. "I suppose we asked for supplies to last a few days, not a picnic. Let's hope this works."

She began to dig around the bump with the tapered end of the pen. To her relief, whatever was keeping it in place was softer than stone – more like wax. Soon she had gouged out a channel around it. She wedged her fingertips around the bump and pulled. It would not budge, so she got to work again.

"Can I ask what you're doing?"

"Yes."

The lump shifted and Sonea tried to pull it free in vain. Gritting her teeth, she returned to digging waxy lumps from the pool.

"So. What *are* you doing?"

"Digging out this *thing*."

"I can see that." He sounded more amused than annoyed. "Why?"

The pen wasn't narrow enough to fit between the hard bump and the edges of the hole it was crammed into. She seized it with her fingertips again. "It's . . . strange . . . ah!" The bump — now a stone — came free. She held it up into the light, working the remains of wax off the surface.

Regin bent over to look at it. "Is it a crystal?"

She nodded. Smooth, flat areas reflected the sunlight. "A natural one. Though by that I only mean uncut."

"And otherwise unnatural?" Regin looked down at the hole it had come out of. "What sort of gemstone is it?"

"Gemstone!" Sonea exclaimed. She sucked in a breath and looked up at Regin, then climbed to her feet. "One of the Traitors' magical gemstones, most likely. I doubt the Duna come this far south, and if the Ichani know about them they'd have used them on us twenty years ago." She considered the way it had drawn in her magic, and her blood went cold again. She looked at Regin and held back the words. Could she tell him her suspicions? What if his mind was read? What if he told somebody? What if . . . ?

When — if — the Traitors arrived, she would need to have already considered all the implications of her discovery. She might not need to tell Regin, to seek his opinion, but she *wanted* to.

Regin was staring back at her, bemused and worried. She drew in a deep breath.

"It is, I suspect, a black magic gemstone," she said, keeping her voice low in case someone, somehow, was watching and listening to them.

242

He drew in a sharp breath and stared at her in horror. Then he looked down at the stone and his eyes narrowed.

"So *that's* why the wasteland never recovered."

She shivered despite the growing heat and looked around them. *It makes sense. If they can make one stone like this they can make hundreds. Thousands. Strewn across the land, they must slowly but relentlessly suck away life. The soil becomes too infertile for plants. Larger, more sophisticated living things like animals starve or move away.*

Which meant the Traitors had been deliberately keeping the wasteland a wasteland.

For centuries.

"All this time it was thought the Guild created this to keep Sachaka weak. Instead it was the Traitors."

Regin frowned. "Well . . . we can't be sure of that. They may have just put the stone here to keep the water clean."

She looked up at him. "I reckon I could find more stones, if any are about."

His gaze sharpened. "Give it a try."

Handing him the stone, which he took gingerly, she walked a few steps away and looked at the ground sloping downward toward the dunes. She closed her eyes and expanded the natural barrier around her skin until it was a globe. Where it overlapped with the rock beneath her feet, she weakened it so that magic began to seep out. Then she began to walk forward slowly.

She had only taken fifty or so paces when she felt the faintest *pull*. It was an illusion — the sense of no resistance where everywhere else there was one. Stopping, she turned and, after losing the sense a few times, managed to narrow down the area the pull was coming from to a few paces in diameter: a stone-filled crack between two sheets of stone.

Regin joined her as she poked around inside the crack. She began sweeping her barrier down the length of the gap, but before she had gone far Regin gave a little crow of triumph and held something up.

Another dark, glossy crystal. Taking it from him she tested it. The magic she sent toward it was drawn into the stone.

"Twice is coincidence," Regin said. "Thrice is . . ."

Nodding, she set off in another direction. This time she found a stone easily, buried in a sand-filled depression. *All in sheltered positions where water might collect or flow through. Nooks and cracks where life might take root.* They returned to the meeting place. She had undone her diversion of the spring, and the pool was full again. Dipping her hand in the water, she confirmed that it was now full of tiny specks of energy.

She looked up at Regin.

"Osen needs to know about this."

He smiled crookedly. "Oh, he most certainly does."

And Lorkin, she thought. *Though he may know already. Ah. If he's not supposed to know, I may endanger his life by telling him. It may not be wise to let the Traitors know we've discovered their dirty little secret, either.*

Still, once the Guild knew, the Traitors would gain nothing from killing her and Regin. Taking Osen's ring from her pocket, she sat down, leaned against a boulder and slipped it on her finger.

—*Osen.*

—*Sonea!*

—*Do you have a moment? You won't want to believe what I've just discovered.*

PART TWO

CHAPTER 16

PLANS AND NEGOTIATIONS

C ery sighed. "Let's run through this again."

"We arrange for Skellin to learn we're living under the Guild," Gol said. "Not being protected by magicians."

"Even if he knows the Guild isn't aware that we're down here, he'll suspect Lilia does," Anyi continued. "We have to make Skellin think Lilia isn't always with us, and let him find out her routine so he'll know when she's not protecting us."

"He'll send others first, to check whether it's true, or to capture me," Cery repeated. "So we've got to set things up so that only a magician can get through to us. Like a magical barrier created by Lilia."

"But won't that make him suspect Lilia is down here?" Anyi asked.

"He's a magician," Cery answered. "He knows a magician can set up a barrier, then go somewhere else."

"Still, it might put him off going any further," Anyi pointed out.

"We put the barrier close enough to us so he can hear us, or see light ahead, making him think he only has to go a little further to find us."

"Him or Lorandra," Gol said. "If he sends Lorandra we spring the trap anyway. At least the Guild will catch one of them, and they could use her as bait in another trap."

"Yes, if they don't let her escape again." Cery smiled wryly.

"Once he breaks through the barrier he'll want to act fast," Anyi continued, "because Lilia will know her barrier has been broken. If he's close enough to see or hear us, we won't have much warning."

"We could put a lamp around the next corner, so it looks like we're close, but we're actually further away," Gol suggested. "And a few more lamps, so it looks like we put them there for our own use."

"Which means getting more lamps and more oil. More stuff for Lilia to bring." Anyi sighed.

"What if Skellin brings others with him?" Gol asked.

Cery considered. "So long as they stick together, they don't matter."

Gol frowned. "But will they? If I were Skellin, I'd send them ahead to look for traps once I got past the barrier."

"Let them find us." Cery shrugged. "They'll either go back to tell Skellin, or wait for him to catch up and give them orders."

"Then, when he does, we spring our trap," Gol said.

Cery nodded. He and Gol hadn't told Anyi their plans to reveal Skellin to the Guild using non-magical means. Cery wasn't entirely sure he understood what the bodyguard had described. It was a method used in mines, that could cause a collapse big enough to open up a hole in the Guild gardens. Gol was confident it would work. Skellin and his men would be either buried or exposed to any magicians who happened to be about.

There was, however, a considerable danger that Cery, Gol

and Anyi would be buried, too. Cery had told Anyi that if Skellin found them before the Guild agreed to the trap, she should run and fetch Lilia. She'd been reluctant to agree, until he'd pointed out that there would be nothing to be gained by her staying. At least if she left, there would be a chance Lilia might arrive in time to stop Skellin.

"I doubt Skellin will be captured by the Guild without a fight," Cery said. "I'd rather not be buried alive. We should get Lilia to strengthen the rooms, too."

Anyi nodded. "She's got plenty of magic right now. Kallen's been teaching her how to use black magic to take and store power."

Cery looked at her and frowned. "He has? That's . . . worrying."

"Why?" Anyi shrugged. "The Guild is supposed to have two black magicians so that one can stop the other . . . Oh, I see." Her eyes widened and she looked at Cery. "You don't think . . . but Kallen's the one teaching her. He wouldn't, if he was planning to do something."

"Who else can teach her?" Cery asked. "Sonea is in Sachaka."

"If Kallen is planning to abuse his power then he may neglect to teach her right," Gol said.

"Hmm." Anyi scowled. "Well, we all know why he might become unreliable. I never thought I'd say it, but I'll be happier when I know the Guild is growing roet."

Cery nodded in agreement, then lifted the lamp and got to his feet. "Now that we've got our plan straight, we need to make sure it'll work down here."

"We should make sure we have an escape route or two in case it goes wrong," Gol added. "Perhaps put a few traps in place in case we're followed."

"We need to practise fighting," Anyi added. She looked at Cery. "All of us."

Cery sighed. She was right, but his body ached just thinking about it. "When we've sorted this out," he said. "There's no point trying to fight magic with knives."

She made a huffing noise. "But it'll be pretty humiliating if we can't deal with Skellin's thugs."

Gol looked at Cery, then turned to Anyi. "Reckon I'm ready for a bit of practice," he said. "If we start slow."

Anyi gave him a considering look, then nodded. "All right then. Later on."

"For now, let's have another look at the passages around here. Anyi, check the escape routes and make sure Skellin can't circle around and approach us from behind. Gol and I will decide where Lilia's barrier should go."

Dannyl frowned as a shadow moved into his office doorway and hovered. He looked up, expecting a slave had come to ask if he wanted food or drink, or to announce the arrival of a visitor. Instead, it was Merria.

"Lady Merria," he said, "what's wrong?"

She shook her head. "Nothing. Silly, isn't it?" Her mouth pulled into a lopsided smile. "Lorkin is safe and everything's back to normal. I should be grateful for that, but all I am is bored."

"This isn't normal," Dannyl told her. "We should be dealing with visitors or invitations. Even Tayend is being ignored now."

Merria looked down. "Actually, I did get an invitation to visit my friends yesterday," she confessed.

Dannyl made himself smile. "That's a good sign." *All I need is for Tayend to come in here and tell us he's off to a dinner or party, and Achati to be the only Ashaki not treating me like an outcast, and everything* will *be back to normal.* But he suspected nothing would ever be the same again between himself and Achati.

Merria looked down at his desk. "Did you finish your notes?"

He followed her gaze to the sheets of paper, and nodded. "Yes. The slaves were finally able to buy more ink yesterday."

"That's good, isn't it?" She paused. "What's wrong?"

He looked up, then realised he'd been scowling. "Ah . . . well, I made two copies so I could send one to the Guild, but I haven't found a safe way to get it there."

She hummed in sympathy. "I wouldn't be trusting them to any ordinary courier. How do you usually get messages to the Guild?"

"With Osen's blood ring."

"You never send anything else?"

Dannyl shook his head. "There are a few traders who travel between Sachaka and Elyne or Kyralia a couple of times each year, and they carry goods for us. Nothing important, though. Just luxury goods. Spices. Raka."

She frowned as she considered the problem. "So . . . you need to rewrite the whole thing in a code, and then send lots of copies via different couriers to Osen to ensure he gets at least one. Then give Osen the key to the code via his blood ring."

He gazed at her in admiration. *Such a simple solution. Why didn't I think of that?* Well, he'd already used a kind of code to hide the more sensitive information.

"Of course, that won't help if you need to get it to Osen quickly," she added.

"Slowly is better than not at all." He drummed his fingers on the table. "So who will I arrange to carry it?" he pondered, more to voice the thought than to ask Merria.

"I reckon my friends might know a few traders going east."

"Could you ask them for me?"

She nodded. "I will. But . . . do you think there's any chance the Ashaki might be about to attack the Traitors? Or the Traitors attack the Ashaki?"

Dannyl blinked at the sudden change of subject. "Why? Have you heard rumours?"

"Not anything specific. But my friends often discuss the possibility, and King Amakira was so determined to get information out of Lorkin."

A chill entered Dannyl's veins. *And Lorkin may have given him that information.* "I don't know."

"It'll be ironic if the Traitors do attack and defeat the Ashaki. All the king's efforts and Lorkin refusing to speak will have been for nothing, because then it won't matter if Sanctuary's location has been revealed."

Dannyl shook his head. "They won't attack. It would be too big a risk. What if they failed? They'd lose everything."

Merria nodded. "You're right, of course. Anyway, I guess you're going to be making more copies of your notes now. Let me know if you'd like some help. I'll take one to my friends tomorrow, if you have it ready."

"Thank you."

As she left, her words repeated in Dannyl's mind: "*. . . then it won't matter if Sanctuary's location has been revealed*". Was this the reason Lorkin had given in and told the king what he wanted to know? *But that would mean . . .*

Shivering, Dannyl drew out the two notebooks that contained his research, and a blank one, and began to make yet another copy.

* * *

252

Regin noticed the approaching Traitors first. From their vantage point, he and Sonea watched as the small group walked across the dunes and up into the rocky hills, their shadows growing longer as the afternoon sun descended. The cool shadow of the mountains rose to meet them, and after they entered it and dusk settled over the land, the figures slowly grew harder to make out. Soon small points of light were glimpsed, low to the ground and moving ever closer. When sounds finally heralded the approach of the strangers, Sonea let Osen know they were about to arrive, then rose, ready to greet them.

The first was a woman who moved with the dignity and tension of a leader, which made her seem taller despite being close to Sonea in height. Her facial features were so Sachakan that, for a brief moment, Sonea's blood turned cold. She had the same broad forehead, high cheekbones, and upward tilting eyes of the Ichani who had invaded Kyralia. But those men, and the sole woman among them, had been heavier in build. The Traitors were smaller and more graceful.

If she had guessed right, the first woman was Savara, the queen. The woman was dressed no differently to the rest of the group. All twelve carried a pack and wore simple clothing. *Eight women and four men.* Sonea's eyes snapped to the tallest of the men and her heart leapt. *Lorkin!*

He smiled as she saw him. She resisted the urge to run forward and hug him, worried that any moves in the Traitors' direction might make them react defensively. And Lorkin might not appreciate her being overly affectionate in front of these people.

So she restrained herself and settled for looking him over closely. *He looks healthy, though tired.* The way he looked at the woman walking beside him, then back to Sonea, made it clear that this was Tyvara, the Traitor who had saved his life. The woman he had agreed to be locked away in Sanctuary for.

She is very attractive, Sonea thought. The young woman returned Sonea's gaze with curiosity and a hint of calculation. *No doubt she's measuring me up as much as I'm appraising her.* That wasn't all that Sonea detected in her manner, however. It wasn't exactly confidence. More a grim determination. *That girl has seen far more than any Kyralian woman her age. I would wager she has experienced more as well. But then, she was posing as a slave when she saved Lorkin, and that would mean enduring a lot of pain and humiliation.*

Sonea looked away from Tyvara back to the leader, who slowed as she took the last steps to meet Sonea and Regin. As she stopped, the others came to a halt behind her.

"Black Magician Sonea?" she asked, smiling at Sonea.

Sonea nodded. "Yes."

"I am Savara, queen of the Traitors." She turned to introduce the rest of the group. None had titles. *Well, Lorkin did say they treat everyone equally – on the surface at least.* "You do not need to be introduced to your son, of course," Savara finished. "It is my pleasure to reunite you, and to finally meet you."

"And you, your majesty," Sonea replied. She gestured to Regin. "This is Lord Regin, my assistant."

Regin inclined his head. "An honour to meet you, Queen Savara, and your people." He placed a hand over his heart. Savara's eyebrows twitched upward, then she inclined her head gracefully.

"Let's sit." She gestured to the flat ground beside the spring. "We have walked far and need to rest, eat and drink."

She turned and nodded to the others, some of whom moved

past her toward the spring. Sonea silently thanked Regin, who had thought to replace the gemstone in the pool. Osen had suggested she keep her knowledge of the gems to herself unless there was an advantage to be gained.

The group began to shrug off packs. They formed a circle, leaving a gap for Sonea and Regin. Lorkin sat down beside Sonea, and Tyvara settled on his other side. Someone created a small globe light and set it glowing in the middle, just above the ground. Food was brought out and placed in the centre. It consisted of simple fare for travelling: hard, flat bread, dried meats and fruit, nuts and pastes for the bread.

Sonea took out the remains of her and Regin's own supplies – pachi fruit, grains and dried beans to be boiled in water, spices, sumi and hard sweets – and offered them. They were taken without any thanks spoken, but with appreciative nods and smiles. She was intrigued to see one of the men place a metal disk with a gemstone embedded in the centre on a flat rock, touch the stone, then place a wide pan full of water on top. Soon the water was boiling and he was adding the grain and beans. *Clearly men aren't forbidden to use magic. That makes their law against men learning magic not as restrictive as it first seems, though they still rely on the women making the stones. I wonder if they have to get permission to use them.*

One of the Traitors was examining the pouch of sumi leaves with puzzlement.

"They're for a hot drink," Sonea explained. "I'll prepare some later."

"Like raka?" one of them asked.

Sonea shook her head. "Same idea, different plant." The supplies provided at the Fort hadn't included raka.

"We have raka."

She straightened. "You do?"

Savara chuckled. "It is a good drink to have while talking. Or negotiating."

The food was passed around, each person taking a portion. Sonea added spices to the beans and grains when they were ready. The Traitors were particularly fond of the sweets. Savara prepared a pot of raka and surprisingly small cups were passed to her for filling. Sonea's own mug returned barely half full, but as she sipped she realised why. The raka was so strong it was syrupy, and after a few sips she felt as if her ears were buzzing.

As each Traitor received their cup they rose and moved away, until only Savara remained. It was full night now, and more globe lights appeared as those who had left gathered in smaller groups several paces away. Savara moved closer, so that they formed a smaller circle.

"We arrived later than we hoped, and you must be anxious to return to Kyralia, so let us begin without delay." She looked at Lorkin. "It was the wish of our late queen, Zarala, that Lorkin act as negotiator today. Are you in agreement on this?"

Sonea looked at her son, who appeared to be holding back a grin. "Yes, your majesty. I carry the blood ring of Lord Osen, Administrator of the Guild. Do you object to me wearing it?"

"No." Savara looked at Lorkin. "Begin, Lord Lorkin."

Sonea slipped Osen's ring on.

—*Osen?*

—*Sonea.*

—*We're about to begin negotiations.*

Lorkin drew in a deep breath. "Queen Zarala asked me to arrange a meeting between the Traitors and the Allied Lands in the hope of negotiating an alliance."

Sonea nodded. "What kind of alliance are we discussing? Are the Traitors seeking to join the Allied Lands? That requires compliance with an agreed core of rules that apply to all and with a few specific to each land."

"What are these core rules?" Savara asked.

"Non-aggression toward other lands in the alliance. Adherence to a set of laws regarding trade, crime and magic. Military support in defence of the Allied Lands. Outlawing slavery."

"The first and last we agree with wholeheartedly." Savara's lips thinned. "What are the laws you speak of?"

Sonea listed them, with Osen's assistance. Savara listened, nodding from time to time. When Sonea finished, the queen laced her fingers together.

"Some of these laws are similar to our own, some are not. It is your control of magicians my people may object to. Especially your restrictions on the knowledge and use of higher magic."

"You have restrictions that we would not agree with as well. I believe magic is only taught to women Traitors, unless the man is a natural."

"Yes, but restrictions based on gender are already catered for in the alliance. The Lonmar people only teach magic to men. If the alliance can accommodate their traditions, could it not accommodate ours?"

"It is likely it could. Black magic, on the other hand, is a more difficult issue."

Savara smiled and gestured toward Sonea. "Yet the Guild has black magicians."

"Only as many as we feel are necessary for our defence."

The queen's expression became serious. "Do you really think three is enough?"

Sonea met and held the woman's eyes. This was no time to be admitting to doubts.

"Yes."

Savara's eyebrows rose. "I hope that a situation never arises to test that. My people are not so willing to put their safety in the hands of a few. We will not agree to an alliance that requires us to stop teaching our daughters higher magic."

"We expected that." Sonea smiled as the queen's gaze sharpened. "We are willing to negotiate an exception in the case of Traitors, with conditions."

"What are these conditions?"

"You have not objected to our law that all magicians be trained at the Guild," Sonea observed.

"No." Savara looked amused. "It would be an opportunity we'd be foolish to turn down."

"The condition is this: your magicians must not be taught black magic until they have graduated, and the teaching of it must be done by Traitors, in Sachaka."

A small line appeared between Savara's brows. She nodded slowly.

"That might be acceptable."

"Of course, if King Amakira learns of an agreement between us he will cause us both trouble. He will try to stop your novices reaching us."

Savara waved a hand dismissively. "Oh, that won't be a problem."

"Once they're in Kyralia it will be harder to conceal what is happening. We could disguise them as Elynes."

"That won't be necessary."

—*She seems a little too confident about that*, Osen noted.

—*Indeed.*

"Perhaps you believe that King Amakira, not knowing where Sanctuary is, is no threat to you, but if you want the young women you send to us for training to be safe you had best remember that he *does* know where Imardin is," Sonea warned.

Savara smiled. "There will be no need for secrecy. By the time we are ready to send magicians to the Guild, if we decide to do so, King Amakira and the Ashaki will be a problem long resolved."

Sonea heard Regin draw in a quick breath. She found herself staring at the queen. A thrill ran through her, followed by a stab of fear.

—*They mean to attack the Ashaki!* Osen exclaimed.

Savara leaned forward. "You said an alliance included military support in *defence* of the Allied Lands. I am guessing that offensive military support is a different matter. Even so, you are old enemies of the Sachakan Empire. Therefore I invite the Allied Lands to join us in ridding Sachaka of the Ashaki and slavery. You may not be able to offer many fighters, since so few of you learn higher magic, but your strength and Healing assistance would be invaluable." She leaned back again. "Will you help us?"

CHAPTER 17

AN ADMISSION

Lorkin watched his mother closely. Though her gaze was still on Savara, it did not quite focus on the queen, but somewhere beyond. He looked down at the ring on her finger. She was communicating with Osen. He noticed another ring that he'd not seen before. It, too, held a gemstone but the setting was decorative, suggesting it was mere jewellery.

"We need time to discuss it," she said. "There are a lot of monarchs to contact."

Savara nodded. "You have until tomorrow night. I'd give you longer, but my people are vulnerable when outside Sanctuary. I know I am behaving as if we cannot lose, but there is no point discussing a future relationship based on the current situation."

"Is there no chance of a future relationship if you lose?"

The queen's expression became grim. "Perhaps a slim one. If we lose it would be likely the Ashaki will find out where Sanctuary is. Without Sanctuary we have no food, shelter and, temporarily, no gemstone-growing caves. We will be more concerned with our survival and recovery than an alliance with the Allied Lands."

Sonea was frowning. "That would put the caves in the Ashaki's hands. Could they begin to grow their own stones?"

"They might discover on their own, in time. It is more likely they would force a captive Traitor to teach them, though they couldn't gain all our knowledge from one or even a handful of Traitors. We have avoided teaching individual stone-makers how to make every kind of stone, instead of spreading the knowledge among many. How dangerous the Ashaki would become would depend on which Traitor or Traitors they captured."

As the two women fell into a thoughtful silence, Lorkin cleared his throat.

"Whether the Traitors win or lose, an exchange of knowledge between them and the Guild would still be beneficial."

Savara turned to look at him, her expression apologetic. "But that exchange has already been made."

"It has and it hasn't." Lorkin shrugged. "As with stone-making, Healing knowledge is too broad to be communicated in a short mind-read. Though you will work out more in time, you will make mistakes along the way. Like stone-making, mistakes can be dangerous. Better to be trained by those already skilled in the art."

His mother was frowning. "They already know Healing?" she asked him.

Savara sighed. "Yes. One of our people disobeyed our law and stole it from Lorkin's mind. She has been punished, and to compensate Lorkin, Queen Zarala decreed that he be taught stone-making."

Lorkin watched his mother closely. A range of expressions crossed her face: shock, anger and gratitude. She gave him a thoughtful look. He concentrated on her presence, wondering if he could pick up surface thoughts again. A faint, distant feeling of pride touched his senses, but he could have been imagining it. At least it wasn't disapproval or disappointment. *Yet. She doesn't know what stone-making involves.*

"So . . ." Sonea said. "One of your people already knows the basics of how Healing works, and one of mine has about the same level of stone-making knowledge. But as Lorkin says, that does not measure up to full training from a teacher with many years of skill and experience. We do still have something worth trading."

"Except . . ." Lorkin interrupted. She turned to regard him, her face calm. "They are not of equal value."

Savara's eyebrows rose slightly. "Which is of greater value?"

"Healing," Lorkin replied.

"Why is that?"

"You need nothing more than knowledge and magic to be a Healer," Lorkin told her. "Stone-making magicians require stone-producing caves."

"What are they, exactly?" his mother asked.

"Caves where the crystalline stones form naturally. Magical gemstones are trained as they grow. I've never heard of any caves like these in the Allied Lands." He spread his hands. "Not that I've been looking for them. It may be that we'll find them if we search. But until we do have our own caves, we cannot apply stone-making knowledge."

"Alchemists may find another way to make them," Regin pointed out. "They already make some kinds of crystals. Perhaps stone-making magic can be applied to those."

Savara's eyes brightened with interest. "Do they really?" Then her lips quirked into a crooked smile. "Ah, but there is another catch. You will have to relax your rules regarding higher magic, since it is needed in stone-making. Your current black magicians may not be suited to the task, either. It demands a level of concentration and patience that not everyone can manage, which will also consume more of your defenders' attention than is wise — and you will only be able to make a handful of stones a year."

Lorkin caught his breath as his mother turned to stare at him. Guilt and fear rose, but he forced himself to meet her gaze levelly. Her eyes flickered back to Savara, then her face went still, her feelings hidden behind a false calm.

"I see," she said. "That does make the exchange a little . . . more costly to us than for you."

Lord Regin had turned to regard Lorkin as well, but his gaze lingered. His eyes were narrowed, but his expression was more thoughtful than disapproving. Lorkin felt a perverse annoyance at the lack of surprise in the man's demeanour.

"Perhaps, then, we could exchange Healing for stones," Savara suggested. "Your Healers could work for us and the Guild would receive stones in payment."

Extending his senses, Lorkin tried again to hear his mother's surface thoughts. What he picked up seemed too out of character, however. He must be imagining it. Though . . . it was also odd that he would imagine his mother thinking such a string of curse words.

"They will be safe," Savara said in reply to whatever had been asked while he was distracted. "The individual who attacked Lorkin did so out of a desire to bring Healing to my people that many sympathise with. But few would use illegal means to achieve it. Hiring Healers to work for us is another way to do so. Did Lorkin tell you of the promise Lord Akkarin made?"

"Yes. Akkarin never told me of it."

"There was much that was concealed in that agreement. Queen Zarala also made a promise that she did not fulfil, though she worked towards doing so all her life."

Lorkin looked at Savara, remembering the former queen referring to such a promise. *"I was never able to uphold one thing I agreed to. Like him, the situation at home was more difficult to overcome than I'd hoped."*

"What was that?" his mother asked.

Savara's expression was serious as she answered. "To do what the Guild failed to do seven centuries ago: destroy the Ashaki and end slavery in Sachaka."

As Tayend entered the Master's Room, Dannyl frowned. "Achati may wish to speak to me alone."

"Too bad. Like it or not, the king's actions have a bearing on Sachakan relations with all Allied Lands," the Elyne said. *"Ambassador,"* he added, to made it clear he considered this something he had the right to do.

Dannyl sighed. "Of course." But his resistance was mostly habit. In truth, he was grateful for Tayend's company. Having a common cause, working together, and Tayend's approval of Achati had changed something. They were no longer at odds. The resentment at their parting was gone, or at least a thing of the past. He felt as if he could call Tayend a friend now and it wouldn't be an insult.

Having Tayend there would keep the meeting formal, too, which might make it easier to ignore his more personal feelings toward Achati. *Like betrayal.*

Yet we know Achati got Lorkin out of Arvice, he reminded himself.

"Lorkin is with Sonea," Dannyl murmured. "I was communicating with Osen when Kai reported Achati's arrival."

Tayend's eyebrows rose. "Good news."

At a sound from the corridor, they turned to face the visitor. Tav, the door slave, arrived first and threw himself on the floor. Achati walked in after him, smiling.

"Welcome Ashaki Achati," Dannyl said. "As always, you seem immune to the disfavour that association with the Guild House seems to engender."

Achati spread his hands. "An advantage of my position, Ambassador Dannyl." He nodded to Tayend. "Ambassador Tayend. It is good to visit the Guild House in more pleasant circumstances than the last time."

"If you mean in the company of the king's spies, then I'd say the circumstances are likely to be much the same."

Achati nodded sympathetically. "The king has far fewer scruples about such things than you expected."

"It is generally good manners to at least *pretend* you aren't spying on others. Even when it's obvious you do so."

Achati shook his head. "Really? Kyralians do have odd ideas about manners. But this is not what I came to talk to you about."

Dannyl crossed his arms. "And that is?"

"I came to explain why I told the king of my part in Lorkin's escape."

"I think we have guessed," Tayend told him. "You saw an opportunity to gain information from Lorkin."

Achati nodded. "One that did not involve abduction, imprisonment, or worse. I took a risk that he would not keep to his word, however. The king thought it reckless, but was eventually persuaded that it was the best course of action." He took a few steps closer. "You do understand that anything I do against the king's wishes would eventually be discovered."

Dannyl nodded. "Next time you wore his blood ring."

"Yes. Initiative is a tricky issue for a king. When does it end and disobedience begin? There's always the danger that knowing what the king needs is interpreted as presuming what the king wants."

"Did the king get what he wanted?"

Achati's shoulder's lifted. "No. He got what he needed. Not everything Lorkin knew, but enough."

"Lorkin betrayed the Traitors?" Tayend shook his head in disbelief.

"He didn't think he had, I suspect." Achati's smile was thin. "He thought he had tricked us, but he told us a lot more than he realised."

"What did he say?" Dannyl did not expect the Ashaki to answer. If the information was so important that the king had let Lorkin go . . .

"He told us where the Traitor home is, just as he said he would."

Tayend narrowed his eyes. "He said something vague, like 'in the mountains'?"

"No. He said 'Sachaka'."

Achati watched expectantly as Tayend turned to frown at Dannyl. Returning the Elyne's gaze, Dannyl nodded in understanding.

"He revealed that the Traitors consider the whole country their rightful home," he explained. "Which means their hope isn't to remain hidden or become a separate people." He turned to regard Achati. "Their hope is to, one day, rule Sachaka."

"Ah," Tayend said. "But that might not happen for years. And they may not win."

"They won't win," Achati said firmly. "There can't be as many of them living in the mountains as there are Sachakans in the lowlands. We are, by far, the greater force. Which is why their usual means of meddling in our affairs is through spying and assassination." His expression became serious. "And that is why we have our own spies everywhere, including the Guild House – though we did not have many here before Lorkin's abduction because we didn't think the Traitors would be interested in Kyralians."

Dannyl frowned at the open admission of spies in the Guild House.

"They are here for your safety," Achati assured him. "Lorkin was a different matter, of course, but that's over now. The king does not wish you harm. He does want good relations between the Allied Lands and Sachaka. As do I, since I enjoy your company." He looked from Dannyl to Tayend, to indicate he included both of them. "I consider you both my friends."

Tayend looked at Dannyl. His eyebrows rose slightly, then lowered as he smiled. There was a hint of mischief in his gaze. He turned back to Achati.

"Well then," he said. "Would you like to stay for an evening drink? I don't know about Dannyl, but I'd like to know more about your plans to thwart a Traitor uprising."

Surprised, Dannyl could only nod to show he approved of the idea. What was Tayend up to? Was he gathering information, or planning to look for holes in Achati's story, or test his declaration of friendship?

Though Dannyl knew he ought to do the same, he had to admit his heart was not in it. *It was easier when I didn't need to trust Achati.* Though he had to admit it only made Dannyl admire Achati more, knowing that he had deftly steered everyone – Lorkin, Dannyl and Tayend, and the Sachakan king – to a solution that satisfied, if not pleased, them all.

Architecture was a subject that all novices learned, though most only received a basic training. Lilia had always thought it was a grand term for what was mostly a menial task for magicians. Few magicians designed buildings, and since the Ichani Invasion the popularity of buildings that relied on magic to stay up had diminished. Most magicians only used what they learned in architecture classes to safely fix structures or speed the construction of new ones.

Both kinds of work required an understanding of non-magical construction techniques. There was no point lifting wall and roof materials into place only to have them crashing down for lack of basic structural knowledge. A magician might also have to deal with a collapsing building, and need to know how best to support it.

Lilia was willing to bet that it had been a long time since any magician had worked on secret underground rooms. The walls Cery wanted her to strengthen were brick, not stone. Even without a layer of mortar between them, they wouldn't bind together like stone did. They didn't have the same property that allowed stone to be suffused with magic, either. Magic slowly leaked out of stone; whereas it dissipated quickly in bricks. Her only choice was to create a barrier at the surface of the bricks to support them.

Drawing magic, she created a dome of force, expanded it until it met the walls, then shaped it to fit the corners. She opened holes for the original door and for the newer hole she'd smashed through to the next room.

"Like the shield blocking the passage, I'll have to hold this in place constantly," she said. "It won't be too hard if I stay close by. It's strong enough to stop a collapse, but it won't hold against a magical attack. If there's pressure on it from above or an attack from below I should sense it." She sighed and shook her head. "Just as well Kallen's been teaching me how to draw power, and I haven't been using it up in fighting practice. This is going to sap some of my strength."

Cery nodded. "Thanks. Again."

His gratitude only made her stomach twist with anxiety.

"You're obviously worried that Skellin might find his way in here before the Guild are ready to help."

"Yes. If Skellin finds us before we're ready to spring the trap, and doesn't want to risk that you or other magicians are close by, he might collapse the roof on us and slip away."

She imagined Anyi suffocating under bricks and dirt, and shuddered. It would not be easy to sleep, knowing that her friends might die if she didn't sense an attack on the barrier.

"If I feel anything happen to the barriers I'll come as quickly as I can," she said.

Cery nodded. "If there are any other signs someone has entered the passages Anyi will go to your room to fetch you. Or get Jonna to. How often is Jonna there?"

"A few times a day. Should I ask her to visit more often?"

"That might be a good idea."

Lilia nodded. "Is there anything else?"

"That's everything." Cery looked at Gol and Anyi, who nodded.

"Then I had better go back," Lilia told them. "I have some studying to do."

"I'll come with you as far as the room," Anyi said.

"Don't distract her too long," Cery told his daughter. The corner of his mouth lifted slightly.

Anyi rolled her eyes as she turned away. Beckoning to Lilia, she led the way toward the Magicians' Quarters.

"Sometimes I wish he didn't know about us," she muttered.

"It's nice that he doesn't mind, though," Lilia reminded her.

"Yeah." Anyi shrugged and smiled reluctantly.

"So why'd you want me to leave earlier tonight?"

Anyi glanced behind. "I'll tell you when we get there."

As always, the climb up the wall to the panel behind Sonea's guest room was uncomfortable in the confined space. Lilia went up first, then lifted up the now-empty lacquer box she always brought food in with magic. Anyi came up after it. They dusted off their clothes.

"My poor old coat," Anyi said, examining the scratches in the leather.

Lilia looked down at herself. "I had better get changed." She took a step toward her room.

A knock came from the door. They exchanged looks of dismay.

"Not Jonna," Lilia said. "She doesn't knock like that."

"Get into your robes," Anyi said. "I'll delay them."

Lilia hurried into her room and stumbled into her robes. It seemed the faster she tried to put them on, the more tangled she got. She could hear voices from the guest room, but Anyi didn't sound alarmed.

At last she was dressed. Opening the door, she looked out and sighed with relief.

"Lord Rothen," she said, bowing to the elderly magician.

A strange, uncomfortable look crossed Anyi's face as she realised she'd forgotten the gesture of respect, and she quickly bent in an awkward bow. Rothen looked amused.

"I came by to see how you are, Lilia," he said. "I've come past on other nights but you've been out."

"Oh. Sorry." Lilia spread her hands.

"I have a hunch I know where you've been, but you can trust me to keep your secret. Sonea told me of Cery's visits." He smiled at Anyi, then turned back and his expression became serious. "So how are you?"

"Um . . ." Lilia gestured at a chair. "Why don't you sit? Can I get you some sumi?"

"Yes, thank you." As he sat down Anyi settled into one of the other seats.

"I'm . . . fine," Lilia told him as she lifted the sumi-making set with magic and moved it to the table, then, as an after-thought, brought over the raka powder. She sat down and set to making the brew. "You know that Cery is in hiding?"

Rothen nodded. "Kallen told us as much."

"*Us*", Lilia thought. *I suppose that means the rest of the Higher Magicians.*

"Well . . . I worry about him." She handed Rothen a steaming cup. "And Anyi." *And Gol, but he may not even know about Gol.*

"That's understandable." Rothen was frowning now. He looked at Anyi. "Is he safe?"

Anyi shrugged. "For now, but how long we can remain undetected . . ." She shook her head. "They could find us tonight, or never find us at all."

Lilia handed her a cup of raka, grimacing at the strong smell of it, and poured some sumi for Rothen.

271

"Well, if there's anything we can do to help keep you hidden, let me know," Rothen said.

Anyi hesitated, then nodded. "Thanks."

The old magician sipped his sumi and turned back to Lilia. "How are your studies?"

It was her turn to hesitate. Should she be honest, or try to delay the inevitable?

Rothen chuckled. "Looks like you are aware of how badly you're failing to keep up. I'm also here to tell you that we've decided that you can drop a few classes for now. You will have more time to finish them – possibly graduate half a year later. Kallen's lessons have added to your workload, and you had much to catch up on from your months of absence. It is better that you learn well, than learn within the allotted time."

At first Lilia only felt relieved. *But it'll be another half-year until graduation.* That made her feel disappointed and tired. Still, less study meant more time with Anyi. She nodded slowly. "Thank you."

Rothen smiled again. "Remember, you can talk to me any time. Even when Sonea is here. I'll do whatever I can to help you."

She nodded. "Thank you, Lord Rothen."

They fell silent, each sipping at their respective hot drinks. Lilia asked if he'd heard from Sonea. He told her that Sonea and Lorkin had been reunited. *Well, that's good. She'll be home soon.*

When they'd finished the drinks, Rothen rose and excused himself. Lilia rose to see him out. After he'd left, Lilia turned to see Anyi sitting with her head in her hands.

"What's wrong?"

Anyi sighed. Dark shadows lay under her eyes as she looked up. "Could you ask Kallen if the Guild will hide Cery here?

We've always assumed they would, but avoided it because . . . well, just out of pride. It's crazy. I should try to talk Cery into coming up here."

"I can ask him tomorrow – unless you want me to tonight."

Anyi shook her head. "Tomorrow if fine. Talking Cery into it will take time."

"What do you fear? That Skellin will come before the Guild are ready to help?"

Anyi frowned. "That Cery will do something stupid. This trap he's setting up . . . I'm not sure if he's planning to wait for Kallen or not."

"He doesn't think, now that Kallen's teaching me to strengthen myself, that I'm strong enough to fight Skellin on my own, does he?"

"No, he didn't know about that until tonight. He started the preparations before then."

Lilia felt a pang of sympathy. If Anyi, who was frustrated by being stuck underground, was concerned that her father was being impatient, then things had to be getting bad down there.

She reached out and drew Anyi into her arms. "I'll talk to him. I'll talk the Guild into it. You talk Cery into it. And if either or both of them won't be sensible, then we'll just have to find a way to trick them into it."

CHAPTER 18

CHOICES

The night sky was clear and the moon bright overhead. Cery breathed a sigh of relief. Though the moonlight made it more likely someone would see them, it also made it easier for them to move about in the forest. Neither he, Gol nor Anyi were used to getting around among trees and vegetation.

Though Lilia was able to supply them with most of what they needed, thanks to Jonna, a few items were beyond her. They'd been back to the farm twice already for more chairs, sacking and straw for making mattresses. Tonight they were after some other practical items.

"A bucket or tub, and more sacks. Nothing else?" Anyi asked.

"No," Cery told her. "Don't go looking for more things to take just 'cause you're there.

"Of course not."

As she slipped away into the forest, he turned to Gol. "Be careful. Don't try to do anything else."

Gol nodded. Cery watched as his friend stumbled off into the trees in the other direction, then cringed as the snap of a branch echoed through the forest. *If Anyi hears him . . . well,*

274

he can give her the story I'm going to tell her when she gets back and finds him missing: that he's looking for the best way to lose pursuit if we ever have to escape this way.

Retreating into the hole, Cery picked up his lamp and headed back down the tunnel. Anyi had insisted that only one of them needed to risk sneaking into the farm. He'd agreed, but only because he wanted to check on the Guild's experiments with roet.

Unless they've moved them after Lilia told them she knew about it.

He found the overhanging roots and pushed them aside. Entering the tunnel, he quietened his steps as he neared the secret cellar door. Everything looked exactly as they'd left it. He bent to the spy hole and saw only darkness. For a moment he could not shake off the idea that there was a dark cloth now covering the spy hole, making it look as if the room was unlit, and there were magicians waiting beyond. Pressing his ear to the door, he listened for some time. All was quiet.

He closed the shutter of the lamp until only a little edge of light spilled out. Slowly he eased the door open. Musty air greeted him, and the sound he made echoed in the room beyond. He opened the shutter of the lamp. Light spilled into an unoccupied room. The same tables stood in the same places as before. He stepped inside and moved over to them. They were covered in small containers. Less than half as many as before, he noted. A pile of broken pots and soil had been swept into a pile to one side. Some of the pots looked burnt. Looking closer, he saw that the ones on the table were seared on one side – and so was the table. He frowned and moved closer. The pots contained only dirt.

Or do they . . . ? He leaned closer. Tiny shoots were emerging from the soil.

Cery smiled. *Grow fast, little plants*, he thought. Then he shook his head. *Never thought I'd think that about roet.*

Moving back to the secret entrance, he re-entered the passage and closed the door behind him. He headed back toward the main network of passages, but instead of returning to the room they were now living in, he checked that the passage to the Thieves' Road was still blocked by Lilia's shield. It was.

By the time he got back to their new room, enough time had passed for Anyi to have returned before him. But she wasn't there. He sat down to wait for her. Soon he felt anxiety rising. It was difficult to judge the passing of time here. Too easy to imagine that hours had passed. Too easy to imagine that something had happened to his daughter.

At least, if she's discovered, it'll probably be by farm servants or magicians. Neither will harm her.

An old memory rose of a much younger Sonea, standing in a city square, staring down at the burned body of a young man. Magicians could make mistakes.

They did so only because they thought they were under attack. Anyi is a lone young woman and, unlike Sonea, doesn't have magic.

Yet his heart was beating too fast, causing an ache that kept growing.

Anyi is smart, he told himself. *She won't be caught.*

But if she was, she wouldn't want to reveal that he was here. They'd throw her out of the Guild. Into the city. Where Skellin was waiting . . .

Stop it, he told himself, rubbing his chest. *There's no point worrying about something until . . .*

A sound came from somewhere outside the room. His blood froze. He held his breath and listened. No sound came again. Then, just as he had decided that he'd imagined the noise, the faintest *whisper* of sound reached him. He stood up, certain that someone was approaching the room taking great care not to be detected. Had Gol been caught as soon as he entered the city. Had Skellin already tortured Cery's location out of him?

He cast about. *We haven't even had a chance to set the trap yet. What should I do?* He turned toward the hole into the next room. Their escape route.

Then five taps echoed in the passage. *The signal!* He breathed a sigh of relief and dropped back onto the chair, almost forgetting to rap on a crate in reply. Footsteps drew closer and light illuminated the corridor wall, moving in a way that suggested Anyi's gait. She peered around the doorway at him and grinned, then came inside carrying two buckets.

"Where's Gol?" she asked as she set them down.

"Scouting in the forest, in case we have to escape that way. What's this?" He peered into the buckets, which were full of more than just sacking.

"Fruit. Seemed a waste not to take some, after they'd done all the picking."

"I told you not to take anything else."

"Yeah, well, you know how obedient I am. And hungry."

He looked up at her and narrowed his eyes. "You said you didn't like fruit."

She looked away. "I said I didn't like *most* fruit." She sat down and yawned.

"Liar."

"Should I take it back?"

He made a rude noise. "Get some sleep."

"But Gol hasn't returned yet."

"He won't for a while. It's late, and the sooner you sleep the sooner *I* can as well."

"Oh, all right then."

Moving to the mattress, she lay down. Soon she was asleep, leaving Cery to wait, and start worrying all over again.

Be careful, Gol, my old friend. Not just for our sakes. I've known you too long to lose you tonight.

As Tyvara left to find out what Savara wanted, Lorkin saw his mother nod.

"She's smart, that one. I'd wager she wasn't counting on you coming into her life."

Lorkin grinned. "She did put up quite a lot of resistance. For a while there I thought I'd only imagined she returned my interest."

"You're sure now?"

"Yes." He felt an echo of doubt. "Mostly."

She chuckled, then her expression grew serious. "So. Black magic."

Lorkin looked away, then forced himself to turn back and meet his mother's gaze. As before, her expression was unreadable. Though her eyes betrayed something. Not disapproval, though.

Sadness, he realised. For some reason that made him feel even more guilty.

"Only so I could learn stone-making, Mother," he said. Her eyebrows rose. "So the *Guild* could learn stone-making," he corrected.

"I thought you volunteered to be Dannyl's assistant because you wanted to find an *alternative* to black magic."

Lorkin sighed. "Yes. I did. I had hoped the Traitors' stones would be that alternative."

"Is it really impossible to make them without black magic?"

"Not impossible, but . . . it is like trying to build a house blindfolded. The way higher magic alters your perceptions and control of magic makes training the stones easier and more accurate."

"Higher magic?" She smiled and looked away. "I find that is the term used by people who embrace black magic."

"And black magic is the term used by people who don't approve of higher magic." Lorkin shrugged. "Whether that disapproval is justified or not."

"Is it justified?"

He thought of Evar, drained of all energy out of revenge. Of himself, kept weak as Kalia's prisoner. But Kalia's supporters would have found another way to punish Evar if they hadn't had black magic, and they'd have found other ways to keep Lorkin prisoner.

"Yes and no. All magic can be abused. All power can be abused. The Traitors are proof that a culture that does embrace higher magic doesn't necessarily turn into Sachaka – the Ashaki kind of Sachaka, that is."

Mother nodded. "Just as Kallen and I are proof that not every magician goes mad and tries to take over the Guild once he or she learns black magic."

"I'd have thought Father was proof of that."

She shrugged. "He's not the best example, since he did use it to win the position of High Lord."

"Yes. He turned out to be a man of *many* secrets."

She let out a bitter laugh. "Plenty. After what you discovered, I . . . I wonder what else he kept hidden."

"So . . ." He took a deep breath. "Will the Guild accept me now that I know black magic?"

Pursing her lips, she did not answer immediately. "Probably.

Stone-making is a new kind of magic with great potential, and they want it."

"Even if it does require black magic?"

"Yes, though that will probably mean only a few will be allowed to learn it. Myself. Kallen. Lilia. You."

"Lilia? Oh – the novice who learned it from a book. Now *that* was unexpected."

"Yes. I have a hunch that she has a particular talent for it, and others might not so easily learn from a description. Though that might be too much to hope for."

"Was it another of Father's deceptions? Did he hope to reduce the danger to the Guild by making us believe it couldn't be learned from a book, so that nobody would try?"

"I don't think so." She frowned. "There is another possibility. Zarala may have told him it could only be taught mind to mind, to reduce the danger of the Guild adopting black magic. He . . ."

She straightened, her eyes widening. Guessing that Osen was communicating with her, Lorkin waited. The cry of a distant bird drew his attention to the surroundings and he realised that the sun was dipping toward the horizon. The mountains loomed to one side. He was suddenly aware that they were just a small gathering of people – isolated, exposed and insignificant.

But we're not. We're magicians. Two of us are powerful figures among our peoples. Important decisions are about to be made. Historic decisions.

His mother sighed. She looked at him, then over at Regin. As if sensing her gaze, Regin looked up. She beckoned, and he rose and moved away from the pair of Traitor women he had been talking to.

"I have an answer," she told him as he reached them. As she moved to stand, Regin extended a hand and, to Lorkin's surprise, she took it and let him help her up. "Could you go tell the queen, Lorkin?"

He did as she asked, finding Savara talking quietly with Tyvara. The two looked a little annoyed at the interruption, until Lorkin told them that Black Magician Sonea had received an answer from the Guild.

Savara rose and dusted off her clothes as his mother walked over to join her. They sat down in a small circle where they had settled the night before.

"Your invitation has been discussed among the leaders of the Allied Lands, your majesty," his mother began. "First, I must convey our thanks. We are honoured that you invited us to join your fight. However, the difference we might make to the outcome is small weighed against the possible consequences of our participation should you lose. As you have already pointed out, we have little to offer an army such as yours at this time. Some in the Allied Lands believe we would be more of a hindrance than a help." Her mouth twitched into a wry smile, to which Savara responded with similar amusement. "Others are not so pessimistic, pointing out that we have more than once in the past proven stronger and more resourceful than we appeared to be. Unfortunately those of the former opinion outnumber those of the latter, and the decision made is that we cannot join you in a conflict against King Amakira."

Lorkin's heart sank. Looking around, he saw looks of disgust on the faces of the Traitors. But not surprise.

"All have expressed support for your aim to end slavery in Sachaka," she continued. "If you delay your plans we may have time to become a more useful ally in such an endeavour. If you do not, we wish you every success and hope to form bonds of trade if not alliance in the future. In the meantime – if the offer still stands – we are willing to trade our Healers' services in exchange for magical gemstones, and I have been instructed to negotiate the details of such a deal now if it is convenient."

Savara nodded. "Please send my thanks for their consideration of our invitation," she said. "Since we do not need to wait for Allied forces to join us, we will not delay our plans. We leave in the morning. However, we still desire to trade Healing for stones." She paused to frown. "How long will it take your Healers to reach Arvice? Wait – before you answer that . . ." She turned to look at Lorkin. "Would you ask Tyvara to bring some raka?"

Lorkin nodded, stood up and hurried over to where Tyvara was sitting alone, watching the meeting.

"Savara said to bring raka," he told her. "Would you like some help?"

She stared up at him searchingly and didn't move.

"What is it?" he asked, lowering his voice.

"What will you do? Where will you go?"

He glanced at his mother, then back at her. "I . . . don't know." Mother would expect him to return to Kyralia, despite the matter of him knowing black magic. He wanted to return – to be able to return – but to leave Sachaka would mean leaving Tyvara. *And the Traitors. I want to see them win. To leave now would be like leaving in the middle of someone telling a story.*

Except that listening to stories wasn't as dangerous as joining in a war. If he stayed with the Traitors he'd be in the middle of the fighting. The Ashaki would consider him another target. They wouldn't hesitate to kill him because he was a Guild magician.

The Guild would not want him to get involved, either. The Allied Lands had shied away from direct conflict with King Amakira for fear that the Traitors would lose, and the king would seek revenge. A Guild magician among the Traitors would make it look as though the Guild supported the Traitors.

But they're going to send Healers. How is that different?

They were simply being hired for their services, and would not join in the fighting. They would probably time their arrival after the battle. They would be of no use before and during it, and it allowed them to retreat to Kyralia, hastily if necessary, if the Traitors lost.

Perhaps he could volunteer to join them. He wasn't a Healer, but he could Heal, and he could be a mediator between Healers and Traitors. *That still means not being there, at the battle. Where Tyvara will be.* He knew that there was no way she would abandon her people and go with him to Kyralia. And that he would do anything to ensure she survived. Even fight with the Traitors.

But if he was going to fight with the Traitors, he could not do so as a Guild magician.

He looked at her. "What do *you* want?"

She stared at him intently. "I want you," she said. "But not if you won't be happy. And not if you won't be safe."

He smiled. *Which is exactly what I want for her. But we can't both be happy and safe.*

Which made the decision easy.

"I won't be happy if I don't at least *try* to make you happy and safe," he told her. "So I guess I'm going to have to come with you and make sure you don't get yourself killed."

Her eyes widened. "But . . . the Guild . . . What's the point of you learning stone-making if—"

"Lord Lorkin," Savara called. "We are getting thirsty."

He leaned down and kissed Tyvara. "Don't worry about the Guild. They'll work something out."

She nodded. "I'll get the raka. You go back."

Turning away, he made his way over to join the queen and his mother. His heart was racing, but he was not sure if it was panic and terror, or joy and excitement. *Probably all of those. Am I really prepared to leave the Guild and join the Traitors? Am I crazy enough to risk my life in battle?*

As he sat down, he looked back at Tyvara. She gazed back at him, her face shifting from happy to worried and back again. He smiled, and her lips widened in reply.

Yes. Yes I am.

As the Guild House carriage rolled through the gates of Achati's mansion, slaves hurried out of sight. All of them – except for the door slave, who threw himself at Dannyl's feet as he climbed out – disappeared. Looking around, Dannyl recalled no female slaves among those he'd seen. Was this because Achati simply preferred male slaves, as with lovers, or did he hope that it would lessen the chance that he had any Traitor spies in his household?

"Take me to Ashaki Achati," Dannyl ordered.

The slave leapt to his feet with all the nimbleness of youth, and led Dannyl through the unadorned, polished wood door into the coolness of the corridor beyond. Achati's invitation had arrived that morning. Dannyl had agonised over whether to accept or decline until midday, when he gave in and consulted Tayend.

"Of course you should go," Tayend had said, barely looking up from his desk. "An Ambassador must maintain good relations, and Achati's the only one here still willing to have any relations with us."

So here Dannyl was, walking down the corridor to the Master's Room, his heart beating a little too fast and his stomach stirring in an annoying and disconcerting way. As he reached the end of the corridor he drew in a deep breath and let it out slowly, schooling his face into a polite smile as he saw the man waiting for him.

"Ambassador Dannyl." Achati stepped forward and grasped Dannyl's arm in the Kyralian manner of greeting.

"Ashaki Achati," Dannyl replied.

"I am so pleased that you accepted my invitation," Achati said, smiling broadly. "Come and sit. I've ordered the kitchen slaves to do their best tonight. Here – I even have Kyralian wine."

He beckoned Dannyl over to the stools and leaned down to pick up a bottle. He held it out to show the label.

"Anuren dark!" Dannyl exclaimed, impressed. "How did you get hold of this?"

"I have my sources." Achati gestured to the stools. "Please sit."

It appeared Achati was determined to behave as if nothing had happened since the last time Dannyl had visited. Perversely, this made Dannyl feel less comfortable. Surely the Ashaki ought to acknowledge in some way the trials his king had put them through. Pretending they hadn't happened would not mend their friendship.

Then, just as Dannyl began to grow annoyed, Achati surprised him.

"I don't expect you to forgive me," he said as he poured a second glass of the wine.

Dannyl paused. "I'm not sure what to say to that," he said honestly.

"Don't say anything. You don't have to lie in order to be diplomatic."

"If you don't expect me to forgive you, I gather you won't be apologising."

Achati smiled. "No. And you won't be thanking me for getting Lorkin out of Arvice, although I did arrange it."

"I should thank you for not handing him over to the king, at least," Dannyl pointed out.

"I'd have never agreed to anything that required me to."

"Agreed . . .?" Dannyl felt his stomach sink. "The king sent you to warn us about the abductor, didn't he? You didn't come out of concern for us."

"Yes, he knew – and no, I *was* motivated out of concern for you all." Achati shrugged. "I persuaded the king to let me warn you in the hope Lorkin would trust me. I didn't think I would get much information out of him, not after what he had done while in prison, but I saw a chance we'd get *some* information, and that was better than nothing."

Dannyl frowned. What had Lorkin done in prison?

Achati chuckled. "Lorkin is a lot tougher than he looks. He proved unexpectedly ruthless. All the more so because he couldn't have known what he did would force the king to free him." His smile faded. "Everyone I questioned had a different view as to the source of the poison. The king isn't admitting to it. The Traitors obviously aren't going to. If it was someone other than the king, they are hardly likely to reveal they acted against his orders – or that he asked them to do it. Whatever the source was, it made it clear that someone had tried to kill a Guild magician, and that upset too many Ashaki."

Someone tried to kill Lorkin? With poison? Dannyl hoped he was hiding his shock well. "So the king let Lorkin go. Only to try to get hold of him again. But in order to put him somewhere safe from the poisoner?"

"Yes."

"Then . . . it couldn't be the king who tried to poison Lorkin."

"I don't believe so, because he let me help Lorkin escape."

"Why did he do that?"

"He agreed that, if I could get Lorkin to tell me anything about the Traitors, he would let me do whatever I judged right." Achati was almost smirking.

"It sounds like a wager. I don't imagine he's the sort of king's who likes losing bets."

"He honours his agreements."

"What did you stand to lose?"

Achati looked smug as he waved a hand. "My house."

"Really?" Dannyl looked around. "Do you own any other land?"

"No."

High stakes, then. But there always were, in politics and war. Dannyl felt familiar feelings of gratitude, affection and admiration, and resisted them. He thought of Tayend's warnings, and was surprised to find the same feelings rising. He resisted those, too. *Tayend is . . . a friend. Perhaps, if it weren't for Achati, we would be more than that again.* But there was Achati . . .

The Ashaki was regarding the wine appreciatively. Dannyl couldn't help thinking that he couldn't be more different from Tayend. Though not as heavily built as the average Sachakan man, Achati was dark and broad, while Tayend was light and slim. *How can I be attracted to such opposites? Ah, but they are both sharp and perceptive. I guess I like smart men. I wonder, though, what he sees in me.*

287

Noticing Dannyl's gaze, Achati turned to meet his eyes. His expression grew speculative. "Do you remember that moment during out journey to Duna? When Tayend interrupted?"

Memories and mixed emotions tumbled into Dannyl's mind. Desire, embarrassment, anxiety and anger.

"How could I forget? Meddling little . . ." he muttered.

Achati laughed. "I'm sure his intentions were good. But I do feel that such moments, such chances, are going to grow rarer for us. Would we still remain friends if we were to go through another difficult time as we've had recently, or would there be too much distrust and suspicion? I wish . . ." He sighed. "It is selfish, I know. I would like us to be more than friends, for a time at least, before circumstances make us feel we must behave like enemies."

Dannyl drew in a deep breath. His heart was beating too quickly again, and there was a strange but familiar fluttering sensation in his stomach. *Which is exactly how I felt when I first arrived*, he realised. Only this time there was something exhilarating about it. What would happen if he welcomed it? Embraced it?

Only one way to find out.

"Well, Tayend isn't here now."

Achati caught his breath. An expression flickered across his face before a look of careful interest replaced it.

Hope.

Dannyl understood then that, for all his power and wealth, Achati was alone. He doubted he could ever take advantage of that loneliness, even if he wanted to. It was not a weakness, it was part of the life Achati had embraced.

"Though I wouldn't put it past him to be heading here right now," Dannyl added.

Achati laughed. "Surely we couldn't have such bad timing twice?"

"That sounds like a theory worth testing. Question is, how closely do we need to replicate the circumstances?"

"Oh, I think we have all the essential ingredients." As Achati stood up, Dannyl followed suit. "And if I'm wrong, at least we can rely on the slaves not letting him in." He paused to stare up at Dannyl. "Ah. Look at you."

Dannyl blinked. "What?"

He reached up to touch Dannyl's jaw. "So very tall and . . . all angles and elegance. It's just as well you Kyralians don't learn higher magic out of habit. You'd be much too intimidating."

Dannyl let out a quick laugh. "You Sachakans are the intimidating ones," he protested. "What with the black magic and—"

Achati silenced him with a shake of his head and a finger to his lips, and the hand on Dannyl's jaw slid behind his neck and pulled him down into a kiss.

Then his mouth was beside Dannyl's ear. "Don't, or you'll remind yourself that we are a brutal people. Let me show you that we can aren't all cruel and heartless." And he stepped back, then beckoned and led Dannyl out of the Master's Room.

CHAPTER 19

AN AGREEMENT

Before the sun had even crested the horizon, the Traitors were getting ready to leave. They weren't preparing to eat first, Sonea noted. *When the Traitors are gone we'll eat the last of our supplies, then head home*, she decided. Though whether that "we" was to comprise two people or three was not a certainty.

She looked over to Lorkin, who had slept next to Tyvara for the last two nights. She'd listened to him closely during the negotiations. He had referred to the Traitors as "we" many times, and to the Allied Lands and Guild as "them". She shivered as a feeling of dread crept over her.

He had changed. Not completely, though. He was still Lorkin. But he had matured. And . . . something else. Something like the brittleness that he'd suffered after having his heart broken, but compensated by a new resilience. She wasn't surprised by the latter. He had been through a lot in the half-year since leaving the Guild. And taken on the burden of black magic.

I ought to be appalled, but all I feel is sadness. He has no idea what he's shouldered. How it will always mark him as untrustworthy, even if they do accept his decision and that it is a cost of stone-making.

"They" being the Guild and other Kyralians. She did not

think they would reject him. How could they, now that they'd accepted Lilia? *But with every magician who learns black magic we seem to be losing something. Perhaps our innocence. Perhaps caution.*

Lorkin had returned from replenishing his supply of water. She thought of the gemstones in her pocket, so far unmentioned to the Traitors. Tyvara smiled up at Lorkin as he handed her the flask. It was hers, not his. Sonea felt a pang of regret that she had no time to get to know the young woman better. The way Tyvara looked at Lorkin sent another shiver of warning through Sonea and she frowned.

For a couple so obviously in love, they are not behaving like they are about to be parted.

As if sensing her gaze, Lorkin turned and met Sonea's eyes. His smile faded, then he looked back at Tyvara and nodded. Her expression became serious. Sympathetic. She nodded and watched as Lorkin made his way over to Sonea.

"Mother," he said. "Can we talk privately?"

"Of course." Standing up, Sonea looked around, then chose a direction at random and began walking. He followed silently. About twenty paces away she stopped and created a sound-containing barrier around them both, then waited for him to speak.

Lorkin suddenly could not meet her gaze. "I . . . ah . . . we . . ."

She sighed and relented. "Are you coming back with me?"

He straightened his shoulders and raised his head. "No."

She stared at him, fighting a rising panic. *I could order him to. I could contact Osen and get him to give the order.* But she suspected that would push Lorkin into doing something even more foolish.

"It's not Tyvara," he said. "Well, not *just* Tyvara." His gaze became intense. She read excitement and hope. "I think the

Traitors will win. When they say they will end slavery . . . I think they'll do that, too. They've been planning it for years. For centuries."

"So . . . if they win, will they be any better than the Ashaki?"

"Yes," he said firmly.

"And if they lose?"

His expression was grim. She suddenly saw in his face what he would look like in ten years or more. *If he makes it through the next few weeks. No, don't think about that.*

"Some things are worth risking lives for," he said. "If you had seen what the Ashaki do – experienced it – you'd want to rid the world of them, too."

At the anger and horror in his voice she felt a pain inside. *What did they do to him?* She wanted to know, and to find whoever had done it, and *hurt* them. *Both for that, and for making my son want to risk his life in this way.*

"The Guild won't like this, but I'm sure you know that," she told him.

He nodded. "Tell them to officially declare me an exile. That way they won't be blamed for my actions, if we lose."

She felt her heart sink. *I ought to be pleased that he's thought this through, but I can't be. If only I could take his place . . . but I don't think that would stop him going to war anyway.*

And suddenly she knew what she would do next. If he would not come home, she would not either. She would follow him. She would do all she could to protect him.

"So you consider yourself a Traitor now." She nodded. "Then there is something you need to know." She reached into her pocket, drew out one of the gemstones and held it out.

He took it, and examined it closely. After a moment his eyes widened.

"I suspected it was possible," he breathed.

As he stared at the stone in avid fascination, Sonea felt a bittersweet joy and pride. Here he was, her son, understanding a magic that no Guild magician had ever explored before. *And he loves it.*

"Where did you get this?" he asked.

She gestured around them. "In the soil and sand. There's one in the spring, too, keeping it clean. I suspect they're all over the wastes. You can detect them, if you know what you're looking for and you're a black magician."

Lorkin's mouth opened and he turned to look at the dry, lifeless land. "Are you saying . . .?"

"Yes. The wasteland ought to have recovered centuries ago, but it didn't because of the Traitors." She touched his arm. "Are you sure you want to leave the Guild to join these people? A people this ruthless? You can still help them to bring about the end of the Ashaki without changing your loyalties."

He looked down at the gem and frowned. Then he closed his fingers around it and nodded. "I am sure. They aren't perfect," his mouth twisted with wry humour, "but they *are* better than the Ashaki."

Turning to her, he placed his hands on her shoulders. "I love you, Mother. I have no intention of dying in this war. I *will* return to the Guild. Queen Zarala gave me stone-making knowledge so that I could pass it on, and I will do that if the Guild wants it. You'll see me again."

Then he hugged her tightly. She held him close, and it took all her will not to resist as he pulled away. He smiled once, then turned and strode back toward the Traitors.

Sonea blinked away tears, sighed and followed.

* * *

Stepping out of the Magicians' Quarters into the bright sunlight, Lilia squinted and set off toward the University. More novices were about than usual for this time of morning, she noted. Most were hanging around the University entrance. As she neared them and stepped into the building's shadow, she realised that all of their faces had turned toward her.

A chill ran down her spine and she slowed.

She recognised a few of them as friends of Bokkin. Two stepped aside. At first she assumed it was to let her through, but a familiar thug filled the gap. He grinned at her as she neared the steps.

"What's you doing coming in here, Lilia?" he asked. "The Lookout is that way." He pointed up the hill.

A few of the novices snickered. They drew closer together. She would have to push her way through them or go around to the front of the University.

"We're not going to let you in," Bokkin said.

Lilia smothered a smile. *Idiot. It's so obvious what they're doing, he didn't need to say it aloud. And now they can't pretend they weren't doing anything wrong.*

She climbed the first few steps and stopped.

"Are you sure?" she asked, meeting and holding the gaze of each novice. "Black Magician Kallen is inside, waiting to teach me all sorts of black magicky secrets. He might not be too happy with you if you stop me getting to his lesson on time."

Some of the novices frowned and exchanged doubtful glances.

"Kallen can only get you to pretend to fight with black magic," Bokkin said. "You can't learn anything else. You haven't even graduated yet."

"I heard you weren't going to be graduating," one of the

girls near Bokkin added. "People say they won't let you. You'll be a novice forever."

Lilia shrugged. "I'll be graduating next year. I have more to learn than the average novice." To make sure the hint sank in, she reached into her robe and pulled out the small, slim knife she had purchased at Kallen's recommendation. She had wondered why he had insisted she needed one when she wasn't supposed to *use* black magic, and suspected it was to be sure he got to approve her choice. He'd told her to buy something plain but good quality. Something more refined than a kitchen knife, but nothing as distastefully flashy as the knives the Sachakans wore. She'd met some knife-makers and chosen an elegant, slim knife with a blade that folded neatly into and out of an ebony and silver handle – an action she had practised doing one-handed.

An action she used now. She resisted a laugh as several of the novices drew in sharp breaths. But she couldn't just stand there waving a knife around. If a magician saw her she'd be in as much trouble as the other novices. Maybe more. Inside her bag, among the books and study notes, was a pachi fruit. Jonna had put it in there when it had been clear Lilia would not have time to eat all of her morning meal.

Taking it out, Lilia began to cut slices from the fruit and eat them.

"Kallen's going to come and find out what's holding me up," she told them between chews. "I wouldn't want to b—"

"What's going on here?" a new voice demanded. Looking up, Lilia saw the head of a magician appear behind the novices. "Find somewhere else to gather and stop blocking the doors."

At once the novices scattered, the closest ones to the

magician sketching a hasty bow. Bokkin was the only one looking disappointed, Lilia noted. The rest looked relieved. He sneered at her as she walked up the stairs, past him. The magician was one she remembered from second year, a middle-aged Alchemist.

"Good morning, Lord Jotin," she said, bowing.

"Lady Lilia." He nodded, then glanced about to make sure the novices weren't going to return before heading back down the corridor. Lilia continued eating the pachi fruit as she made her way to the room Kallen held his lessons in, putting all thought of Bokkin behind her. At some point she would pose Anyi's question to Kallen, and she had to consider how best to do it. She paused to wipe the knife and gather her thoughts, before pushing through the door into the room.

"Good morning Lady Lilia," Kallen said, his lips widening into a half-smile as she entered.

"Black Magician Kallen." She bowed and sat down, then opened her mouth to speak but stopped as she noticed the items on the table. A ceramic bowl stood next to some of the hollow tubes of glass Alchemists used when they needed to shape vessels and pipes to a particular use.

"Today I will teach you how to make blood gems," Kallen told her.

She felt a thrill go through her. This was a part of black magic that most people regarded as acceptable and safe. Kallen picked up a tube and indicated that she should do the same.

"The process is easiest communicated mind to mind. The former High Lord discovered it by examining an ancient blood ring. I've seen and examined this ring, and I have to say I'm glad I didn't have to work that riddle out for myself. First, melt some glass, keeping it spinning in the air to maintain the shape."

She put aside Anyi's question until later and followed his instructions. When they both held revolving spheres of molten glass in the air, he told her to take his hand and focus on his thoughts. She watched him shape his magic and impose his will on the glass, somehow altering its structure, then letting it cool. Then he watched her attempt the same on her piece.

They repeated this a few times, re-melting and shaping the glass, before he felt she was adept enough to try adding blood to the glass. To her surprise, this did nothing more than imprint an identity on it.

"The blood gem only works when someone is touching it," he told her. "Do you understand the difference between how it works for the one who provided the blood, and the one who touches the gem?"

"The creator can see what the wearer sees, even if he doesn't want to. The wearer can't see what the creator sees but can receive mental communications without anyone else hearing them."

"Yes, but the gem conveys not only what the wearer sees, but their thoughts. Unless the wearer is carrying a blocking stone."

She blinked in surprise. This was new. "What's that?"

"Something the Traitors make. Something we may soon have. Instead of glass, these stones are crystals trained as they grow to do a magical task. A blocking stone prevents a mind-read and allows the wearer to project the thoughts they want a searcher to see."

Cold shivered down Lilia's spine. "Naki's ring."

He looked surprised, then apologetic. "I am sorry. I forgot that you had already encountered a blocking stone."

297

She shook her head. "Don't worry about it. What else can these stones do?"

"Anything a magician can do."

"Even a black magician."

"In that they can draw in and store power? Yes – but you must keep that to yourself for now."

Lilia whistled quietly. "Tell me we're making friends with these Traitors. They don't sound like enemies we'd ever want."

Kallen frowned. "We're working towards that, hoping to trade for the knowledge of stone-making." He waved a hand dismissively. "I'll tell you more about that another time. The important thing is that stone-making requires black magic."

She felt a thrill of excitement. "I'll be learning to make these stones?" That would mean she'd be one of the first Guild magicians to be able to use this new magic.

"Perhaps."

"Will I have to travel to Sachaka?"

"No." But by the way he paused and looked thoughtful, she guessed that the answer was not that straightforward. He shook his head. "Well, that is all for this morning. Do you have any questions?"

Her heart skipped as she remembered Anyi's question. "Yes. Would the Guild let Cery and his two bodyguards stay here?"

Kallen's eyebrows lowered. "Has his situation grown worse?" he asked.

"Possibly. Would they?"

"I will have to get the agreement of the Higher Magicians, but it is likely they would grant it. When would he come here?"

"Soon." Then, realising that could mean anything, she elaborated. "In a few days."

He nodded. "I will let you know as soon as I can." He

smiled thinly. "We managed to get some seed from a perfume-maker, thanks to you. The plants aren't big enough yet to confirm if they're roet, but it will not be long. If Cery is still willing to help us catch Skellin, we may be able to do so soon."

She nodded. There was that "soon" word again.

"He'll be very willing," she told him. "Of that I'm sure."

As Anyi and Lilia disappeared into the darkness, heading back to the Magicians' Quarters and Sonea's rooms, Gol looked at Cery and raised his eyebrows.

"Yes," Cery answered, keeping his voice low. "Tell me what you found out."

Gol leaned forward. "Everything has changed. The rest of the Thieves . . . well, they don't go calling themselves that any more. They call themselves 'princes'. Skellin they call 'king'."

"Of course," Cery rolled his eyes. "King of the Underworld. What do people on the street think?"

"That they've all got big-headed. But nobody says it aloud. They're scared. They know Skellin is a rogue magician and his mother is the Thief Hunter. Both have done nasty things to people who wouldn't do what they wanted." Gol grimaced. "Good thing is, everyone hates him now."

"What do they think of me?"

Gol shrugged. "They think you're dead."

"And if they knew I was hiding?"

"I suggested it, and a few said they hoped so. They said they hoped you were working out a way to get rid of Skellin."

"No one thought I'd abandoned my workers?"

"No one said as much to me. Interesting thing is, in one bolhouse the people I got chatting to had an argument about

299

whether you were hiding in the Guild or not. The one who doubted it said you couldn't be, because the Guild is working with Skellin."

Cery frowned. "That could just be a rumour."

"One that would help keep people scared of Skellin."

"If they knew it wasn't true, they wouldn't be as scared."

Gol shook his head. "They'd still be too scared to do anything."

Hooking his fingers around the edge of his seat, Cery drummed his fingers on the underside. "What about the supplier?"

"Saski's still there. Still got the minefire. He's been trying to sell a new tool that uses it. Some sort of blowpipe that people warned me was as likely to blow up as work. His most popular product is little packets that people throw into the fire to make a bang and a flash of light. People liked the bangers, but they couldn't see much other use for minefire when magicians can do the same things it can do."

"They don't see that it could let ordinary people do things magicians can do?"

"Not the sort of things they want to do, like Heal or levitate or move things at a distance. Who needs to explode things here in the city? And Saski puts customers off with all his warnings about how dangerous and unpredictable it is. Magic sounds a lot safer."

Cery nodded. "It does. It's not just that minefire might explode when we don't want it to, but that it might *not* when we need it to. Are you sure this trap will work?"

"Mostly. Before, when I got friendly with Saski, he often described how minefire was used in the mines of the far north. We'll be using the same method."

"How are we going to buy it? Could we get a street kid to buy some of these bangers for us?"

Gol nodded. "That'd be wise. Saski doesn't seem the type to run off and sell us to Skellin, but who knows? It'd be tempting. He can't be making much money."

"But we do need Skellin to find out where we are."

"Not through Saski. Then Skellin would know that we'd bought minefire, and wonder what we were up to down here. Wouldn't take much thinking to work out we were setting a trap."

"True." Cery looked around the room. "Well, you're going to have to set things up here without Anyi suspecting something odd is going on."

"Once I get the tubes into the walls, they won't be all that noticeable, especially if we put them in the holes and hollows in the mortar."

"But you'll have to do it while she's not here."

"You don't want to wait until they're sure the plants are roet? Once we have the trap set up, there's always going to be a danger it'll go off before we're ready."

Cery shook his head. "Not after what Lilia said about the Higher Magicians being prepared to let us live in the Guild in the meantime. Anyi was too keen to do it. Too ready to argue with me about it." He shook his head. "Something tells me her patience is running out. Or that she knows something that we don't."

"Like that the plants aren't roet?"

"Maybe."

Gol shrugged. "She's right though. There's no need for us to be uncomfortable or risk getting Lilia into trouble for hiding us here."

"But if the rumours you heard were right and someone in the Guild is working with Skellin we could put ourselves right in their hands. They'll make sure the Guild doesn't work with us to catch Skellin, or make sure something goes wrong and we're all killed. Otherwise we may expose their dirty little secret."

Gol looked up at the roof. "Well, if Anyi is right and we're under the gardens between the University and Magicians' Quarters, our trap will definitely expose Skellin to the Guild."

Cery smiled. "Yes. But let's make sure it doesn't kill us all in the process."

CHAPTER 20

FIRST ENCOUNTER

From high above, the sun poured heat and brightness down onto the wasteland, which threw it back up again in protest. Assailed from the sky and ground, Lorkin trudged along with the Traitors and tried not to imagine facing an Ashaki in battle.

Instead, he thought about the gemstone in his pocket. He had tried last night, after everyone was asleep or on watch, to see if he could sense other stones buried in the area, but his mental search had detected nothing. Yet that was no proof his mother was wrong. She had said he would only find them because he knew black magic, and there had been nothing of black magic in his method of searching.

I should have asked her to explain. But he'd only had one last moment with her, the morning of the previous day, and he'd used the opportunity to question her about another magical puzzle. Her gaze had grown keener as he'd asked if she'd heard of magicians able to read surface thoughts.

"Your father was supposed to have been able to," she'd told him. "I always assumed he encouraged the rumour in order to maintain the fear or awe people regarded him with – and if questions were raised about other abilities he shouldn't have, he could point to that rumour as an example of the silly things people thought about him."

"It might not have been a lie," Lorkin had told her.

Her surprise had, as always, turned to thoughtful calculation. What she'd said next he hadn't expected. "Best keep that to yourself," she'd advised. "It will make even those closest to you uncomfortable. Be careful you don't learn more about others than you really want to."

She has a point. He could imagine many situations where hearing someone's stray thoughts might be embarrassing. Fortunately, it was only the clearest surface thoughts that he could hear, and only when he was concentrating hard.

"Lorkin."

Tyvara had returned to his side. She had been called over by Savara and the pair had been chatting for some time.

"Yes?"

She smiled. "Tell me more about Lord Regin. Is he particularly important to the Guild? Why do you think he was with your mother?"

Lorkin frowned. "He's not important. Well, he's from an important House, but he doesn't hold a position within the Guild."

"So is he just a source of magic for your mother?"

He tried to imagine that scenario, and failed. But then, he'd pictured Regin behaving like a Sachakan source slave, when the man didn't have to. *All he has to do is send power out and Mother will take and store it.* It would involve touching, of course, but nothing more than clasping hands.

"Maybe," Lorkin replied. "Well . . . probably."

"So how are they related? Friends? Lovers?"

"No. In fact, he and Mother hated each other as novices.

304

He bullied her until she challenged him to a duel. She thrashed him, and after that he left her alone."

"A duel?" Tyvara's eyebrows rose and her smile widened. "Interesting custom."

Lorkin narrowed his eyes at her. "Are you mocking my people's ways?"

"Not at all." She tried to look serious.

"You are," he accused her. Then he grinned. "It is a silly custom. As far as I know, nobody had challenged anyone to a duel for years before, and nobody has since."

"It must have been her last resort, then." Tyvara looked thoughtful. "So, did they become good friends after their big confrontation, as so often is the case?"

"No. Mother hasn't forgiven him." Though Lorkin could not remember her saying so. If anything, she always pointed out how brave Regin had been during the invasion. Grudgingly.

Tyvara said nothing to that, and he turned to see she was frowning.

"Why do you ask?"

She looked up. "Well . . . Savara and I both thought that it was odd that the Guild would send two people with such obvious regard for each other on such a mission. If they were captured it would be harder on them, if one was threatened to blackmail the other."

"My mother and Regin?" Lorkin shook his head. "Impossible. You've got the wrong idea."

She shrugged. "Maybe you're right. Or maybe the seeming impossibility of it led to the Guild not realising what a bad choice Regin is. Or maybe Sonea and Regin don't realise it either."

Lorkin shook his head and sighed.

"What?"

"The most powerful women in Sachaka, and all you do is waste time gossiping and matchmaking. Ow!" He rubbed her arm where she'd hit him.

"Men gossip more," she said. "And it's not a waste of time, when it has political and martial consequences."

"It does?"

"It will." Her head lifted and her eyes narrowed. "Ah."

He turned to stare ahead. Past Savara and the Traitors walking ahead, he saw that they were cresting the top of a dune. Ahead lay a flat plain covered in sparse vegetation and, a few hours walk away, a sprawl of buildings.

"You can still change your mind," she told him. "Nobody will stop you going back to Kyralia. There are no Ichani around the Pass to fear."

Am I really brave enough – foolish enough – to join a people I have no ties of blood with and dare to wage war on the legendary black magicians my people have feared for centuries?

He looked at Tyvara and smiled. "Where you go, I go."

She gazed at him and shook her head. "Whenever I find myself thinking I don't deserve someone as good as you, Lorkin, I remind myself that, if you're willing to come with me, you may be a little bit mad."

"You think my mother and Lord Regin are in love. It's not *my* sanity in question here."

She smirked and looked away. "We'll see."

As they walked on in silence, her words repeated in his mind – "*. . . someone as good as you, Lorkin*" – and he felt his smile fade. Would she still think of him as good if she knew what he'd done to the slave girl? He hadn't told her yet. So far there had been no reason to. *No, that's not entirely true. There have been opportunities. Every time, I decided it would spoil the* *moment, or sour the conversation. But I shouldn't put it off. The Traitors might need to know what happened to the girl. If she was a Traitor.*

But what if she wasn't? That was what he was most afraid of: to discover that the girl hadn't known the water was poisoned. It was much easier to live with his decision, believing that she had deliberately taken her own life.

If this is what it feels like to have killed someone when they wanted it, what is it going to be like when the war starts and I kill people who don't want it? Maybe it wouldn't be so difficult, given that they had enslaved, tortured and killed others. *Maybe it will be easier.*

He looked around at the Traitors. Their expressions were grim and determined. Talk had ceased but for the occasional low murmur. Slowly they made their way down the last dune and onto the plain, then toward the sprawling buildings. The first people they encountered were two slaves, watching over a small herd of reber. Both young boys, the pair rushed over to throw themselves on the ground before Savara. She told them to stand, and never to lower themselves before another man or woman again.

"It's time?" one of them asked, gazing up at her eagerly.

"Yes," she said, then nodded toward the buildings. "You know what to do?"

"Stay out of reach," he replied. "Move away from the city. But we can't get much further away than here."

"No. Just stay away from the house until we are done."

He frowned. "If I go back I can tell the others to get out."

"That would be very brave. You must not let the Ashaki suspect we're coming, though."

"We won't. We've all been planning for this for years."

"Go, then."

As the boy ran toward the buildings, Savara straightened and beckoned to the Traitors. They continued on, quickening their pace. A thrill of excitement and fear ran down Lorkin's spine. Some of these outer estates were run by trusted slave masters, so they might not encounter an Ashaki. Or the Ashaki could be out visiting or tending to business. But the boy would have told Savara if that was so.

There's little chance we're not heading toward our first fight.

All too soon they were within a few hundred paces of the buildings. Then they were stepping through a gate in the low wall that surrounded them. As the Traitors spread out, in twos and threes, to approach the building from different sides, slaves emerged. They hurried, some running, past the invaders and the low wall, and out onto the plain in all directions.

Spreading out, so that even if the Ashaki used magic to drag them back, he'd have to use more magic and time collecting all of them. Some might still escape.

The Traitors split into smaller groups so that they could enter the buildings from different directions. Tyvara grabbed Lorkin's hand and drew him toward what looked like a stable.

"Stay with me." She plucked at her vest. "I'm carrying plenty of stones, but we're supposed to avoid using them until the battle. Our own power can be replaced, but most stones are single-use." She glanced at him. "I'll make sure you have your own set, for the final battle."

Once in the stable he saw the stalls were furnished with benches covered in blankets. He realised with a shock that this was where the slaves lived. Several were hiding there now, looking confused. Tyvara ordered them out, telling them to run away and come back in a few hours. One very pregnant woman shrank back into her stall, shaking her head.

"Come on," Tyvara said, extending her hand and smiling. "We'll protect you. It won't be for long."

"What's going on?" a voice demanded.

They turned to see a slave with a red cloth wrapped around his brow emerge from another building. Judging from the smoke wafting up from a chimney pipe, it contained the kitchen and perhaps other domestic rooms. Lorkin's stomach turned as he saw the man was carrying a short whip.

From somewhere beyond the building the man had emerged from came a boom. They all jumped and looked up to see fragments of what might be roof tiles flying into the air.

The man turned back and stared at Lorkin and Tyvara, his eyes widening. "It's time?" he asked.

"It is," Tyvara replied.

He grinned and tossed the whip onto a pile of firewood. "At last." Turning from them, he strode away from the buildings.

Lorkin looked at Tyvara, expecting her to stop him, but she only smiled.

"Wherever we could, we let the slave masters know that if they weren't unnecessarily cruel, we'd consider giving them some of their Ashaki's estate when we took over."

More slaves darted from the buildings, some looking terrified. Tyvara glanced back to the pregnant woman, then turned to Lorkin. "We'll stay here and keep watch in case the Ashaki comes after them."

Lorkin did as she asked, but the next person to emerge was a Traitor, Adiya. The woman looked around and, seeing Lorkin and Tyvara, walked over to meet them.

"It's done," she said.

Tyvara nodded and looked over her shoulder at the pregnant slave. "You're free now. Our work here is finished. Soon the others will come back and join you. They'll keep you safe."

The woman stared at her and said nothing, but she seemed a little less afraid now. Tyvara started toward the building Adiya had emerged from. Lorkin followed her inside. They wound through the familiar layout of passages and emerged at what must have once been the Master's Room. The roof had been blasted away, and the walls bulged outwards or had toppled into rubble.

A middle-aged Sachakan man lay slumped on the floor, blood seeping from a shallow cut on his arm.

Dead? Yes. Lorkin stared at the corpse and remembered the Ashaki who he and Dannyl had stayed with, when they'd first entered Sachaka. The man had been friendly and generous. Perhaps this dead man had been kind too. Perhaps he had kept slaves only because it was what powerful Sachakans like him had always done. Perhaps he would have surrendered if given the chance. Surely he didn't deserve to die like this?

It was impossible to know. The Traitors couldn't imprison all Ashaki and put them on trial to decide if death was an appropriate punishment. To imprison them would take too much of the Traitors' time and energy.

The Traitors are at war with a way of life, not the individual people, but individuals will pay the price. He suspected, though, that many of the Ashaki would refuse to change their ways, even if they were given a choice.

He looked around and saw that Tyvara had picked her way across the room to one of the collapsed walls. Making his way to her, they helped each other over a pile of rubble into a courtyard. There, a richly dressed woman stood glaring at Savara, her face streaked with tears.

"The Ashaki's wife," Tyvara murmured. "We're hoping it won't be necessary to kill the women and children."

"They won't obey you," the queen was saying to the woman. "You had better get used to that. My people will do what they can to protect you, but they won't guard you day and night. The rest is up to you."

Two Traitors stood behind the queen. As Savara turned away they moved to stand beside her. Tyvara and Lorkin walked over to join her.

"We're done here," the queen said. "Time to gather everyone together and move on." She looked over her shoulder at the broken building, her expression grim. "It's too much to hope all estates will be this trouble-free."

More Traitors arrived. As the last pair appeared, one hurried forward to the queen.

"I just heard that Chiva's group had to fight four Ashaki – a father and his three sons. Vinyi was killed."

Savara stopped to regard the woman with dismay. "A loss already." She sighed and started toward the main gates of the courtyard. As she reached it, she stopped abruptly. Lorkin looked beyond and saw what had surprised her.

A crowd of about twenty slaves – ex-slaves, Lorkin corrected – waited outside. As they saw Savara they hurried forward, stopping a few paces away. From the adoring way they looked at the Traitor queen, Lorkin expected them to throw themselves at her feet. None did, though a few looked as if they had to work hard to resist the habit, bending forward then jerking upright again.

Nobody spoke. The foremost ex-slaves glanced at each other, then one held out his wrists to the queen.

"We want to give you . . . we have nothing to give you . . . do you need to take power from us?"

Savara drew in a quick breath. "We don't need to yet but . . ."

"Take it," Tyvara murmured. "They will feel they had a part in the fight for their freedom."

The queen smiled. "I would be honoured." She looked down at the knife at her belt. "But not with this. This is for our enemies."

One of the ex-slaves stepped forward. "Then use this."

In his hand was a small knife obviously meant for a domestic task like tailoring or wood carving. Savara took it and felt the edge for sharpness. She nodded and handed it back. The man looked confused.

"You must make the cut," she said. "I will not deliberately harm my own people."

He ran the blade across the back of his thumb, then held out his hand to her. Touching the cut lightly, Savara closed her eyes and bowed her head. The man closed his eyes.

A short time passed. As Savara withdrew her hand she looked up at the rest of the ex-slaves. "We cannot stay long. I cannot take power from all of you."

"Then we'll give it to your fighters," the first speaker declared. The rest nodded and turned their attention to the other Traitors. Lorkin noted that, as domestic knives were found to be lacking, the Traitors were handing over their own knives. When a woman offered her wrists to Lorkin he blinked in surprise.

"Um . . . Tyvara?"

She chuckled. "You're one of us now," she said. "Better get used to it."

"Oh, that's not the problem." He put a hand to his sheath-less belt. "I don't have a knife."

She looked at him and smiled. "Then I guess we'd better see to that at the first opportunity. For now," she looked at the man facing her with hand extended, "we'll have to share."

The sun was hovering above the mountains when Sonea and Regin neared the first Ashaki estate. Gold-tinged light bathed the walls the colour of old parchment. In contrast the hole in the roof was an ominous black.

The estate was swarming with people.

"Slaves," Regin said. "Looting?"

Sonea shook her head. She could see a line of men hauling rubble out of the building. "Cleaning up."

Regin frowned. "Surely they'd have run away when the Traitors attacked – and stayed away now they have their freedom."

"They've got to live somewhere, and there's food and shelter here. I wonder: if the Traitors win will they take over the estates or give them to the slaves?"

"Hmm." Was Regin's only answer. "They've seen us."

Sure enough, a group of about a dozen slaves had stepped out of the gates and were walking toward them. Sonea pictured what she and Regin must look like. Their robes clearly marked them as Kyralian magicians. As Kyralians they might not be welcome here, but she doubted even newly freed slaves flushed with victory would dare to attack them.

"What do you want to do?" Regin asked.

Sonea stopped. "Meet them. Better to know what reception we're going to get now, than later, when we'll be further from the border."

About twenty strides away, the group slowed to a halt.

"Who are you? Why are you here?" one of them called out.

"I am Black Magician Sonea and this is Lord Regin, of the Magicians' Guild of Kyralia. We are here as representatives of the Allied Lands."

"Who invited you here?" the man demanded again.

"We met Queen Savara two days and three nights ago."

"Why are you following a few days behind, then?"

"To avoid being caught up in the fighting."

The slaves began discussing this. Osen had agreed that Sonea and Regin could follow the Traitors to Arvice, keeping a safe distance from the fighting, so that the Guild would keep track of the Traitors' progress. He'd suggested that Sonea use the excuse that she was checking the way was safe for the Healers the Guild was sending – but only if she had to. The fewer who knew of the deal, the less chance the Sachakan king would learn of it. If the Traitors lost but enough of them survived and were still willing to trade their stones, it would be easier to get Healers to them if the king didn't know about it.

The slave who had spoken strode forward, the others hurrying after him. Regin straightened and crossed his arms, but the man ignored him. The lead slave stopped a few steps from Sonea, staring at her intently, his eyes narrowing.

"We'll have to check that is the truth."

She nodded. "Of course." Inwardly she cursed. If they did manage to contact Savara, the queen would learn that Sonea and Regin were following her. She might try to stop them.

The main straightened. "In the meantime, you must stay here. It will be night soon and we Sachakans pride ourselves on our hospitality."

She inclined her head. "We would be honoured. With whom are we staying?"

314

The man paused and looked down, his confidence disappearing as if he had suddenly realised his behaviour had been unnecessarily confrontational. "I am Farchi," he said. He turned to introduce the others. Too many names to remember, Sonea decided. She took note of the names of the boldest, and the sole woman in the group.

With a gracious movement, Farchi invited her and Regin to accompany him to the estate. As they walked, Sonea figured she might as well find out what had happened here.

"If it is not rude of me to ask, is the damage here from a Traitor attack?"

Farchi nodded. "The queen and her fighters killed the Ashaki and freed his slaves."

"What will you do now?"

"Try to run things on our own, and with the Traitors' help."

"So the Traitors aren't going to take ownership of this place?"

"Some estates they will take. Most will go to ex-slaves. Some will be divided up."

"And the rest of the ex-slaves?"

"Will be paid for their work. And be free to live where they want, marry who they want, and keep their children."

She smiled. "I hope with all my heart that you achieve this."

Farchi's chin rose and his back straightened. "We will. The Traitors are Sachakans. They will not abandon the task, as the Guild did."

She looked at him closely. "How do you know they did? Our records indicate no decision by the Guild or Kyralia to stop trying to end slavery in Sachaka."

He frowned. "It's . . . what everyone says."

"They also say that the Guild created the wasteland to weaken Sachaka, but historical records found here in Sachaka

315

point toward it being the action of one madman, and many Guild magicians died trying to stop him."

And we now know that the Traitors are to blame for the wasteland never recovering. She resisted telling him that. The Traitors were the ex-slaves' rescuers. Even if they did believe her, it would undermine the Traitors' efforts to prevent Sachakan society falling into chaos once the Ashaki no longer controlled it. *But one day the truth will come out. I wonder what the ex-slaves will think of the Traitors then.*

"Was this madman Kyralian or Sachakan?"

"Kyralian."

"So it is still your fault."

Sonea sighed. "Yes, whether it was deliberate or a mistake, it was still the fault of a Kyralian. Just as it was the fault of all Sachakans that Ichani attacked Kyralia and murdered many of my people." She met his gaze and held it, and he quickly looked away. "If I don't blame you for the crimes of the Ichani twenty years ago, can you try to forgive me the act of a madman six hundred years ago?"

Farchi gave her a long, appraising look, then nodded. "That's fair."

She smiled, and followed him through the gates into a scene of destruction and hope, grief and newfound freedom.

As Cery joined Gol he drew in a deep breath of clean, forest air.

"Smells like spring."

"Yes," Gol agreed. "It's warm at night now, too."

"Warm*er*," Cery corrected. "As in warmer than cold enough to freeze your eyeballs."

Gol chuckled. "We'll have to skirt around the farm to get to the part of wall nearest the meeting place."

316

"Lead on, then."

With most of the undergrowth hidden in the night shadows cast by the forest, it was impossible to walk quietly and without stumbling. The passages below were a lot easier to get around, even in complete darkness. By the time they got to the wall that separated the Guild grounds from the city, Cery was sure that they must have attracted someone's attention with all the snapped twigs, rustling leaves and stifled curses. They waited for a while to make sure nobody and was coming to investigate, but no magician, servant or guard emerged from the darkness. Satisfied, they scaled the wall with the help of a nearby tree branch. From the top Cery could look over the eastern end of the North Quarter. Houses were built up against the wall, their yards divided by lower brick walls topped with an upside-down "v" embedded with broken glass to discourage climbing. The one below them contained a neat little garden.

Gol looped the end of a rope ladder around the tree branch they'd climbed to get on top of the wall, and knotted it. The rope had been another item stolen from the farm, and Gol had used short branches found in the forest as the rungs. He climbed down into the yard first, the rope creaking. Cery followed. They skirted the garden beds, paused to oil the hinges of the side gate to the yard, then slipped out into the shadows of the street beyond.

To walk the streets of the city felt like freedom. As they made their way through the neighbourhood, Cery wavered between excitement and worry at the risk they were taking. At least Anyi was safely back in the Guild with Lilia. He hadn't told her his plans for the evening, knowing that she would either try to stop him, or insist on coming. Even if he had talked her into staying behind, she'd have wanted to know why he was going into the city, and he could not think of a good enough reason.

Other than the truth. But I doubt she'd have found that a good enough reason anyway, he thought. *She wants me to live in the Guild and leave catching Skellin to the magicians.* She trusted the Guild too much. *And I don't?* He shook his head. *Not with Sonea gone and Kallen in charge of finding Skellin.*

He hadn't completely given up on the Guild, though. They weren't going to stop trying to find and deal with rogue magicians. But they'd take longer at it than he was prepared to wait.

To force their hand I need minefire, to buy that I need money, and the only caches I had that Skellin hasn't found are in the hands of minders.

Minders who didn't believe Cery was alive, and had refused to give the cache to Gol.

The risk of a trap was high, of course. He and Gol had selected the minder least likely to betray them to meet tonight. His name was Perin. Gol had hired three different street urchins as guides, each to take Perin on a winding journey through three Quarters of the city. The last instructions were written down, so that not even the urchins would see where Perin went. The meeting place was within a hundred paces of the wall, so if Cery and Gol had to run they had a fighting chance of reaching the grounds.

Reaching a crossroads, they stopped and looked around. Here the doorways were shallow and the street lamps bright. Nowhere to hide for several strides, so it would be difficult for someone to ambush them. A man stood on the opposite corner, watching them. Though Cery could not see all of the man's face, what was visible was familiar.

"Perin," Gol murmured.

Cery nodded. He crossed the road and approached the man. Perin stared at him intently, his eyes widening as he recognised Cery.

"Well, well. You're alive and breathing."

"I am," Cery said, stopping a few paces away.

"Here." Perin held out a wrapped parcel. "Send a messenger if you want the rest."

"Thanks. I owe you."

The minder grimaced. "No you don't. I have my fee, and the satisfaction of knowing the bastard who calls himself king didn't get to everyone." He held out a hand. Cery hesitated, then moved closer so the man could briefly clasp his arm, and did the same in return. "Best of luck and health," Perin said, his brows lowering as his gaze moved over Cery's face. "Looks like you could do with some."

Then the man stepped back, smiled tiredly and turned to walk away. Cery heard Gol quietly move closer behind him.

Did he mean luck or health? Or both? Am I looking as old and tired as I feel lately?

He felt a touch on his elbow. Shaking his head, he turned and followed Gol back to the house by the wall, through the gate and up the rope ladder. It was harder climbing up than down, but as they made their way through the forest he felt his mood lift. Their journey had been worth the risk. Gol had money to buy minefire. They were closer to being ready to lure Skellin into their trap.

And it was nice to know that someone, even if just a minder, was pleased to know Cery was still alive.

CHAPTER 21

INTRUDER

Sitting down at his desk, Dannyl took Osen's blood ring out of his pocket. *Oh, how I wish I could put this off a little longer.* But he couldn't. Osen expected Dannyl to report back to him every two or three days. He would be annoyed or alarmed if Dannyl didn't.

Even so, Dannyl hesitated. *I've never been able to tell how much of my mind Osen can read during our communications. I always assumed he, knowing my preferences, doesn't look too deeply – and that he would have objected already if they thought I was getting too friendly with Achati.* And that Osen could only read the thoughts Dannyl was actively *thinking* while wearing the ring, not all his memories.

It should be enough, then, to avoid thinking about his night with Achati while communicating with Osen. Of course, the subject a person was most worried about was the one their mind would most likely turn to. Overcoming that took concentration and control, skills Dannyl had painstakingly cultivated as a novice.

He closed his eyes and practised some mind-calming exercises. When he felt he had control over his thoughts, he slipped on the ring. Osen's mental voice immediately spoke.

—*Dannyl. Good. I have urgent news for you. Sonea met with the Traitors a few nights ago. Their queen, Savara, revealed their intention to overthrow Amakira and the Ashaki, and free all slaves.*

He needn't have worried how much Osen would see in his mind. The Administrator would be well distracted by this news. Dannyl felt his heart skip as Osen told him of the declined invitation to the Allied Lands to join them, and the deal they'd struck instead.

—*Lorkin has joined the Traitors. Sonea and Regin are heading to Arvice, following them.*

—*The Traitors are on their way?!*

—*Yes. They attacked the first estates yesterday. I don't know how long it will take them to get to Arvice, if they get that far at all.*

—*Do you think they'll win?* If Lorkin was with them, surely he believed they could. But if Lorkin's loyalty was with the Traitors now, he might choose to help them *because* their chances weren't good.

—*Impossible to say. Sonea believes they've been organising this for a very long time. They weren't forced into confronting the Ashaki. She doesn't think they'd risk everything they have if they didn't think they'd win.*

And yet Achati didn't think they had a chance. The man's face rose in Dannyl's mind and he felt a stab of apprehension before he pushed it aside.

—*I'm sorry, Dannyl. I know you regard Achati as a friend, but you cannot warn him. It would alert Amakira to the fact that we knew about this before he did. Do not do anything to raise suspicions of our foreknowledge of this.*

—*I understand. What should we do?*

—*Stay where you are. Stay together — and that includes Tayend. Stay out of sight. The Traitors won't harm you. The Ashaki shouldn't, if they don't suspect we're siding with the Traitors. Make sure Merria and Tayend understand all I have told you.*

—I will. Any messages for them?

—No. Sonea and Regin will join you when they get there, but I doubt they'll reach you until after the conflict is over.

—We'll stay put. At least they'll know where to find us.

—Yes. From now on report to me once a day, or as soon as you learn anything new. Take care, Dannyl. Contact me if anything happens.

Slipping off the ring, Dannyl stared at it again. *Sachaka is at war*, he thought. *An army is heading this way. An army of black magicians. Who will no doubt encounter an army of King Amakira's black magicians – a conflict of a kind not seen in over six centuries.*

He pocketed the ring, rose and strode out of the room, slaves scattering before him. He'd only taken twenty or so steps down the corridor when a female voice called out.

"Ambassador!"

He turned to see Merria hurrying toward him.

"I heard something last night you will find interesting," she said.

"Should Tayend know this, too?"

She nodded.

He beckoned and heard her fall into step behind him. They passed through the Master's Room, entered the corridor beyond and soon reached the door to Tayend's rooms. The female slave waiting attentively inside the main door threw herself onto the floor.

"Is Tay – Ambassador Tayend there?" Dannyl asked.

She nodded.

"Tell him we are here to see him."

She scrambled up and disappeared into one of the rooms. A moment later there was a low groan and a curse.

"Out!"

The slave darted out again and hurried over to Dannyl and Merria.

"Don't," Dannyl said as she went to prostrate herself again.

"The Ambassador is dressing," she said, then moved over to a wall and stood with her back to it, eyes lowered.

Osen said the Traitors are going to free the slaves, Dannyl thought. *If they succeed, where will the slaves here go?* Perhaps they would stay on as paid servants. He hoped so. It would be a relief when they stopped behaving so submissively. *Though I may, perhaps, think differently should they start pushing us around like some Kyralian servants do.* He blinked as something else occurred to him. *If the Traitors win, end slavery and join the Allied Lands, could some of these ex-slaves one day become magicians?*

He thought of the lengths to which Fergun had gone in order to prevent Sonea entering the Guild. If he'd felt Sonea didn't deserve to become a magician, what would he have thought of Sachakan slaves?

The idea made Dannyl feeling oddly cheerful, but the mood dissipated as Tayend appeared, looking dishevelled in his hastily donned elaborate clothing.

"Ambassador. Lady Merria," Tayend said, beckoning. He ushered them to the stools arranged in the middle of the central room, then sat down on a particularly large pillow and rubbed at his eyes.

"Late night?" Dannyl asked.

Tayend made a face. "Late and well irrigated. My Sachakan friends were particularly determined to drown their worries." He turned to the slave girl. "Bring some water and bread."

323

Once she had left, Dannyl drew magic and surrounded them in a sound-blocking barrier. He leaned toward Tayend. "They have reason to."

The Elyne's eyes widened and he straightened. "Oh?"

As Dannyl told them of Osen's news, both Tayend and Merria began to nod.

"That explains it," Merria said. "Last night my friends told me that female slaves suspected of being Traitors are being tortured and killed." She paused and frowned. "Well, that explains something else, too. My friends were making arrangements to travel to a country estate for the summer, and invited me along. I said I couldn't go. I had to stay with you." She nodded to Dannyl. "And they said you and Tayend could come as well, if you needed to."

"'Needed to'?" Tayend echoed. "Hmm."

"They've probably left already. I suppose I could find out where they are." Merria looked worried.

Dannyl shook his head. "We can't go with them."

"But should we stay here?" Tayend asked, looking at Dannyl. "Mistakes happen in wars. People can be killed by being in the wrong place, or by a stray bit of magic that misses its intended target." His pursed his lips. "I don't suppose we and Achati could go on another research trip."

The suggestion brought a pang of gratitude and anxiety. *Though he likes Achati, I doubt he'd have included him if it weren't for me.* "If we suggest it he'll suspect we knew the Traitors planned to invade," Dannyl replied.

"Unless he doesn't know. We could get him out of the way. He'd never forgive us for preventing him from doing his duty though," Tayend added, looking away.

Tayend was right. Achati's loyalty was with his king and

people. *He'll never leave Sachaka. Not for me.* He'd always known that.

"What will the Traitors do to the free women, and their children?" Merria asked.

They exchanged grim looks.

"I don't think they'd kill anyone who wasn't a magician," Tayend said slowly.

"It may depend on how well they treated their slaves," Dannyl added.

Merria shrugged. "Well, for all that they say they don't like the Traitors, my friends do seem to have some connection with them. Surely that means they'll be all right." She looked at Dannyl. "It's your friend I'd be worried about."

He was saved from having to respond by the return of the slave girl. As Dannyl rose to leave, Merria did the same.

"Stay a while, Dannyl?" Tayend asked. The Elyne waited until Merria and the slave girl had gone before he spoke. "You're worried. I can tell. But remember, the Traitors might lose."

"Lorkin is with them."

Tayend grimaced. "Ah. Yes. There is no good end to this, is there?"

Dannyl shook his head. "All we can hope for is that, whatever the outcome, the people we care about survive and escape." He turned and walked toward the door.

"You do care about him, don't you?"

Dannyl stopped and looked back to see Tayend had got to his feet. He thought about Achati's words: *"I would like us to be more than friends, for a time at least, before circumstances make us feel we must behave like enemies."* He sighed.

"I'm not in love, Tayend."

"No?" Tayend walked over and placed a hand on Dannyl's shoulder. "Are you sure?"

"Yes. I've never thought it would last. I just . . . I expected that if it ended it would be for more mundane political reasons."

"You fear for him."

"As I'd fear for any friend."

Tayend eyebrows rose in disbelief. "You two are more than just friends, Dannyl."

"You and I are more than just friends, Tayend. We were together too long to say otherwise. I'd fear for you in this situation, as well."

Tayend smiled, and his hand on Dannyl's shoulder squeezed. "And I for you. The only difference is I'd take you back without a second thought. You wouldn't." He turned away and walked back to the stools.

Breath catching in his throat, Dannyl gazed at Tayend. As the Elyne glanced back, Dannyl tore his eyes away and stepped out of the room. It wasn't until he reached his own suite that his mind snapped out of its surprise and began to churn with all that he'd learned and feared.

Pushing through the door into the inner passages of the University, Lilia took a few steps before she saw the novices ahead. They didn't move out of the way as she neared them. Instead, they turned to face her, the three of them blocking the way.

Lilia slowed. From behind her came the sound of the door opening again, then a "ha" of triumph. She turned to see Bokkin and two more novices approaching, all grinning.

"Lilia," Bokkin called. "Just who we were looking for, weren't we?" He glanced back at his followers and they nodded.

She shook her head. *I can't believe how stupid they are. Don't they think about the future? Do they think I won't remember any of this when I've graduated?* But that was in the far future, to them. They knew she would never be allowed to use black magic except in exceptional circumstances, and they couldn't imagine any other way she might gain revenge.

"You know what I heard, Lilia?" Bokkin asked. "I heard someone saying that novices haven't united against someone like you for years. Someone who doesn't know her place. Last time it was real effective, I heard."

They mean Sonea, she realised. "Effective?" she replied. "She beat her rival in a challenge and became a Higher Magician. If that's effective, I ought to encourage novices to unite against me."

She held back a laugh at the surprise on the other novice's faces.

Bokkin scowled. "*Before* then. Before—"

The door behind him opened and a black-robed magician strode through. Lilia felt a rush of relief, then quickly schooled her face. If anything had shown, she hoped they were too busy staring at Kallen to see it.

Kallen looked at them, his frown deepening as he took in the scene. The novices bowed. His eyes narrowed.

"Lady Lilia," he said. "We only need *one* volunteer." He scanned the faces. "Which of you would like the honour?"

Bokkin's followers turned to frown at him. Kallen followed their gaze and nodded. "You'll do, Lord Bokkin. Follow me."

The novices flattened themselves against the wall as he moved past. Not wanting to trail behind Kallen with Bokkin, Lilia turned and led the way to the small room Kallen used for her training. When she reached the door she turned back, expecting to see that Bokkin had fled.

327

But the boy had obediently followed. He was pale and frowning. *Worried*, she thought, smothering a smile. *I would be too. What on earth does Kallen want with him?*

Kallen opened the door and ushered Bokkin inside. Lilia followed. Kallen pointed to a seat. Bokkin sat down, his eyes downcast.

"Thank you for volunteering," Kallen said, taking the other chair. "Lilia has explained that it will not hurt?"

"Nnn—" Bokkin began, his eyes widening.

"Not yet," Lilia injected. "I haven't had time to explain much."

Kallen looked at her. Though he was frowning in disapproval, she caught a glint of something else in his gaze. *What is he up to?*

He turned back to the young man. "In fact, done correctly the subject cannot sense their mind being read at all." Bokkin's eyes went very wide, but Kallen didn't appear to notice. "Now, I did arrive a little late, and don't want to delay your arrival at your first class, so we'd best begin." He beckoned to Lilia. "Stand behind him."

She was glad he'd given her a reason to move out of Bokkin's sight, as she doubted she could have resisted smiling much longer. As she obeyed, Bokkin tried to turn to look at her.

"This wasn't . . . I didn't . . ."

Kallen leaned forward and fixed Bokkin with a challenging stare. "Changed your mind, have you? I guess we can always put the word out that we need someone else."

Bokkin stilled. Lilia could imagine him weighing up the options. Be labelled a coward or have his mind read by one of the feared Black Magicians and Lilia. To her amusement, Bokkin stayed put.

"You won't go looking through my memories?" he asked.

Kallen shook his head. "Of course not."

Bokkin nodded. "All right then."

Standing up, Kallen nodded to Lilia. "I will connect with your mind; you connect with his."

Taking a deep breath, Lilia placed her hands on either side of Bokkin's head and, as she felt Kallen's hands press against her temples, started a simple exercise to clear and focus her mind.

—*Lilia*, Kallen spoke.

—*Kallen*.

All she sensed was his presence and mind-voice. In other lessons involving mind-to-mind instruction, he had discouraged her from imagining her mind as a room. Sometimes it made the lessons harder, but it meant her grasp of concepts was less conscious and more instinctive. It made using magic feel like moving a limb – as much reflex as deliberate.

—*Bokkin will report us if you search through his memories, but I doubt he has much control of his mind. He'll probably show us what he doesn't want us to see anyway. If you remain alert, you may see something you can use to stop him harassing you.*

Lilia could not hide her shock from him.

—*But . . . we ought to ignore those memories!*

—*Yes. However, the Guild does allow some bending of the rules, in exceptional cases. We have learned that it is better to do so and stop the harassment of novices, than ignore it and risk those novices breaking rules and laws later.*

—*Because of Sonea?*

—*And conflicts brought about by opening the Guild to lower-class entrants.*

—*I'm not sure I could bring myself to use anything very private . . .*

—You may not need to. The threat of it may be enough to deter him.

—I hope so.

—Now, focus on Bokkin's mind. Sense his instinctive resistance to a mind-read.

She did as he instructed and sensed a surge of triumph from Bokkin as she failed.

—Now watch . . .

Kallen's presence expanded and weakened, like a beam of light softened by passing through a window screen. Bokkin's mind did not sense a focused effort at intrusion, and did not fight it. A moment later Kallen's presence sharpened again.

—Now you. Clear your mind of everything but the one intention: to drift into his mind like smoke.

Smoke or light, it seemed easy enough, but it took Lilia a few attempts before she was no longer detectable by Bokkin's mind. He must have sensed something in her approach changing, because by the time she did manage to enter his mind he was worried about her succeeding.

It's not right, he thought. *She broke a law. She shouldn't be allowed to learn these things.*

A memory rose. A face. Lilia instantly knew it was Bokkin's father. *"Someone will always grow stronger than you – if you let them. You have to sort them out while they're weak. Stop them getting strong."* Bokkin caught himself, forcing himself to stop remembering, but not before Lilia caught three quick flashes of emotion-laden images. Love and hurt. Beatings. Anger. Grief.

She understood, then, that Bokkin believed this fiercely and completely, and thought it the best piece of wisdom his father had taught him. After all, his father had proven it by beating

330

his own son into obeying and fearing him. Then his father had been killed by a man he had admitted he should have been harder on.

That's what he's trying to do to me, she realised. *He* is *thinking about the future. I'm going to be stronger than him, so he's trying to weaken me now.* She shuddered at the thought of the kind of magician he would become. *By then he'll be stronger than most people. It's only other magicians he'll be threatened by. Like me.*

—*Lilia?* Kallen spoke.

She moved out of Bokkin's mind.

—*Yes?*

—*You have done well. That is enough for now.*

She felt his hands leave her head, so she opened her eyes and released Bokkin. Kallen moved around to the chair and sat down. The door behind him opened.

"You can go now, Lord Bokkin. Thank you for your assistance. Tell one of the others to be here tomorrow morning, at the same time."

"Yes, Black Magician Kallen." Bokkin bowed and hurried out of the room.

The door closed behind him. Lilia leaned against the back of the chair, delaying sitting down. She didn't even want to feel the residual warmth of Bokkin from it.

"What did you learn?" Kallen asked.

Lilia grimaced. "That he believes anyone who might grow stronger than him is a threat, so he has to find a way to dominate them before they dominate him." Then it occurred to her he was probably asking about mind-reading. "Which is the opposite to how mind-reading works. You don't succeed by trying to dominate."

Kallen nodded. "Yes." He shook his head. "Magicians like

Bokkin are the reason we do not teach this level of mind-reading to all magicians."

"Wait . . . you mean *anyone* can learn to do this?"

"Unfortunately, yes. High Lord Akkarin was the first Guild magician to learn how to read the mind of an uncooperative person, so it has always been assumed that it was a skill that required black magic. He revealed to Black Magician Sonea that this was not true by teaching her how to read minds before he taught her how to take and store magic. Sonea agreed to keep that fact to herself. You must do so as well."

"Oh. Definitely." The thought of what Bokkin might do with such knowledge sent a shiver down Lilia's spine.

"You have a fresh and interesting way of approaching things, Lilia," Kallen said. "Like this idea of using a quick, strong stab of forcestrike as a substitute for a knife when performing black magic. It is ingenious. I have described it to Lady Vinara, and we have discussed ways we could experiment safely."

She felt her face warm at the praise and looked down. "Well . . . I hope it works."

"Even if it doesn't, it's worth trying. Well, that's all for today. You had best get to your first class."

As the door opened again, Lilia bowed and murmured his name. She made her way to her first class of the day feeling alternately cheered and worried. *I'm learning so much from Kallen, and he seems to approve of me more now that our lessons aren't all about Warrior practice.*

Yet while she now knew why Bokkin was harassing her, she had no idea how to stop him. *He's always going to be working against me. I'm always going to be stronger than him, though, and he's too stupid to ever be a threat in other ways, so it could be worse, I suppose.*

But she was going to have to keep a constant eye on him, and that was going to get very, very annoying.

Once Anyi's footsteps had faded from hearing, Gol stood up and retrieved his tools from under his mattress. As he got back to work, Cery inspected the holes his friend had drilled into a section of wall earlier, each one piercing mortar and the earth beyond. Anyi hadn't noticed them. The bricks were rough and cracked in places, and Gol had chosen positions where the lamplight cast heavy shadows.

He had to bend close to see the end of the tubes Gol had inserted in each hole, each with a little tongue of oily paper protruding.

"How many more do you want to do?" Cery asked.

Gol had moved to the opposite wall. "Depends how quick you think we can light them. You don't want the first lot to go off while we're lighting the rest. If I do five in each wall and we do a wall's worth each, we might get them all lit. Bring me a tube, will you?"

Moving to the box of fruit Lilia had brought them the night before, Cery emptied it and lifted the sacking at the bottom. He'd stored the minefire underneath, relying on Anyi's dislike of fruit to keep her from discovering it.

As he carried the first tube to Gol, he noticed a fine stream of dust leaking from a fold in the paper at one end.

"It's broken. Is that bad?"

Gol turned and his eyes widened. "Hold it so the hole's at the top," he said urgently.

Cery did so and the leak stopped. "Is it that dangerous?"

"Yes." Gol's expression was serious. "Get too much of this floating in the air, a candle or lamp could set it off." He looked down at the tube, then tipped a little powder into his palm before stuffing it into the wall. "I'll show you. Take a candle out into the passage and put it down about twenty paces away."

No more than a pinch of the dust lay in Gol's hand. Cery picked up a burning candle and took it out of the room, setting it down in the passage. Gol beckoned, then shooed Cery behind him. "You'd better cover your ears."

Cery did as Gol advised.

"Watch this."

He gathered the powder between two fingers, dashed forward and threw it at the candle. A flash of light dazzled Cery's eyes, and at the same time a sound like a very large hand slapping a table echoed in the passage. Dust and dirt trickled and puffed out of the walls near the candle, which was suddenly much shorter and surrounded by a molten pool of wax.

Cery removed his hands. *That, from just a pinch. And we have a lot more of it in those tubes.*

"Are you sure you want to put that many tubes in the wall?"

Gol shrugged. "Gotta put it somewhere. Safer if it's in the wall, than in the room with us."

Of course. Even if we leave it in the fruit bowl, it could still go off when the rest does. Better it fries the inside of a wall than us. "How long do the delay strips take to burn?"

"A count to twenty." Gol retrieved the candle, gave it to Cery and moved back into the room. "If we don't have enough time, we might get away with only lighting one on each side. When it goes it should set the others off."

"So we each light one, then run."

Gol frowned. "Is that Anyi coming back already?"

Cery listened. As he heard the faint sound of footsteps he hurried over to the fruit box and placed the sacking and fruit over the tubes again, while Gol hid his drilling tools. Just in case it wasn't Anyi, they kept hold of their candles. A moment later a low whistle echoed quietly in the passage and they relaxed.

Cery whistled back and a moment later Anyi hurried inside clutching her lamp. He realised that he'd assumed she was further away because her steps had been so faint. As she saw them, she let out a quick breath.

"One of the walls has collapsed near Lilia's barrier. Or it was broken. Whatever the reason, there's now another way to get through to here without breaking her barrier."

Cery's heart skipped a beat. "Any tracks?"

Her shoulders lifted. "I couldn't see. I shuttered the lamp so they wouldn't notice the light and came straight here. I didn't hear anything, though."

Cery looked at Gol. His bodyguard stared back, his face full of concern.

"I think you should get Lilia," Gol said.

"She'll be in class. I can't just—"

"Go to Sonea's room," Cery said firmly. "Tell Jonna to fetch Lilia."

"You should come with me. Hide in Sonea's room."

"If we hear anything, we'll follow you," Cery told her. "Now *go*."

She paused, biting her lip, then hurried away. Gol didn't even wait until her footsteps had faded. He dove for the drill and all but attacked the wall with it. Cery tipped the fruit out of the box and carried it over to his friend. Four more tubes of minefire lay in the base. Gol's words repeated in his mind even as he listened, straining his ears, for any sound in the passages.

"Safer if it's in the wall, than in the room with us."

He wasn't sure if his heart was racing more from anticipation or fear. Was Skellin approaching? Would they get to spring their trap at last? Would it create a big hole in the Gardens and expose the Rogue to the Guild, as they'd planned? Or would Skellin, not expecting the blast, die?

Whatever happens, at least Anyi is out of the way. I have no intention of dying along with Skellin, but the fewer of us around the less chance that one of us will be hurt.

CHAPTER 22

AN OLD ENEMY

S quinting at the dark smudge on the road ahead, Lorkin wasn't able to make out much more than the impression of movement. *Looks like a group of people on horseback.* He glanced at Savara. The queen's attention was on the road so she could not have missed them, yet she did not look concerned.

He turned to Tyvara, riding beside him, catching her shifting her weight in the saddle and grimacing. Seeing him notice, she smiled. "Only been a few hours and I'm chafing already."

Ex-slaves had given them horses at one of the estates they'd freed that morning. "Freed" simply meant walking in and executing the Ashaki owners and his magician brethren. Often the men had no more warning of an imminent attack than their slaves suddenly disappearing. Though they all put up a fight, most of them obviously weren't in the habit of keeping their store of magic well boosted. *Why would they? They're not Ichani, constantly under threat from other black magicians. They probably only stock up on power when they need it for a particular task.* It made their death seem less like casualties of war. More like murders.

It feels like we're breaking into these people's homes and killing husbands, sons and fathers, not waging a war. If we faced them in a unified front we'd still be killing husbands, sons and fathers, but it would seem justified. Yet the Traitors weren't triumphant victors, casually or vengefully killing off the families, looting and torturing. If they had been, Lorkin might have regretted his decision to join them. Instead they were merciful and efficient.

But ruthless.

He thought of the gemstone his mother had given him.

He reminded himself that his father had extracted a promise from Zarala that the Traitors would end slavery. His father had wanted this to happen. Every time Lorkin doubted, or lost courage, he looked to the newly freed slaves, and told himself this was all for a good cause.

He had expected the Traitors would encounter better-prepared Ashaki once the invasion began, but it was clear each was surprised by the attack. Perhaps those killed earlier were too occupied in their own defence to send a warning to others. Perhaps they relied on slaves to send messages, but the slaves who supported the Traitors ensured that those loyal to their masters did not leave to warn others.

Eventually a warning would get through, Lorkin knew. Maybe an Ashaki would mentally send a warning, either broadcasting it or communicating through a blood ring. Even if Savara's team managed to kill them before they got the chance, other teams might not. Once the news got ahead of the advancing Traitors, nothing would stop it spreading to the city. When it did, the Traitors would not be attacking one or two magicians at each estate, but an army of them. Which was why the shadow on the road ahead had set his heart racing.

He focused on Tyvara's mind and sensed eager expectation, with only a small pang of worry. *No more Traitors have died*, he caught. *But it won't be long . . .* She noticed him frowning at her, and smiled.

"Don't worry. It's just another team. As we all get closer to the city, teams will meet and join up."

Relieved, he turned to watch as the other Traitors approached. Shadows resolved into figures on horseback. Riders became women and men. Faces became recognisable. He heard Tyvara curse at the same time as he realised one face was familiar.

"What is *she* doing here?" he muttered.

Tyvara sighed. "Kalia's punishment was suspended for the duration of the invasion," she told him. "As was mine. It would be unfortunate if we lost, but for the power of two magicians."

He watched as Kalia's eyes moved over Savara's group, then her expression turned sour as she saw him and Tyvara.

"We are all on the same side," Tyvara said. "But I do wish Kalia had been put in a team attacking the opposite side of the city," she added in a lower tone.

Savara turned to look at them both. "I will be keeping an eye on her. And an ear." She looked back at the approaching team and urged her horse forward to meet them. To Lorkin's relief, the woman who came to meet her was not Kalia. It was Speaker Halana, leader of the stone-makers.

"At least she's not leading the team," he said.

Tyvara chuckled. "We aren't *that* stupid."

Halana placed a hand over her heart briefly, then took hold of the reins again to guide her horse to a stop next to Savara's mount.

"Any news?" Savara asked.

"We've lost Vilanya and Sarva," Halana replied. "They were ambushed."

"So the Ashaki are warned."

"Most likely. Any trouble?"

"A few slaves getting a little too eager," Savara replied. She sighed. "Those in one estate killed an entire family and the head slave, who was one of our allies. I told them this isn't our intention, but I don't think they were listening."

Halana nodded. "There will be more trouble of that kind. I have been hinting that we want to deal with the families ourselves, later."

"That might work, so long as they don't take on the role of jailor too enthusiastically." Savara looked around. "Let's continue."

The two groups mingled to become one. Lorkin noted that Kalia positioned herself so that Savara and Halana were between her and Tyvara. The two leaders discussed what they would do if freed slaves were unable to provide the Traitors with food. Not long had passed when Savara suddenly spoke loud enough for all to hear.

"What is this problem you are discussing, Kalia?"

Lorkin looked over to see the woman glance at him, then back at the queen. Her back straightened.

"We have a non-Traitor among us. I was merely advising Cyria that she be careful."

"Cyria need not be wary of anybody here. We are all Traitors."

"Lorkin is Kyralian."

"Kyralian born. Now a Traitor. There are ex-slaves and women who were formerly wives and sisters of the Ashaki among us. All chose to join us. All are needed."

"But he is a Guild magician, and a *man*."

Savara smiled. "If my meeting with his mother had achieved its purpose, we would be marching toward Arvice along with many hundred Guild magicians, among them quite a few men. Would so much masculine company alarm you, Kalia?"

"Of course not! Though I would not so easily trust them, as you might." Kalia gave Savara a sidelong look. "So . . . the Guild won't go to war with the Ashaki. And he is still here? Are you *sure* he isn't a spy?"

"I am sure."

"Do you really expect . . .?" Kalia fell silent as one of the Traitors at the rear called Savara's name. All turned to see the man pointing back along the road. Several hundred strides back, a cloud of dust billowed up behind a rider galloping toward them.

"Stop," Savara ordered. "And shield."

It was not long before the rider reached them, the horse slowing to a walk, sides heaving and dark with sweat. The rider was a young man wearing fine clothing, but his build and colouring suggested he was an ex-slave.

"Queen Savara," he said, placing a hand over his heart briefly. "I have been sent to warn you that two Kyralians are following you." He paused to think. "Black Magician Sonea and Asha – Lord Regin. We tried to keep them at the estate, but they disobeyed our order to stay and forced their way out with magic."

Lorkin suppressed a sigh. He should have expected it. *But if I couldn't let Tyvara go to war without me, why would I expect my mother to do the same?*

"Was anyone hurt?"

The man shook his head.

Kalia muttered something. Savara stared at the woman through narrowed eyes. Then she turned to Lorkin, her eyebrows rising in question.

341

He shrugged. "I don't know. She didn't say she was planning to follow me – us."

"Spy," Kalia said.

The queen scowled. "Enough, Kalia." She looked around the group, her gaze settling on two of the Traitors, one male and one female. "Saral, Temi. Go meet Black Magician Sonea and ask her to explain herself." She reached into a pouch at her waist and drew out a ring. As she tossed it to the woman, a glint of yellow reflected the sunlight. "Use this to tell me what they say."

The pair nodded and, frowing with obvious annoyance at the task, rode away with the messenger. Savara nudged her horse into a walk and set her gaze on the road ahead. In grim silence, the two teams continued, heading for the next estate, and the next battle.

Lilia drew in a deep breath and sighed it out again as she set pen to paper and tried to make sense of her notes from the morning's Healing demonstration. Though the number of subjects she was studying had been reduced and her graduation delayed, she still found it hard to concentrate at times like these.

It was easier to be motivated when I thought I might choose the Healing discipline. Now that I won't get to choose a discipline at all, what's the point? She'd be a black magician, and it was more important that she was ready to fight than Heal. *Not that I've suddenly become enthusiastic about Warrior lessons. But these new lessons with Kallen have been interesting. Perhaps because there is a lot we can discover about black magic. It's not as though the Guild has been studying it for centuries and knows everything about it.*

This morning's Healing demonstration had been on a man

who had been stabbed accidentally during a sword-fighting lesson. The wooden practice sword had pierced the toughened leather armour, but hadn't penetrated deeply. It was a rare occurrence. A slash with a sword usually slid across the armour, and stabs weren't supposed to be made with full force. But he'd been leaping toward his fighting partner, who had been angry and used more force than he'd realised.

A quick, forceful stab, she thought. *Which is what I want to do with magic, instead of using a knife, to break the skin's natural barrier before using black magic to take power.* Something caught her attention, and she looked up to find the teacher watching her. She realised she had been staring at nothing, her notes forgotten. *And thinking about how to kill someone with black magic.*

Other faces turned toward her, but she ignored them. When she'd entered the University that morning, and then the Foodhall later, the stares and whispering of other novices had been almost as bad as when she'd first returned to the University. Most likely Bokkin had said something about her lesson with Kallen. Not the truth, of course. Bokkin wouldn't want to admit he'd got himself into a situation where his mind had been read, so he had probably made something up. She wished Kallen had said what he wanted from Bokkin in front of the other novices. Then they would know she'd read Bokkin's mind, and if she revealed anything about him he couldn't deny it was true.

Not that I'm going to be telling people what I saw in his mind, she thought. *It just seems wrong.* Though Bokkin hadn't been tricked or coerced, and he could have left at any time. *He could claim otherwise. He can't accuse Kallen or me of anything, because he'd have to let a magician read his mind to confirm it. Still, he could insinuate that something else happened.*

343

She considered his plan – his need – to weaken others before they became stronger than him. If he didn't like anyone being stronger than him, then he was never going to be happy. He was surrounded by stronger magicians and, since his magical strength was average, he always would be.

Maybe he'll go somewhere else, once he graduates. Somewhere everyone else is weaker. She shuddered. What would he do in order to assure himself that he was the strongest, and make sure others knew it, too? *Someone needs to keep an eye on him.* Perhaps Kallen would, or the other Higher Magicians. Or her. One day she would be a Higher Magician. She could end up being the one who had to watch Bokkin.

"Lady Lilia."

Her heart skipped as she realised she had been staring at nothing again. The teacher didn't stare disapprovingly, however. She pointed toward the door. Following the woman's gaze, Lilia saw a familiar face and felt her heart jump again.

Jonna. The servant beckoned.

Rising from her seat, Lilia bowed to the teacher, then slipped between the desks and out of the room.

"What is it?" she asked as Jonna glanced up and down the corridor.

"Anyi was in Sonea's rooms," she said. "She said there might be an intruder down . . . you know where."

Lilia caught her breath. "How long ago?"

"She'd been waiting for a time, but I'm not sure how long. Took me a while to find which classroom you were in."

"I should hurry . . ." Lilia took a step down the corridor, then stopped. "I should go the other way. It'll be faster. Could you go back and tell her?"

Jonna shook her head. "She went straight back." The servant

frowned. "If you mean the way I think you mean . . . I'll come and make sure nobody sees you using it."

"Thanks, Jonna." Lilia headed toward a side passage and led Jonna deeper into the University. When they reached the hidden door Anyi had unblocked, Jonna moved to the next side corridor and peered down it.

She nodded. "All clear. Be careful," she whispered.

"I will," Lilia told her. Then she pulled the lever that opened the door, and stepped into the darkness beyond.

"It's incredible to think that all these people were slaves," Regin said.

"Yes," Sonea agreed.

They had just crested a long, low hill. Before them, the road stretched in a nearly straight line and was busy with people and carts — even the occasional fancy carriage. At first she had wondered what reason the former slaves had for roaming about, other than to exercise their newfound freedom to go where they wanted. Surely it made sense to take over the estates they had worked on, so that they would have food and shelter.

Then they'd witnessed the reunion between two women, one older and one younger, and realised they were mother and daughter. A young woman cried out with joy as she was handed a baby by a man. Two young men hurried to meet each other, calling out "brother!" Couples of all ages embraced, walked and talked with each other.

Their masters may have forbidden them to marry, she thought. *They may have bred them like domestic animals, but they could not stop them from feeling the bonds of love and family, despite slavery existing here for more than a thousand years.*

"I always believed slavery was wrong and was proud Kyralia ended it as soon as we were free to," Regin said. "But that happened centuries ago. We Kyralians never really comprehended it, because we never saw it for ourselves."

Sonea nodded. Looking at Regin, she felt an unexpected affection. *If the Traitors lose, then at least I got the chance to see the compassion and humility in him.*

"Perhaps that's why we failed to end it," he continued, "when we conquered Sachaka. It had been too long since we'd endured it ourselves."

Sonea shook her head. "But it had only been a few hundred years since Kyralia and Elyne regained their independence and ended slavery."

"Enough time for those who knew what it was like to die of old age, and the concept to become an abstract idea to their descendants."

"And yet we still have an aversion to it, passed down for a further seven hundred years."

"Only because it is something we associated with Sachakans."

Sonea chuckled darkly. "Ah, yes. Because that made them hateful, which made us morally superior. Never underestimate the pleasure of seeing faults in others."

Regin turned to frown at her. "You don't think slavery is—"

"Of course not. I just wish we'd done this when we had the chance." She gestured to the people before them. "And that the Allied Lands had accepted the Traitors' invitation."

"You'd have us go to war, when most of us are too weak to make a difference?"

"Yes. But in our own way."

Regin looked at her, then his eyes widened. "By the Guild giving you and Kallen all our power."

"Which I have taken already. All we had to do was prepare and send for Kallen."

"Or Lilia?" Regin frowned. "No . . . she is too young."

"Not much younger than I was when I fought in my first war, but yes, I wouldn't wish that on her and we shouldn't risk losing all magicians with knowledge of black magic."

Regin smiled. "Though it appears it can be learned from a book, after all."

"Yes." Sonea sighed. "I suspect the Guild will lose its battle against black magic soon. If the Traitors win it'll be even harder to . . ." She paused as she saw a couple on horseback riding toward them. They wore Traitor garb, and looked familiar. The pair were looking at her and Regin. "Those two look like they're coming to meet us."

Regin squinted against the bright sunlight. "And they don't look surprised to see us either. I expect someone has told them we didn't go home."

They watched as the pair drew closer. *A man and a woman,* Sonea noted. *Is she the magician and he a source of power?* she wondered. *Or did the Traitors train their men to use magic so they could fight?* A few strides away, the couple turned their horses to block Sonea's path.

"Black Magician Sonea," the woman said. "Lord Regin. I am Saral, this is Temi. Queen Savara asks why you have not returned home."

Sonea paused as if to consider her answer. She had expected the question, but didn't want her answer to seem too well rehearsed.

"The Guild is obliged to ensure its members will be safe, when in other lands," she told them. "I am here to ensure our Healers will not be in danger."

347

The woman's eyes went blank, then focused on Sonea again. "We will make sure all Guild magicians entering Sachaka are unharmed."

"So you have the time to patrol the roads, and have Traitors free to act as guards and escorts, at the same time as fighting the Ashaki? I would rather you put your resources into achieving your aims." Sonea stepped forward until she was looking up at Saral, addressing the woman she knew was watching her through the ring Saral was wearing. "Not the least because you have my son with you," she added, lowering and hardening her tone. "Do you really expect me to go home? I am one magician, and no threat to you or your people, Queen Savara." She smiled. "Whether you have Lorkin with you or not."

Saral's chin lifted, then her gaze flickered away again and she scowled. Her face fell and she looked down at Sonea.

"You may continue to Arvice," she said. "On the condition that you do not enter the city before we do, and you do not side with the Ashaki. I can't guarantee your safety if you get in the way, and if you or your lover influence the battle against us you will both be killed."

Sonea inclined her head. "I give you my word that we will keep to these conditions."

Saral's lips thinned and her shoulders slumped. "Temi and I will escort you," she said. Beside her, Temi made a small noise of protest.

Sonea nodded again. "Thank you. For the sake of avoiding embarrassment, I should point out that you are wrong in one matter."

"What?" Saral's eyes narrowed.

"Lord Regin is not my lover."

The woman's eyebrows rose into a disbelieving expression. She said nothing in reply, instead turning her horse so that it faced the way she had come. Temi did the same, smirking as he moved to take a position on the other side of Sonea. Regin stepped forward to stand beside Sonea. He met her eyes briefly.

"Traitors like gossip as much as everyone else," he murmured, smiling.

Sonea shrugged and started walking. Such gossip could be dangerous. An enemy, thinking they were a couple, might try to harm Regin in order to blackmail her. But, as she'd hinted to Savara through Saral, if the Traitors wanted to blackmail her, they already had Lorkin. *Still . . . Regin would be a better target, if Tyvara cares for Lorkin and Savara cares about Tyvara's feelings.*

She looked at Regin, and he turned to meet her gaze. If he was worried, he was keeping it well hidden. His eyebrows rose in question, then his mouth twitched into a small, secretive smile. She looked away. *Anyone watching him would think we were a couple.* She looked back at the days they'd spent together since leaving Imardin. It had been a relief to find they got along with each other. That she didn't mind his company, and he didn't seem to mind hers. But what was it that others saw to make them think more was going on? *I'm not doing anything*, she thought. *Is it Regin, then? Surely . . .*

She shook her head. *No. He's not in love with me. Don't be ridiculous.*

But what if he was? She thought back. Tried to remember everything he'd said. Tried to recall how he'd spoken to her, behaved around her, *looked* at her. She remembered how she had started to ask herself the same question before, in the carriage after leaving the Fort. What had he said to make her wonder? That he had admired her for years.

Was he trying to tell me more? She shook her head again. *Does it only seem that way now that I'm wondering about it?*

She couldn't ask him, because the Traitors would hear. But if an opportunity came to talk with Regin privately . . . The thought of it made her throat close up. *I can't do that. What if I'm wrong? It would be embarrassing for the both of us. Or would it be worse if I'm right? At least I'm sure I'm not in love with him.*

A tangle of contradictory feelings and thoughts followed. It took all her self-control to keep her steps regular and her face calm. Then, as quickly as it had risen, the conflict ended, leaving her surprised and dismayed.

So. I do. No, I could. That's different. The potential is there, but it isn't so. Yet, she thought. But she wouldn't say anything of it to Regin. And if he hinted of feelings for her she would have to discourage him. *It's not that I haven't forgiven him. He's become a person so much better than the novice I hated. It's not that I haven't got over Akkarin – well, got over him enough to love another. It's not even that it makes Regin vulnerable, should someone seek to blackmail me. It's because . . .*

She felt a stab of annoyance. Why was it that the only men who showed any romantic interest in her had no right to? Not that she had any real proof of Regin's interest. Which was just as well because, though Regin had parted from his wife, he was still legally married.

CHAPTER 23

THE ULTIMATUM

Dannyl paced his rooms.

There must be some way I can warn Achati without revealing how we know the Traitors are coming. It would be a few days before the Traitors arrived and they needed to behave as if nothing extraordinary was happening, so Tayend had left to visit an Ashaki merchant, and Merria was making an afternoon visit to the market with a friend who hadn't left the city yet, leaving Dannyl alone to ponder his dilemma. *I could pretend one of the slaves told me the Traitors are coming. Or passed on a message to me. But what if that leads to the Ashaki torturing more slaves?*

A movement in the doorway caught his attention. He turned to see Kai drop to the floor.

"Ashaki Achati is here to see you."

He's here! Dannyl felt his heart lift, then plunge downward again. *And I don't have a solution yet.* Then he shook his head. *Well, it has only been half a day. Even if I'd thought of something, I ought to run it past Tayend first, so I'll have to behave as if I know nothing for this meeting anyway.*

"Have some food and wine brought."

The slave rose and hurried away. Entering the corridor,

Dannyl strode down it to the Master's Room. He felt a wave of affection as Achati turned and smiled at him.

"Ambassador Dannyl."

"Ashaki Achati." Dannyl inclined his head. "A pleasure to see you again."

The Sachakan's smile vanished. "Ah, I hope it always will be." He sighed. "I have news."

"Good or bad?" Dannyl ushered the man to a stool and sat down in his usual place.

Achati considered. "Not good. Not overly bad. Possibly advantageous."

"You're being mysterious now."

"Just answering the question." The corner of Achati's eyes crinkled, then smoothed as he sobered. Two slaves appeared with the wine and food. Achati waited until they had gone before speaking again.

"The Traitors have ventured out of the mountains and have begun attacking estates all around the country," he said in a low voice. "They've killed every magician they encountered and are heading toward Arvice. It appears they are intent on taking over Sachaka."

A wave of relief swept over Dannyl, which he hoped he hid well. *He knows! I don't have to warn him. But I can't admit that we knew already.* He drank a mouthful of wine, considering how to respond. *Not with surprise. He's mentioned the possibility of a Traitor rebellion before.*

"You thought this might happen," he said, "but doubted they were strong enough to be a threat."

"I still do." Achati shrugged. "Which is why this is not good news, yet is possibly advantageous. The Traitors are unlikely to survive, so we will finally be rid of them.

352

Unfortunately we will lose many good men in the process. The king doesn't want to send forces out to meet them. They are attacking from all directions, so it would thin our ranks if we tried to tackle them all. He has sent messages ordering Ashaki and their families to retreat to the city."

"Will they obey him?"

Achati nodded. "Most will, but whether they do so quickly enough is another matter. And there is one setback we didn't anticipate." He paused to look around the room. "Slaves have taken the opportunity to rebel. Mostly by fleeing from estates just before the Traitors arrive, but a few have attacked their owners."

"And succeeded?"

"Only in a few cases – with poison. Which is one of the reasons I am telling you this. Be careful of your slaves, Ambassador Dannyl."

Dannyl looked at the wineglass in Achati's hand. The man hadn't even sipped it yet. Did he fear the slaves here? The Guild House slaves belonged to the king, but that hadn't prevented the Traitors putting their spies among them. Dannyl had drunk only a little of the wine, and hadn't touched the food. He sent his mind within but found no sign of distress.

"I should be able to counteract the effect of poison with Healing magic," he told Achati.

Achati chuckled and raised the glass to his lips. "Handy skill, that one."

Dannyl nodded. "Do Ambassador Tayend, Lady Merria and I have anything to fear from the Traitors?"

Achati shook his head. "I see no reason why they would attack you, so long as you keep out of the way. If by some ill chance this goes badly, and the Traitors reach the city . . ."

He paused and sighed, his shoulders dropping. "I confess I fear you would be in more danger from my people than theirs. The king has treated you as if you had colluded with the Traitors. If the rebels do a lot of damage, some Ashaki may come here to seek retribution. Or, if the battle goes badly, they may seek to replenish their store of power."

Dannyl stared at Achati. For the man to admit his people might do this . . . there must be a real danger.

"What should we do?"

Achati held Dannyl's gaze. "There is a ship in the harbour called *The Kala*. The captain has been told to take you, Ambassador Tayend and Lady Merria on board if you request it. He will sail you back to Kyralia."

But Osen told us to stay . . . ah, I can't tell him that without revealing we already knew about the attack. Still, Osen might change his mind once I tell him what Achati fears.

"Thank you. I'll have to ask the Guild what they want us to do. Would you . . .?" Dannyl paused, wondering what Osen would think of the proposal. *If it meant we were safe, he'd agree to it.* "Would you come with us?"

The Sachakan's eyes widened a little. He smiled and reached out to touch Dannyl's arm in a gesture of reassurance and fondness. "My place is here, with my king and people." He waved his other hand, holding the wineglass. "And it is very unlikely the Traitors will reach the city anyway. The ship is just a precaution." He squeezed Dannyl's arm gently, then let go. "And an excellent excuse to visit you."

"I appreciate the warning. And the visit." Dannyl put his wineglass aside. "You've missed Tayend, though. And Merria."

"A pity. I may not have much time spare to visit again until after this little crisis is over."

354

Dannyl's heart skipped. *If he is wrong about the Traitors, it might be the last time we are together.*

"But I do have the House all to myself for the evening. Can you stay long?"

Achati's eyebrows rose, then he smiled. "Perhaps for an hour or two."

The room shivered with candlelight. Though the effect looked as if it was the result of the flickering flames, Cery knew some of the movement was from the shaking of his hand. He felt hot wax drip over his knuckles and looked down. Though it felt like they had been standing like this for an hour, the candle wasn't visibly shorter.

He looked across the room at Gol, who was also holding a candle at the ready. Cery frowned as Gol shifted his weight and the flame came perilously close to lighting a timer strip. He could hear Gol's quick breathing. His own seemed too loud. He tried to breathe deeper and quietly, to will his racing heart to slow down, worried that either would drown out the sound of someone approaching.

Skellin – if it is Skellin – is going to hear us and know we're waiting for him. The only reason we'd stay put is if we knew he was coming was if we had set a trap. I'd realise that. Surely he would, too.

Several ways that his plan could go wrong went through his mind. He knew the trap wasn't perfect. The minefire might go off before he and Gol had a chance to get safely away. It might go off too late to harm Skellin. While they hoped that it would kill him, their aim was to blow a hole in the Gardens above and reveal the Rogue Thief to the Guild. But what if it didn't? What if there was no hole, and Skellin survived?

355

What if Skellin didn't come personally to deal with Cery? What if Cery and Gol blew a hole in the Gardens, and possibly themselves, only to reveal Skellin's minions to the Guild?

Gol was looking at Cery now, and shaking his head. In his eyes was a question. How long would they stand like this before they decided Anyi had been wrong, and no intruder was in the passages? Cery looked at his candle. Should they take turns instead? Should they . . .?

From somewhere down the corridor came a sharp intake of breath. Cery looked at Gol, then followed his bodyguard's surprised gaze to the doorway.

Someone was standing there. *No*, Cery realised. *Someone is* floating *there.* Someone all too familiar.

"So this is where you've been all this time," Skellin said. Then he whistled. From further back in the tunnels came a piercing reply.

Cery moved his hand in the direction he'd feared to go moments earlier, and heard a sizzle as the timer strip caught alight. He saw a spark flare in Gol's direction, then turned and dashed for the door to the next room.

And slammed into the wall.

No, not the wall. A barrier of magic. Cery cursed as he realised Gol had encountered the same invisible obstruction. Light filled the room – the distinctive glare of a magic globe light. His friend looked at him, his expression grim and frightened. Cery met Gol's eyes and grimaced. *So that's it, then. We might have had time to escape if we'd heard Skellin coming . . .* But Skellin had levitated to avoid his footsteps being heard. As Cery turned to face his enemy he saw the flame of the timer strip Gol had lit retreat in its hole. He closed his eyes and held his breath. *At least Anyi got away.*

"Now, now. No need to brace yourself. It would be rude of me to kill you without having a bit of a chat first. Hmm. Not much of a hideout."

Cery opened his eyes to see the Thief magician, his shoes now touching the floor, walking toward him. Two men stepped into the doorway behind him. They were young and well muscled. Skellin looked around the room, then over Cery's shoulder at the next one. "Not as nice as your old one, from what my mother tells me, though perhaps that was your wife's taste in decoration and you've reverted to the habits of your namesake since she died."

My wife . . . the hideout . . . Cold shock and then hate rushed through Cery. *Lorandra did murder my family. Though why would she do so when Skellin and I weren't enemies then?*

"Though perhaps you were glad to be rid of her. You were supposed to be so angry that you'd form an alliance with me so I'd find the Thief Hunter for you," Skellin said.

Cery stared at Skellin. *He killed my family to make me want to join forces with him. After he "found" the Thief Hunter — or some poor scapegoat — I'd be indebted to him.* He looked at the other wall, seeking the flame of the timer he'd set alight. He saw no spark of light. It, too, had burned back into the wall, toward the tubes of minefire. Soon it would blast Skellin into . . .

Gol cursed and bowed his head. "Sorry, Cery," he muttered. "It should have gone by now."

Cery cursed as he realised the trap had failed. Gol had shown him that the minefire worked. Why not now?

"What are you chatting about?" Skellin came closer, his strange eyes narrowing. He leaned toward Cery and his mouth stretched into a humourless smile. "There's someone missing, isn't there? Where is your daughter, Ceryni?"

357

Cery's heart began to shrink inside his chest, but he forced himself to laugh. "Do you really expect me to tell you that?"

Skellin shrugged, then straightened and looked around. "No. But my sources in the Guild tell me she is down here with you. I wonder where she could be."

"Safe from you," Cery told him. *Sources in the Guild? So the rumours are true. But how do they know Anyi is here?*

"Is she?" Skellin must have removed the barrier, as he moved past Cery into the next room, his globe light floating before him. "Who sleeps on the third bed, then?"

"Someone you don't want to meet."

Skellin didn't reply. He was looking at the doorway to the passage leading to the Magicians' Quarters. Though his face was turned away from Cery, the set of his shoulders suggested he was listening to something.

Anyi and Lilia? Cery felt a rush of hope followed by fear. *I hope Lilia is ready for this, and Anyi has the sense to stay out of the way.*

Skellin took a step toward the doorway, then another. Cery sensed that Gol had crouched down. He looked away and saw that his bodyguard had picked up a still-burning candle. Skellin's two henchmen had moved into the room, however. They would be able to stop Gol getting to any of the minefire tubes set into the walls.

A laugh drew Cery's attention back to Skellin. The Rogue had stepped into the passage. He extended a hand toward something out of Cery's view. An all-too-familiar voice cursed. Anyi appeared, struggling as an invisible force pushed her into Skellin's reach.

At the sight of her Cery felt his heart jump and twist like an animal struggling to escape – and it *hurt*. He clenched his fists against the pain and started forward, but something caught and held his legs. Gol, too, lurched to a halt.

Where is Lilia? As Skellin reached out to grab Anyi, she stopped resisting and darted forward. *Surely Anyi didn't come back without Lilia.* But the hand that stabbed toward Skellin twisted as it encountered his torso and she cursed in pain. Skellin grabbed her wrist and prised the knife out of her grip. *But if she couldn't find Lilia then . . .*

The Thief looked up at him, grinning. "Safe from me, eh? Looks like you've failed to protect your family again, Ceryni."

Cery gritted his teeth. *Had Anyi at least sent a message to Lilia? Was Lilia on her way?* Cery wanted to ask Anyi, but the pain in his chest made it hard to breathe and he didn't want to warn Skellin that Lilia was coming. *We have to delay him. Give Lilia time to get her.*

Anyi was still fighting, but she could do nothing to harm or unbalance Skellin. Cery swayed as a wave of dizziness hit him, and the room darkened. When his sight cleared he saw that Skellin had pushed Anyi against a wall. She stayed there, held in place with magic. Skellin whistled, and the men pushed past Cery.

"Search and bind her."

Anyi's jaw tightened as the men stripped off her coat and felt for weapons. Cery wrapped aching arms around his chest and dragged in a breath to speak.

"You want me, not her," he managed.

Skellin laughed. "I want all three of you. But you have to die in the right order. And . . ." Skellin looked up and around as if he could see the magicians above them. "Not here." He turned to face them, his eyes moving from Cery to Gol. His nose wrinkled and he shook his head. "You're not worth the trouble." His eyes narrowed and Cery heard a sickening crack. Gol cried out in agony and surprise, and fell to the floor.

No! I have to stop him killing Gol. Slow him down! Cery tried to think past the fire in his chest. Find some way to delay Skellin a little longer. He opened his mouth to speak but only ended up gasping out a breath. Another wave of blackness consumed him and he felt his knees go weak. He suspected that only Skellin's magic was holding him up. *What has he done to me?*

"Wait a moment," he heard Skellin say. "There's something wrong with him."

Cery felt a growing fear as he realised Skellin was right. *It's not him. It's me. My body . . . my heart . . .* Though his eyes were open, darkness still obscured his vision. A bitter triumph rose. *At least Skellin didn't get the satisfaction of killing me. But . . . Anyi . . .*

The force holding Cery melted away and he felt himself land on the hard floor. Whatever Skellin said next, he said at such a distance that Cery could not hear it. Then, after a stretch of silence, he felt cool hands on his face and he heard Gol talking from far, far away.

"Don't worry. He won't kill Anyi. He wants to make a trade. Lilia will get her back. If Anyi doesn't kill him first. Those two will always look after each other. You know it. Don't worry. It'll all be fine. Anyi will be fine. We'll make sure of it."

Lilia hurried down the passage, keeping a tiny globe light floating before her.

Should I extinguish it? The intruder might see the light and know I'm coming. But if I do that, I'll have to feel my way in the dark. It'll slow me down. What's more important? Speed or remaining undetected?

Her footsteps sounded loud in the narrow space. They would betray her approach anyway. She decided to keep the light burning.

Aside from her own footsteps, she heard no other sounds. The secret entrance to the passages that Anyi had cleared was on the far side of the University, so Lilia had to make her way around the foundations of the building. Fortunately, the passages were no labyrinth here. They were straight and turned at right angles until they led away from the University, under the gardens. Lilia's heart was pounding by the time she reached the first curved wall.

I don't think I've been so scared in all my life, she thought. *I think I'd even consider having a little roet right now, if someone offered it to me.*

The intruder might be someone harmless – a novice or servant venturing where they shouldn't. Anyi might be wrong, and there was no intruder at all. Or it could be Skellin's people, come snooping or looking for Cery. In that case, she had to hope that, if they'd found Cery, then he, Gol and Anyi had been able to hide until she got there.

But if it was Skellin or Lorandra. Or Skellin *and* Lorandra . . .

I have to hope, if both of them are here, that I've gained enough extra power from Kallen to fight them. And enough skill.

She'd considered this many times before. It was unlikely Skellin or Lorandra had much training in fighting. Lorandra might have learned something before she left her homeland, but she and Skellin would have had no training here. The most they could have done was practise on each other.

She was not far from the rooms now. As she started down the last stretch of passage she slowed, staring into the darkness ahead.

Should I whistle to warn them it's me? It'll warn Skellin if he's already there. But if he is, wouldn't I be able to see light and hear voices?

She added more magic to her shield and crept forward. A faint noise reached her. A low, murmuring voice. The doorway was dark, but as she drew closer she saw a faint, flickering light. Reaching it, she peered around the opening and saw a single candle burning, braced between two rocks, and a hunched figure sitting on the floor. At the same time she heard a choking sound.

Something about that sound made her stomach sink.

The man's head lifted and the shadows concealing his face retreated from her globe light. Gol's cheeks glistened.

"Lilia," he said.

She brightened the light and saw what he was sitting beside.

"Oh no." She hurried forward and knelt on the floor. Cery's face was pale, his eyes closed. She could see no sign of injury. Placing her hand on his forehead, she sent her senses out – and immediately recoiled. "Oh no."

"It's too late, isn't it?" Gol said, his voice tight.

She felt her heart twist, then looked around the room. *Where is Anyi?*

"Yes. What happened?"

"I don't know. Skellin did nothing to him. Was going to take him away. But . . . he just collapsed."

Reluctantly she reached out and touched Cery's body, forcing herself to examine him again. She had never used her Healing skills on a dead person before. The lack of presence, the mental silence within, the lack of a natural barrier to repel the will of another, all were shocking to her. But if Skellin had done this . . .

No. The damage was clear, once she found it. Cery's heart had failed. *Not that Skellin didn't cause it indirectly, by forcing Cery to live here, constantly fearing for his safety. And Anyi's.*

Anyi. She withdrew her senses, opened her eyes and looked at Gol. He had slumped forward, and was breathing quickly. His face was contorted with pain, but she suddenly understood it was not just the pain of grief.

"What's . . . are you hurt?" She reached out and grabbed his arm, then jumped as her senses opened to a flood of agony. It was coming from somewhere lower. His legs. Letting go of his arm, she crawled over to him and grabbed his shoulders. "Lie down."

He did as she told him, sucking in sharp breaths as he moved. Once he was lying flat, she moved her light over to his legs.

"Don't," he said. "Go. Find . . . her. Find . . . Anyi."

She froze. From somewhere deep inside her rose a terrible dread. "*Where is she?*"

"Skellin . . . took her."

"When?" Her mind raced ahead. She climbed to her feet. Cery had not been dead long. Skellin could still be in the passages. If she left now, she might catch him. Save Anyi. "But why take her? Why not kill her?"

"You." Gol gasped, sucked in a breath, held it. "Wants you. Will send . . . a message. Where . . . to meet."

She pictured herself catching up with Skellin. Fighting Skellin. She shook her head. *He won't fight me. He'll put a knife to Anyi's throat. Or do something with magic. He'll use her to get away. And take me with him. And make me teach him black magic.*

Would it work out any differently if she waited for his message? Perhaps he'd torture Anyi in the meantime.

363

No. He won't harm her. Not if he wants me to teach him.

He might accidentally hurt her if she rushed upon him now.

If she waited for the message, waited for the meeting, she would have time to work out how to rescue Anyi without teaching Skellin black magic. Time to strengthen herself. *Time to decide how I'm going to tell Anyi her father is dead.*

She may know already. Oh, Anyi. I'm sorry I didn't get here faster.

It took more strength of will than anything she had done before to not run after her. Forcing herself to kneel down next to Gol, ignoring his protests, she set to work mending his shattered bones. And hoped, desperately, that she had made the right decision.

CHAPTER 24

DANGEROUS MINDS

The sky was streaked with orange and black when Saral and Temi moved off the main road towards another estate. Sonea and Regin followed. Every night since the Traitor escort had met them, they had stayed at freed estates. Horses had been given to them at Saral's request on the second morning, though they had not ridden at any great speed since then.

I'm surprised we haven't caught up with Savara's group. It must take time to confront and subdue the Ashaki. But maybe that's why we're travelling so slowly. She doesn't want us catching up – or getting to Arvice before her.

They'd travelled mostly in silence. Saral and Temi clearly weren't happy about their role as escort to two inconvenient foreigners, but neither complained. They did not strike up a conversation either. At the estates it was a different story. The newly freed slaves were euphoric and endlessly talkative, asking questions of Saral and Temi and assuming Sonea and Regin were welcome visitors in Traitor eyes. Now, as the four horses neared the estate's walls, ex-slaves poured out to greet them.

"Welcome, Traitors!" they called. "Will you stay here?" They came forward in a surge, then the foremost slowed as they saw Sonea and Regin.

"I am Saral and this is Temi," Saral told them. "This is Black Magician Sonea and Lord Regin, of the Magicians' Guild of Kyralia. We are escorting them."

One of the slaves stepped forward. "I am Veli, chosen leader of this estate." He looked up at Sonea. "Welcome to Sachaka."

"Thank you, Veli," Sonea replied, inclining her head respectfully.

Veli's attention returned to Saral. "Will you be staying? Queen Savara and her team were our guests last night."

"Yes, we will stay, and we would all like news of your previous guests."

Saral looked at Sonea and almost seemed to smile. Sonea inclined her head again in gratitude. At every estate where the queen had stopped, Sonea had asked after Lorkin.

The ex-slaves led them into the estate, where they dismounted and the horses were taken away. A middle-aged woman and her two daughters approached and welcomed them.

"Tiatia is the former owner's wife," Veli explained. "She welcomed Queen Savara into her home when she arrived."

"And her husband?"

"Is in the east. He is a good man and we did not want him to die. We knew there was a chance that he would be forced to fight along with the other Ashaki, or that we would not have a chance to speak in his defence, so we arranged for him to be out of the country."

"What did the queen think of this?"

"She said she was impressed with our loyalty. But it was not simple loyalty."

Saral frowned. "No? What was it?"

"Friendship." As Saral regarded him closely, his gaze faltered. But then he lifted his head and stared back at her. "He is a good man," he said defensively. "If you want proof, take a look at our slave quarters. They are clean and warm. He allowed men and women to choose each other and live together, and to keep their children. He only required us to make obeisance when visitors were here."

Saral's eyebrows rose. "Remarkable. What will happen to him now?"

"His ship slaves will tell him everything in a few days, and warn him that he may have to seek permission to return. Do you think it will be granted?"

The two Traitors exchanged looks. Temi shrugged. "Perhaps. He will have no land. He will have to live on equal terms with you."

"He will be honoured to," Tiatia said.

Saral looked at the woman, then Veli, and nodded. "Queen Savara did say there would be circumstances like these and that we must know when to balance caution with compassion."

"Come inside," Veli said, smiling. "Rooms and a meal are already being prepared for you."

As with all previous estates, a surprisingly humble main door led down a corridor to a bigger room, which in each home has been put to different uses: sometimes storage, sometimes sleeping quarters, sometimes a gathering place.

"Sit," Veli invited. "It will be a while before the food is ready."

Sonea chose a pair of stools for her and Regin. *Sitting on pillows is for younger people than me*, she mused. Veli, Saral and Temi did the same.

"While we wait, can I prepare some raka for you?" Tiatia asked.

Saral looked at Veli, her eyebrows raised in question. He nodded. "Yes, that would be appreciated," Saral replied.

Tiatia smiled, and settled with her daughters onto pillows at the centre of the room. Beneath a stool was a raka pot and a canister of the powder. As more ex-slaves arrived carrying water and cups, she set to work. While Saral and Veli talked about the estate's produce and future, Sonea watched, amused to see such a familiar ritual of preparation in a place so unfamiliar. To her surprise, steam began to waft from the pot's spout.

"You are a magician?" Sonea asked Tiatia.

All conversation abruptly ceased. Sonea looked around. Veli was biting his lip and frowning at Saral. The two Traitors were both gazing at Tiatia in surprise. Sonea's stomach sank as she realised that Veli had wanted to keep this a secret, and she might have condemned the woman in their eyes by revealing it.

"Yes," Tiatia said in a quiet voice. "My husband taught me."

Saral let go an in-held breath. *Now* I'm willing to think your husband may be all you claim he is," she said.

"Why do you believe this, and not us?" Veli asked, scowling.

"Because treating slaves well is – was – never going to threaten an Ashaki's power over others. But teaching his wife magic might."

Unless he did not teach her higher magic, Sonea thought. She knew Sachakans looked down on magicians who did not know higher magic. If Tiatia's husband hadn't taught it to her, she would still be lower than him in status as well as power.

As would Regin be, to Sachakans, if he and I were . . .

She pushed the thought away, suddenly conscious of Regin sitting silently beside her. It was strange and disturbing how a stray thought could change her awareness of his presence from simply knowing his location to sensing a much more *physical* nearness. She would suddenly notice his breathing, and imagine she could feel warmth radiating from him.

"On behalf of all the people here," Veli said, his formal tone drawing her attention away. "I offer our strength to you. We gave strength to Queen Savara and her team this morning. We will have recovered enough to do the same for you tomorrow."

He was looking directly at Saral.

The Traitor smiled and looked down. "You are very generous."

Veli shrugged. "We want you to win."

Saral nodded. "As do I. Temi is strong, but it may be that I will join the battle at a time when extra strength will turn it in our favour. I accept your offer with gratitude."

In the corner of her eye, Sonea saw Regin turn to look at her. Each morning, as they had begun their ride for the day, he had reached across to touch her arm and send power to her. With Saral and Temi within hearing, she had been unable to object.

Not that I should. It is what I brought him for. If he wasn't so determined that we do it, I wouldn't be able to bring myself to ask for it. Especially not now.

But she couldn't fault his timing. Mornings were better times for transferring power than evenings since they'd joined their Traitor guides. After giving her his power, he was vulnerable. When riding with the Traitors, Sonea was unlikely to be separated from him, and Saral was probably obliged to protect them. If someone tried to attack him, it would most likely be during their stay in estates. Perhaps a slave who, like the first they'd met, resented the Guild for not freeing them after the Sachakan War. Perhaps an Ashaki's wife, mother or daughter, thinking that the Guild had colluded with the Traitors. By evening most of Regin's powers were restored and he was better able to protect himself.

"So tell us of Queen Savara's team." Saral glanced at Sonea. "First tell us, how fares the pale young man, Lorkin?"

Veli shrugged. "He was well." He looked at Sonea and frowned. "Is he Kyralian?"

"Yes," Saral nodded. "He is Black Magician Sonea's son."

The ex-slave glanced at Sonea in surprise. "A Kyralian fighting with Traitors?"

"He is a Traitor now. He has joined us." Saral smiled. "What of the rest? How many were there in the queen's team?"

"Thirty-two," he told her.

"Good. Another team has joined them. It is good to know everything is going to plan, more or less. Any news of losses?"

Veli nodded. As he listed names, Sonea tried to ignore the sudden, panicked surge of her heartbeat. *It's hard enough hearing the words "Lorkin" and "fighting" spoken in relation to each other, but it is worse to then contemplate that even Traitors who have trained and prepared for this battle are dying. Be careful, Lorkin. Please, don't let me outlive you as well.*

Staring up at the ceiling, Lorkin cursed silently. Once again, he couldn't get to sleep.

The building they were in was the average size for a country estate, but two more teams had joined Savara's and there simply weren't enough beds for everyone. Most Traitors now slept on the floor each night. Neither discomfort nor the sound of breathing should have prevented him from getting any sleep. He was tired after a long day of travelling.

It's being so close to so many minds, he told himself. But that wasn't entirely true, either. He could only hear the occasional surface thought, and only if he concentrated hard. No, it was the place to which his mind kept wandering whenever he let it drift that kept him awake.

Or places. When I'm not remembering the slave girl I gave the poisoned water to, and wondering if she was a Traitor, I'm worrying about Tyvara getting killed in battle. Or me. Or Mother getting caught up in it – why couldn't she have just gone home!

And then there was Kalia.

At least the woman had stopped muttering "spy" all the time. Or she'd stopped doing so when he could hear her. She still gave him and Tyvara looks filled with hatred, but that didn't bother him. It was the way she looked at Savara that had him worried.

Never with open dislike, he thought. *It's the way she's all humble and obedient whenever Savara looks her way, then she narrows her eyes and smiles whenever Savara's attention is elsewhere. It's the feeling of expectation I sense whenever I concentrate on her presence.*

So far he hadn't picked up any distinct surface thoughts from her. Kalia appeared to be as sly in thought as she was in nature. She kept her mind quiet, her main surface thoughts being short and mostly criticisms of others. He'd lost count of the times he'd heard the word "idiot!" burst from her mind.

What is she expecting? Is she hoping Savara will fail or be killed, or is she actually scheming to ensure either happens?

Kalia was sleeping on the other side of the room. Though he knew he'd probably have no better success reading her mind than before, he steadied his breathing and began to concentrate. Anything to turn his mind from less pleasant memories. Slowly he shifted his senses outward. From most of the Traitors he sensed little more than their presence. Though a few were still awake, their thoughts were too quiet to hear.

Then he heard a familiar mental voice and he felt cold rush through his body. It was the same mental voice that had spoken into his own mind months before in Sanctuary, the same presence that had gone seeking information he did not want to give.

—*. . . they'll blame her. All the deaths. I'll make sure they do . . . can't let Savara rule . . . better if she dies in battle . . . arrange that . . . but how? When she's weak . . . Speakers will falter. Tyvara is too young . . . foolish to pick her . . . nobody will follow her . . . better if she dies too . . . but how?*

Lorkin realised he had been holding his breath, and made himself exhale slowly and quietly. *I was wrong. Now that she's not subconsciously hiding her thoughts they are loud and clear. They've been amplified by malice and glee. She's going to make sure Savara dies in the coming battle. Tyvara too, if she can.*

Did Savara know? Surely she saw that Kalia would take advantage of any situation that would weaken her position or get rid of her. But Savara didn't know how far Kalia was prepared to go.

If I tell her, I'll have to reveal that I can read surface thoughts. Mother warned me not to do that. He had to admit, his mother was right. He wouldn't like to know that someone could read his thoughts so easily. Not even someone he liked. Even if he understood their ability was very limited he'd still be constantly wondering which thoughts they'd heard. He'd want to stay away from them, in case he let slip something private or a secret entrusted to him.

Would Tyvara feel that way? How would I feel if Tyvara could read my surface thoughts? He looked at her, lying beside him, eyes closed and breathing slowly. *I trust her.* Then why hadn't he told her about the slave girl he'd killed? *I don't want her to think I could do that.*

But he had. Perhaps it was time he told her. *No. One challenging admission at a time. Warning her about Kalia is more important. And I have to warn her, even if it means revealing my ability to Tyvara. If Kalia's plan works, they'll both die.*

He reached out to touch Tyvara's arm. She frowned but her eyes remained closed.

—*Tyvara.*

Her eyes fluttered open. As her gaze met his he felt a rush of affection. She was so beautiful, even in the dim light. She must have sensed it, as he felt surprise, pleasure and then a mix of fondness and, gratifyingly, desire.

—*Lorkin? What's going on?* Her mental voice was fuzzy with sleep.

—*Kalia is planning to betray Savara.*

Her eyes widened and he felt her stiffen under his touch, and sensed alarm sweep aside affection.

—*How do you know?*

—*I can only tell you if you promise not to tell anybody else.*

She stared at him.

—*I promise, but only if it doesn't endanger my people.*

—*It won't.* He explained, and told her what he had overheard. Tyvara's eyes widened as he did.

—*You can . . . how long have you been able to do this?*

—*Since I was in the palace prison. Mother says people believed my father could do it. She thought it was an exaggeration. That he was unusually observant.*

—*How often have you picked up surface thoughts from me?*

—*Not often. When we were reunited I heard a few words. That was when I realised I hadn't been imagining it before. Since then . . . not deliberately. Only once or twice by accident. I have to concentrate hard, and it doesn't seem polite to listen in on other people's thoughts.*

—*Except with Kalia.* She sounded amused.

—*No. I was certain she was planning something. Now I know for sure. Savara is in danger. You are too.*

—*And you. Savara's approval and confidence in you goes a long way to convince others that you can be trusted.* She frowned as if something had occurred to her.

—*What is it?*

—*How does someone accidentally concentrate hard?*

His heart skipped and he sensed suspicion. Was she repelled by him now? He searched for an answer that she might approve of.

—*When I'm paying particularly close attention to you.*

Abruptly her frown vanished and she grinned.

—*There could be some interesting advantages in having someone around who knows when you want something.*

He rolled his eyes.

—*How about we stop thinking of ways you can order me around and work out what to do about Kalia.*

Her smile faded.

—*We have to tell Savara.*

—*Can we do that without revealing my new ability to her? Can we just tell her that we overheard Kalia speaking?*

—*Lie to Savara? I can't do that. Besides, she'll want to know who Kalia was talking to.*

—*Not lie, avoid telling more than we have to for now. We'll say she was talking to herself.*

—*Kalia debating betrayal aloud? She isn't that stupid. Savara is going to need proof if she's to deal with Kalia.*

—*Then she'll have to prove to everyone that I can do this and that my word can be trusted. Kalia will point out that I've kept a secret from them all and say it's proof I'm a spy.*

Savara let out a little sigh of frustration. Lorkin took her hand and squeezed it.

—*At least we know Kalia is planning something. We can keep an eye on her. Wait until she makes her move, then stop her.*

—*That's not going to look good. Savara will be angry that we didn't warn her. Kalia will claim we set her up. No. We have to tell Savara. I can't see any other way. But I don't think she'll tell anyone else. It will make people distrust you, and that will cause too many problems for us right now.*

Lorkin thought of his mother's warning, then sighed.

—*I hope you're right. When do you want to do it?*

—*Now. It's our best chance of getting her alone.*

As Tyvara stood up Lorkin followed suit. He resisted looking over to Kalia as they crept out of the room. *I hope I'm not going to regret this.*

Savara was in the kitchen, sitting at a long wooden table with two of the estate's former slaves. She sent the women away, invited him and Tyvara to sit opposite her, then listened as Tyvara explained what Lorkin had heard from Kalia. Savara's gaze fixed on Lorkin, her eyes slowly narrowing.

"So," she said in a quiet but slightly clipped tone, "what else haven't you told us, Lorkin?"

Lorkin immediately thought of the slave girl. He winced, then instantly regretted it. He felt Tyvara move away from him, and turned to see her staring at him.

"There's something *else?*"

He looked from her to Savara. In unison, the two women crossed their arms and fixed him with a stare of expectation. It would have been funny, if he wasn't facing an admission he'd been dreading.

He dropped his gaze to the table, took a deep breath and

forced the words out from where he'd locked them away. "When I was in the prison, they tortured a slave girl to see if it would make me speak. I . . . I gave her water I knew was poisoned. It had the warning glyphs you said to watch for. I thought she was a Traitor and knew what she was doing."

He heard Tyvara's indrawn breath, but could not bring himself to look up and see if it was from horror at what he'd done, or sympathy.

"You want to know if she was a Traitor," Savara said.

He made himself meet her eyes. "Yes."

"You know it won't make a difference."

He shrugged. "But I won't be wondering any more."

She sighed and shook her head. "She was not, as far as I know. You made a hard and terrible choice, and one you can never know was right or wrong." Savara reached across the table, took his hand and squeezed it.

"Our spies make these choices all the time," Tyvara told him. "We can hardly hold it against you."

Savara let go of his hand and smiled. "Anything else you wish to confess?" she asked lightly.

He thought of the stone he was carrying. *Either I reveal what I know now, or never confront them with the truth. If the Traitors find out later that I've learned about it, and that the Guild has discovered their secret, they* will *be angry. And with Kalia trying to make them mistrust me, and Savara now having reason to worry about me because of my ability to read surface thoughts . . .*

"You're not actually *looking* for things to confess, are you?" Tyvara asked, shaking her head.

"Not exactly," he said. He turned to Savara. "There are going to be things I won't want to tell you. Things about the Guild.

I may not be a Guild magician any more, but I don't want to make them my enemy, either. Or yours."

Savara nodded. "I understand."

"I also don't want to bring about harm to the Traitors from not having told you something."

"I'm pleased to hear it."

He reached into his pocket and brought out the stone from the wasteland. As he placed it on the table in front of Savara her expression changed to dismay.

"Ah."

He looked at Tyvara. She looked a little sheepish, he was glad to see.

"Mother gave it to me," he told them.

Tyvara cursed.

"Indeed," Savara agreed. "But we've been very lucky that nobody worked out what they were before now. We'd be even more so if what our predecessors did was never discovered." She looked up at him. "You understand why they did, don't you?"

"To do what the Guild was accused of: ruin the land to keep Sachaka weak."

She nodded. "Not permanently. It will recover."

"And you'll get the credit for restoring it."

She reached out to take the stone. "Now that the Guild knows, I doubt we will." She placed her elbows on the table and rested her chin on her hands. "In the long term, it won't matter. We will win, repair the damage and be forgiven, or we will lose and the Ashaki will do it and we'll be forever hated. The land will be restored either way."

"So what do we do about Kalia?" Tyvara asked. "Can we lure her into making her move?"

Savara straightened. "No. If we do she'll claim we set her up, by taking advantage of her doubts. We do nothing."

"But . . ."

The queen looked up at Tyvara. "Don't think that I'll ignore her, or trust her." She shook her head and sighed. "When offering a person a chance at redemption, you can't force them to take it."

"And Lorkin's ability?"

"Tell nobody of that, either. The Traitors are tolerant, but this *will* stretch their trust too far." She stood up. "Halana is always telling me I need guards. I choose you two. You'll have to stay close to me at all times, even sleep nearby, but at least you can keep an eye on Kalia when my attention has to be elsewhere."

Tyvara smiled. "You know I'd be the first to offer. And you know we'll be good company as well."

"Yes." Savara sighed, then she looked at Lorkin and narrowed her eyes. "No reading my surface thoughts, though."

He shook his head. "I would never dream of it."

As more pages broke from the spine of the old record, Dannyl sighed. He really ought to leave it be, but he needed something to fill the long, empty hours so he was rereading some of the books he'd acquired. It had been days since Achati's visit. Nobody else had visited the Guild House. Tayend had received no invitations. Merria had heard nothing from her friends.

A sense of expectation filled the House. They came together at meals and talked for long hours afterwards, going their separate ways once they realised they were circling around the same old worries and speculations one time too many. Dannyl consulted Osen twice a day now. The Administrator would report on Sonea and Regin's progress and a few Guild matters that would have seemed more important if Dannyl hadn't been stuck in a city about to be overtaken by civil war.

"Ambassador Dannyl."

Looking up from the record, Dannyl found Kai standing in the doorway of his office.

"Kai," Dannyl replied. "What can I do for you?"

The slave smiled and Dannyl felt a strange confusion. It was as if Kai had become a stranger. He realised he'd never seen Kai smile. And then something else occurred to him.

Kai had not thrown himself to the floor. He had addressed Dannyl by name.

"You Kyralians are strange," Kai said. "But it is a good strange."

Dannyl's mind was racing. What did this mean? *You know what it means.*

"They're here, aren't they? The Traitors."

Kai shook his head. "Not yet. Tomorrow. We have decided to leave now. The Ashaki know. They are killing slaves."

Dannyl frowned. "But surely you are safer here. We won't harm you."

"I know." Kai smiled again. "You can't stop others, though. They will come seeking power. Or revenge. Or both. You should leave, too."

"Our orders are to stay." Dannyl pushed away a simmering fear.

"Then I wish you good luck."

"And I to you." Dannyl forced himself to meet the slave's eyes. "And I apologise, on behalf of the magicians who stayed here, if we have done anything . . . ah, who am I kidding?" He spread his hands. "The whole slave and master thing was wrong. And disturbingly easy to get used to."

"We made it so." Kai shrugged. "It was what we were trained to do. But not any more."

"No." Dannyl smiled. "I hope the Traitors succeed."

"I hope you will be safe and stay alive." The slave took a step back, then hesitated. "Have you ever explored the parts of the House the slaves occupied?"

"Not fully," Dannyl admitted.

"Do so," Kai advised. "More than just the kitchens when you get hungry. There are places you might hide in, and other exits. They may save you."

Dannyl nodded. "I will. Thank you."

Kai grinned. Then he stepped away from the door and walked, shoulders straight, out of the suite.

For a long time Dannyl stared through the empty doorway, then he got to his feet. *No point in wasting time or Kai's advice. He didn't say* when *the Traitors would arrive tomorrow. It could happen first thing in the morning. Or the Ashaki might attack us overnight. I can't help thinking that if both Achati and the slaves think we're in danger, we are. Best start making plans to get out of here if we need to.*

Leaving his suite, he made his way through the Guild House to find Tayend and Merria.

CHAPTER 25

BEFORE THE BATTLE

As Lilia neared the door to Sonea's rooms she quickened her steps. The days since Skellin abducted Anyi had been unbearably long. It was hard to pretend nothing had happened. Hard to behave as if her lessons still mattered. Harder still to concentrate enough to learn anything. Hardest of all was to be around Kallen, when she couldn't help thinking that, if he had just found and dealt with Skellin as he was supposed to have done, Cery would be alive and Anyi safe.

Reaching the door, she reached for the handle eagerly. Once inside she could stop pretending. Already she could feel the prickle of tears coming. Every day, as the strain of hiding her feelings disappeared, she had curled up on her bed and cried.

It's all my fault. If I'd arrived earlier I might have been able to save Cery. I might have stopped Skellin taking Anyi.

Gol and Jonna argued otherwise. Gol had explained about the minefire trap he and Cery had set. As soon as she had healed his leg bones, despite her warning that he should not put weight on them yet, he had climbed to his feet and walked to the walls on either side, plucking tubes of powder out of holes and cursing.

"Why didn't it work?" he said, over and over, she recalled. *Then*

he asked me to bring my globe light closer. Showed me how the paper was stained with damp. Moisture in the walls had got in and ruined them. Not all, but he and Cery had only lit two of them, and they'd picked two of the damp ones.

Lilia suspected that Cery's heart had been slowly failing for a long time. It could have stopped at any moment. If she had been around to help him when it happened he would have survived. She told Gol this, and hoped it made him feel a little less guilty.

Jonna had lamented that she hadn't found Lilia quickly enough. She told how a magician had stopped her, concerned that she looked upset. When she'd told him she was looking for Lilia, he'd directed her to the wrong classroom. It would have been an easy mistake for the magician to make. Lilia's timetable had changed a lot recently. He had probably made a guess, hoping to be helpful.

Turning the handle, she opened the door and stepped inside. Seeing Lord Rothen standing there, she blinked away the threatening tears and swallowed hard.

"Lord Rothen," she said, bowing. Gol was sitting in one of the chairs, Jonna standing behind him. She and Jonna had smuggled Cery's bodyguard, disguised as a servant, up to Sonea's rooms, the night after Skellin's attack.

Jonna had persuaded Lilia to tell Rothen everything. *"You need a magician ally,"* Lilia recalled her saying. *"Rothen can be trusted to keep a secret. He's kept plenty for Sonea over the years."* To Lilia's relief, Rothen had been as discreet and helpful as Jonna had promised. He'd wanted to tell Kallen, until Gol repeated Skellin's claim of having sources in the Guild.

As Lilia closed the door, Rothen's mouth thinned in a sympathetic smile. "Lady Lilia." He looked at Jonna, then down at the table. Following his gaze, Lilia felt her heart lurch. A square of paper lay there, with her name scrawled on it.

"Is it . . .?"

"From Skellin?" Rothen grimaced. "Probably. We haven't opened it. We guessed you'd want to read it first. Sit down before you do."

She slid into a chair, Rothen and Jonna taking the other seats. With trembling hands, she picked up the message and turned it over. The seal, she noted, was a simple crown hovering over a knife. *King of the Thieves.* Disgust and anger steadied her. She broke the seal and unfolded the paper. Her eyes moved over the words. As their meaning became clear, she dropped it back on the table.

"It's an address," she told them. "It says 'tomorrow' and a time. And he says to tell no one and come alone."

"No surprises there," Gol muttered.

"Where is the address?" Jonna asked.

"In Northside." *Cery's old territory. He's rubbing it in.* She looked at Rothen. "I have to go. I have to try to save Anyi."

He nodded. His agreement sent a perverse anger through her.

"Shouldn't you tell me I can't?" she asked. "You know what he wants. It's bad enough we have a rogue magician ruling the underworld. A rogue black magician will be so much worse."

"It may not be what he wants. He may already have found a book on black magic and learned it for himself, though that is unlikely. If there are any more books out there, they're well hidden." Rothen sighed. "Even so, we Higher Magicians have considered what to do if he does learn black magic." He smiled thinly. "It won't mean we can't catch and deal with him, it'll just be a little more dramatic when we do."

"But many more people will die before you do. And we don't even know if Anyi is still alive." She felt her throat close and fought back tears again.

"He won't have killed her," Gol assured her. "He knows you'll ask to see her before you teach him anything."

Lilia took a few breaths to steady herself. "Even if she is alive, how do I know he'll let her go after I've taught him?"

"You have to make sure she can get away before you teach him anything," Rothen said.

"It would be easier if I could take another magician."

"He'll never let you," Jonna said. "You can't even take a magician disguised as a servant. He said you must be alone."

Rothen nodded. "If he has sources here, a disguise may not work anyway." He sighed. "If it weren't for these sources, I'd suggest we go to the Higher Magicians. They could have Kallen make a blood ring so we can track Lilia with it. If the exchange goes badly we'll be close enough to help."

Lilia looked up at him in surprise. *A blood ring! Why hadn't I thought of that?* "I can make blood rings. Kallen taught me."

His eyes widened. "You can? Well then . . ." He straightened and rubbed his hands together. "We could have the beginning of a plan."

Gol looked away. "Don't ask me to help. Last plan I made wasn't very good."

"You did what you could with the few resources you had," Rothen told him. "It was impressively bold. I'd never heard of minefire before. Intriguing stuff. If your trap had worked, you'd have delivered Skellin right to our door, so to speak." He smiled briefly. "I'd appreciate your advice, Gol. You know the underworld and the city better than we do."

Gol frowned. "Well . . . this idea of using a blood gem, if I'm getting it right how they work, will only be any good to us if you can pick the places you're seeing through it," Gol pointed out. "What if you don't know where they are? What if you're blindfolded?"

"Both would be a problem." Rothen drummed his fingers on the chair, his brows creased in thought.

"Does Skellin know what a blood ring is?" Jonna asked. "He might notice it and make her take it off."

Lilia shook her head. "I'm not supposed to wear a blood ring made from anyone else's blood — except Sonea's and Kallen's."

Rothen nodded. "Of course. Whoever supplied the blood would be able to read your thoughts and might learn about black magic. So Gol must wear one made of your blood."

Lilia turned to Gol. "And you must smash it if anyone tries to get hold of it."

"Otherwise it could be used against Lilia." Rothen shook his head. "If only there was another way to follow you. It's not like we have to track magicians often . . ." He drew in a quick breath and his eyebrows shot upward. "Ah! Of course! Sonea! We located Sonea before she joined the Guild by sensing her using magic." He looked at Lilia. "All you have to do is use magic without hiding it. Concealing the use of magic was one of your earliest lessons."

She nodded. Every year, when new novices joined the Guild, she detected a few of them using magic before they were taught how to conceal it. "But won't Skellin sense that, too?"

"Only if he's trying to. If you do something small and constant, like holding a shield, that may lessen the chance he'd notice, too."

"So you track me using magic," Lilia said, "while Gol wears my blood ring because he's more likely to recognise where I am."

"Once you have tracked Lilia to Skellin, are you strong enough to fight him if something goes wrong?" Jonna asked Rothen.

"Skellin *and* Lorandra," Gol added.

Rothen frowned and shook his head. "I doubt it. But between Lilia and me, we may be strong enough. We can't risk recruiting another magician in case they are Skellin's source. I wish Dannyl was here," he added in a murmur.

"I can be as strong as I need to be," Lilia pointed out, meeting Rothen's gaze and holding it.

He grimaced. "It would be better if you avoided breaking the law against using black magic without permission. But . . . perhaps we can bend it a little. I will give you permission, as a Higher Magician, but that doesn't comply with the law completely since it is supposed to be agreed upon by all Higher Magicians."

Lilia looked down. *If anything goes wrong, and the Guild doesn't agree with him bending the law, he'll lose his position.* "Are you sure?"

"Yes. Allowing you to go to this meeting, when there's a chance you'll be forced to teach a rogue black magic, is far worse than allowing you to strengthen yourself using willing volunteers. I can give you my strength tonight."

"And mine," Jonna said.

"Mine, too," Gol added.

Rothen nodded. "I will recover my strength overnight."

"Will we?" Jonna asked.

"Yes."

"Then take strength from me tomorrow as well," Jonna said. "It's not as if I use it. Perhaps, if we give Lilia enough magic, she'll be able drag Skellin back here with her."

"Let's concentrate on getting Anyi back," Rothen said.

"Of course," Jonna agreed. "But if there's an opportunity to catch Skellin at the same time, let's do it. It's about time the King of the Underworld became the Inmate of the Lookout."

The dusk sky was slowly darkening. No clouds hovered overhead for the sun to paint in colourful shades. Looking down from the rooftop, Lorkin wondered how this could be the same city he'd entered with Dannyl so long ago, excited at the prospect of being assistant to the Guild Ambassador to Sachaka. *It feels like years ago, but not even one year has passed since we arrived.*

Though the walls and buildings had not changed since Lorkin had left Arvice in the slave cart, the population had. Before, slaves had hurried up and down the streets, keeping their distance from carriages bearing their masters. Now the streets were crowded as ex-slaves fled the city centre, most on foot, some clinging to stolen carriages and carts.

A small group had been waiting when Savara and her team arrived at the mansion chosen as the gathering place before the battle. After taking the strength offered by the ex-slaves, Savara had sent them away, then split her team – now over sixty Traitors – into two groups: one to watch and guard, the other to arrange a meal and bedding. As the arrangements were made, Savara had headed for the roof.

"Why aren't the Ashaki trying to stop them leaving?" Lorkin wondered aloud.

"Another man's slave is another man's problem," Savara

quoted. "They're probably too busy trying to stop their own slaves escaping than worrying about everyone else's."

"In most estates, slaves came and went all the time," Tyvara told him. "How else could they get food and other goods to the estate? All that kept them in place was the fact that there was nowhere to run to. An escaped slave would eventually be caught, and sent back to his master."

"Unless an Ashaki manages to round up and imprison all of his slaves in one place, he can't stop some of them getting away." Savara's eyes narrowed as she looked over the rooftops. "And plenty of Ashaki are away from home, fighting us."

Lorkin followed her gaze. *How many of these mansions house Ashaki preparing to face us in battle? How many are empty?* So far Savara's team had only fought small groups of Ashaki. He'd wondered at that, but reports via message stones had told of a larger, more organised army of Ashaki west of the city. After it had surprised and defeated one of her teams, Savara had ordered Traitors in that area to avoid it by circling around and joining teams to the north and south.

King Amakira must expect the Traitors to join together to form one army once they reached the city. Savara had indicated they would do so eventually, but for now the Traitors remained in smaller groups, taking advantage of most of the populace of Sachaka being on their side. While the Ashaki were out hunting for them, the Traitors were lying low, growing stronger on the strength of the Ashaki's slaves.

While Lorkin saw the advantage in that, he was also worried that keeping the Traitor army divided made it vulnerable. The king's army could easily defeat one of the smaller Traitor groups. It would be weakened by the fight, but in time would regain its strength, while the Traitors . . . once dead they stayed that way. *But if the Ashaki are relying on slaves to replace the power they use, they will have a problem. The slaves have left.*

Still, it would be better that no Traitor group confronted the army on its own in case, some fell into the king's hands. He would torture information out of them, learn of Savara's plans, the threat of gemstones . . . He would *possess* gemstones, too.

"The city will be empty by tomorrow," Savara murmured. "Except for the Ashaki. The ones returning from the west will join those still here, and then we'll see if our strategy and preparations and losses lead to the freedoms we seek."

She sighed and looked up. Lorkin followed her gaze. Stars had begun to dust the sky and a chill had crept into the air. He frowned as they rippled, as if reflected in water.

Then something slammed into his right side and propelled him into Tyvara.

They both tumbled onto the roof. Tyvara scrambled into a crouch and he did the same, though more awkwardly than she. Pain speared through his right arm. *Broken*, he thought. Instinctively he sent Healing power to numb the pain, but he resisted mending the bone. He might need his strength for more important things. Like avoiding a more fatal strike.

If I hadn't been holding a shield when the forcestrike hit, I would already be dead, he thought, restoring his shield. Though his barrier had been overcome, it had absorbed most of the strike.

Savara was standing straight, head high and glaring at some- thing to his right. The air rippled as she sent strikes in reply to another attack. Tyvara was standing between him and the unseen attacker. She placed a hand on Savara's arm, no doubt ready to give power if needed. Moving closer, he looked over Tyvara's shoulder.

Four Ashaki were standing on a nearby rooftop. As they struck out with firestrike, their faces were bathed in red light. None looked much older than Lorkin. *Too impatient to wait for their elders to join them?*

Below, ex-slaves had noticed the battle. Some were running away, some had stayed to watch. Lorkin realised his heart was pounding. In all the confrontations between Savara's group and Ashaki, he'd been part of a larger group. Now they were three against four. He tried not to think of all the power raging between this rooftop and the next, and failed. His knees felt weak. He placed a hand on Savara's other shoulder and told himself it wasn't for support. A memory of his Warrior lessons flashed through his mind. *It is normal to be frightened during battle. What matters is that you follow your training.*

But I've never been trained to use black magic in battle.

A shout came from below, then a streak of light shot up from the street between the buildings. The Traitor watchers below had noticed the battle and joined in. The Ashaki looked down and, realising that they were outnumbered, retreated. Three disappeared into a hatch, but the last, forced to defend with no help, faltered. A strike from Savara sent him tumbling away from the hatch, then over the far edge of the roof.

Suddenly the air was still. Savara, Tyvara and Lorkin stood frozen, silently watching. A rumbling mix of muffled shouts, banging doors and the occasional boom came from below. A flickering light drew Lorkin's eyes to a window of the house the Ashaki had disappeared into. The building was on fire.

Abruptly, Savara turned and led the way back to the hatch behind them. As she started down the rope ladder to the stair-well below, Tyvara grabbed his arm — thankfully the unbroken one — and pulled him after her.

"You first," he said as they reached the hatch. "Give me a moment to sort out my other arm."

Her eyes widened. "You're hurt?"

"Not for long."

"Then I'll stay and protect you until . . ."

"Don't be stupid. The Ashaki are gone and it won't take long to heal. Someone has to protect Savara."

She looked from him to the hatch, then sighed and started to climb down. "Don't take too long," she growled.

When she was out of the way, he strengthened his shield, sat with his legs dangling down the hatch opening and concentrated on Healing. He only needed the bone and tissues to mend sufficiently for him to climb down the ladder. Soon he was stepping off the last swinging rung, the hatch closed and bolted above him, and hurrying down the stairs after Tyvara and the queen.

At the bottom he pushed through a door into the corridor beyond, only to find it was now part of the Master's Room, the wall between reduced to rubble. Traitors stood in a circle around their queen. As Lorkin came closer he saw she stood over three bodies, her expression grim. Two were Ashaki but the third . . . Lorkin's breath caught in his throat as he recognised the woman as Speaker Halana.

The room seemed to spin for a moment. He remembered how Halana had called for volunteers to take the first watch. He also remembered her teaching him stone-making — her encouragement, her understanding of the sacrifice he'd made in learning black magic. The vast knowledge and great skill she'd had, now lost . . .

Tyvara moved to his side and leaned close.

"She and a few others were setting barrier and warning

stones around the house," she murmured. "The others lost sight of her just as the Ashaki attacked. She killed three of them before they overcame—"

"We must move," Savara declared. "If we did miss one of them, he may be reporting his estimate of our numbers right now. They may come back with a greater force. If we are lucky we will relocate without them tracing us. It may be that we won't get to rest tonight at all. What matters is we avoid outright battle with the Ashaki until we join the other teams." She looked up and swept her gaze over all. "Pack, and take what food can be easily carried and eaten while we move."

The Traitors scattered. Tyvara took Lorkin's hand and dragged him away to the room they had planned to share with Savara. Since they hadn't had a chance to unpack, all they had to do was shoulder their packs. Tyvara grabbed Savara's and they returned to the Master's room.

". . . want us to do with her body?" a Traitor was asking.

"Leave her here. If we win we will come back for her," Savara replied. She took her pack and shouldered it, but, as she turned away, Lorkin caught a glint of moisture in her eyes.

The Traitors were returning to the room now. One stepped out of a side passage near Lorkin, and as he turned his heart darkened. Kalia stared at him blankly, then gave him a wide berth.

Which is . . . odd. I'd expect a glare at least. He narrowed his eyes at her back and *concentrated.*

He caught no surface thought, just a wracking feeling of guilt.

"It's her fault," he gasped.

Nobody looked up. They hadn't heard him. The room was too noisy. He turned to find Tyvara staring at him. Then a hand grasped his arm. He looked up to see Savara standing behind them, her other hand resting on Tyvara's arm.

—*Say nothing*, she sent. *This is not the time.*

Choking back a protest, he nodded and followed the Traitor queen out into the street.

As Saral and Temi stopped in front of the gate and pushed it open with magic, Sonea let out a sigh of relief. The sun had set hours before, and she had begun to wonder if the escort planned to travel through the night. The Traitors steered their mounts through the entrance. As Sonea and Regin followed, Temi slid off his horse and walked over to close the gates again, glancing up and down the street before retreating.

Saral dismounted and handed the reins of her horse to Temi, then indicated that Sonea and Regin should do the same.

"We need to check the house," she said in a low voice. "Looks like the slaves have gone, but there's always a chance a few ones loyal to their master have stayed. While the Ashaki has most likely joined the king's army, he too may have stayed behind, or might return for something, or may have sent a friend to watch over his house. Stay here."

Sonea nodded. "Need help?"

"No."

Saral straightened and looked at Temi, then stalked away toward a nearby door. It was unlocked, and she disappeared inside. Sonea looked around. It made sense to stand with Temi. If they were attacked it would be easier to protect everyone under one shield. But as she started towards him she saw that he was holding up a small object. She sensed a faint vibration in the air and realised that he, and the horses, were already within a shield. The object must be a magical gemstone.

So, it's up to us to shield ourselves now. Why waste power that could be needed in battle on a couple of uninvited foreigners? Well, I suppose they are about to go into battle, and we can look after ourselves. Sighing, she veered away and headed for the shadow of a wall nearby. In the protection of darkness, she extended her barrier around Regin. He glanced at her and moved closer, but said nothing.

A long wait followed. Temi said nothing, but his anxiety was plain to see. The horses were quiet, heads hanging wearily. They'd been ridden with few pauses all day. *Longer and faster than we travelled before. I wonder . . . are we in the city now?* Low walls and houses set within fields had been replaced by high walls protecting buildings much closer to the road. Most structures were single storey, but the occasional one – as in the country – had a small tower protruding above the roof. She hadn't been able to see if fields were hidden behind them, or how large the estates were. Even now, all she could see was the courtyard they stood within. There could be sprawling fields on the other side of the buildings, or another mansion.

It doesn't sound like a city, though. It's too quiet.

Regin shifted his weight from one leg to the other, and his shoulder brushed against her own, leaving an impression of warmth. She felt a shock go through her, not entirely unpleasant.

Stop it, she told herself.

A door opened to their left and her heart skipped a beat. Then a globe light appeared and she was relieved to see it was Saral returning.

"Empty," she told them. "The stables are over there." Temi nodded and led the horses in the direction she'd pointed. Saral looked at Sonea. "Come inside."

They entered the mansion by the door Saral had first used.

As with so many Sachakan homes, a short corridor led to a bigger room. Corridors led off on either side to suites of rooms, a bathhouse, and the kitchens and other service areas.

"If you use these later," Saral said of the baths, "don't take too long. If Tovira does return, you won't want to be caught there."

"No," Sonea agreed. "It would be rather disconcerting having to fight an Ashaki while naked."

In the corner of her eye, she saw Regin cover his mouth. Saral hesitated, then looked away. "And it has only one entrance," she said.

Sonea could not see if the woman was smiling, or hear amusement in her voice. *Too close to battle to maintain a sense of humour.* They went to the kitchen next, where Saral helped herself to food and told Sonea and Regin to do the same.

"You're not worried the slaves might have poisoned it in the hope of weakening the Ashaki?"

Saral shook her head. "If they had, they'd have left a warning. A glyph our spies use. Now, I'm going up to the tower. You can stay here if you like."

"I'll come with you," Sonea said firmly. "I want to see where we are."

Saral looked as if she might argue, then shook her head. "Follow me, then."

A short journey followed. The tower was reached through what must have been the Ashaki's suite of rooms. Sonea noted female clothing along with male.

"I wonder where his wife is."

"Sent away somewhere safer, most likely," Saral replied. "We are on the outskirts. A more central location would be easier to defend."

The outskirts, Sonea mused. *So we have reached the city.*

At the top of a spiral staircase was a small, round room.

"Stay to one side of the windows so nobody out there will see your shape," Saral instructed. She approached one from the left, peering around the edge. Sonea looked out from the other side. Rooftops spread before her. Somewhere several hundred paces to the left a building was on fire. A greater number of two-storey buildings stood directly ahead, and what looked like domes rose behind them.

"Welcome to Arvice," Saral said. "Savara has communicated orders that we stay here until she summons us. Unless, of course, we are forced to leave. What are your orders?"

Nothing so specific, Sonea thought. *But since she had the courtesy to ask* . . . "I will check."

Reaching into her robe pocket, she drew out Osen's ring and slipped it on her finger.

—*Osen?*

—*Sonea.*

—*We've arrived at the city and are hiding in an empty estate belonging to Ashaki Tovira, who is most likely in the king's army. Our Traitor escort says we must stay here until Queen Savara summons us.*

—*No doubt they want to ensure you don't interfere.*

—*What should we do?*

—*What she says.*

—*I won't be able to see the fighting from here.* Which meant she would not see what happened to Lorkin, or be able to help him.

—*Hmm. If you and Dannyl both wear my blood rings, you may be able to see what he communicates to me. Though I have told him to stay in the Guild House. Maybe I should ask him to find a vantage point from which to watch the battle instead.*

396

—So long as he doesn't put himself at risk doing so.

—There is always risk, being close to a magical battle. The Guild needs to know what the outcome is. Our Healer volunteers left this morning. We don't want them walking into a dangerous situation.

—Are you sure you want us to stay put?

—Yes. As a figure of greater authority than Dannyl, and as a black magician, you are more likely to be seen as a threat by both sides. If it weren't for Lorkin, we would have ordered you home.

—Ah. Well. I'm grateful that you didn't.

—Those of us in favour of you remaining in Sachaka argued that, when the conflict is over, you may persuade Lorkin to return or at least ensure the Traitors uphold their side of the exchange.

—Let's hope they don't use up all their stones in the battle, then. I must go. Saral is waiting for my answer.

—Take care, Sonea.

—I will. Sonea slipped off the ring and pocketed it.

"We're to stay here for now," she told Saral.

The woman nodded, then led the way back down to the kitchen. Temi had arrived and was chatting to Regin. Seeing the two men together, their differences were more obvious. Regin was taller, Temi was leaner. But Temi was not much darker than Regin. The Traitor's skin tone was lighter than the usual Sachakan, and Regin had gained a tan while travelling. *It suits him.* They fell silent as Sonea and Saral entered the room. When Temi offered to keep a watch for the first half of the night, Regin offered to keep him company.

"No," Saral said. "I will take the first watch. Alone."

Regin shrugged. "Then where should we sleep?"

"The second suite. If Tovira returns in the middle of the night, he'll probably head straight for his bedroom."

Regin nodded, then looked at Sonea and headed for the

door. She followed, amused that he had taken the lead, when in most instances since the Traitors had joined them he had waited for her decisions.

The second suite had beds in three of the rooms. Sonea picked one at random and sat down on the bed. Looking around, she noticed smaller versions of Ashaki clothing hanging on a hook. A jewelled jacket overlapping plain trousers . . .

"What did Osen say?"

She looked up to see Regin standing in the doorway.

"How'd you know I contacted him?"

He shrugged. "An easy guess."

"Saral said we must stay here until Savara summons us, then asked if that was okay. Osen said it was fine. They want to be sure we don't interfere."

"If Lorkin was in trouble, you would."

She looked up to find him smiling knowingly. "Only to save him."

"That's still interference. Not that I wouldn't understand."

"Osen thinks that if Dannyl and I both wear his blood rings, I may get to witnesses the battle through Dannyl."

Regin looked thoughtful. "That would be a good way around the Traitors' restrictions." He frowned. "If the Traitors are struggling, we'll know because Saral will leave to help them. Will you follow her?"

Sonea looked away. "Maybe. Probably. But you should stay here."

"I go wherever you go."

She felt her heart skip. *That would sound so romantic in less dangerous circumstances.* "No. You'll put yourself in danger for no reason."

"You'll be more of a target than me," he told her. "Which

reminds me . . ." He moved over to the bed and sat down. "You should take my power."

Conscious of how close he was, Sonea turned to face him. "What if Tovira returns tonight? You won't even be able to shield yourself."

"I doubt I'd last long anyway." He held out his hands.

She stared at them as reluctance welled up inside her. *Too intimate*, she thought. *What if he senses something? It wasn't likely when we were on the road. We only touched as long as was necessary. Others were watching.*

"You really need to get over your fear of your black magic," he told her.

"I'm not afraid," she told him. Not entirely a lie. *Not exactly the truth, either.*

"If you take my power, I promise I won't go with you into the city," he offered.

She met his eyes. He looked back at her, his gaze level and his expression serious. She felt a flash of amusement.

"You won't go into the city because I ordered you not to," she told him.

He shrugged. "So we have an agreement?"

Sighing, she took his hands and tried to ignore how warm they were. Closing her eyes, she took the power that flowed from him and stored it away.

CHAPTER 26

BEGINNINGS AND ENDINGS

Dannyl stared up at the ceiling, blinked and then pushed himself up onto his elbows. *What . . . ? Something woke me.* He frowned. *Someone called my name? Or was I dreaming?* He created a globe light and peered out of his bedroom door to the main room of his suite.

Was it Tayend? Or Merria? Has someone broken into the Guild House, as Achati and Kai warned?

—*Dannyl.*

He jumped at the mental call. *Osen!* He sighed in relief that the source of disturbance was in his mind, not the Guild House. Then relief melted away. Osen had called him openly, which any other magician could hear. He wouldn't do that unless he had something important to tell or ask Dannyl. Getting up, Dannyl dug into the pockets of yesterday's robes, found Osen's ring and put it on.

—*Osen. Sorry. I was asleep.*

—*Then I apologise for waking you. You hadn't contacted me at our agreed time.*

Dannyl paused. He wasn't entirely sure what time it was. With no slaves to wake him, and no windows in the suite, it could be midnight or midday.

—What time is it?

—An hour before the first classes start here.

Since the sun always rose a little earlier in Sachaka, it was mid-morning. Was the battle over? Or had it not even begun yet? He was amazed that he'd been able to sleep at all. But then, he, Tayend and Merria had stayed up late, and drunk more than a little of the Guild House's supply of wine to ease their anxiety over being stuck in a city at war, and the possibility of being killed out of vengeance or for their magical strength.

—I spoke to Sonea last night, Osen continued. *She and Regin are staying in a house on the outskirts of the city. The Traitors have ordered them to stay there until summoned – which will most likely be when the battle is over.*

To know that Sonea was close was reassuring, though Dannyl wasn't sure why. Perhaps she could come to his rescue, if the House was attacked.

—Unfortunately this means she will not see how Lorkin fares, or know who is the victor. I have been considering the warning Achati and your former slave gave you, that the Guild House may be targeted. Is there anywhere else you can go?

—Somewhere we might witness the battle?

—If that can be arranged without compromising your safety and that of Merria and Tayend.

Dannyl considered. The ship Achati had arranged to wait for them would be a safe place to be, but one of the reasons for that was that the docks were far from where fighting was likely to take place – so not a good vantage point. Where would the battle most likely occur? *The palace, eventually. And Achati's mansion has a view of the parade leading to the palace. Perhaps if we climbed onto the roof . . .*

—Can you get there safely? Osen asked.

Dannyl felt a chill at this reminder that his thoughts were open to the Administrator, thanks to the blood ring.

—Sorry. I am finding it hard to curb my impatience. Merin wants news and I was hoping you or Sonea would have contacted me by now, Osen sent.

Dannyl smiled in sympathy. For the Kyralian king to be putting pressure on the Administrator directly meant that he'd grown so anxious about the Sachakan situation he wasn't content with High Lord Balkan's reports.

—I suspect getting to Achati's house will be the dangerous part, but we will see if it can be done, Dannyl sent back.

—Don't take any unnecessary risks. Oh, and Sonea will be wearing one of my blood rings. We're hoping she will also be able to see what you see.

—And come rescue me if something goes wrong?

—That would create less of a political mess than if she has to rescue Lorkin. Hmm. It could be a way to get the Traitors to let her enter the city. They'd find it harder to justify preventing her coming to the aid of the Guild Ambassador than of her son.

Dannyl's heart skipped.

—You want me to get into trouble so she has an excuse to enter the city?

—No. But maybe we could pretend you are . . . No. Not unless we have to. Get yourselves to Achati's house first, then we'll consider other ideas.

—Very well.

—Good luck, Dannyl.

—Thanks, Osen.

Slipping off the ring, Dannyl dressed quickly in fresh robes. He paused to look back at the room. Was there anything else he ought to take with him? *My notes? No. They'll be safer left here than with me. If I'm killed, this place might be looted, but no looter will want notebooks. Later someone might go through our belongings more carefully. Hopefully a Guild magician, who will see the value in them. Maybe Achati . . . if he survives.*

Pushing that thought aside, Dannyl turned and strode out of his suite in search of Merria and Tayend.

Lorkin sat cross-legged, his back against a wall. The Master's Room of the estate the Traitors had gathered in was crowded, but they were taking care to keep clear a narrow path from corridor to corridor so that messengers could move about quickly and without tripping.

This was the third location Savara's team had moved to during the night. The second had been another abandoned mansion; then, towards morning, they'd slunk through the silent city streets to a more defendable house chosen to be the gathering place before the final confrontation with the Ashaki. Lorkin hadn't slept, and doubted that anyone else had either. *Not that I would have been able to if I'd had the chance or there'd been room to lie down.* A Traitor entered the room and looked towards him. He turned to see who it was and his heartbeat quickened as he saw it was Tyvara. She smiled and made her way over to him. There was no space for her to sit beside him, so he stood up. She handed him a vest.

"This is for you," she said, raising her voice so he could hear her in the noisy room.

He felt his stomach do a little flip as the weight of it settled into his hands. All of the Traitors wore these vests. They were covered in small pockets, each holding gemstones fixed into settings of wood, stone or precious metal. He'd assumed he would be fighting without stones, since he'd had no training in using them in battle.

"It's easier to use if you put it on," Tyvara told him.

"Give me a moment," he retorted. Shrugging into the vest, he found it was a little tight around the arms.

"I thought it would be a bit small," Tyvara said, trying and failing to bring the buckles and straps at the front together. "But it's the only one we could spare."

"Well, it's what's in it that's important," he said.

"How the stones are arranged helps you find them if you can't look away from the enemy, so if the fronts are flapping about you might grab the wrong one. But I guess you aren't familiar with their positions anyway." She sighed and looked up at him, her expression serious. "Just remember: the left side is for defensive stones, the right for offensive. The stronger ones are to the centre, the weaker to the sides. Make sure that if you take the vest off you don't turn it upside down with the pockets unbuttoned, because if they fall out you won't know which is stronger or weaker."

Lorkin repeated what she'd said. He hadn't seen the Traitors using stones when fighting up to this point. He guessed that they were saving them for the main battle, or that the stones were more useful in a bigger confrontation. The only stones he'd seen used so far were defensive, like the barrier stones that Halana had been setting when she'd been ambushed. Those had created simple shields, but others had been activated that used a shield as an alarm, not strong enough to prevent a person passing though but emitting a noise when they did. He had also seen a stone, accidentally activated, produce an opaque white non-resistant shield, and Savara had a stone that would block noise.

"The bigger pockets hold basic shield and strike stones," Tyvara told him, patting a row of larger pockets near his waist. "The shield stones are all strong enough to hold against a few strikes, but how many or how powerful depends on the limits of each stone. Always be ready for their depletion with a shield of your own magic."

She flipped open the top flap of a pocket and pulled out one of the stones. The setting was like a short spoon, with the gem filling the bowl. "Hold it like this." She pinched the handle between two fingers and turned the concave side outwards. "Press your finger into the back of the gem to activate it. Face the gem away or you'll direct the shield or strike at yourself."

"That would be embarrassing," he noted.

A glint of humour entered her gaze. "And potentially fatal. Which would be embarrassing to me. I'll be forever known for choosing a very stupid man."

He chuckled. "What about the other stones?"

"This will be harder to remember. Shield stones have stone settings, strike stones have wooden ones. The rest use bronze, copper, gold and silver, with different textures on the handle so you can recognise them by touch." She took these out one by one, describing what they could do. One was for noise-blocking, another would make an ear-splitting sound. A few could produce light, for illumination or signalling. One made a short, constant firestrike for cutting or burning, another used forcestrike to project any small missile set into the bowl. Another pair were designed to explode after a delay, though she warned him that it could be after anything from a count to ten to a few hundred.

Then she pulled out a handful of rings from her pockets.

"Most of the vest stones are single-use stones. These are multiple-use ones, so don't throw them away when they're depleted. The smallest are for communication," she said, slipping two rings holding iridescent gems onto his little fingers. "They don't activate until you press them down into the setting, against your skin. The one on your left hand connects with the ring I'm wearing, the other was going to connect with Halana, but Savara will now be wearing her rings. Don't use hers except in urgent situations. You could distract her at a bad moment.

"The dark red ones are strike stones. The pale blue are shield stones." She pressed them onto his first and second fingers, then held out the last two. "These are new to us, and we don't have many of them. The clear one . . . you gave Halana the idea, actually. We'd never bothered to make stones with the *sole* purpose of storing magic to be retrieved later as pure magic, rather than to be channelled to a purpose."

"A storestone!"

"Yes. We have about twenty of them. They have only the strength of three average magicians stored in them. Halana didn't want to risk adding more, and most of Sanctuary's strength was being taken and held by Traitor magicians — which made it instantly accessible rather than having to reach for a ring. If these were strengthened in peace time, however, they could be more useful."

He took the ring and slipped it on the last free finger of his right hand.

"And the other?

"The purplish one," she grinned, "is a Healing stone."

"*Kalia* made it?"

"No. A stone-maker read her mind, tested what she'd learned

406

on a volunteer, then made a few stones. She says the stones have been taught to boost the body in whatever Healing it's already trying to do."

Lorkin picked up the ring and examined it. "Smart. That way, if it works, it won't matter what kind of wound needs Healing. The wearer only needs to know how to use magical force to hold bones in the right position so they don't heal crooked, or the sides of wounds together, or to remove poisons, infection or a build-up of blood. It wouldn't work for using Healing beyond what the body needs, like easing pain, or tiredness, though. How many did she make?"

"Five. Wait . . . easing tiredness?" Tyvara frowned. "You can stop yourself feeling tired?"

"Ah . . . yes. I didn't mention that when I was in Sanctuary, in case it made people feel more . . . well . . . annoyed with me."

"Does it take much magic?"

"No."

"Could you ease my weariness, or Savara's?"

"Yes."

She waved a hand as he tried to give the ring back to her. He looked at her hands. She wasn't yet wearing any of her rings. "Do you have one?"

"No."

"Then take it. There's no point in me having it. I can do all these things already."

"Savara said you'd say that, but insisted I offer one to you anyway."

"I appreciate the offer, but she'd be doing me more of a favour if you wore it."

"Why would I need one, when I have you?" Taking the ring, she smiled. "She wants to see you."

She caught his hand in hers, and led him across the room and into a corridor. Savara was in the main suite, surrounded by people talking in groups or arriving and leaving. Looking around, Lorkin recognised all of the Speakers – except Halana, of course. Seeing him, Savara held up a hand to the woman she was talking to, then walked over to meet him.

"Lorkin," she said, her eyes dropping to his vest then up to meet his gaze. "All prepared for the fight?"

He patted his chest. "Yes, thanks to you and whoever prepared this for me."

Tyvara held out the purple ring. The queen smiled and nodded. "Give it to Speaker Lanna."

As Tyvara moved away, Savara stepped a little closer and suddenly all sound ceased as a barrier surrounded them. Her expression became hard.

"Has she given anything away?"

Guessing she meant Kalia, Lorkin frowned. "No. All I sense is guilt. I've caught her thinking that she is a fool a few more times."

"Not even a hint that she is planning something?"

He shook his head. "I wouldn't lower your guard, though."

Her lips pressed into a grim smile. "No. She will be well away from me, watched closely." She sighed. "I suspect whatever she did backfired and got Halana killed, and she doesn't want to risk making the same mistake."

"I hope so, though it will make proving what she did impossible. Unless you want me to reveal what I can do?"

"Not when I am her only target." She looked down and let out a bitter laugh. "However, you may find your life's task is to keep an eye on her until she dies. If we win this battle."

408

He shrugged. "I'd do it anyway," he admitted. "If not for your safety, then for mine and Tyvara's. And . . ."

The queen put up a hand to silence him. The sounds of the room abruptly returned as Tyvara rejoined them.

"Lorkin was just telling me that he can heal away tiredness," she told Savara. "It would give you an advantage, going into battle with your mind fresh and sharp."

The queen's eyebrows rose. "It would."

"Is that wise?" another voice said. Lorkin turned to see Speaker Lanna step closer. She looked apologetic but also determined. "Mere hours before the final battle, can you afford to put that much trust in someone not born a Traitor?"

As Tyvara turned to glare at the woman, Lorkin placed a hand on her arm. "It's a fair question."

Savara nodded. "It is. And entirely unnecessary. After Halana learned what she could of Healing from Kalia, she and I have been – were, in her case – experimenting." A look of pain flashed across her face. "She succeeded in working out how to Heal weariness a few days ago." She straightened and turned to Lorkin. "But if she had not, I would accept your offer. The benefit is worth it, and there are competent people ready to take my place, should trusting you prove a bad decision." Her gaze shifted to something behind him. "And here's another messenger."

Lorkin turned to see a tired-looking man hovering behind him, and felt a jolt of recognition.

"Evar!" he exclaimed.

The man grinned. "Lorkin. I was hoping I'd run into you one last time." He turned back to the queen and placed a hand over his heart. "The Ashaki are gathering in the parade, your majesty, and look ready to advance."

Savara's eyes widened a little, then she straightened her back. "It is time." She looked around the room. "Gather everyone outside the gates. I will say a few words, then . . . then we'll finally confront our enemy directly."

Lilia followed her sixth guide for the morning out of a cluttered alley behind several smaller shops and into the tidier one between two large buildings. The alley was shadowed and she tried not to flinch at the stares of a group of men leaning against the walls. She was dressed in threadbare servants' clothing and probably looked as tired, nervous and vulnerable as she felt.

The journey had begun before dawn. The guides had taken her all over the city, through all of the main districts. At first there had been few people about, then only servants and the employees of businesses with jobs that required early rising. Slowly the city streets had filled as more people emerged.

Though only a few hours had passed, it felt like far longer. Lilia longed for the journey to end. Wanted the exchange with Skellin over with. And yet she dreaded the confrontation.

She'd spent most of the night awake, imagining every possible way things might go badly. The few times she'd fallen asleep, she'd started awake again from dreams in which Anyi was calling for her, but couldn't hear her replies. Remembering the dreams sent a shiver down her spine, so she thought back to Rothen, Gol and Jonna's discussion the previous night.

"Sonea once killed an Ichani with Healing power," Rothen had told her. *"He imprisoned her within his shield, thinking her too weak to be dangerous and not realising that Healing magic can overcome the body's natural barrier. She stopped his heart. It would be better if you didn't kill Skellin, even if it means letting him escape,*

so we have a chance to catch him and find out who his allies and sources are. But if you have no other choice . . ."

To kill with Healing magic, Lilia would have to touch Skellin's skin and have time to send her mind within. If he detected what she was doing it would only take a small effort to push her out. The Ichani hadn't known anything about Healing magic, but Skellin did. He would be suspicious of any attempt she made to touch him anyway, in case it was an attempt to use black magic.

No. My plan is better. Not much better, and I have to ignore the fact that, unlike using Healing to kill, I have no idea if it will work.

Her own shield would have earned her the mockery of any first-year novice, but not for its lack of strength. It had taken her a while to work out how to stop hiding her use of magic so that Rothen could sense it. The magician was somewhere in the centre of the city. He'd guessed that Skellin's men would realise he could track Lilia if he was spotted following her around, so he was waiting with Gol until she let them know she was about to meet Skellin. Once she did, he would move as close as he could without attracting attention, so that if something went wrong he could, hopefully, get to her in time to help.

She could sense Gol's mind at the edge of her own. It was less distracting than she'd feared. He and Rothen were in a quiet room of a house belonging to a friend of Rothen's. A rather nice house, judging the impressions she was getting from Gol. With his mind so constantly open to her, it was easy to forget that he could not see into hers, and she had to speak to him consciously in order to communicate.

Emerging from the alleyway, Lilia paused as a gust of

fragrant air battered her. She looked around and felt her stomach twitch in anxiety. The docks stretched before and to either side of her.

The guide noticed that she'd stopped and made an impatient gesture. Taking a deep breath, Lilia followed him toward a long pier. They skirted around stacks of goods and wharf workers. Ships rocked gently on either side. As the guide started along the pier, she framed a question in her mind.

—Gol! What if he tells me to get on a ship?

There was a pause before Gol answered.

—Rothen says he's thinking about it.

After they'd passed four ships, the guide stopped before a plank leading up to one of the vessels and pointed to it. She looked up at the vessel. The crew stared back down at her expectantly.

—They look ready to sail. What should I do?

—Get on board. You may only get one chance to save Anyi, Gol replied.

Which was better than no chance. She drew in a deep breath, let it out, then started up the plank. Nobody spoke to her. As soon as she had reached the deck the crew turned away and set to work.

How will Rothen follow? Does the Guild have a ship? Will he be able to use it without having to tell the Higher Magicians what I'm doing?

She moved down the deck, searching the faces. Skellin was not there. Nor Lorandra. Nor Anyi. The crew must be taking her to meet Skellin — but how far away was he? Surely not in another country. It would take weeks to get there.

She imagined what she might feel like if she had been a lone young servant girl surrounded by these tough-looking men. Their expressions were not leering, though, but cold. They avoided her gaze. Nobody paid attention to her except to skirt around her when she got in the way.

Which happened a lot. There wasn't much room on the deck of a ship. Certainly not on a small vessel designed for transporting goods rather than people. By noting the movements of the crew, she found a place to stand out of their way. From there she watched as the ship drifted away from the pier, out of the Marina and towards the sea.

The deck began to rock under her, and she had to brace herself. Many more ships surrounded them, sailing to or from the mouth of the Tarali River, but as their vessel drew further from land they pulled away from most of the others. All but one, which had its sails furled. The man who was barking out most of the orders – from which she guessed he was the captain – pointed in its direction.

She stared at the tiny figures on the other ship. Details grew clearer as they sailed closer. Among the people on board was a trio standing together at the railing. Soon she could tell that one was male and the other two female. She recognised Anyi first. How could she not? *I would know her by her shadow. By her presence.* Her heart twisted. *I can't mess this up. She'll die. Perhaps I should abandon my plan and do whatever Skellin orders. But will he really let her go if I do? Will he keep her and force me to stay and teach him everything I know about magic?*

Steeling herself, she looked at the other two people. The vessels were close enough now for her to see that the woman was Lorandra. Which meant the other man was her son.

So this is Skellin. He was tall like a Lans but dark like a Lonmar. *But since both peoples are known for their honour and strict moral code, I doubt they'd like the comparison. Still, he's probably not the best example of his own people. I wonder . . . It took an outsider, someone willing to break our rules and laws, to show us our weaknesses. What could we have learned about ourselves if the first people to visit us from Igra had been decent and law-abiding?*

The ship slowed and turned so that the vessels now floated alongside each other. She could hear activity around her —the anchor lowering and sails furling, she assumed – but she could not take her eyes off the trio on the other ship. They were only twenty or thirty paces from her.

—Rothen says do whatever you have to, to get Anyi away safe, Gol sent.

Lilia nodded, then hoped that if Skellin had noticed her movement he'd taken it as a gesture of recognition. The rogue magician beckoned.

"Come join us, Lilia," he called.

She looked down at the gap between the ships, then at the crew watching her. They were making no move to direct her to a boat. How was she supposed to transfer to the other vessel?

—Can you levitate? Gol asked.

—Yes, but it will use up some of my magic.

Which was probably Skellin's intention. Still, levitation over that small distance wouldn't use up too much magic, if she was quick about it.

Drawing power, she created a small disc of force beneath her feet and lifted herself up and forward. Skellin, Lorandra and Anyi stepped away from the railing to make room for her. Lorandra was holding onto Anyi's arm. Once her feet were on the deck, Lilia looked up and saw that the woman was holding a knife to Anyi's throat. Her stomach clenched and a chill ran over her skin. Anyi stood stiffly, braced against the rocking of the deck, and as she looked at Lilia her eyes were full of apology, anger and fear.

"Lady Lilia," Skellin said. "So glad you accepted my invitation."

She made herself meet his gaze without flinching. *You may think you're the king of the underworld*, she thought. *But I am a black magician, defender of the Guild.* The pride she felt was surprising and maybe a little inappropriate, but she didn't care so long as it gave her the confidence to stand up to him.

Unlike his mother, he had no unfamiliar accent. He paused as if waiting for a reply, and when she said nothing he smiled. "Well, you have been up for some hours and early mornings don't suit all of us. Perhaps we should get to business. I have a proposition for you. A trade. Teach me black magic and I will hand this lovely young woman into your care. I believe you know her?"

As he gestured to Anyi, the knife at the girl's throat turned in Lorandra's hand, reflecting a flash of sunlight into Lilia's eyes.

Lilia ignored it. "Let her go now."

Skellin shook his head and laughed.

"How do I know you won't kill her," Lilia continued, "once I've given you what you want?"

"How do I know you won't kill me, once I let her go? You are the black magician, after all."

"And you are the murdering rogue magician and Thief."

His eyebrows rose. "Now, now. When have you ever seen me kill someone?"

She opened her mouth to reply, then closed it again. She hadn't. Not even Cery had. Anyi's father had died when his heart failed, though that was likely caused by the strain of being hunted by Skellin. Lorandra was the Thief Hunter.

But that was the way of Thieves, wasn't it? They didn't get blood on their hands. They got someone to do it for them.

She crossed her arms. "Let's get this over with."

He grinned. "My, aren't we impatient?" He took a few steps towards her, then stopped. "But first you need to take off your clothes."

She stared at him. "*What?*" The word burst out of her.

His smile vanished. "I've done my research, Lady Lilia," he said in a low voice. "I know black magic requires the skin to be cut. I require assurance that you aren't carrying any sharp objects. You can be sure I am not, since I would rather not risk you'd turn them against me. I could get one of the crew to check you over, but you might kill him, and would probably rather not be man-handled. I only need you to undress to the point where it is clear you are weaponless."

Swallowing hard, she pulled off the worn old tunic and trousers. Then she glared at Skellin, daring him to insist she remove the simple undergarments that Guild women wore beneath their robes. From the crew of the ships came low whistles, but they fell silent as Skellin glanced around, his expression stern.

"Kick the clothes away and turn around," he ordered. Sighing, she obeyed. "Now, to begin you will teach me how to read minds."

Lilia froze, then cursed silently. If she protested that the deal was only to teach him black magic, he'd laugh. She was in no position to argue.

"You need someone to practise on," she told him.

"You'll do," came the reply she expected.

She felt an unexpected admiration. *Oh, he's not stupid. He's thought this through. Far better than I have. It never occurred to me*

416

he'd demand this. If I do it, he'll see everything. My plan will never work.

"I haven't tried to teach it that way before." It was not hard to sound uncertain and honest. She *hadn't* taught mind-reading before. To anyone.

"Then you don't know it won't work." He took a step toward her, then another. *It's time to decide. Give him everything he wants, try to kill him with Healing, or try my plan.* She flinched as he reached out, but made herself stand still. Looking over his shoulder, she met Anyi's frightened, angry gaze and hoped she did not look as uncertain as she felt.

This had better work . . .

CHAPTER 27

OLD BATTLES, NEW WEAPONS

Being dressed all in black had been an advantage when Sonea had slipped out of the mansion in the early hours of the morning, but now that the sun was up she was all too visible against the pale walls of the Sachakan capital.

At least I'm closer to the centre of the city.

As dawn had arrived, she'd chosen another mansion with a tower to hide in. The side door she'd slipped through hadn't been locked, but she'd discovered the building wasn't completely empty when she'd heard voices from somewhere inside. When she'd tried to leave, a quick check of the outside revealed a group of men hurrying along the street, so she'd crept back through the house as silently as she could. She'd found the stairs and ascended to the tower, telling herself that if she heard anyone coming up she would climb out of one of the tower windows and escape across the rooftop outside.

Hours had passed and the only sound she'd heard below had been distant and muffled. The tower windows were open, perhaps to let in the cool morning breeze. From the street below she'd heard footsteps and more voices, but the city was mostly quiet.

The windows looked onto the furthest side of the street

below and a sea of rooftops. *It's tempting to slip out and find a better vantage point. But the risk of being seen isn't worth it. I don't know where the fight is going to be.* Once it started there should be noises and lights to tell her where it was located. *I'll be able to move closer then. Perhaps go across the rooftops, like Cery and I used to do, back when we were children of the slums . . .*

"The view's no better here," a voice said behind her.

She jumped and spun around. Regin stood near the top of the stairs, arms crossed. Embarrassment at being found, then a selfish relief that he was here, was followed by a flash of concern and annoyance.

"Regin!" she hissed. "What are you doing here?"

He shrugged and uncrossed his arms. "I followed you, of course, though I got stuck downstairs for the last few hours, hiding from the people down there. They just left, by the way."

"You told me you wouldn't come with me. We had an agreement."

"I lied." He shrugged again and continued up the stairs. "I knew you wouldn't take my power if I didn't agree to stay behind. Besides, you lied too. You told the Traitors you would stay put."

"That's different. I should be able to trust another Guild magician to keep his word. And they left without telling us."

"I think the Guild would disapprove more of you risking making the Traitors an enemy than of me ignoring you. I'm only trying to protect you."

She placed her hands on her hips. "You can't. If we're attacked, *I* will have to protect *you*. All you are is another person I have to worry about. You could get us both killed."

He smiled, not bothered by her brutal honesty and she found herself wondering if she was attracted to him because he wasn't

419

the least bit intimidated by her. "Protecting one person won't take more power than protecting two." His gaze moved to the window, and she could not help following it. "Is Dannyl in place yet?"

Sonea reached into her robe for Osen's ring. "I don't know."

"You haven't contacted Osen yet?"

"I did earlier. Nothing was happening. I didn't want to keep the ring on in case someone came up the stairs and I was too distracted to notice."

"No need to worry about that now. I can keep watch." He chuckled. "See? You do need me."

Biting back a retort, she felt her fingers close on the ring. She drew it out, slipped it on her finger and sought Osen and Dannyl's minds.

Peering around the corner of the building, Dannyl searched the street and was relieved to see it was empty. Beckoning to Tayend and Merria, he stepped out and hurried forward. Their footsteps and breathing told him they followed close behind.

So far the only people they'd seen roaming the city were slaves and a carriage driven by a man too well dressed to be a slave. All had been in a hurry. All had been moving away from the centre of the city, whereas Dannyl and his companions were moving inward.

Unfortunately, what made Ashaki's home attractive also made it dangerous: its proximity to the wide parade leading to the palace. Getting close enough to see the battle also meant getting close to the very people he'd been warned to stay away from.

But we should be fine, once we get there. Once we're inside and out of sight.

He'd always been aware of the prestigious location of Achati's house, but had never been in any rooms on the parade side. Master's Rooms and private suites were usually central, and did not have windows. Sachakans preferred privacy and to be away from the heat of the summer sun over nice views.

He reached a larger thoroughfare – one that joined to the parade. Achati's house was on the corner. After checking that the street was empty, he led the others around the corner. Keeping close to the wall on one side, he tried to walk softly and quickly. Even so, the rap of his and Merria's boots echoed in the street.

Tayend's shoes made little more than a soft tap, he noted. As if to make up for that, the buttons and clasps of his elaborate courtier garb clinked and chimed as he moved. The noise would normally be unnoticeable, but in the eerie quiet it sounded like . . . He frowned as he tried to think of a comparable racket. *Like the rattle of roughly handled cutlery.*

A door across the street opened and he froze. He heard Merria stop and out of the corner of his eye he saw Tayend casting about for somewhere to hide, but it was too late. A man emerged, looked up and, as he saw them, he stopped.

Ashaki. Dannyl's heart pounded. The man stared at them, then he straightened and started toward them.

"Run?" Merria asked quietly.

Dannyl shook his head. To run would make them look guilty. To show fear would make it obvious they had reason to. Warrior lessons from long ago repeated in his mind. *You can't tell how strong another magician is, nor he you. A confident attitude will give your adversary reason to doubt he is stronger, even if all evidence points to him being so.* Following the other man's lead, he straightened his back and walked forward to meet him.

The man was about sixty, Dannyl estimated. Grey streaked his hair and the typical Sachakan broadness was well softened by fat.

"You are the Ambassadors from the Guild House?" the man asked briskly. He was tense, Dannyl noticed. *In a hurry. Perhaps I can use that to my advantage.*

"We are," Dannyl said slowly and with formality. "I am Guild Ambassador Dannyl." He gestured to Tayend. "This is Elyne Ambassador Tayend. And this—" he turned to Merria.

The man cut him off. "Why are you not at the Guild House? You do know what is about to occur? You may be heading toward a magical battle."

"I have been appraised of the situation," Dannyl assured him. "I assure you, we do not intend to get in the—"

"Then why are you here?"

"We were offered a safer alternative to the Guild House." That much was true. Achati had told him there was a ship waiting.

The man frowned. "Here? Close to the palace. How can here be safer?"

Dannyl shrugged. "The Traitors are unlikely to get this far."

That had the desired effect. The man's chin lifted. "Yes. Of course. Well, then. It is not far to the palace and I am heading that way. I will escort you there."

Uh, oh. The last place Dannyl wanted to be was among the Ashaki, if they started to lose and were desperate for more power. He ducked his head in apology.

"I'm afraid we aren't going to the palace. Both of our rulers are keen to avoid any impression of interference by the Guild." Then, knowing the man was not going to let them wander off without knowing their destination, especially after mentioning the possibility of interference, he added: "We are going to Ashaki Achati's house."

The man's eyebrows rose, then he nodded. "I will take you to the door."

He strode away, his strides long and fast. Dannyl followed, relying on the sound of Merria's footsteps and Tayend's noisy buttons to tell him they were keeping up. The temptation to look back and meet Tayend's eyes was strong, but he resisted. Looking confident meant also looking as though he was in charge.

Peering over the Ashaki's shoulder, he saw movement. A crowd large enough to block the broad street had gathered, and probably filled the parade beyond. Men in trousers and short coats stood watching something within the parade that Dannyl couldn't see. Precious stones glittered in the sunlight. *Ashaki. Many, many Ashaki. At any moment one is going to look up, see us and draw the attention of the others to us. What will happen then?* He could not help imagining a horde of them coming at him, ready to harvest power from the three foreigners.

But none did. As the self-appointed escort neared the door of Achati's house the crowd began to move. The Ashaki army was leaving. Dannyl hoped this would persuade the escort to abandon them, but the man only scowled and stepped up to the door. He rapped on it.

A long silence followed. The Ashaki rapped again. As time stretched, Dannyl felt his heart beating fast. Achati would be with the king. The slaves had probably gone. What would the escort do when it became clear nobody was going to answer? The man knocked a third time, waited, sighed, then turned to face Dannyl.

Then, as his mouth opened to speak, the door swung inward. A slave peered out.

"Ambassador Dannyl."

Tayend let out an in-held breath and Merria sighed. The Ashaki turned to look back at the slave, then at Dannyl, then towards the parade. Following his gaze, Dannyl saw the last of the Ashaki stride out of sight behind the building opposite.

"Thank you, Ashaki . . ."

The man didn't offer his name. He took a step back. "Stay out of sight," he advised, then he turned and broke into a run.

Dannyl looked at Tayend and Merria. Their eyes were wide as they stared back at him. "Let's get inside."

The slave didn't protest as they pushed through the door. Once all were in the Master's Room he threw himself on the floor. Hearing a movement, Dannyl saw another slave on the floor near another corridor. He looked from one to the other and frowned. Why were these two still here?

"Stand up," he ordered. The pair obeyed. "What are your names?"

"Lak."

"Vata."

"Why haven't you left with the rest of the city's slaves?"

Lak glanced at Vata. "He may need us," he said.

"He" must be Achati. Dannyl felt a wry admiration for their loyalty.

"What's the best place we can see the parade from?" Tayend asked.

Vata looked up. "The roof."

Tayend's eyebrows rose and he looked at Dannyl. "Well?"

Dannyl nodded. "Then take us there."

*   *   *

Traitors filled the street, milling before the mansion's gates. Lorkin and Tyvara had found their way out through a slave's entrance to a side street and hurried around to the front of the building where the Traitors were gathering. Looking around, Lorkin noted that half of the fighters were women, half men. Magicians and sources. All wore vests like his. *For most of the men, the stones will be their only source of magic*, he realised. *Non-magicians participating in battle. That must be a first.*

Just before the crowd swelled to fill the space between the houses, Lorkin glimpsed the street stretching on towards the centre of the city. It might have been his imagination, but in the distance the street appeared to be blocked by a shadow. And that shadow seemed to be moving.

Calls for quiet settled the crowd and he realised a familiar voice was coming from somewhere in the centre.

". . . protect all. We must all stay together. Our strength is in our unity and purpose. We are united. The Ashaki are not. We have prepared ourselves for centuries. The Ashaki have not. We have the support of the slaves. The Ashaki do not. *And we have stones.*"

Taller than most Traitors, Lorkin looked over their heads in the direction of the voice and saw Savara standing higher than the crowd, visible to all.

"Can you see her? We have to get to her," Tyvara whispered in his ear.

"She's over by the gates."

Grabbing his hand, she pulled him around the crowd to the wall of the mansion. Savara's voice grew louder as they neared, filled with confidence and passion.

"Do not spare the stones. This is what they were made for.

425

Tools for breaking bonds, for making our future, for making everyone equal. To bring freedom to Sachaka."

"Freedom!" the Traitors shouted.

Lorkin's heart jumped at the unexpected noise. The second time it came, he was ready for it and this time his pulse quickened at the building excitement. Once at the wall, Tyvara wove through people gazing at their queen with rapt expressions. Finally they broke through the crowd to find the queen standing on a cart, surrounded by the Speakers, just as her speech ended.

"Today we bring Sachakans together, united in freedom!" she finished.

"Freedom!" everyone shouted again. It became a chant as Savara stepped down from the cart and strode forward, the crowd parting to let her through. The Speakers hurried after, and Tyvara all but dove forward, dragging Lorkin after her so that they joined the Speakers before the Traitors fell in behind them.

They reached Savara just as the queen left the crowd. The Speakers moved out to either side, forming a line across the street. Chaos finally shifted into order as the Traitors moved to follow the Speakers who led their teams. Tyvara looked around, then over each shoulder.

"I can't see Kalia," she hissed. "You?"

"No." Lorkin shook his head as he sought the woman.

"Oh, she's staying behind," a voice said to his left. He looked over to see that Chari, the woman who had helped them escape to Sanctuary, had appeared beside him. "Ready to treat the injured."

"Well, that's one less thing to worry about," Tyvara muttered. "Now we only have to deal with *them*."

Following her gaze, Lorkin looked past the queen's shoulder to see that he hadn't been imagining it: the street beyond was blocked by another crowd several paces away and marching rapidly closer. Sunlight glinted off jewelled jackets.

All those gemstones. I wonder . . . Lorkin thought. *Did the Ashaki of the distant past decorate their clothing with magical stones? Has the tradition persisted though the knowledge of stone-making was lost?*

Though only moving at a walk, the two armies seemed to rush towards each other. Lorkin realised his heart was racing. *This is it. Either I'll be alive at the end of this, or not. Curse it – I was going to contact Mother.* All around him, Traitors were reaching into their vests for the first stones. *Too late now.* Taking a deep breath, Lorkin did the same, taking one strike and one shield stone. As Tyvara moved to the queen's right side, he stepped up to take his place on the left.

The gap between the two armies shrank from a few hundred paces to less than a hundred. The Queen held up a stone, ready to strike. The Speakers did the same. Looking at the enemy, Lorkin saw the determined faces of the Ashaki. Saw the scowls of hatred and the grins of anticipation. He saw the king and his blood went cold. The old man regarded the invaders of his city with a haughty stare. *I'd like to personally smack that look off his—*

At some signal Lorkin did not catch, both sides attacked. He could not tell who struck first. One moment the space between the armies was charged with expectation, the next it sizzled with magic. He automatically pressed on the shield stone and felt it activate and bounce against that held by the queen and the Speaker to his left until it settled between them. Savara was attacking, but Tyvara only held her strike stone at the ready, as she had instructed him to do. They would join the battle later; for now they were to protect the queen.

Both sides had come to a halt. Lorkin fought the urge to flinch away from the dangerous forces streaking between them. *They did not even attempt to address each other*, he realised. *Not even to throw insults.* According to history books, leaders of armies always invited the enemy to surrender. Not this time.

It's not that the Traitors and Ashaki believe the other side would never accept. It's because they aren't offering. Each side means to eradicate the other. To kill every last Traitor or Ashaki. He shivered. *Even the Ichani offered to let the Guild give in and avoid a battle.*

Not striking meant he had the opportunity to watch. The Ashaki stood unmoving, whereas the Traitors were in constant motion. He had been fascinated by the method of battle they'd developed and was keen to see it in action. The queen and Speakers remained at the front and he and Tyvara stayed as the queen's protectors. The rest of the Traitors formed columns behind the Speakers. As each reached the front they moved to stand beside a Speaker. If they took a place to the left of the Speaker, they shielded the front line; if they moved to the right, they used a strike stone. When their stone was depleted they retreated to the end of the column to let others have their turn.

This ensured that most Traitors weakened at the same rate, and that most stones were used before the magicians of the army began using their own store of power. It was much easier to respond quickly to abrupt and unexpected attacks with personal magic than with stones, so it was held in reserve.

Warning shouts came from behind. Lorkin looked back. Something was going on to the right of the Traitor army.

"What's happening?" Savara asked.

Traitors in the columns to the right were calling out to each other. The ones closest turned to relay what they were hearing to Tyvara. Lorkin caught snatches of their report.

"Attack from the right," Tyvara repeated. "Seven Ashaki. All dealt with."

Lorkin saw Savara smile in relief and satisfaction and felt a small surge of triumph.

The Ashaki are fools if they think we're not ready for this sort of attack.

"Lorkin," Tyvara hissed.

He turned to see her frowning in worry. She jerked her head and flicked her eyes back towards the Traitor army, at the same time silently mouthing a word. His blood went cold.

Kalia.

Twisting around, he searched the faces in the columns behind her, but saw no sign of the woman. *Maybe Tyvara saw someone who looked a bit like Kalia. No, she doesn't not look at all doubtful. So where is Kalia?*

Not behind Tyvara. He turned to look at the Traitors behind him and his heart turned to ice. Kalia was just a few steps away, slipping into the closest column where a Traitor was distracted, fiddling with his vest. Lorkin gasped out her name, drew magic and threw up a shield behind himself, Savara and Tyvara. It bumped up against another, and he realised Tyvara had already done the same.

"Kalia?" Savara said, her voice full of surprise. She turned to face the woman. Traitors stared in surprise as their leader's attention shifted from the enemy. Strikes burst against Savara's shield, but she seemed unconcerned as she faced Kalia. "What are you doing here?"

Kalia looked around at all the faces watching and paled. "I came to help."

"I gave you an order," Savara reminded her, an edge of annoyance and forced patience in her voice.

Kalia paused. The battle raged on. The air before Savara vibrated as the attack on her shield increased, the Ashaki hoping her distraction was a sign of weakness. The Traitors stepping up to fight did so without hesitation, while those who retreated did so a touch slower, eyeing Kalia and the queen with interest.

"But you need every—" Kalia began.

"I need you to follow orders." Savara's tone and expression were cold now. "How do expect to regain our trust if you will not do what you are told?" She turned away. "Go to the back and stay there."

As Kalia retreated, Savara leaned toward Lorkin.

"What is she thinking?"

He concentrated. As before, he picked up few words, but disappointment radiated from her. Not the annoyance or anger of a foiled plan, though. Kalia's sense of failure was laced with fear and shame. Dislike still filled her, but not murderous intent.

"I don't think she was planning anything," he said.

Savara nodded. "Shield me."

"Already am," he heard Tyvara say quietly. "Someone should go back and keep an eye on her."

Savara shook her head. "No. It is us she hates. She will not deliberately harm other Traitors." Her gaze was fixed on the Ashaki. She took a step forward. A moment later the Speakers followed suit. Looking ahead, Lorkin saw some of the Ashaki shuffle backwards. A ripple of excitement went through the Traitors.

Savara chuckled. "Either they're weakening, losing confidence, or are leading us into a trap."

"What do we do?" Tyvara asked.

"See which one it is," the queen answered. "It's time you made use of your strike stones. If we spot a trap and you suddenly start striking, we'll warn them that we know what they're up to. I'd rather leave them guessing whether we've noticed it for as long as possible."

Smiling, she took a longer step forward, and then another.

CHAPTER 28

VICTORY AND DEFEAT

As Skellin's fingers touched Lilia's forehead she could not help flinching away. He reached for her again, his eyes boring into hers.

"If I think you're delaying, or you cause me pain, my mother will cut your friend's ears and nose off," he growled.

Heart racing, Lilia lowered her eyes. *And once I do, he'll want more. He'll threaten to hurt her until I've taught him everything. Then he'll kill us both. I may as well stick with my plan. If I fail, at least we'd get the pain and dying over with sooner. But I will have to be quick. Give him no time to react.*

Reaching out, she grabbed his wrists as if to stop him, then let him press his hands to her temples. Taking a deep breath, she closed her eyes, gathered enough power to smash through a strong shield and sent it out from her right palm in a stabbing forcestrike.

She felt the barrier beneath her fingers part under the unexpected and finely focused attack. *It worked!* Surprised, she started drawing power, relying on the paralysing effect to keep him from struggling or speaking. With his back to Lorandra, hopefully she wouldn't notice.

His grip on her head loosened as the weakening effect of

black magic took hold, but she held his hands in place. Opening her eyes, she sent magic out to stop him sinking to the ground. He stared back at her, his pupils wide with anger and fear.

Yes. Fear me, she thought. *This time you've underestimated your victim. Too eager to get hold of what you want.*

But she must not underestimate him, either. Or his mother. Right now Lorandra was more of a danger than Skellin. She would notice something was wrong eventually, and she still had the knife at Anyi's throat. Lilia felt a pang of doubt and slowed her drawing of power. She did not know how long it would take to strip away most of it, and she needed to decide what she'd do once she had.

I must protect Anyi before Lorandra realises I'm draining Skellin. She turned her head slightly, so that she could see Anyi, and extended her senses and magic. Somehow she must place a barrier between the knife and Anyi's skin without either of them noticing. Concentrating on drawing power and using it at the same time was challenging. *Kallen should have taught me to do this . . .*

Her magic encountered a resistance.

A barrier! Lorandra's barrier. It can only be hers. Skellin can't use his power.

At once she knew she'd made a mistake. Lorandra frowned. *She knows I shouldn't be doing anything with magic. Skellin would stop me.* In horror, she watched Lorandra's eyes widen with realisation, then narrow with fury.

Lilia drew power and sent it out toward Lorandra even as the woman's hand moved. Red burst from Anyi's throat.

No! Lilia let Skellin fall. As Lorandra's barrier shattered she caught Anyi and pressed her hand to the girl's throat. Blood poured between her fingers. She wrapped herself and Anyi in a shield, lowered her friend to the deck and sent her mind into her body. *Close!* she commanded of the rent tubes that carried Anyi's blood. Healing power poured from her, knitting together flesh. The tubes became whole, the muscle repaired. Hope rushed through Lilia, but as skin melded to skin she loosened her grip on Anyi's throat. *Was I fast enough? Did she lose too much blood?*

Anyi lay still, her eyes staring at the sails and sky above them. Her face was pale. Her lips blue. *But she's alive. Heart beating. Still breathing. Alive but . . .*

A scream burst from somewhere close by. Startled, Lilia turned to see Lorandra getting up out of a crouch, Skellin at her feet. He, too, was staring at the sky. Lorandra turned to face Lilia. At the fury twisting the woman's face Lilia instinctively strengthened her shield, but no strike came.

Instead the air before Lorandra rippled. Lilia felt heat and caught an impression of skin and cloth darkening to black. Flames flared, outlining Lorandra's form. The woman shrieked, staggered backwards and toppled over the railing.

Stunned by the image still burned into her mind, Lilia could not move for a moment. Then she realised the crew around her were shouting, and objects were raining down from above. Sails. Rope. A wooden beam bounced off her shield. Something was destroying the ship's rigging. Probably the same something that had struck Lorandra. Straightening and stretching her neck, she looked around and glimpsed another vessel, a purple-robed figure standing at the helm, approaching from the other side of the ship.

"Lilia?"

Catching her breath she looked down at Anyi. The girl's eyes were open. Lilia's heart leapt with joy and relief.

"You're alive! You're alive." Lilia lay down next to Anyi and pulled her close. "How are you feeling?"

"Awful. But not as bad as I think that bitch is – if she's still alive."

"You saw that?"

"Yeah. Thought I was dreaming." Anyi's lips were still tinged with blue. She frowned. "Is Skellin dead?"

Lilia looked over to the Thief, lying still a few paces away. "He looks it, but he could just be exhausted. Either way, he can't harm us."

"Do me a favour and check."

Looking around, she saw that the crew were giving them a wide berth. Reluctantly, Lilia got up and walked over to Skellin. His face was locked in an expression of pain and surprise. He wasn't breathing. Touching him, she sensed no energy within him. *Deader than dead. But I hadn't finished draining him when Lorandra cut Anyi's throat.* Remembering how she had drawn power in order to break Lorandra's shield, she realised where she had drawn it from. She'd defeated Lorandra with Skellin's power.

Lilia looked over the railing. She had expected to see Lorandra's body floating nearby, but there was no sign of it. She returned to Anyi and sat down. "Yes. He's dead. The Guild isn't going to be happy about that."

Anyi made a rude noise.

"Not because of roet," Lilia said. "They wanted to find out who his allies are, especially those in the Guild."

"Don't worry," Anyi scowled. "Father will find who they are."

Lilia's breath caught in her throat. *She doesn't know . . .*

Anyi's eyes went wide. "He . . . he wasn't pretending, was he?"

Biting her lip, Lilia shook her head.

A look of pain creased Anyi's face. She swore. But as Lilia reached out to embrace her, Anyi shook her head, her face hardening. "Time for that later. We still have a lot to do, and we can't let . . . Father made sure what was done to his family made him stronger, not weaker. I have to be strong, too." Anyi pushed herself up onto her elbows, but her face went even paler and she sank back down again.

"Rest," Lilia told her. "You've lost a lot of blood and your body needs time to make more."

"How long will that take?"

Lilia shrugged. "I'm not sure. A few days, maybe." She smiled sadly at Anyi's grimace of impatience. *I fear it'll take a lot longer for her heart to mend than her body, though.* "You need food and water. Rothen will be here any moment." She craned her neck to see that the other vessel was drawing alongside the ship.

Anyi nodded. Looking around, Lilia spotted the tattered clothing she had been wearing. "I should get dressed."

"Yes. Why did Skellin make you strip down to your underclothes?" One of Anyi's eyebrows rose. "Not that I'm complaining."

"Just making sure I wasn't carrying a knife."

"Sounds strange, a magician worrying about knives when people who carry knives usually fear magic, but I guess black magic turns things around a bit."

"Not any more." As Anyi frowned, Lilia shook her head. "I'll explain later."

—Osen? The battle has started. I can hear sounds and flashes of light several streets away.

—Can you see the fighting?

436

—No. What about Dannyl?

—He contacted me to say they've arrived at Achati's place, but I've heard nothing since then. The house is on the parade, so they'll only see the battle if the Ashaki have to retreat.

—Do you want me to try getting closer?

—No. Stay where you are. Keep the ring on. Dannyl is sure to put his on soon, and I suspect having both of you wearing rings will be a bit . . . overwhelming, though Naki's mind-read-blocking ring appears to be protecting me from your thoughts.

Sonea looked down at the other ring on her finger. She hadn't told him about slipping away from the house that the Traitors' guards had told them to stay in. If all went well, she wouldn't have to.

The Traitors are only worried that we'll interfere. So long as I don't, I think they'll forgive me for wanting to know what happens to my son.

The trouble was, she was no closer to seeing Lorkin than she had been earlier. She was going to have to rely on Dannyl to show her what was happening. And he wouldn't be able to, if the Ashaki didn't fall back. If they didn't it would mean they were winning.

Not for the first time that morning, she felt anxiety rising up like a suffocating wave. Taking a deep breath, she pushed it away and weighed up her options. Could she get a little closer, without putting Regin in danger or the future relationship between the Allied Lands and Sachaka?

From the roof of Achati's house Dannyl could see the city spread around him, but mostly it was a view of rooftops. He could guess at where the battle was, however. The rumble and crack of strikes impacting on shields or stone echoed across the city. Smoke billowed up from a building at least a thousand paces away, flashes of magic constantly brightening the cloud's underbelly.

"Do you think Achati's slaves will be all right, if the Traitors win?" Merria asked. "Or will they be killed for remaining loyal?"

"I fear the latter is more likely," Tayend replied.

"Could we protect them?"

"You will have to ask the Guild. Dannyl?"

"Soon," Dannyl replied, not taking his eyes from the distant signs of battle. "Osen will be with King Merin and the Higher Magicians. I don't want to distract him again until there's something to report."

But that wasn't the only reason Dannyl was hesitating. Once he put Osen's blood ring on he would have to push aside all thought of Achati, and he wasn't sure how long he could keep that up. *Especially when Merria and Tayend are talking as if the Traitors will win.*

"They're getting closer," Merria said.

No, Dannyl thought, looking at the cloud of smoke. *It's no nearer. Achati is safe.* But was Lorkin? He felt a pang of anxiety, then a bitterness. *As Tayend said, no matter which way this goes, something bad will come of it.*

"I think you're right," Tayend replied. "The flashes were lighting the underside of the pillar of smoke before. Now they're lighting *this* side of it."

Dannyl's stomach sank as he saw Tayend was correct. *Maybe the Ashaki will gather their strength and regain ground again. Maybe the Traitors will run out of magic.*

His companions were silent for a long time as nothing else happened to indicate any change in the battle. Then a building halfway between the parade and the distant smoke cloud sank out of sight. The boom and rumble followed a heartbeat later, then dust billowed up. Merria gasped. Tayend muttered a curse.

"Maybe this isn't the safest place to be," Tayend said in a thin voice. "If they get this far."

"We'll be fine," Merria said, the waver in her voice betraying her lie. "We'll just levitate away."

"I guess I should stay close, then."

"We should all stay close together," Merria agreed.

As the pair moved to stand on either side of him, Dannyl glanced at them, amused that they should be drawn to him for protection. It made sense that Tayend would. Though Merria was a magician, Dannyl had been close to Tayend for a long time. But Merria should have the confidence of knowing she could protect herself.

Dannyl looked out towards where the collapsed building had been. *Unlike me, being caught up in the fight is the last thing Merria wants. But me . . . I wish I had some excuse to help Achati. Even if just to ensure he survives should the Ashaki lose . . .*

"They're here!" Merria exclaimed.

Dannyl's heart plunged as he saw people running out of a nearby side street. All men, all wearing Ashaki garb, some coated in dust. They stopped when they reached the parade, forming a line one, then two, then three deep across the street entrance as more Ashaki emerged to join them. He estimated there were about a hundred of them.

"Is that King Amakira?" Tayend asked.

Dannyl narrowed his eyes. An older man stood at the centre, but many other grey-haired Ashaki were in the line and it was impossible to identify which was the king. From streets on either side spilled more Ashaki. Perhaps they had tried to circle around and attack the Traitors from behind. Whatever they had done had not weakened their enemy enough, though. The edge of the Traitor front line was moving into sight. Their strikes were driving the Ashaki back. Men at one edge of the line stumbled back and fell. They did not rise again.

The Ashaki in the line struck in unison, and the Traitors retaliated. At once, holes began to form in the defensive wall of Ashaki. The line thinned as men stepped into gaps to replace the fallen. At a distant shout the defenders began to retreat rapidly, no longer striking, concentrating all their efforts in shielding.

They're losing. They've lost. Unless they've put something in place at the palace . . .

"Dannyl," Merria said.

"What?" he asked, then felt a flash of guilt at the sharpness of his tone.

"Osen's ring?"

Dannyl cursed, then apologised, as he fumbled in his robe for the blood ring. Taking a deep breath, he slipped it on his finger.

—Dannyl?

—Yes, Osen. It's me. The conflict has moved into sight. The Ashaki formed a line at the entrance to the parade, but they're now in retreat.

—Sonea, can you see?

—Yes, came Sonea's reply. Her mental voice was clear, but he could sense nothing of her presence or thoughts. Below, the retreating Ashaki were fifty paces from Achati's house and getting closer. Soon Dannyl would be able to see more than the back of their heads. See if Achati was still among them.

A strike slammed two of them back into the men behind. Dannyl caught a glimpse of crushed, bloodied faces.

—*The Ashaki are losing*, Osen noted.

—*They may have another force waiting at the palace*, Dannyl replied.

—*Can you see Lorkin?* Sonea asked.

Dannyl dragged his eyes away from the Ashaki to the Traitors. He caught his breath. Hundreds of them were moving into the parade. They walked in columns, their orderly formation a telling contrast to the crowd of retreating Ashaki. As he watched, a few of the foremost Traitors stepped aside and let those behind take their places.

He had assumed it would be easy to pick Lorkin out as the one man among many women, but there appeared to be as many male Traitor magicians as women and they were all dressed the same. Male or female, they were dipping into the pockets of the vests they wore, then holding out whatever it was they'd removed. He caught a glint of light, then another, and realised what they were doing.

Stones. They're using stones.

Then his eyes found a familiar face and he felt recognition and relief rush through him. Lorkin was standing at the centre of the Traitor line, behind and a step to the side of a shorter, older woman. *Tyvara? No. None of the personal slaves at the Guild House had been that woman's age.* So who was the older woman?

—*The queen*, Sonea sent.

Looking at the older woman again, Dannyl noted her position at the centre and the determination in her face. *Queen Savara*, he thought. *Who, unless the Ashaki come up with some last-moment winning manoeuvre, will be the woman I will soon have to kneel before and negotiate with.*

441

The Ashaki . . . were drawing level with Achati's house. They were a much smaller group now. He steeled himself as he looked down and sought a familiar face. A head turned to look up toward him, and all the fear and affection he'd meant to hide from Osen and Sonea surged up and paralysed him. Achati smiled as if he had known Dannyl would be watching from atop his home all along, then turned his attention back to the Traitors.

Dannyl couldn't move. His heart hammered in his chest as the Ashaki continued backing towards the palace. *He can't die.* King Amakira was flanked by Achati and one of his other advisers. More Ashaki fell. *He won't*, he told himself. *He'll be fine if they get back to the palace.*

"Oh." Merria said. "Look."

Tearing his gaze away, Dannyl saw she was pointing towards the grand palace building. People were pouring out of the entrance. At first he felt a surge of hope and triumph, thinking they were more Ashaki, then Tayend whistled quietly as he always did when impressed, and at the same time Dannyl realised he wasn't seeing glittering Ashaki garb.

"The Traitors have already overtaken it." Tayend sighed. "And the Ashaki haven't even noticed."

Looking down again, Dannyl felt sick as he waited for signs that the Ashaki had realised the truth. *When they do, they'll surrender. They have no other choice.* The Ashaki were bunching together around the king. No more than twenty now. Some were looking back at the palace. The ones at the back stopped, shouting a warning. He saw the king begin to turn, then stop. Saw Amakira's lips move, and Achati's nod. The king and the other adviser continued to retreat, but Achati stopped. The strikes from the Traitors suddenly intensified, perhaps at the sight of their enemy's leader moving out of sight.

Achati staggered.

Then he made an impossible leap backwards, contorting in the air and crashed to the ground.

Dannyl's heart stopped. He stared at the twisted, limp form of his friend in disbelief.

But . . . why? Why didn't he retreat with the king? Why sacrifice himself then, when he didn't have to. The king must have known they had lost. He should have surrendered. I should have done something. If I'd known he'd do this I would have done something . . .

Hands were restraining his arms. He looked down to see both Merria and Tayend holding him. He looked at them in surprise. Then he realised he was very close to the edge of the roof.

"I'm sorry," Tayend said. As he met Tayend's gaze he saw understanding and sympathy there. Merria had said something at the same time, and it took Dannyl a moment to realise what it was.

"Don't what?" he asked.

She stared at him intently. "Try to save them."

Dannyl stepped back from the edge and shook them off. "For a moment I thought you were worried about *me*," he said bitterly. He flinched at the petulance in his tone. Then anger filled him, and something else. Something that threatened to overwhelm him. Suddenly he had to get away from them. Away from the sight below. He took a few steps toward the hatch they'd climbed through to get onto the roof.

"Wait." Merria hurried to him and grabbed his hand. He pulled away and felt something slip from his finger. *Osen's ring.* He'd forgotten about it. *Everything I saw and felt would have*

443

been seen by . . . But he didn't care. Achati was dead. *Dead. And I stood by and watched and did nothing.*

Tayend walked over and placed a hand lightly on Dannyl's shoulder. It was both unwelcome and yet soothing.

"Let's go inside and wait," he suggested. "Merria can take over from here."

Resentment faded. Tayend understood. He followed his friend down into Achati's house, along corridors and into the Master's Room. There they stopped, looked around the room, then at each other. Tayend's eyes glittered with tears. He walked over and wrapped his arms around Dannyl.

"I thought you didn't like him," Dannyl whispered.

"I did. Just not as much as you did."

No. Not as much as I did. Dannyl bowed his head and let the tears come. When the worst of it had passed he was surprised to find he could feel affection and gratitude at the same time as grief and horror. *I am so lucky Tayend is here with me. He has always understood me better than anyone. Even if we are never more than friends again, I hope we will always have this.*

With Tayend beside him he would not mourn Achati alone. With Tayend close by he would be able to face the people who had killed Achati. With Tayend he had someone who would remember how fine a man Achati had been.

And now that I've seen how ruthless the Traitors can be, I must do what I can to ensure they don't decide the Allied Lands need "freeing", too.

Without taking his eyes from the Ashaki, Lorkin explored the pockets of his vest in case he had missed any strike or shield stones, but found none. The red and blue rings were depleted, so he had been using his own store of power. He didn't want to use the power within the storestone until he had to.

He suspected it wouldn't be necessary. The Traitors who had emerged from the palace were now joining with the main army, encircling the remaining Ashaki. Only a dozen or so Ashaki were left, surrounding and protecting the king.

He was not sure how long had passed since the battle had begun. A few hours, perhaps? From the angle and length of his shadow he guessed it was afternoon, but the smoke from the burning houses was giving the sunlight a deceptive golden glow that suggested the day was older than it was.

The battle had been surprisingly uncomplicated, with few Traitor deaths. Twenty or so had been lost during one side attack. While the Traitors on the right had defended themselves successfully, those on the left had been taken by surprise when the building beside them had exploded and Ashaki had surged out into their midst.

But the Ashaki had never stopped retreating. The battle had become a steady Traitor advance to the city centre. The Ashaki began to fall long before they reached it, and by the time they were driven to the parade their numbers were down to a third.

No magical battle that he'd ever read of had resembled this one. *The parameters of magical fighting have changed. Gemstones have made it into something completely new. The Guild knows that it needs gemstones for defence, but it has no idea how badly. If it doesn't adapt it will be left behind.*

Still, the battle wasn't over yet. He was all too aware that he wasn't the only Traitor who had run out of stones. Their method of fighting ensured that, barring surprise attacks, all were protected until the entire army was exhausted. Only Savara knew how strong the army was now, through communication with the other Speakers, who received reports from each Traitor as he or she left the front. *We could be onto our last stones or still bursting with power*, Lorkin thought. *Savara has shown no sign of concern, but then she's very good at looking calm and confident.*

He looked at her again. She was taking in the scene with narrowed eyes. Straightening, she raised an arm, palm facing outward – the signal to stop.

At once the Traitors stopped striking the Ashaki. The hum of power streaking through the air ended. The shuffle of feet ceased. Voices fell silent. The few sounds that followed were muted, as if all noise had been dampened.

A circle of Traitors surrounded the remaining Ashaki, who stared back defiantly. Lorkin looked from them to Savara.

What will she do? So far the order has been to kill all Ashaki. I've seen no Ashaki attempt to surrender. The few we heard about who were sympathetic to the slaves and did not want to fight the Traitors have left the country.

The order to kill all Ashakis had been to ensure their defeat. Now that they were defeated, would they remain unharmed if they surrendered? He thought of the stones keeping the wasteland lifeless. The Traitors could be ruthless . . .

Savara took a step forward, then another. Lorkin saw Tyvara tense. He turned the ring holding the storestone around so he could curl his fingers around it, ready to draw power if he needed it. Savara stopped.

"King Amakira," she called.

The Ashaki did not move. Lorkin searched for some glimpse of the king among them. The silence lengthened.

"You are defeated," Savara said. "Come forth, or are you too cowardly to show your face?"

Low voices were heard from the Ashaki now, then Lorkin saw movement.

"You expect me to *surrender?*"

Lorkin shivered at the voice. A memory rose of an old man on a throne, followed by the palace prison, the slave girl . . . He blinked them away and concentrated on the scene before him. The Ashaki parted and the king stepped out.

"We do not submit to Traitors," he said.

As he spoke, his hand moved to his belt and closed around the hilt of a knife. Gems glittered in the sunlight as he drew the blade. He extended his arm toward Savara, pointing at her. He let the knife go. It hovered in the air. His arm dropped to his side.

Then, in a movement almost too fast to follow, it reversed and shot backward, plunging into his chest.

Lorkin sucked in a breath, and heard gasps from all around. *Well, I didn't expect that*, he thought as the king fell, and was caught and lowered to the ground by the Ashaki behind him. *Did he just commit suicide, or did he ask one of the Ashaki to—?*

The rest of the Ashaki stepped back hastily as a bright light enveloped the king's body. A sharp crack, followed by a roar like a fire flaring before a gust of wind, echoed between the buildings. *The king's remaining power, released as his control failed.* Lorkin shuddered.

The light vanished, and all that was left was ash.

Then the air before Savara began to vibrate. Lorkin looked up to see that the remaining Ashaki's gazes were fixed on her. Realising that the men were striking at their queen, the Traitors attacked. Lorkin winced at the dull thuds and crack of bones, as the last Ashaki fell before the onslaught. *They didn't bother to shield. They used their last magic in a final vain attempt to kill the Traitor queen, and to ensure they would die.*

The Traitor strikes ended as quickly as they had begun, and a different kind of silence fell. One filled with relief as well as horror. Savara's shoulders lifted and dropped and she bowed her head. She didn't look up or speak, and as time stretched the Traitors began to frown and exchange glances. As Tyvara stepped forward, concern in her eyes, Lorkin followed, but he kept a few steps back, ready to help but leaving Tyvara to speak.

Savara looked at Tyvara and shook her head. "Ashaki and Traitors. We are so different. And yet we are the same. So determined we are right.

"The Traitors are no more too. We will have soon destroyed what we rebelled against. We should now call ourselves Sachakans."

"We are not the same," Tyvara told her. "The Ashaki are no more."

Savara looked back at Lorkin. "What do you think? Are we the same?"

Lorkin shook his head. "No. Yes, you are determined, but that is no bad thing in itself. Only a stronger determination to end their power would overcome their determination to hold onto it."

Savara eyebrows rose. "An interesting observation from a Kyralian and former Guild magician."

He shrugged, then managed a smile. "But don't tell me you've succeeded where the Guild failed until you've successfully held onto power here for a few decades — and have done so without being as ruthless as the Ashaki."

A faint smile thinned her lips, then she straightened and

looked around the circle of Traitors. "The battle is over," she called out. "The hard work now begins. You know what to do."

Lorkin saw wry expressions and weary resignation as the circle of Traitors broke apart. The Speakers started forward and Savara walked over to meet them. The rest of the Traitors gathered into teams. Listening to a group nearby, Lorkin heard the leader asking how many stones were left. As they counted, she asked for a volunteer to take messages to the former slaves, telling them it was safe to return to the city.

He felt something poke him in the ribs and turned to see Tyvara nodding toward Savara. The queen and the Speakers were moving away. He fell into step beside her as she followed them. *Savara will need guarding for some time yet*, he realised. Then he shook his head. *Somehow I've wound up as a royal body-guard. I never would have predicted that.*

"There are many, many dead slaves in the palace," Speaker Shaiya was saying. "I can't estimate how long it will take to remove the bodies. Even if we could clear them tonight, we won't know it's completely safe until we search all rooms."

"And the free servants?"

Shaiya shook her head. "Most resisted us. The rest fled."

"They were raised to be loyal," Savara said. "And, unlike slaves, they had something to lose. We were never going to win them over." She sighed. "We need a safe base from which to organise. Somewhere central. What about one of these houses?"

Shaiya looked around. "I'll send teams in to investigate."

CHAPTER 29

A NEW AND FRIGHTENING FREEDOM

Despite the way that the crew rushed around, nothing seemed to happen quickly on a ship, Lilia reflected. But as the vessel drifted toward the docks she looked at Anyi and decided she didn't mind. Rothen had ordered that food and water be brought, and while Anyi was still very tired she had regained some colour and could sit up.

Anyi's expression was distant and pained, which made Lilia's heart ache with sympathy, but then her friend shook her head and her face hardened with determination. *She has more self-control that I'd ever have, in her situation*, Lilia thought. *Suddenly I can see Cery in her.* He'd had the same habit of looking distracted, then snapping into focus, she realised. She just hadn't understood why.

He probably grieved for the loss of his family when alone, or with Gol. Lilia frowned. *Losing* him *is going to catch up with Anyi eventually. I will be there for her when it does, even if I have to sneak out of the Guild.*

They watched in silence as the last manoeuvres were made to bring the ship dockside. Rothen stood beside the captain, talking quietly. The two magicians he had recruited at the docks stood guard over the crew taken from Skellin's ship. Seeing them following his orders unquestioningly, though they clearly had no idea of the reasons for them, had amazed her. Magicians weren't usually so cooperative, at least not from what she'd seen. But then she saw the respect in their faces and remembered that Rothen was not just a Higher Magician, but had been Black Magician Sonea's guardian and teacher, and had no small part in fighting the Ichani Invasion.

It's easy to forget that, with Rothen. He doesn't push people around or look down on them. He's approachable. I bet he doesn't think he's all that important.

Rothen turned to look at her, then walked over. He smiled at Anyi. "How are you feeling? Ready to go?"

Anyi nodded but, as she stood up, she looked down at herself and grimaced.

"Dizzy?" Rothen asked, reaching out to steady her.

Anyi shook her head. "No. I'm fine."

He nodded, then beckoned and headed towards the long plank the crew had strung between the ship and dock. Anyi took a few unsteady steps.

"Are you sure you're all right?" Lilia asked in a low voice.

"I look a mess. I *feel* a mess. And I don't think this coat is ever going to be the same."

Lilia shuddered. Anyi's clothes were stiff and stained with her blood. She hooked her arm through her friend's. "I'll buy you another one."

"Maybe it'll be a good thing, me looking like this. Might make the Higher Magicians feel guilty they didn't catch Skellin sooner." She sighed. "At least you're clean."

Lilia looked down at her robes. Rothen had brought them, so she wouldn't have to return to the Guild wearing the tattered disguise. *Assuming I did return. It could have all gone very badly.* She still couldn't believe her trick had worked. Looking over at Skellin's body, which was covered by an old piece of sacking, she shuddered. *I killed a person. With black magic.* But she didn't want to think about that now.

They caught up with Rothen at the railing. "Will the Higher Magicians want to see us straightaway, Lord Rothen?" she asked as they reached him.

He nodded. "I'm afr—"

"What's *he* doing here?" Anyi interrupted, her words a low growl.

Lilia followed Anyi's gaze and her heart sank as she saw the black-robed magician waiting on the dock.

"Kallen is – was – in charge of finding Skellin," Rothen reminded her.

"A fine job he did of it, too."

"Are we going to tell him what happened?" Lilia asked. "What if he is Skellin's source."

Rothen's eyes narrowed. "Say nothing until the meeting." He gave them a grim smile. "Don't worry. We'll work out who the source is. If it is a Higher Magician, well, it wouldn't be the first time one of us had a nasty secret. We'll deal with it."

As they started down the gangplank, Lilia gave Anyi a re-assuring nod. "He sounds confident."

Anyi shrugged, then followed. As they reached the dock, Kallen stepped forward to meet them. Lilia bowed, but Anyi remained unbending, her eyes dark and jaw stiff.

"Lord Rothen. Lady Lilia. Anyi." Kallen turned to Rothen. "You asked me to meet you here?"

"Yes, Black Magician Kallen. I will explain more when we

return to the Guild, but I can tell you that Skellin is dead and his mother too. His body is on board, if you wish to inspect it. Lorandra's is somewhere under the sea."

Kallen's eyebrows rose. Without saying another word, he strode up the gangplank and headed for the body. His back was to them as he crouched and lifted the sacking, so Lilia could not see his expression. *I would have liked to*, she mused. Kallen returned to the dock. He looked straight at Lilia and smiled. "You have some explaining to do." His tone was not disapproving, she noted.

"Not until we return to the Guild," Rothen said firmly. "I've made arrangements for the crew to be imprisoned until we can question them, and for the body to be delivered to the Guild."

Kallen nodded and gestured to the end of the dock. "The carriage that brought me is still here, if you would like to take it."

Rothen nodded. They walked to the carriage in silence. Looking around, Lilia noted how the dock workers paused to stare at Kallen. They looked curious, but also uneasy. *But then, that's how novices react to Sonea walking past, too. Impressed, but also intimidated.* Then it occurred to her that people would regard her in the same way one day, when she had graduated and had to wear black robes. *I used to look forward to the day I didn't have to wear novice robes. Now I dread it.*

The journey to the Guild was not a long one, since a wide road led directly from the Marina to the grounds, only detouring around the palace, but it seemed a lot longer. Nobody spoke. Kallen's gaze moved from Lilia to Anyi to Rothen, staying mostly on Rothen.

He looks perplexed. And worried. I'd have thought he'd be more annoyed than this that we've been dealing with Skellin without consulting him. Whenever he met her eyes she looked away.

When they arrived, Rothen started toward the University entrance while Kallen paused to instruct the driver.

"The Administrator is at the palace," Kallen called after him.

Rothen stopped and looked back. "High Lord Balkan?"

"Also with the king."

"Will they return soon?"

Kallen's shoulders lifted and fell. "I doubt they'll return until late."

Rothen blinked, then his eyes widened suddenly. "You were at the palace when I sent for you, weren't you? It's happening, isn't it?"

Kallen nodded. "But I knew you would only send for me if it was important. Can I have a word privately?"

Leaving Lilia and Anyi at the steps, Rothen rejoined Kallen. Lilia saw that Anyi's expression was full of suspicion. She looked back at the magicians. While their mouths were moving, she could hear nothing. Most likely they were using a sound-blocking shield. *Looks like something important, and something Rothen was expecting.*

"Are you sure it was him?" Rothen asked, his voice suddenly loud and clear. Kallen nodded. "Well, then. Unfortunately I must reveal what I have learned first to the Administrator and High Lord so we'll have to wait until they return."

"It may be a day or two before they are free to meet with you."

"Yes, that is likely. Do you think the king will summon all the Higher Magicians to the palace?"

"No." Kallen replied. "He doesn't like having too many magicians flapping about. Would you like me to tell the

Administrator and High Lord that you have found Skellin and wish to meet with them?"

"Yes, thank you."

Rothen waited as Kallen climbed back into the carriage. The driver urged the horses into motion. They picked up speed as they neared the gates, Lilia noted.

"He's in a hurry," Anyi said in a low voice. She looked at Rothen. "What's so important that it trumps the death of Skellin and tracking down his spies in the Guild?"

Rothen's expression was serious as he replied. "Something *very* important. You will find out soon enough."

Anyi looked thoughtful. "We're not about to be invaded again, are we?"

Rothen shook his head. "No."

"Or invade someone else?"

"No. Enough guessing. I'll take you both to Sonea's rooms, then I'll bring Gol back here. I told him to wait at—"

"Gol's alive?" Anyi interrupted.

Lilia smiled. "Yes. He helped us find you. He's going to be very happy we got you back."

Anyi winced. "He must be so . . ." She sighed. "Well . . . let's go get cleaned up."

Lilia smiled. "At least there's one benefit to the delay."

Oh, Dannyl. Sonea pulled Osen's ring from her finger and wiped tears from her eyes. *To lose someone you love like that . . .* It had brought back a flood of memories and emotions, and she had been thankful that Naki's ring had kept both from Osen. The Administrator had been a little shocked. He'd known that Dannyl was fond of his Ashaki friend, but clearly Dannyl had managed to conceal just *how* fond he had been.

455

She suspected Osen hadn't wanted to consider it was even possible. *Not that Dannyl could love another man – he knew about Tayend – but that he could fall for a Sachakan. Especially an Ashaki. Or that so powerful a Sachakan could fall for Dannyl.*

She felt a pang of sympathy as she recalled Dannyl's anger. If she'd known that he might witness the death of a lover, she would not have suggested Dannyl watch the battle and communicate the result to her and Osen. *I don't think Dannyl believed the Traitors would win, though. He was more concerned for Lorkin.*

"I'm sorry, Sonea," a familiar voice said. "I'm so sorry."

Regin. She would have to tell him what had happened. Looking up, she caught a glimpse of eyes glinting with moisture before finding herself pressed against a warm chest, hands stroking her back.

"There was nothing more you could do," he said. "He chose a brave path, and I admire him for it."

The stiffness of surprise eased and she felt herself relaxing against him, soothed by his warmth and concern, even as she realised the mistake he'd made. *He saw tears and thought Lorkin had died. Curse it. He thinks Lorkin is dead, and he's upset.* She had to let him know otherwise, but a selfish part of her wanted to let this moment last a little longer. *He cares about Lorkin. And me . . .*

Stop it! she told herself. *You'll only end up wanting what you can't have.*

"It's fine. He's fine," she blurted out. She forced herself to push him away so she could look up at him. "Lorkin's fine." She met and held his gaze to show she wasn't lying. "The Traitors won."

Understanding dawned in his eyes. His face reddened a little

and he smiled ruefully. Then he frowned again. "Then why
. . .?" His eyes widened. "Dannyl?"

"He's fine, too. So are Merria and Tayend. It just that . . ."
She shook her head. "I'll explain later."

She felt his arms loosen. He began to step back. Catching
his hands, she squeezed them once before letting go.

"Thank you."

His eyes shone for a moment, then he looked away and his
expression became serious. "So what now?"

She turned to the window. "Osen wants us to find Dannyl.
Then we're to congratulate the queen, tell her our Healers
aren't far away and see if she'll let us keep a Guild ambassador
in Arvice."

"How will we find them?"

"We go in that direction." She pointed. "At some point we'll
reach the street on which the battle took place. I suspect
we'll know it by the Ashaki bodies. If Dannyl's observations
are a good guide, the street out front leads to the parade that
leads to the palace. We'll find Dannyl in a house on the parade."
She started toward the stairs.

Regin followed. "It'll be night soon."

As she descended, Sonea wondered at the elation she felt. *I
shouldn't be this cheerful.* But Lorkin had survived the battle,
and the relief she felt was overwhelming. Perhaps she would
be able to talk him into coming home now. At that thought
she felt worry return. *He'll want to stay with Tyvara. If he's as
in love with her as I was with Akkarin he'll follow her anywhere.
I shouldn't want to stop him.* But she did. *And yet, I want him to
be happy. I would never want him to suffer what I did.*

Reaching the ground floor, Regin led the way through the
house, moving silently and checking for other occupants before

he stepped into a corridor or room. They reached the kitchen and peered through the slave entrance to the street beyond. It was empty.

Sonea moved through, Regin following close behind. The city was quiet, a luminous twilight settling over all as they made their way towards the centre. Once again, Sonea felt conspicuous in her black robes, but they were not as stark against the white walls now as they had been in the morning light. She held a strong shield around them both. The first side street they turned into was also empty, but there were distant figures in the next main street.

"Well, they're going to spot us eventually," Sonea said, then stepped into the street. Regin's only reply was a chuckle.

If the people saw them, they were not concerned. No one moved from their position. At the next turn Sonea saw two Traitors further down the street, a man and woman walking arm in arm away from them. From the way they leaned against each other, they were either exhausted or had already enjoyed a celebratory drink. She shrugged and followed, Regin beside her.

They had only taken twenty steps or so when two more people stepped out of a door, after the Traitors had passed it. Regin stopped and she heard his breath catch at the same time that she froze, recognising the cut of the men's jackets and the glint of the knives in their hands.

Ashaki.

"Watch out!" she shouted.

The pair looked over their shoulders, saw the two men and spun about to face them. One of the Ashaki glanced back at Sonea and Regin, then made a dismissive gesture and turned back to the Traitors. The other struck at the woman, who flinched and pushed her companion behind her. They both began to back away.

"They're weak," Regin said. Sonea knew he did not mean the Ashaki, who had seen two Kyralian magicians and remained unconcerned.

They must have enough strength left to think they can ignore us. Perhaps they're assuming neither of us could be a black magician, since we're Kyralian.

"Are you going to do something?" Regin asked. "Because I can't stand by and watch them kill those two. Not when the Traitors have won anyway."

"I wish we could." She looked at him. "But that would be interfering."

"I'm sure the Traitors would forgive you if you saved two of them.

"My actions will be taken as actions of the Guild, and the Allied Lands."

"Good. I wouldn't want to belong to a Guild that didn't help in this situation. Besides, you don't have to kill the Ashaki. Just scare them off."

The two Ashaki had separated and were circling around the two Traitors. The woman looked toward Sonea and Regin, her eyes wide with fear.

Regin's right. The Traitors and Guild can sort out the consequences later. Drawing power, she sent it in two strikes at the Ashaki. As they struck, the men staggered, then recovered and turned to face her. The Traitors took the opportunity to flee, running to the corner of the next main street.

The Ashaki exchanged a look, then one started toward Sonea and Regin. The other hesitated and followed.

"They don't look scared," Sonea observed.

Regin chuckled. "They don't know who you are."

Strikes flashed toward her, and she strengthened her shield. They weren't particularly strong – probably only meant to test her. She responded with an array of firestrike to intimidate them. They stopped and she heard the murmur of a conversation too low to hear.

Then the two Traitors reappeared at the corner. Followed by four more. The Ashaki stumbled forward from a new attack at their rear. They turned to see their intended victims lift their arms, holding something toward them, then they glanced back at Sonea and Regin.

Trapped, Sonea thought. *But this is the Traitors' fight now.* She watched as the Traitors wore the Ashaki down until their shields failed, then winced as they fell under a final blow. Regin made a small noise of surprise, but as she glanced at him he shrugged.

"They don't take prisoners, do they?"

She shook her head, remembering the Sachakan king's suicide. The Traitors walked past the dead Ashaki toward Sonea and Regin, one of the newcomers leading.

"You are Black Magician Sonea?" the woman asked.

"Yes. This is Lord Regin."

"I am Speaker Lanna. You should have stayed where we put you." She made an imperious gesture. "Come with me."

As the woman turned away, Sonea looked at Regin and saw a flicker of annoyance and amusement. She fell into step behind Speaker Lanna, suppressing a smile as the other Traitors moved into position on either side, flanking them as they were escorted toward the city centre.

At the sound of approaching footsteps in the corridor, Tayend looked up at Dannyl. They had been sitting on either side of

Achati's chair in the Master's Room, mostly silent, for the hour or so since they'd descended from the roof.

"Responsibility and duty returns." Tayend sighed. "Are you ready to face the people who killed him? We could go find Achati's ship and take the long route back to Imardin instead."

Dannyl shook his head. "No. That would ruin both of our careers. The Traitors . . . though I wish that they could have spared him, they did not know him. They did not know he was worth sparing. How could they? He was an adviser to the king, who represented all they hate. And . . ." He sighed. "Despite everything, I want to stay here in Arvice. Not forever but . . ."

From the corridor entrance Merria walked in.

She looked different, and it took a moment for Dannyl to pinpoint the change. *She looks older. Not aged, but mature. Almost stern. She reminds me of Lady Vinara. Hmm. Shouldering responsibility clearly agrees with her.*

But it was time he took charge again.

"Lady Merria," he said, standing up and holding out his hand. "Thank you for your help."

She hesitated, then reached into her robe and brought out the ring. As he took it she gave him a measuring look. Judging whether he was fit for resuming his ambassadorial role? He nearly smiled at that.

"King Amakira is dead, as are the rest of the Ashaki," she told him. "He killed himself, and the rest forced the Traitors to kill them by attacking the Traitor queen. Sonea and Regin are making their way here to meet you. Osen says we are to join together and request an audience with the queen."

"What are the Traitors doing now?"

"Entering the nearby houses. They've already found and killed an Ashaki who hid during the battle."

Tayend drew in a quick breath. "Achati's slaves."

Dannyl felt his heart skip a beat. "They'll kill them."

"Will they?" Merria asked. "They might not."

"We can't take that chance. We must warn then." Tayend took a few steps toward the corridor.

Merria frowned. "If they can get away, they will have done."

Tayend stopped and looked back at Dannyl. "But if they can't . . ."

"Then we'll take them with us," Dannyl said. "If they choose to come with us. They are free men now."

"You'd hire them as servants?" Merria asked, frowning. "When they don't have much choice. Surely that's no different than slavery."

Dannyl shook his head. "It's better than death. But I think . . . we will simply offer to take them with us. The rest is up to them."

"We have to find them first," Tayend reminded them. "If they're here, they're hiding. And we might not have much time."

"Then we split up," Dannyl decided. "You go with Merria for protection. They may attack you if they can't see you, thinking you are a Traitor. I'll look upstairs, you stay on this level."

Dannyl headed down the corridor to the stairs. As he explored Achati's house, he found parts he had never seen before. All were decorated in the same subdued, earthly colours that Achati had preferred over the stark white walls of Sachakan tradition. Dannyl felt as though he was surrounded by Achati's presence, and his heart ached.

At the back of the house he pushed open a door, looked around and sucked in a breath in astonishment.

Why didn't he tell me about this?

Dannyl had seen Achati's library. It was a modest room

within the man's private suite, the books and scrolls contained in finely crafted cabinets. The room Dannyl stood within now was several times larger and lined with shelves. A large table stood at the centre, bare but for a piece of paper, folded and sealed.

Behind the table stood two men. Achati's slaves.

They were not wearing the usual slave wrap now, but were dressed in simple trousers and tunic. They lowered their gaze as Dannyl looked at them.

"The master left this for you," one said, gesturing at the letter.

Dannyl opened his mouth to speak, then changed his mind. *First, see what the letter says.* He walked over to the table and picked it up. His stomach clenched as he saw his name written across the front in Achati's elegant hand.

Taking a deep breath, Dannyl broke the seal, opened the letter and read.

Ambassador Dannyl of the Magicians' Guild of Kyralia

The trouble with collecting the best of anything is that there must also be the mediocre and the worst to compare it to. I have endeavoured to discard the latter in most things, but found that I could not always do so when it came to my family, my king, or my library.

If they will allow it, I give you my library. The rest of my belongings they will surely take or destroy, and I only hope that my slaves will benefit from some of it.

Ashaki Achati, formerly adviser to King Amakira of Sachaka

Dannyl closed his eyes, swallowed hard, then cleared his throat and looked up at the slaves.

"Well, Lak and Vata, I may not have much time to explain, so I will have to be forthright. Your master is . . ." Dannyl's throat closed up.

"We know," they said together.

"The Traitors are entering the houses around the parade, and I suspect they may perceive your staying here as an indication of loyalty to your master. So Ambassador Tayend and I are offering to take you with us."

"Must we leave?" Vata asked, his eyes wide.

"Probably," Dannyl replied. He shook his head. "I honestly don't know what the Traitors will do. I don't know if it's better that you become our companions or servants — or if you'll even find that acceptable. But I promise that we will do what we can to protect you."

The two men looked at each other, then Lak nodded. "The master said we should do whatever you tell us."

"Then I'm telling you to come with me," Dannyl said, beckoning and heading back to the library door. "But not in a slave-like way," he added. "Behave like the free men that you now are. Not in the way the Ashaki were free men, of course. I don't think the Traitors will look kindly on that."

"I'm not sure how to be a free man," Vata said in a low voice.

"You'll work it out," Dannyl assured him. He placed Achati's letter in his pocket and led the man's former slaves out of the library into a new and frightening freedom.

CHAPTER 30

NEGOTIATING THE FUTURE

O nce again, Savara had occupied the main suite of rooms in the mansion she had commandeered as a base. This time the Master's Room was where those wanting audience with or summoned by the queen were waiting. As people came and went, reporting on the Traitors' progress in gaining control of the city, Lorkin and Tyvara sat to her left, keeping watch.

All of the houses around the parade had been searched now. A few Ashaki had been found hiding within to ambush Traitors and had been disposed of. Several free women and their children had been discovered, too. Their husbands, fathers and sons had been so confident that they would win that they hadn't bothered to send their families somewhere safe. Some of the mansions were full of the bodies of slaves who had not been able to escape before their masters killed them for their magical strength.

A mansion had been chosen to house the healthy and uninjured free women and children until the Traitors decided what to do with them. *Which will probably be the same as with the other families we encountered*, Lorkin thought. *They'll have to find their place among the freed slaves, which probably means working for the first time in their lives.*

"Some slaves attacked their former owner's families before leaving the city," Speaker Shaiya told the queen. "Some free women lashed out at slaves after they heard of the Ashaki's defeat. We've sent all the injured to a mansion across the parade from here. A few slaves and one free woman have gone into childbirth, too. All of the Traitors with healing experience have been sent to treat them."

"Are they enough?"

Shaiya shook her head. "We need more. When do the Kyralians arrive?"

"In a day or so."

"I'll go," Lorkin offered.

"No." Savara turned to look at him. "I need you here, for now."

The Speaker looked down. "I know how you feel about Kalia, but . . ."

Savara scowled and shook her head. "I don't trust her."

"You don't have to. Just let her do what she is trained to do."

Lorkin held his breath as Savara regarded the Speaker. The queen could not reveal Kalia's guilt to the Traitors without also revealing his ability to read surface thoughts. *Then I guess I'd better brace myself for the consequences.*

"Bring her here," she said.

When Shaiya's footsteps had faded out of hearing, Savara turned to him.

"This ability of yours could prove very useful to me, Lorkin. Are you willing to use it in the service of the Traitors?"

He blinked at her in surprise. "I . . . I guess so. Do you want me to use it on Kalia? I can't promise I will be able to tell you much."

Savara smiled. "Just tell me if you detect her lying. Don't

say how. Do not mention your ability to anyone unless I tell you to."

The sound of Shaiya's footsteps returned, along with another's. As Kalia entered she looked up at Savara, then her gaze dropped to the floor. She placed a hand over her heart.

"Leave us, Shaiya."

The Speaker paused, then nodded and left. Rising to her feet, Savara walked slowly over to stand in front of Kalia. The woman did not look up. Her eyes were wide and her breathing fast. Lorkin concentrated on her until he felt a familiar presence, and guilt.

"I know what you did," Savara told her. She glanced at Lorkin and Tyvara. "*We* know what you did."

From Kalia came a surge of fear and shame.

"What I don't understand is: why Halana?" Savara continued. "Everyone loved her. She had no enemies." She shook her head. "The experience and understanding of stone-making she had. The talent. Even if you hated her, how could you take that from us?"

"I didn't hate her," Kalia protested. "I . . ." She looked up, then quickly down again.

"You *what*?"

"I didn't intend for her to get killed."

"Just us." Savara moved back to her chair. "I have no proof of that, but I can prove you had something to do with Halana's death. If you can convince me it was an accident I . . ." She sighed. "Much as I hate to say it, we need you Kalia. Convince me, and see to the injured, and I won't distract and demoralise our people at this crucial time with accusations of attempted murder against one of their own."

467

Kalia swallowed, then nodded. "When you were on the roof last night," she began. "I saw you were alone with . . ." Her eyes flickered toward Lorkin and Tyvara. "Nobody else would be harmed if you were attacked. I just had to draw attention to you. So I slipped out of a slave entrance, found some Ashaki, and led them back. They saw you, but as I ran to the slave entrance Halana stepped out of another. I think she was setting shield stones. She . . . didn't see them. She . . ." A sob escaped her. "I tried to warn her but it happened so fast. I didn't mean for her to be killed."

Savara glanced at him. He shook his head. Everything Kalia had said was true. The queen turned back to stare at Kalia She looked as if she had taken a bite of something especially vile. But it wasn't just revulsion at Kalia's actions. *She wants to punish Kalia, but she won't. If I was Savara, I'd have her locked up and send me to heal the injured.* Kalia's healing skills weren't unique. Then he felt a bolt of realisation. *But my mind-reading abilities are.*

"Then swear you will never speak of it, to anyone, unless on my orders," the queen said. "And swear you will never attempt to cause me, Tyvara and Lorkin harm again."

Kalia bowed her head. "I swear."

"Go. Shaiya will direct you to the mansion housing the injured."

As the woman hurried away, Savara rubbed her hands on her knees as if wiping them clean.

"Well, at least we have something to use to keep her in line from now on."

Footsteps hurried down the corridor, but this time Speaker Lanna entered the room.

"Are you ready to see the Kyralians yet?"

Savara drew in a deep breath then let it out slowly. "Am I?" she asked herself.

Lanna frowned. "There's something I should tell you first."

"Oh?"

The Speaker's lips thinned into a forced smile. "When I found Black Magician Sonea she was fending off a pair of Ashaki. Tayvla and Call, the pair who found them, told me that the Ashaki had attacked them first. Sonea intervened, allowing them to get away."

Lorkin turned to look at Savara and was puzzled to see she was frowning at this news. The queen glanced at him, then snorted softly.

"Well, that spoiled my plans." She turned to Lorkin and uncrossed her arms. "Your mother disobeyed an order to stay where her escort left her. I was looking forward to raising that with her, and seeing if I could get something out of her by way of apology."

He raised his eyebrows. "I doubt you'd succeed."

"How do you suggest I go about persuading her to grant us a favour, then?"

"I am the last person who can tell you. She knows me far too well."

"But you are her son. Perhaps I should use that."

Lorkin winced. "Only if you're feeling particularly brave. I, ah, advise you to learn more about her before you push her too far."

Savara pursed her lips and considered him, then nodded. "You would like to see her, and your homeland, again one day."

"Eventually. I'd like to take Tyvara with me, so it would be nice if Sachaka and the Allied Lands stayed on good terms."

Savara turned back to Lanna. "Send in the Kyralians. And the Elyne, too."

Lorkin felt his heart begin to beat a little faster. *Mother and Dannyl and everyone else cannot have any doubts where my loyalties lie now. I guess I'm about to find out how they feel about that.*

His mother led the others into the room. They lined up before Savara, then knelt. A silence followed, full of surprise and a tinge of embarrassment. Lorkin felt an odd little shiver go down his spine. To Kyralians and Elynes, this was the traditional genuflection made to a ruler, but to Traitors it was far more than was expected.

"Rise," Savara said, her voice subdued. As the five foreigners stood, she smiled. "Later, Lorkin will tell you the Traitor way of greeting a leader." Her gaze moved along the line. "I am Queen Savara and this is Tyvara and Lorkin. Please introduce yourselves."

"I am, as you know from our previous meeting, Black Magician Sonea of the Magicians' Guild of Kyralia," his mother began. She then introduced the others according to status, beginning with Dannyl.

Dannyl looks . . . not uncomfortable but like he's trying to conceal discomfort, thought Lorkin. *Is he injured? No, it is something else. Perhaps merely the unease of having just seen these people kill a whole lot of people he . . .* A heavy feeling dragged at his stomach as he realised that Dannyl, Tayend and Merria had formed friendships with the Sachakan elite. *They've possibly just seen their friends killed.*

As his mother spoke Regin's name, Lorkin remembered Tyvara's suggestion that he was more than Sonea's source and assistant. Regin's expression was solemn. His gaze shifted to

Lorkin's and he inclined his head slightly. Lorkin returned the nod. *That didn't tell me anything*, he concluded.

"So," Savara said, rising from her seat. She moved to stand before Dannyl. "Do you intend to stay in Sachaka, Ambassador Dannyl? I imagine we'll need a Guild representative here, once the Healers arrive."

Lorkin noticed his mother's brows lower a fraction. As the figure of greatest authority, among the Guild magicians, she ought to have been asked the question. Perhaps, by posing the question to Dannyl, Savara was indicating that she preferred him as a representative of the Guild over Sonea.

"If the Guild allows it, and you approve, your majesty." Dannyl replied.

Savara nodded. "You'll do for now." She moved to face Tayend. "And you, Ambassador Tayend – will you continue to represent Elyne?"

"I have already received instruction from my king to request my continuation in the role, your majesty," Tayend replied. "In fact, he gave me a short message to memorise and deliver to you, to stand in for a later, longer missive."

"He has? Then relay it."

Tayend bent in a courtly bow. "King Lerend of Elyne congratulates you on the successful conquest of Sachaka. He hopes he will have an opportunity to meet you and discuss the many ways our lands may engage in mutually beneficial relations. May a peaceful and prosperous future await you."

Savara smiled. "Convey my appreciation of his good wishes next time you communicate. I look forward to his longer missive. I see no reason you should not stay on as ambassador." She moved past Merria and Regin, and stopped.

Lorkin watched his mother's face as the queen turned to face

471

her. He saw the familiar shift in her expression, from the usual slightly pained, thoughtful look she wore most of the time to the still, all-knowing stare that he'd never been able to hold for long.

"Black Magician Sonea," Savara said, her tone no longer friendly, but not cold either. "You disobeyed my order to stay in the house where your escort left you."

"I did, your majesty."

"I was not pleased to learn that."

"I did not expect you to be."

"Why did you disobey?"

"Ambassadors Dannyl and Tayend, and Lady Merria believed themselves to be in some danger. Saral and Temi had left, so I could not seek permission to go to the aid of my colleagues, or request that they be protected. I kept to your earlier condition that I would not side with the Ashaki, and to the Allied Lands' wishes that we should not intervene in the battle."

"Yet you did intervene, later."

Sonea's eyebrows rose. "Should I have not?"

Savara's head tilted a little to one side. "How do the Allied Lands regard it?"

"I haven't had the opportunity to ask them, yet. They know some decisions must be made quickly. The battle was already won and they do want to be sure our Healers will be safe here."

"They will be." Savara took a step backwards, and returned to her seat. "The Healers are a full day's ride away, however. In the meantime, would you and the other Guild magicians here tend the worst injuries?"

Sonea's chin rose and a light entered her eyes that Lorkin knew only too well. He caught his breath, then let it out in a quiet sigh.

"Of course," she replied.

Savara nodded. "Lorkin will escort you to the mansion where the sick and injured are being housed, after I speak with him privately. You may go."

Lorkin watched his mother, former colleagues and friends leave. As they disappeared into the corridor, Savara turned to him.

"Was asking them to Heal unwise?"

So she'd heard his reaction. He shrugged. "Mother set up the hospices in Imardin. Give her this work to do and she may never go home."

Savara frowned. "And I thought *you* would be the reason she'd try to stay. I did not mean to make your task more difficult."

"My task?"

"To persuade or arrange for your mother to go home. It's nothing personal, and I don't think ill of her, but I suspect she is someone I will not like having around."

"No," he agreed. He paused to think. "The way to get Mother to go home is to have Dannyl recommend it to the Guild. He may agree to do so if I can convince him it is a good idea, or perhaps as a favour to me. But I suspect just trying will make him suspect my motives. Though . . . there's something else we can offer him to prove our intentions are peaceful, if you'll agree to it."

Savara leaned forward. "And what is that?"

As Lorkin led them out of the mansion, Sonea examined him critically. He looked thinner, though it might only be the Traitor style of clothing that gave the impression. Magician robes tended to conceal a lot, emphasising the shoulders and waist but hiding the rest. The close-fitting Traitor vest hugged his body. The fabric of his tunic and pants was rustic and undyed. In contrast to this humble garb, his fingers were clustered with rings, which would normally have given the impression of indulgence and wealth if she hadn't guessed the stones were magical.

He started out towards the other side of the parade. His walk was relaxed and confident, she noted, but he was also constantly alert, his gaze roving over their surroundings. *He feels secure in his place among the Traitors and has nothing to fear from the Guild except, perhaps, disapproval, but he knows the city isn't completely safe yet.*

Glancing back at her, he slowed until he was walking beside her.

"I wanted to contact you before the battle," he said. "But everything happened so fast. We were making plans one moment and rushing out to meet the Ashaki the next."

"What did you do with my blood ring?"

He grimaced in apology. "I have it with me. I should have hid it, but—"

"No, I would rather you had it with you to use if you needed."

"Well . . . I suppose there's a chance that if I'd been killed it would have been destroyed too."

A chill ran down her spine. "Let's not talk about you being killed."

He grinned. "Fine with me."

"So what will you do next?"

Lorkin's expression became serious. "That depends on Savara. And Tyvara. It's clear Savara has plans for Tyvara and, since Traitor women have all the responsibility and power and their

men are expected to go along with it, I'll end up going wherever she goes."

"Will you be happy about that?"

He grinned. "Mostly. I love Tyvara, Mother. I love how
being in charge is natural and normal to her, even though it
can be frustrating at times. I also enjoy being the one who
challenges that."

Sonea resisted a sigh. "So you're not coming home."

He shook his head. "Not any time soon, I expect. Savara
knows I'd like to be able to visit you, and the Guild. I'd still
like to pass on the basic knowledge of stone-making, as Queen
Zarala wished. Perhaps the Guild can do something else with
it. Perhaps stone-producing caves will be found in the Allied
Lands. If they do exist, the most likely place is the northern
part of the Elyne mountains, where . . ."

A whoop came from a group of people entering the parade
from a side street nearby. Lorkin stopped, placing himself
between the newcomers and Sonea, then turned back to
her and smiled. "Looks like there will be some celebrating
tonight."

Sonea looked beyond him to see that the men and women
were carrying furniture. They weren't dressed in Traitor garb,
so she guessed they were freed slaves. Looking around, she
realised there were several more groups of ex-slaves gathering
along the road. Further away, a fire was burning. She heard
Dannyl mutter a curse as they tossed the furniture on the
ground and began to break it up. As two of the ex-slaves
headed back to a nearby house, one called after them.

"Get some tinder!"

"And the wine!"

Lorkin ignored them and continued across the parade.

"They're going to ransack the houses, aren't they?" Dannyl asked, to nobody in particular.

"Probably," Merria replied.

Dannyl sighed. "I should have locked the library," he muttered.

The mansion Lorkin led them to was larger than most. A pair of Traitors stood by the door. They stared at the foreigners, but did not object as Lorkin led them through. Inside, they were confronted by chaos and noise. The usual short corridor was lined with people, and the Master's Room was crowded with more. Some lay on the floor, injuries poorly bandaged or not at all. Others hovered over them, clearly not injured, sometimes four for every patient. Traitors hurried from the corridor on one side to the one on the other, tripping on limbs and all manner of objects from baskets of food to bottles of wine. One of the injured was clutching a large gold box even as the wound in her leg bled freely. From somewhere beyond the room came muffled screams and shouting.

"This is a mess!" Sonea exclaimed. "Isn't anybody in charge here?"

The noise in the room diminished slightly. Heads had turned toward her. A Traitor who had just stepped into the room stopped and glared at her. Sonea cursed inwardly. She hadn't meant to speak so loudly.

"Where's Kalia?" Lorkin asked the Traitor.

"Treating someone," the woman said.

"Who is checking the new patients?"

The woman shrugged and looked around. "Someone . . ."

Lorkin waved her on. "Go do whatever you were doing. I'll sort this out."

The woman hurried way. Lorkin looked down at his rings

and pressed the stone of one of them. His gaze shifted to the distance and he was still for a long moment, then he nodded and straightened. He turned to Sonea.

"Savara is sending a Speaker over. She'll make sure everyone here follows your orders. Kalia used to be in charge of the treatment of the sick in Sanctuary, but she broke a few laws and . . . well, she's not herself at the moment. She's only here because we need her expertise." His dislike was obvious. "She knows a little Healing. The best way to handle her, I think, will be to give her patients to treat but not decisions to make."

Sonea raised her eyebrows in disbelief. "Savara is putting me in charge?"

"For tonight." He grimaced. "It took a lot of persuading. We thought we could rely on Kalia but . . ." He shrugged. "I can't tell you the details but she made a bad decision and it has shattered her confidence. She is a good Healer. Dedicated. You can trust her to do her job well." He took a step toward the entrance. "Speaker Yvali will be here in a moment. I have to go. Ambassador Dannyl is to come back with me."

Dannyl's eyebrows rose, but he did not appear concerned as he followed Lorkin out. Sonea looked at Merria, who was staring around the room and shaking her head.

"It won't take long to sort this out," Sonea assured her. "So long as people do as we say."

Merria nodded eagerly. "I've always wanted to set up a hospice. After I'd explored the world."

Sonea regarded the young woman with new interest. *Where were you hiding this one, Vinara?* she thought. She had often suspected the Head of Healers was keeping the best of the new Healers for herself. *Not that I wouldn't do it, too, if I was in her position. But it looks like she let this one slip through her fingers. Maybe one day, after Merria has satisfied her wanderlust, she'll come back to work with me.*

A Traitor woman stepped out of the shadows of the crowded entrance corridor and met Sonea's gaze. Sonea straightened and smiled. Putting all plans for Merria's future aside, she stepped forward and began to explain what she and the sick and injured of Arvice needed.

Celebratory bonfires were not confined to the parade, Dannyl discovered, as he, Tayend, Lorkin and Achati's former slaves made their way to the Guild House. They were being lit all over Arvice, and the thought of all the beautiful and precious things being used to fuel them made him feel a bit ill.

They're just objects, he told himself. But it still saddened him, and he could not delude himself that precious knowledge wasn't being destroyed along with the merely beautiful. How could ex-slaves, most of whom did not know how to read, realise that they might be burning something that could benefit them and their descendants? Maybe the two following them would. They had been hiding in Achati's library, after all. *Is Achati's library being burned right now? If it isn't, can I persuade the Traitors to protect it?*

He looked at the young man walking beside him. Lorkin would understand. He might not be able to do anything, but Dannyl at least had to ask, in case there was a chance that he could.

What had kept him from trying was the memory of Lorkin fighting alongside the Traitors. Of the Ashaki falling before their strikes. Of the thought that Lorkin might have been the one who killed Achati.

From the awkward silence between them, Dannyl guessed

Lorkin was at least aware that fighting with the Traitors had strained his relationship with Dannyl and the Guild. *But he can't know why, in my case. Only Tayend knew that Achati and I were more than friends.* And Tayend wasn't saying anything.

"Have you made any progress on your book?" Lorkin asked.

"Not for some time," Dannyl replied.

"Did the copies you made reach the Guild?"

"Not yet."

They continued on without speaking for several minutes, dodging another group of revellers. Finally they rounded a corner and came in sight of the gates of the Guild House. No bonfires, thankfully, but, as a result, the street was dark. As they drew closer Dannyl heard Tayend draw in a quick breath. At the same time, he saw that the gates were hanging oddly. Someone had broken through them.

Lorkin reached into his vest and drew out something. He held it between two fingers, at the level of his chest, as he approached the gates. Bending to examine the twisted metal, he made a low noise.

"Only magic could have done this," he murmured. He straightened and frowned at the building beyond. "The door is open."

They stood, unmoving, as Lorkin stared at the open door, frowning. "I think we should go back and get—"

"I'll go in and check," Lak said, striding forward, followed by Vata.

"Wait, you don't—" Lorkin began, but the former slaves ignored him, walking silently across the courtyard and into the building. Lorkin sighed and looked at Dannyl. "They must like you."

Dannyl met his gaze. "They were Achati's slaves."

Lorkin blinked, then his expression became pained. "He didn't survive, did he?"

"Of course not. He was one of the king's closest advisers."

"A fine way to pay him back for getting me out of Arvice." Lorkin's tone was heavy with regret.

"He'd have just as easily turned you over to the king, if he had thought it would benefit Sachaka," Tayend said.

Dannyl looked at Tayend sharply. The Elyne stared back at him. *Daring me to deny it*, thought Dannyl, ruefully. *I can't. Though I'd like to think Achati would have felt bad about it, if he'd turned Lorkin over.*

Lorkin looked down at the object he was holding and shook his head. Looking closer, Dannyl saw light reflect off something in the centre.

"It's not right they take such a risk for us. Stay here. Out of sight." He started toward the door. Dannyl looked at Tayend, and they both hurried after Lorkin. As Lorkin noticed this he sighed. "Stay close, then. Inside my shield."

As they entered the building Dannyl felt the vibration of a shield surround them. It was dark inside. Lorkin created a globe light and sent it floating before them. They emerged into an empty Master's Room. Lorkin chose the right-hand corridor. *If the invaders were after magic or valuables to steal, they'd head for the suite of the highest-status person in the house.* Reaching Dannyl's rooms, Lorkin stepped inside. The rooms were empty, but someone had gone through the chests and cupboards, tossing most of the contents aside from the look of it. They turned to go, only to be met by Lak, holding a lamp.

"Nobody in the house," the slave reported. "Vata is checking the stables and slave quarters. Don't think any Ashaki would hide there, though."

Lorkin let out a sigh of relief. He turned to Tayend. "Would you like me to come with you while you fetch the blood ring?"

Tayend shook his head. "I'll be right back." He beckoned to Lak, and the pair disappeared into the corridor.

The house was very quiet. Dannyl inspected the room. *Very little has been taken. Why would anyone want Guild robes or old books? Should I take my research materials back with me? Where would I put them? There's nowhere safe. But maybe I can do something about that.* He looked at Lorkin, then reached into his robe for Achati's letter and held it out. Lorkin took it, unfolded and read it. He winced and then handed it back.

"Will the Traitors let me have Achati's library?" Dannyl asked. "If it isn't ransacked."

Lorkin frowned, then toyed with his rings as he considered.

"Savara says you may have access to them," Lorkin replied. "If you let her know where it is, she'll send someone over to guard it."

Savara says? Dannyl looked at the rings and saw that Lorkin was touching one of the stones. *Interesting.*

Lorkin dropped his hands to his sides again. "Can you do me a favour in return?"

Dannyl shrugged. "Depends on the favour."

"Get my mother to go home as soon as possible." Lorkin grimaced. "She won't deliberately interfere, but she will cause problems just by being here. I'm not talking about for me, but for the Traitors. They need to be the ones taking charge here."

"Of the Guild's Healers as well?"

"Did they put her in charge?"

"No, actually." Dannyl shrugged. "They will report to their own leader, and then to me."

481

Lorkin looked relieved. "So there's no other reason for her to be here?"

"Other than to make sure you, me and Merria are safe . . . no. But Savara has put her in charge of the hospice."

"It's only for the night," Lorkin said firmly. He massaged his temples and sighed. "Can you suggest to Osen that having her here will put a strain on relations between Sachaka and the Allied Lands?"

"I can convey your concerns and the queen's wishes."

Lorkin shook his head. "If Mother gets the slightest hint that it came from me she'll be more determined to stay. It has to come from you, Dannyl. And . . . well . . . I'm not a Guild magician any more."

Dannyl paused to consider the young magician he'd brought to Sachaka as an assistant. *He really means to stay with the Traitors. He gave up everything for them. And for love, too, I suspect. I don't think I could have done that. Not even for Achati. Would I have done it for Tayend, back when we were young and so dedicated to each other?* He felt an echo of that feeling. *Yes, I think I would have.*

Lorkin looked down at his hands again. He took one of the rings and slipped it off his finger, then held it out to Dannyl.

"This is why you should have my mother sent home. This is why the Allied Lands should establish good relations with Sachaka."

Taking the ring, Dannyl examined it. The setting was silver, and the stone within it was clear. "What is it?"

"A storestone."

Dannyl's breath caught in his throat. He remembered what Achati had said: *"If one should still exist, or was created, it could be terrible for all countries."*

"It contains the strength of only a few magicians. The trouble with storestones is that you can't know how much power they can hold. Too much and they will shatter, releasing all their power. It would be safer to have several storestones holding a little power than a few holding a lot. But even then, it could be the solution to defending the Allied Lands without resorting to black magic."

"So the Traitors lied. They *did* know how to make them," Dannyl breathed.

"No, though they have stones that are very similar. I'm afraid I — we — gave them the idea to try. They have made only a few so far, but I can see no reason why they couldn't make more, or improve the method." Lorkin looked at the ring, then back at Dannyl. "Savara said you can keep it."

Dannyl frowned. "A bribe?"

"The first payment for the Healers' services."

"How do I use it?"

"Touch it. Draw power as if you were taking it from another magician. You'll have to use it straightaway, since you don't know how to store magic. Strengthening it is the same. Just send it power as if you were sending it to another."

"And don't store too much power in it."

"No."

Dannyl let his hand and the ring drop to his side. He looked at Lorkin, weighing up all that his former assistant had said. Then he nodded.

"This will definitely persuade the Guild to order your mother home."

Lorkin smiled. "Thanks. Though I'll make sure I get the chance to spend some time with her before she goes. I do miss her. And my friends. And Rothen. Ah. And there's something

I wanted to ask you about Lord Regin. Are he and . . .?" He stopped and turned toward the door. "Ambassador. Did you find it?"

Tayend had stepped into the room with Lak and Vata. He held up a small ring, his connection to the Elyne king. "Exactly where I left it."

"Good," Lorkin said. "Now, do you want to stay here, or come back with me?" He looked at Dannyl. "By the time we get back we'll know if Achati's library is intact. The best way to prevent it being ransacked would be to occupy the building, and I think Savara will approve of her main links to the Guild and Allied Lands staying close by."

Dannyl sighed with relief and saw Tayend's eyes brighten with hope. "I'll just grab a few things, then we'll gladly take up your offer of accommodation."

CHAPTER 31

REWARDS

That haunted look has crept into Anyi's gaze again, Lilia noted as she emerged from her bedroom. She knelt down beside the chair and wound her arms around her. Anyi sniffed once, and turned to look at Lilia.

"I know you buried him out in the forest, but it's not right. We have to put him with his family."

"Where are they buried?"

"I'm not sure. Gol will know."

Lilia kissed her. As Anyi's arms began to slide around her a knock came from the door and they froze. Lilia pulled away and sighed. Getting to her feet, she sent a little magic to the door to open it.

"Gol," Anyi said with obvious relief, as the big man stepped inside with Lord Rothen. "How did it go?"

He sat down. "Things are going back to the way they used to be real fast. The Thieves stopped calling themselves 'princes' straightaway, and they're taking back what they had control of beforehand – and anything else they can grab. If you want to take Cery's territory, you need to move now."

Anyi frowned. "Will his people work for me?"

Gol nodded. "Those I asked were keen. They'd rather you

than any of the neighbours. It helps that you are Cery's daughter, but in some ways it'll make it harder. Cery had no favours left to call in, and plenty he owed, but he had money stashed away and was respected for keeping promises."

Lilia watched Anyi's face, her stomach sinking as her friend's expression hardened.

"I'll do it." She looked up at Gol. "But only if you help me."

Gol smiled. "I was hoping you'd want me. Not that I wouldn't like to retire."

"I *am* retiring you," Anyi said. "You won't be my bodyguard, you'll be my second. Like you were for my father. I don't know why he didn't just call you that and be done with it."

"To make me less of a target," Gol told her.

"Well, you can't pretend to be a bodyguard any more. Nobody'll believe I'd choose a bodyguard twice my age."

Gol crossed his arms. "I'd still beat you, any day."

Anyi stood up. "Oh, really? Let's see—"

"I apologise for interrupting," Rothen injected, "but may I suggest you test that theory somewhere other than Sonea's quarters? And the Higher Magicians will not look favourably on us arriving late, especially after we insisted this meeting take place as soon as could be arranged."

Anyi looked at him thoughtfully, then at Lilia. Her expression was apologetic.

"I'm sorry Lilia, but if I am going to take my father's place, I can't go to this meeting."

Lilia stared at her. "But . . . we need you to tell your story."

"No, you don't. It will make no difference whether I tell it, or you, or Lord Rothen." Anyi's expression was serious. "We know Skellin had allies in the Guild. Who knows which Thief has adopted or inherited those allies? If these spies don't know what I look like, then I should keep it that way. If they do, I shouldn't remind them."

Lilia's heart had begun to race. "But . . . how will you visit? I'm not supposed to leave the grounds. Once the Guild finds out a Thief was living in the tunnels and that Skellin was there, they'll fill in all the passages."

Anyi walked over to Lilia and hugged her. "We'll find other ways. You didn't think we could live here together, did you?"

"I suppose not."

"You'll graduate soon. They'll let you out of the Guild grounds then. Maybe they'll even let you live in the city, like other magicians do. Whatever happens, we'll still see each other. Nobody is going to stop us being together." Anyi pulled away, then turned to Gol. "I'll go out the other way. *You* won't fit and people might've seen you come in, so you'd better leave with Rothen. I'll meet you at Donia's."

"Are you sure you want to go that way?" Gol asked.

Anyi nodded. "I'll be fine."

"Just . . . keep the lamp flame covered. I don't know how much minefire got spilled."

Anyi nodded, then looked at Lilia expectantly. Taking the hint, Lilia moved to the door and led Rothen and Gol out. She looked back and saw Anyi wave before the door closed. *I hope she'll be safe going back into the city on her own.*

She worried about that all of the way to the Administrator's office. They detoured to the front of the University, where Rothen arranged for a carriage for Gol. There they found Jonna waiting for them outside Osen's door. The servant looked a little pale, but she smiled and squeezed Lilia's hand as Rothen knocked.

"I've done this before," Lilia reminded Jonna in a whisper.

"I haven't," Jonna replied.

The door swung inward and they stepped into a room full of Higher Magicians.

"Ah, good," Osen said as Lilia, and Jonna bowed. He frowned. "Were there more witnesses wishing to tell their stories, Lord Rothen?"

"No, Administrator," Rothen replied. "You may wish to interrogate the crew I took into custody two days ago, but for now I, Lady Lilia and Jonna, Sonea's servant, should be able to describe the events and cover the issues without any unnecessary repetition."

"Good. Who will begin?"

"I think Lady Lilia is best placed to explain where it all started," Rothen said, turning to look at her.

Lilia took a deep breath. "For some time now Anyi – my friend and the Thief Cery's bodyguard – have been visiting me in the Guild via the underground passages . . ." Watching the faces of the Higher Magicians, Lilia saw eyes sharpen and jaws harden, but as she told of the arrival of Cery and his injured bodyguard some softened with understanding. Kallen frowned, but she could not tell if it was from disapproval at her keeping this secret from him, or guilt that his failure to find Skellin had led to the situation.

A few smiled at the trap Cery had planned, arranging for Skellin to walk right into their midst. But then all signs of amusement faded as she described how the trap had failed, of Cery's death and Anyi's abduction and, she saw with satisfaction, displeasure in all faces at Skellin's claim that he had sources in the Guild.

Rothen then took over, telling of their plans to rescue Anyi without the help or approval of the Guild for fear of alerting

488

Skellin's source. He stopped at the point where Lilia boarded the ship, then looked to her to finish the story.

It was harder than she had expected to describe how she had defeated Skellin and Lorandra. *I killed someone with black magic. And yet Skellin's death wasn't as nasty as Lorandra's.* Now and then she remembered the woman's screams. What had been easy to forget on the day had turned into a memory that refused to fade.

When she had finished, the inevitable questions came.

"You left the grounds and used black magic without permission," Lady Vinara said.

Lilia nodded and bowed her head.

"Actually, she didn't," Rothen told them. "I gave her permission to do both."

"Permission ought to be obtained from all Higher Magicians, or at least the High Lord," Osen said, but then he smiled and spread his hands. "However, there was reason to suspect corruption among us. Caution was the best approach, in this instance."

"If Lilia is to fulfil her role as a black magician in future, she should not regard us with unquestioning trust," Kallen agreed.

Balkan nodded. "I agree. It is more important that we discover who Skellin's source is."

"We have a new clue: the magician who delayed Jonna reaching Lilia," Vinara pointed out. She turned to the servant. "Who was it?"

Jonna's eyes widened as all attention turned to her. Then her gaze flickered across the room. "Lord Telano."

All turned to regard the Head of Healing Studies. He looked around the room, then threw up his hands.

"A coincidence," he protested. "So I tried to help her find Lady Lilia and got the room wrong. That proves nothing."

"But it is interesting, in light of your recent behaviour," Vinara said. "It would explain why—"

"Wait," Osen interrupted. "Lady Lilia. Jonna. Is there anything else you would like to tell us?" As they shook their heads he nodded. "Please wait outside the room."

"Lilia should stay," Kallen said. "We may have need of her."

Lilia stared at him in surprise. *Surely, if he was one of Skellin's spies, he wouldn't want me here.* Osen looked around the rooms and she was even more astonished to see most of the magicians nodding. Except Lord Telano. What had Vinara said? *". . . in light of your recent behaviour."* What had he done?

"Very well," Osen said. "Stay, Lilia."

Jonna took that as her cue to leave. Rothen moved to an empty chair and sat down, leaving Lilia as the only one standing. All attention had returned to Telano.

"Lord Telano," Vinara said. "Were you Skellin's source in the Guild?"

"No," Telano replied firmly.

"Then why is it that the roet most of the magicians and novices acquired can be traced back to you?"

"Why have my assistants seen you visiting members of the underworld and bringing back packages?" Kallen asked.

"I like smoking roet," Telano said, throwing his hands in the air again. "So do others. There is no law against it."

"There will be soon," Vinara said quietly.

"But there *is* a law against working with criminals," Osen pointed out.

"I didn't *work* with anyone. I just happened to have bought their products. Plenty of magicians do this, often unwittingly."

Telano gestured to Lilia. "She has knowingly worked for a Thief. Nobody is questioning *that*."

"We'll get to it," Vinara assured him. "You've defended yourself with this reasoning for a while now, Lord Telano, but it doesn't explain your attempt to destroy our roet crop. For someone who likes roet, that seems . . . odd."

He shook his head. "I thought the Thieves had somehow set themselves up here."

"Really? That wasn't your excuse when we first caught you."

"I didn't know who to trust. You could have been colluding with them. After all, it turns out there *is* a spy in the Guild."

"A simple mind-read would establish your innocence," Lord Peakin said.

The room fell silent. Looking around, Lilia saw both reluctance and hope. *They've wanted it done for a while, but are worried what the consequences will be if he's innocent. He'll resent them for distrusting him, at the least.*

But what if he was guilty? That would be even worse.

"Will you . . .?" Osen began.

"No," Telano said, the word echoing in the room.

"Your lack of cooperation does not encourage us," Osen pointed out.

"Then demote me." Telano's tone was sullen.

"No." All eyes shifted to Balkan. The High Lord was sitting with his elbows on the arms of his chair, his fingertips touching. "With Sachaka now under the rule of the Traitors and our attention needed elsewhere, we need this matter settled. Read his mind, Kallen."

The mood in the room changed to surprise. Telano's eyes had gone wide, but his face smoothed again. As Kallen stood up he slowly got to his feet.

491

"Well, if you must. At least we have something in common," he muttered.

Lilia drew in a sharp breath. "I . . . I'm not sure that's a good idea," she forced herself to say, lowering her eyes as attention shifted to her. "I've occasionally suspected Black Magician Kallen was . . . the one."

This roused mutters of surprise and frustration. "We could wait until Sonea returns," someone suggested.

Looking up, Lilia forced herself to meet Kallen's eyes. He smiled. "As I said, we have need of Lilia. Distrusting me will soon be part of her responsibilities. I suggest she read my mind as well, to put everyone's at ease."

Lilia stared at him, feeling doubt and a little guilt creep over her. *If he's innocent I'm going to feel very bad about suggesting he's Skellin's source, after all he's taught me. But if he's not . . . will he use this opportunity to secretly blackmail me?*

Osen was nodding his head. So was Balkan. Kallen beckoned. There would be no avoiding it. If this had been his intention all along, she had well and truly fallen into his trap. Her mouth dry, Lilia approached him. He took her hands and, still smiling, lifted them to his head.

"You remember what to do?"

She nodded. Then closed her eyes.

It was impossible to tell how much time had passed when she stepped away from him again. She felt guilt for distrusting him, but mostly she felt relief. *I can see why the Guild chose him. He would rather die than betray the Guild. He hates himself for allowing himself to be trapped by roet – and I had no idea the craving could be that bad. I* am *lucky to have not been caught by it.* He had expressed admiration for her risking her life to save Anyi, and she had seen his frustration and shame that he hadn't been able to find and deal with Skellin. *He did try very hard. I know that now. I can forgive him for failing.*

He'd also warned her that, if Lord Telano was guilty, she might have an unpleasant time reading his mind. Lilia turned to the magician. The man looked around the room, then scowled and stood up. He held himself stiffly as she reached out to touch his temples.

It wasn't pleasant. He tried to block her. He tried to think only of other things – things that might shock her into turning her attention away. He tried to show her lies. But she saw through everything. She saw where it had begun, at brazier houses. She saw that suppliers had suggested he avoid purchasing through the Houses and buy direct. She saw how he had grown concerned that the Guild would disapprove of the drug, so he had begun to encourage its use by more and more magicians so they would resist a ban. All his thoughts were laced with a ferocious ache for roet. He feared he wouldn't be able to buy it now that Lilia had killed Skellin. He hated her for that. His only consolation was that so many other magicians would be suffering the same pain.

It was a relief to withdraw her mind and return to the room. As she relayed what she had learned to the Higher Magicians she wondered how it could be that roet could do this to Telano, who must have been a man of integrity to have become a Higher Magician – and a *Healer* – while Kallen hadn't been corrupted, and she hadn't become addicted. *It would have been easier for the Guild to decide what to do about roet if the results were always the same.*

"She's lying," Telano declared. "Why would you believe her over me? She has already admitted to working with a Thief."

493

"We did give you the opportunity to allow a simple mind-read," Osen pointed out. "Have you changed your mind?"

Telano stared at Osen, then straightened. "No. I will prove my innocence in more convincing ways."

"You'll have your chance, when we hold a Hearing to judge you," Osen said. He turned to Kallen. "Take him away."

Telano scowled as he was ushered out of the room. Lilia stood awkwardly as the Higher Magicians exchanged glances.

"Did you see any hint of other spies in the Guild, Lilia?" Osen asked quietly.

She shook her head.

"That's a relief." He looked at the others. "We should wait for Sonea to return before holding this Hearing, but announce the ban on roet and our intention to find a cure as soon as possible." He looked at Vinara. "I want you to involve Sonea in the search for a cure." Vinara frowned and opened her mouth to protest, but Osen stalled her with a raised hand. "She identified the problem first, and it is time you two were seen to work together. It's also the best way I can think of to keep her occupied and out of Sachakan matters."

Lilia frowned. *Why would they . . . ?* She saw Vinara nod in her direction, then Osen turned to her.

"Thank you Lilia. We will need you to speak at the Hearing, but for now you can go."

Lilia bowed and headed for the door. As she passed Rothen he smiled and nodded.

It's all over, she thought, *as much as it can be "over". Anyi is as safe as any new Thief can be, which is not particularly safe but better than when Skellin was around. I can now finish my studies. Even though I have no choice about what I'll be doing after that, I don't mind so much now. As long as I still get to see Anyi.*

494

How they'd manage that, she didn't know. But one thing she was sure of: Anyi would find a way.

Sonea slipped Osen's ring off her finger and put it away.

"Well, *that* was interesting."

Regin turned from the window of the carriage to regard her. "Oh? What news from the Guild?"

"The Rogue Skellin is dead. So is his mother, Lorandra. I don't have the details yet. Osen said they can wait until I get home."

"That's good news."

"Yes, but there's bad as well. Lord Telano was working as Skellin's spy, and had set himself up as the main supplier of roet to the Guild. His powers have been blocked and he now resides in the Lookout."

Regin's eyebrows rose. *"Telano?* The Head of Healing Studies?"

"Yes. Of all people." She shook her head. "The only good to come of that is they've finally banned roet."

"What about the magicians who are addicted to it?"

"Vinara managed to acquire roet seed, so the Guild can wean magicians off it. She has started looking for a cure, too. Osen wants me to help her." Sonea looked out of the window at the wasteland. "Now I understand why he was so insistent that I come home."

Regin smiled. "I'm sure that's not the only reason."

"Why? Do you think there's another reason?"

He shrugged and looked away. "Lilia isn't quite Kallen's equal, yet. You're the only one who can keep him in check."

"Ah. Kallen." Sonea grimaced. "Until you mentioned him, I was looking forward to getting home."

Regin turned so that his elbow rested on the top of the seat back. "I got the impression you wanted to take charge of Healing in Sachaka. Perhaps start a hospice."

Sonea shook her head. "No, not really. I would like to see things change for the better in Sachaka, but I don't think they need me to do it for them. I just . . . I don't want to be so far from Lorkin." She sighed. "Are you looking forward to seeing your daughters?"

He shrugged. "Yes. But they don't need me. In fact, I'm not looking forward to getting back at all."

"No? You want to stay here?"

"Not particularly. But . . ." His eyes narrowed. "I'm not sure I've quite figured you out yet."

Sonea blinked. "Me? What's there to figure out?"

Regin eyebrows rose. "Oh. Plenty."

Crossing her arms, she turned to face him. "Really? What have you figured out so far?"

He smiled. "That you are attracted to me."

Sonea stared at him and felt her heartbeat suddenly increase. *Curse him. How did he work that out?* She drew in a deep breath, let it out slowly, and considered all the ways she'd thought of to let him down gently.

"Lord Regin. I—"

"I also know that *you* have worked out that I am attracted to you," Regin interrupted. "You took your time with that one, though I supposed you first had to forgive me for being a malicious, bigoted bastard when I was a novice."

This was not going to be easy. *For either of us*, she had to admit. "Regin, I'm not . . ."

"Attracted to me?" His eyebrows rose. "So you deny it?"

She hesitated, then forced herself to straighten and look him straight in the eyes. "Yes, I do."

496

His eyes narrowed. "Liar."

What am I doing wrong? Uncrossing her arms, she attempted to place her hands on her hips, but it proved too difficult in a moving carriage, so she settled on shaking one finger at him.

"Don't you call me a liar when . . ."

He laughed. "Ah, Sonea. If I'd known it was so much fun to tease you, I'd have started sooner."

The panicky feeling that had been growing in her eased. *He's only having fun with me. He's not serious.* Relief was followed by disappointment. *Oh, don't be silly*, she told herself. She sighed, straightened in the seat and leaned against the back.

"You may not be a malicious, bigoted bastard any more, but you are still just as manipulative, Lord Regin."

Regin shrugged. "Well, that's not news. I hope you agree, I always do it for a good cause." He leaned toward her. "But I would like to know what you have against the idea of you and me being a couple."

She paused before answering. *At least he wants to discuss it sensibly. Maybe we should. Get the idea aired and out of our heads.*

"It would be . . . well, a lot of people would object to it. I'm a black magician. You're . . . married."

"Is that all?" He shook his head. "How *conventional* of you. Sonea, the woman who changed everything – the Guild, Kyralian society, the way we regard black magic – is worried about *gossip*?"

"Of course. It took years for me to gain people's trust. I can't risk losing that."

"You won't. They'd be happier seeing you settled with another magician."

She looked away. "You can't know that."

"I know Kyralia's gossips better than you," he retorted. "I have the dubious pleasure of knowing them personally."

He sighed. Glancing at him, she felt her heart twist a little. He looked disappointed. *Maybe he's right. No, he doesn't know what it was like, these last twenty years. People constantly weighing in on every move I made, every friend or lover I had.*

But as she stole another glance, she knew he was right about one thing. She did find him attractive. A lot. *Crazy as that may be.*

"So," he said quietly, "would it be acceptable if I was divorced?"

"No!" she protested, though whether at his question or at him continuing to pursue this she wasn't sure.

"Maybe I should rephrase that. Would it be acceptable *to you* if I was divorced?" He leaned closer and she turned to face him. "If nobody else's opinion mattered, would you want me then?"

He was staring right into her eyes. It would not be easy to lie to him. She hesitated, then opened her mouth to try.

But the words never came out because he was suddenly kissing her. As she froze in surprise he slipped his arms around her, drawing her closer, and she found she could not quite get coordinated enough to do anything about it. Her body did what it wanted to: it relaxed against the warmth of him.

It was, she had to admit, a very good kiss. She was disappointed when it ended, though she was a little out of breath. He looked at her, but not with the full confidence he'd had a moment before. *He will stop this now, if I tell him to.*

I don't want to tell him to.

She searched for something else to say.

"You're not divorced yet," she reminded him.

He smiled. "Oh, but I am. The king granted it before I left."

"What? You never told me that!"

"Of course not. I know you too well. You might have guessed my intentions, and kept me at arm's length," he told her. "Well, more than usual."

"You planned this all along. You scheming, manipulative—"

"Always for a good cause," he said. Then he kissed her again.

As Lorkin stepped into Savara's suite of rooms the queen looked up from the papers she was reading and smiled. Lorkin stopped and put a hand to his heart, but she made a face and waved him past.

"Stop that. Nobody's watching. And Tyvara's waiting for you," she said.

He walked over to the room he and Tyvara had been sleeping in. Tapping lightly on the door, he heard a faint reply, and pushed it open. Tyvara was lying on the narrow bed reading yet more documents, dressed only in a short shift. He closed the door, leaned back on it and hoped he wouldn't have a reason to move again too soon.

She looked up, then rolled her eyes. "Stop that."

"Can't," he said.

"Very well then. Stay there. You'll get bored eventually."

"I doubt it."

She tried to ignore him, but he could see that her eyes were moving back and forth without actually descending down the page. Eventually she closed them, sighed, and looked up at him again.

"I suppose there is a way to make you stop which would be mutually agreeable to both of us."

He widened his eyes in mock innocence. "Mutually agreeable?"

"Definitely. Come here and let's do some experimenting with your new ability. I suspect there are some mutually agreeable ways that skill could be applied."

Some time later Lorkin found himself on the floor, lying beside her with the bedding serving as a not-entirely-comfortable substitute for a mattress. He had been tired before, and now he was more so, but it was a pleasant sort of weariness and he resisted the temptation to Heal it away.

"We really need a bigger bed," Tyvara said.

"Yes."

"How are our Ambassadors?"

Lorkin resisted a smile. Savara had begun to refer to Dannyl and Tayend as "our" Ambassadors the day after she'd met them. "They're fine. They were in the library, happy as children with new toys. I think they'd just found something for Dannyl's book."

"Are those two what I think they are? Are they a couple?"

"They used to be. For a long time, actually. Until Dannyl came here. They'd parted company, but I don't know why."

"And now?"

He shrugged. "I don't know. They seem close again. But they seemed that way just before Dannyl came here, so maybe I can't tell with them." He frowned. "Though there was a tension between them then that isn't there now."

She turned to look at him. "Aren't you going to ask me what Savara wanted to talk about?"

He rolled onto his side. "What did Savara want to talk about?"

"We talked about her plans for Sachaka."

"Now there's a surprise."

Tyvara poked him in the ribs. "Listen. We figure the country estates will maintain themselves without too much assistance for now. There are a few we still have to liberate. They were too out of the way for us to deal with before moving on Arvice. But once they're done, the main challenge is to revive the wasteland.

"Before then, however, we need to sort out the city. It's structurally unsuited to the changes that need to happen. It's nearly all mansions, because the Ashaki were mostly self-sufficient. Though each mansion could house many ex-slaves, they'll want their own homes eventually. We also want to gather people with the same kinds of expertise to work together. That all means lots of buildings will have to be demolished and new ones constructed."

"That will take years."

She nodded. "In the meantime, we need to establish good relations with the Allied Lands. Savara is worried that other lands will hear of the upheaval here and try to take advantage of it. Maybe not by invading. The stones will hopefully deter anyone from trying that. But there are other ways, through trade and politics, to hobble a new and recovering country."

Lorkin held his breath. This was the mission the former queen had sent him on. It was what he was best suited to. He knew how both Traitors and the Allied Lands worked.

"Savara has decided to send me to Kyralia to continue exploring trade options and the possibility of an alliance."

He stared at her as confusion was followed by disappointment and then dismay.

"You don't mean . . .?"

"Yes." Tyvara smiled. "We're going to Kyralia. You'll be my guide and assistant."

He sighed. *Well, it wasn't what I was expecting, but it's good enough I suppose.*

"Ah, Lorkin." She reached out to touch his cheek. "You would never have been chosen for that role. You haven't been a Traitor long enough to negotiate on behalf of Traitors."

"And I'm a man."

She nodded. "That, too."

"You do realise that no other land thinks like that. Everything you believe men aren't suited to, everyone else believes women aren't suited to."

"I know. They are going to have to get used to us as much as we have to get used to them." Then she laughed. "Besides, if I'm ever going to be queen, as Savara intends, then I can't be seen to follow some man around. Least of all a Kyralian."

His stomach flipped over. "You're . . . you're planning to be *queen?*"

"*Savara* is planning for me to be queen." She shrugged. "I'm not sure I want to be. But a lot can change. If it does happen, it won't happen for a long, long time, I hope. I'm hoping she will live as long as Zarala. Being queen is a lot of responsibility, and there's a lot I want to do first. Like have some children." She tilted her head slightly. "Does that sound like a life you might want to live?"

His head spun with the possibilities. *This is all just a bit too incredible. I just want to be with Tyvara. And . . . yes, children would be great eventually.* He looked at her, and felt his heart warm yet again.

"It sounds wonderful. Well, except maybe the bit about us being in charge of a whole country. But I suppose if the Traitors can bear the idea of a Kyralian as their king . . . sure, I'll put up with that if it means I get to spend my life with you."

She rolled her eyes. "You won't be king. We don't have kings."

"Not even through marriage?"

"Not even then. Were you really hoping to be king?"

"Of course not. I can think of nothing worse." He grinned. "Though it does seem unfair. I bet the queen's husband still has to work incredibly hard, with no hope of retirement, talk to annoying people and attend boring ceremonies and events, and listen to his wife complain about how hard life is while having to obey her every whim – and look after her children while she's off doing queenly things. All while getting no credit for it." Which was probably what the Kyralian queen had to endure, he realised.

Tyvara shrugged. "None of them have complained before."

Lorkin snorted. "You Traitors aren't as equal as you claim you are. But, as you said, a lot can change."

She poked him in the ribs again, hard. "Not *that* much. Now let's get this bed back together and get some sleep. Tomorrow we have a lot of work to do."

EPILOGUE

"**Y**ou were dreaming about Cery again, weren't you?"

Sonea looked up at Regin. He held a steaming cup of raka out to her. She pushed herself into a sitting position on the bed and took it. The flavour of good Sachakan raka filled her senses and she felt the last threads of the dream loosen their hold.

"I miss him." She sighed and wiped her eyes. Knowing that she would never see Cery again was like discovering something vital inside her had been stolen. "Even though I didn't see him that often before his family died. I wish I could have done something." She saw him open his mouth and shook her head. "No, you don't have to remind me. It wasn't my fault. Things may not have gone differently if I'd been here . . ."

". . . and you couldn't have been in two places at once," Regin finished. "At least, it's not something the Guild has worked out how to do yet."

"I suspect the tasks of finding a cure for roet and discovering how to make stones without the need of gemstone-producing caves are more urgent." She sipped the raka, then looked towards the window screens. "What time is it? The sun's only just rising, from the looks of it. Why did you get up?"

504

"A message arrived. The king has summoned the Higher Magicians to the palace."

She swung her legs down to the floor and stood up. "When?"

"Not so soon that I haven't time for this." He drew her close and kissed her.

"Hmm." She slipped her arms around him as he began to pull away again. "Time enough for anything more?"

"Not now. The king did me a favour. I shouldn't repay him by making you late." He pushed her towards the clothes cupboard, then got back into the bed.

Sonea dressed quickly, and gulped a few more mouthfuls of raka before slipping out of Regin's rooms. Moving in with him had been her way of stopping the rumours that she and Regin were lovers. It wasn't a rumour any more when it was an obvious fact. She was sure Lilia was enjoying having rooms all to herself. Anyi visited now and then with Jonna's help, disguised as a servant. The Guild had finally removed the problem of the underground tunnels by having them filled in. Though she checked on Lilia regularly and monitored her progress, it was more out of concern that Lilia wasn't completely recovered from everything that had happened to her.

After all, she killed someone with black magic. That isn't as easy to live with as most would think, even when your victim was a bad person.

A door opened further down the corridor. Recognising Lady Indria, Lord Telano's replacement, Sonea waited for the woman to catch up.

"Any idea what this is about?" Indria asked.

"Not yet." Sonea smiled. "How are you settling in to your new role?"

Indria shrugged. "It's both harder and easier than I expected.

I've been teaching for years, so I understand teachers' complaints and needs. But there are so many *records* I didn't have to deal with before."

Sonea chuckled. "Yes. The only advice I can give is that you get yourself an assistant or three."

"I will." As they stepped out of the Magicians' Quarters, Indria glanced around. "It doesn't help that Telano left everything in such a mess," she added in a low voice. "I guess he stopped caring. Have you got any closer to finding a cure for roet?"

Sonea shook her head. "No."

Indria sighed. "These things take time. How are the hospices?"

"Full of addicts in withdrawal. Some responding to Healing, some not. Thankfully, those magicians resistant to roet have automatically healed, so we only have to deal with the forty or so who can't."

They discussed the ongoing roet problem as they walked through the garden. Reaching the front of the University, they saw Osen, Balkan and Kallen standing beside a carriage, and another carriage waiting behind. Osen looked up, saw them and beckoned.

"There's room for you in here Lady Indria," Osen said. "The rest have gone ahead. We'll take the other."

As Indria climbed inside, Osen led the way to the second carriage. Once they were all inside and the carriage began moving, Sonea looked at Osen and raised her eyebrows. He met her gaze and shook his head.

"No, I don't know exactly what this is about, but the King's Adviser assured me there is no invasion and Lorkin is fine."

Sonea smiled. *They're afraid I'll go rushing back to Sachaka at the slightest sign of trouble. Still, it is good to know this isn't anything to do with him.*

"Have you read Dannyl's research notes yet?" Kallen asked the Administrator.

"I'm halfway through." Osen's eyebrows rose. "They're actually rather fascinating, especially the Duna's stories. I'm looking forward to reading the whole book, once he finishes and prints it."

"He'll have to write a new chapter on the Sachakan Civil War and magical gemstones first," Kallen said.

"And I have a feeling there'll be another chapter to add after that," Balkan added.

Osen's eyes narrowed at the High Lord. "Are you still worried about minestrike and that contraption the king's spy says they have in Igra?"

"The ballshooter." Balkan nodded. "Dargin thinks it is what enabled the Igrese priests to conquer all their neighbouring lands."

"More likely the Igrese magicians weren't very powerful or skilled," Osen replied. "I can't see how a ball sent through a tube can threaten a magician, if he or she is shielding well enough."

"I suspect it works much like Lilia's innovative idea of stabbing with magic rather than using a knife when performing black magic. A focused force sent quickly enough will overcome all but the strongest shield."

"The spy said there's little chance an Igrese army would survive a desert crossing," Kallen reminded him. "And we know they do not have black magic or gemstones."

As Balkan shook his head, Osen turned to the window and rolled his eyes. "It's not the Igrese I'm worried about," Balkan said. "The minefire the Thief Cery used was unlike the usual—"

"We'll have to leave that argument to another time," Osen said, turning back from the window. "We've arrived."

The carriage slowed to a stop, and the door opened. Osen gave a little sigh of relief as Balkan stepped out. He, Kallen and Sonea followed. They were in a small courtyard within the palace where magicians were taken when the king wanted to avoid the delay of formal greetings. The other carriage was pulling away and the occupants had already disappeared inside.

A palace attendant ushered them through a door and into a sumptuously decorated hall, then led them along a corridor to a dining room. Sonea had eaten here a few times before, along with other Higher Magicians, sometimes as a guest of the king, sometimes in order to meet important foreign visitors. Today the chairs were occupied only by the Higher Magicians and four of the king's non-magician advisers. Rothen smiled and nodded as she saw him seated at the end of the table. As she, Osen, Balkan and Kallen took the four unoccupied chairs a man strode into the room and all rose to their feet.

"Your majesty," Osen began.

The king waved a hand. "Sit. You have important decisions to make, and knowing how quickly magicians make decisions you'd best get started without delay." Sonea suppressed a smile at his dry tone. He moved to the end of the table and planted his palms flat on the surface.

"Yesterday the new Sachakan Ambassador arrived. As you know, she is a black magician – or, as she calls it, a *higher* magician. As you also know, her not being a member of the Guild makes her a rogue magician. So her presence here means two of our most serious laws regarding magic are being broken right now.

"So, either I send her home or we change our laws."

He paused to look around the table, meeting each magician's gaze.

"I do not intend to send her home, so we had better change our laws. That is what you are here for. You've been arguing about this for months, and it is time you came to an agreement. Between yourselves and my advisers, before the end of the day, you will draft new laws that will allow foreign, non-Guild magicians to live and trade here legally and with effective, workable restrictions. Those restrictions must regulate both the use of black magic and the possession of magical gemstones. Your predecessors had good reason to fear black magic, but we need a better method of control than banning it.

"It has also been pointed out to me that gemstones put magic into the hands of non-magicians, and we don't want them hearing about the Igrese and deciding to rid the Allied Lands of magicians. Though I think it is unlikely they'd succeed, I do not want to deal with a civil uprising. We must have some kind of regulation of gemstones, even if only to prevent the Thieves from getting hold of them. The rise of the Rogue Skellin should be a warning to you: we must keep magic out of the underworld.

"I also expect that these laws will go some way toward improving the behaviour of Guild magicians. It is clear from the corruption roet has revealed in the Guild's ranks that some magicians aren't immune to vice and profiting at the expense of others. It is time their excesses and activities were curtailed."

The king straightened. "You have a lot to discuss, so I will leave you to it. Bring me a summary of your progress at midday." He pausing for a last look around the table, then turned and strode out of the room.

All were quiet, listening to the king's footsteps fading in the background, then Osen cleared his throat and looked at the advisers.

"If it is acceptable, I will lead the discussions."

The advisers nodded. As Osen started to speak, Sonea felt an unexpected sadness. *And so everything changes again. Just like after the Ichani Invasion, when we knew we had to accept black magic as our only form of defence, and restore the Guild by taking in lower-class novices. There were so many unforeseen consequences, like the Thieves battling each other and the city overtaking the slums. We can try to make laws that control the changes that magical gemstones and an alliance with Sachaka will bring, but they will have effects we don't anticipate.*

All they could do was try. And, for her part, attempt to ensure that when Lorkin returned to Kyralia, even if only to visit, he – and the family he might eventually have – would be safe and welcome.

GLOSSARY

ANIMALS

aga moths – pests that eat clothing

anyi – sea mammals with short spines

ceryni – small rodent

enka – horned domestic animal, bred for meat

eyoma – sea leeches

faren – general term for arachnids

gorin – large domestic animal used for food and to haul boats and wagons

harrel – small domestic animal bred for meat

inava – insect believed to bestow good luck

limek – wild predatory dog

mullook – wild nocturnal bird

quannea – rare shells

rassook – domestic bird used for meat and feathers

ravi – rodent, larger than ceryni

reber – domestic animal, bred for wool and meat

safly – woodland insect

sevli – poisonous lizard

squimp – squirrel-like creature that steals food

yeel – small domesticated breed of limek used for tracking

zill – small, intelligent mammal sometimes kept as a pet

PLANTS/FOOD

anivope vine – plant sensitive to mental projection

bellspice – spice grown in Sachaka

bol – (also means "river scum") strong liquor made from tugors

brasi – green leafy vegetable with small buds

briskbark – bark with decongestant properties

cabbas – hollow, bell-shaped vegetable

chebol sauce – rich meat sauce made from bol

cone cakes – bite-sized cakes

creamflower – flower used as a soporific

crots – large, purple beans

curem – smooth, nutty spice

curren – coarse grain with robust flavour

dall – long fruit with tart orange, seedy flesh

dunda – root chewed as a stimulating drug

gan-gan – flowering bush from Lan

husroot – herb used for cleansing wounds

iker – stimulating drug, reputed to have aphrodisiac properties

jerras – long yellow beans

kreppa – foul-smelling medicinal herb

marin – red citrus fruit

monyo – bulb

myk – mind-affecting drug

nalar – pungent root

nemmin – sleep-inducing drug

nightwood – hardwood timber

pachi – crisp, sweet fruit

papea – pepper-like spice

piorres – small, bell-shaped fruit

raka/suka – stimulating drink made from roasted beans, originally from Sachaka

roet – plant from which a soporific drug and a perfume are derived

rot – slang term for the drug roet

shem – edible reed-like plant

sumi – bitter drink

sweetdrops – candies

telk – seed from which an oil is extracted

tenn – grain that can be cooked as is, broken into small pieces, or ground to make a flour

tiro – edible nuts

tugor – parsnip-like root

ukkas – carnivorous plants

vare – berries from which most wine is produced

whitewater – pure spirits made from tugors

yellowseed – crop grown in Sachaka

CLOTHING AND WEAPONRY

incal – square symbol, not unlike a family shield, sewn onto sleeve or cuff

kebin – iron bar with hook for catching attacker's knife, carried by guards

longcoat – ankle-length coat

quan – tiny disc-shaped beads made of shell

undershift – Kyralian women's undergarment

PUBLIC HOUSES

bathhouse – establishment selling bathing facilities and other grooming services

bolhouse – establishment selling bol and short term accommodation

brewhouse – bol manufacturer

hole – building constructed from scavenged materials

stayhouse – rented building, a family to a room

COUNTRIES/PEOPLES IN THE REGION

Duna – tribes who live in volcanic desert north of Sachaka

Elyne – neighbour to Kyralia and Sachaka and once ruled by Sachaka

Igra – country far to the north of the Allied Lands where magic is forbidden

Kyralia – neighbour to Elyne and

Sachaka and once ruled by
Sachaka

Lan – a mountainous land peopled
by warrior tribes

Lonmar – a desert land home to the
strict Mahga religion

Sachaka – home of the once great
Sachakan Empire, where all but
the most powerful are slaves

Vin – an island nation known for
their seamanship

TITLES/POSITIONS

Administrator – magician who sees
to the running of the Guild

Ashaki – Sachakan landowner

Black Magician – one of two
magicians allowed to know
black magic

Directors – magicians in charge
of managing novices within and
outside of the University

Heads of Disciplines – in charge
of magicians of the three
disciplines of Healing, Warrior
and Alchemy

Heads of Studies – in charge of
teaching the three disciplines
of Healing, Warrior and
Alchemy

High Lord – the official leader
of the Magicians' Guild of
Kyralia

Ichani – Sachakan free man or
woman who has been declared
outcast

King's Advisors – magicians who
advise, Heal and protect the
Kyralian king

Lord/Lady – any magician of the
Magician's Guild without a
greater title

Master – free Sachakan

OTHER TERMS

the approach – main corridor to the
Master's Room in Sachakan
houses

blood gem – artificial gemstone
that allows maker to hear the
thoughts of wearer

earthblood – term the Duna tribes
use for lava

lowie – slang term used in the
Guild for novices from middle-
and lower-class origins

Master's Room – main room in
Sachakan houses for greeting
guests

obin – separate house joined to the
main house of a Naguh Valley
house

snootie – slang term used in the
Guild for novices and magicians
from the Houses

slavehouse – part of Sachakan homes
where the slaves live and work

slavespot – sexually transmitted
disease

storestone – gemstone that can store
magic

The Slig – a hidden people who live
in the passages underneath
Imardin

vyer – stringed instrument
from Elyne

LORD DANNYL'S GUIDE
TO SLUM SLANG

blood money – payment for assassination

boot – refuse/refusal (don't boot us)

capper – man who frequents brothels

clicked – occurred

client – person who has an obligation or agreement with a Thief

counter – whore

done – murdered

dull – persuade to keep silent

dunghead – fool

dwells – term used to describe slum dwellers

eye – keep watch

fired – angry (got fired about it)

fish – propose/ask/look for (also someone fleeing the Guard)

gauntlet – guard who is bribeable or in the control of a Thief

goldmine – man who prefers boys

good go – a reasonable try

got – caught

grandmother – pimp

gutter – dealer in stolen goods

hai – a call for attention or expression of surprise or inquiry

heavies – important people

kin – a Thief's closest and most trusted

knife – assassin/hired killer

messenger – thug who delivers or carries out a threat

mind – hide (minds his business/I'll mind that for you)

mug – mouth (as in vessel for bol)

out for – looking for

pick – recognise/understand

punt – smuggler

right-sided – trustworthy/heart in the right place

rope – freedom

rub – trouble (got into some rub over it)

shine – attraction (got a shine for him)

show – introduce

space – allowances/permission

squimp – someone who double-crosses the Thieves

style – manner of performing business

tag – recognise (also means a spy, usually undercover)

thief – leader of a criminal group

watcher – posted to observe

something or someone

wild – difficult

visitor – burglar

ACKNOWLEDGEMENTS

Writing this sequel trilogy has been hard work of the most enjoyable kind. Which is why I appreciate the work done by everyone behind the scenes, and the support of all the wonderful booksellers and readers who embrace my books when they finally launch into the world.

Thanks go to Anne Clarke and the Orbit team; my agent, Fran and her wonderful assistant, Liz; the feedback readers Paul, Donna and Nicole. You all had a part in making this book as good as it could be.

A special extra thanks to Fran for coordinating the organisation of my big European tour, along with Rose at Orbit and Berit at Verlagsgruppe Random House; to all the staff at the stores that hosted readings and/or signings – I wish there was room to list you all; my wonderful Polish publishers, Galeria Książki, who treated me like royalty during two fabulous days in Warsaw; the marvelous Imaginales Festival in France; and the amazing team brought together for the German author nights by Verlagsgruppe Random House.

And most of all, to my readers: a special extra thanks to everyone who came to see me on my European tour, or at a signing elsewhere in the world. It is always a fabulous treat to meet you. And to all readers: I hope you enjoyed revisiting the world of the Black Magician trilogy as much as I did, and will join me on the next adventure of the imagination.

ABOUT THE AUTHOR

Trudi Canavan published her first story in 1999 and it received an Aurealis Award for Best Fantasy Short Story. Her debut series, the Black Magician trilogy, made her an international success, and all three volumes of the Age of the Five trilogy were *Sunday Times* bestsellers. Trudi Canavan lives with her partner in Melbourne, Australia, and spends her time knitting, painting and writing bestselling fantasy novels. For more information about Trudi and her writing go to www trudicanavan.com

Find out more about Trudi Canavan and other Orbit authors by registering for the free monthly newslettter at www.orbit-books.net